THE WORLD OUTSIDE MY WINDOW

CLARE SWATMAN

Boldwood

First published in Great Britain in 2023 by Boldwood Books Ltd.

Cover Design by Leah Jacobs-Gordon

Cover Photography: Shutterstock

A CIP catalogue record for this book is available from the British Library.

Paperback ISBN 978-1-80280-683-0

Large Print ISBN 978-1-80280-682-3

Hardback ISBN 978-1-80280-681-6

Ebook ISBN 978-1-80280-684-7

Kindle ISBN 978-1-80280-685-4

Audio CD ISBN 978-1-80280-676-2

MP3 CD ISBN 978-1-80280-677-9

Digital audio download ISBN 978-1-80280-680-9

Boldwood Books Ltd
23 Bowerdean Street
London SW6 3TN
www.boldwoodbooks.com

For Jeanne with love

PROLOGUE
MARCH 1991

It was almost midnight, as it often was by the time I staggered out of the restaurant after a long shift. Rain had transformed the pavements and roads into slick, shimmering lakes, and as I pulled my car out of the tiny staff car park I smiled. There was something special about London at this time of night. It felt as though the city had fallen into a deep slumber, and the roads were deathly quiet as I wound my way northwards towards East Finchley.

Fifteen minutes later I turned onto my street. The rain had begun again in earnest and I squinted through the windscreen, the ancient wipers losing their battle against the sudden downpour as I searched fruitlessly for a parking space.

I crawled past my flat and slowly down the street until finally I found a space a couple of hundred metres from my front door, just big enough to squeeze my little Fiat into. It felt like a small triumph.

As I locked the doors I felt a rumble of anxiety in the pit of my stomach. The sudden downpour had ended as quickly as it had begun, and while the pin-drop peace might seem magical from the safety of a car, there was a menacing undertone to a darkened London street, and I hurried my pace, key wedged firmly between my fingers as a weapon, just in case.

The moment my flat loomed into sight, the tension began to drop from my shoulders. Although my husband, Jim, was away, the hallway light I'd left on earlier still glowed like a welcoming beacon. I checked my watch: 12.24 a.m.

I'd be inside any second, stepping through the door into the safety of our flat. I hitched my bag up onto my shoulder and took a few more steps.

It happened without warning. Staccato movements. Beats of terror.

A knock against my elbow.

A hand on my mouth.

A stifled scream.

A stumble; blinding pain.

Primal, all-consuming panic.

Fury rose in me as I tried to jab my elbow into my attacker's face. But his vicelike grip held me firm. Fury turned to terror as I was dragged towards a narrow pathway between two houses. I dug my heels in, frantic, desperate, but it was hopeless. He was stronger than me. I stood no chance.

Then we were engulfed in blackness, the street lights positioned so that no one passing the end of the alleyway would ever see us. A face loomed, tiny eyes in a black balaclava.

'Make a noise, and I'll kill you,' he hissed. His body pressed against me, and I realised I was trapped between him and the wall. I frantically dragged air in through my nostrils, in two, three, four, out two, three, four. Breathing was all I could concentrate on. He tugged at my waistband and I screamed, but no sound came out. Terror rose in me with every second.

I couldn't let this happen, just yards from home.

His hand moved inside my trousers and pulled hard. I heard a rip and tried to kick out, but he pushed my legs apart roughly.

Then a glint in the darkness and I froze, paralysed with dread. A knife.

For a few seconds we were both utterly still. Then adrenaline kicked in and I sucked in as much air as I could and tried to scream again. But a dizzying pain filled my head, my neck, my face. He'd smacked my head against the wall. I slumped down, all fight gone as my body roared with pain.

This was it. This was the end.

A shout then, and the eyes in the mask froze. Hands ripped away, footsteps receded. I was suddenly alone again, hunched on the cold wet ground like a puppet whose strings had been cut.

As quickly as it had begun, it was over.

I stayed there, curled into a ball, for what could have been seconds or hours. Then someone spoke in the dark – 'Are you all right?' – and I knew I was saved. A man had been walking his dog, had heard noises from the alleyway. He'd given chase, and called the police. My saviour.

He helped me up, walked me home and stayed with me until the police arrived. He made tea and spoke to the officers and gave a brief description of the man who'd attacked me, for what it was worth. We all knew he'd never be caught.

I stayed up for the rest of that night, too terrified to sleep. The police wanted me to go to the station and give a statement, but I refused. When Jim returned from work the following day he begged me to go, but I still said no.

Two weeks he stayed at home with me, desperately trying to get me to see the GP, the police, to consider returning to work.

But I couldn't do it. I couldn't even contemplate crossing the threshold of the flat. Because something told me that if I just stayed in the safety of my own four walls, nothing bad could ever happen to me again.

I haven't been outside since.

PART I

LOST

1

Laura Parks hasn't left her home for more than eighteen months. Neither has she spoken to another soul apart from her husband, Jim, and best friend, Debbie, in all that time. She's only aware of the passing of the seasons thanks to occasional snapshots of the outside world through gauzy net curtains, and slices of life glimpsed through narrow gaps between blinds.

And now, Laura has been abandoned. At least, it's beginning to look that way.

Because Jim hasn't come home.

Here she is, hovering by the window, squinting into the cul-de-sac, making deals with herself. Perhaps, she reasons, if she stands here for ten more seconds, he'll appear.

Ten seconds pass. Another thirty seconds, then. That should be enough.

She feels her heart skitter inside her chest as she peers through the blinds, angling herself so that she won't miss her husband's familiar figure the second he rounds the corner, while avoiding revealing the whole street at once. Her gaze flicks to the clock above the fireplace and back again. He's now an hour late. He's never an hour late.

She inches closer to the glass until her nose lightly touches one of the vinyl slats. Dust shoots up her nostrils, making her want to sneeze, and as she breathes out, the glass behind the blind mists, clears, then mists over again. It's getting darker now, spaces between the houses opposite rapidly turning grey, smudged with shadows. An early evening breeze tickles the treetops, making the leaves dance, and a few float to the ground, zigzagging through the air before brushing the earth with barely a murmur. It's peaceful outside now, everyone finished with their lawn mowing, hedge cutting, car washing. Lights are being switched on in living rooms, smoke rises from chimneys. There isn't even the usual bored teenager doing keepy-uppies by the kerb to disturb the peace.

She starts suddenly, her pulse quickstepping as a movement catches the corner of her eye by next door's hedge. But when she looks more closely, it's gone. A fox, probably, or next door's cat.

She pulls back, angry with herself, and picks up a glass from the coffee table. There's less than an inch of clear liquid left in the bottom, so she tips it down her throat and stalks into the kitchen to top it up, the vodka splashing onto the worktop as she pours with shaking hands. She takes another gulp and closes her eyes, leaning against the counter for support, and listens to the drum of her pulse in her chest, her temple, her limbs. She feels weak with worry.

The sudden peal of the telephone breaks into her thoughts and she almost screams with fright.

'Jim?' Her voice fires out like a bullet, hope flaring in her chest as she smacks the plastic receiver against her ear, the twisted wire swinging forlornly.

'It's me.'

Her shoulders sag, stomach dropping with disappointment.

'Oh, hi, Debs.'

'Don't sound too pleased to hear from me.' She hears her best friend swallow and pictures her sipping the cup of tea she always has on the go. There's a rumble of the TV in the background and she imagines Debbie's kids stretched across the carpet on their bellies watching *Blue Peter* or *Pingu*, their favourite.

'Sorry. I just—' The words stick in her throat.

'Has something happened?' The concern in Debbie's voice is clear now, and she feels a stab of guilt that she always puts her best friend through so much worry when she has such a lot on her plate already.

'It's Jim,' she croaks. 'He's missing.'

A second of silence, then: 'What do you mean, missing?'

A pulse beats in her temple, and she swallows. 'He's not home yet.' Saying the words out loud make it feel all too real and she starts to shake.

'Do you want me to come over when Steve gets home?'

She hates that she's so needy, that Debbie even has to ask this question. She's thirty-three years old, she should be more than capable of looking after herself. But she's always had someone there as a crutch – Mum, Dad before he disappeared like a wisp of smoke; Debbie and, for the last seven years, Jim. The thought of being alone makes her feel as though she's been hollowed out, or lost a limb.

'No, it's fine. I'll be fine. You stay with the kids.' She takes a sip of her vodka and realises the glass is already empty. 'Jim will be home soon, I'm just being silly.'

'You're not being silly, darling, you never are.' Laura can hear the concern in her friend's voice. 'But I do think you're right. I'm sure Jim will be home soon.'

Laura swallows down a sob at her kindness and whispers, 'Thank you.'

'Don't be daft.' Debbie goes quiet for a minute but Laura knows she's still there. 'Will you let me know when he gets back?'

'Course I will.'

'And, Lau?'

'Yes?'

'Try not to drink too much, promise?'

Laura looks down at her empty glass, at the half-full bottle next to it, and replies: 'Guide's honour.'

When she replaces the handset she stares at it for a while, willing it to ring. Just like when she was watching out of the window, she makes deals with herself. Maybe if she stares at it for thirty seconds, it will ring, and she'll hear Jim's voice, telling her everything is okay. A minute; two minutes.

Eventually she gives up and splashes some more vodka into her tumbler, knocking it back in one. She never used to be much of a drinker. Back when she met Jim she only really drank when she went dancing with her friends, and even then she'd mainly stick to wine or the occasional gin and tonic. She wasn't a lonely drunk, stuck at home knocking back vodka night after night, passing out rather than falling asleep. But ever since the attack she's felt like a broken window, pieces of herself lying splintered and discarded on the ground, and as though booze is the only thing that can start to patch those pieces back together again, however ragged and makeshift the repair job is.

Who cares if it's a temporary solution, if it helps for a few moments?

She snatches up the bottle, refills her glass and takes them both out into the hallway. She hurries past the front door and runs up the stairs, stumbling as she reaches the top, almost spilling the drink from her glass. She takes the last few steps more carefully, and heads into their bedroom. The curtains are drawn in here, the same as every other room, and it's dim, barely any light filtering through the heavy fabric. She slams the bottle and glass on her bedside table with a crack.

A bath. She'll take a bath. Perhaps by the time she's run it, Jim will be home. She'll tell him how worried she was, and he'll laugh at her indulgently, and say, 'Oh, Lau, you're such a worry wart,' and she'll wonder why she ever felt this tense and panicked in the first place.

She sticks the plug in and sets the taps running, tipping in bubble bath. As she waits for the bath to fill she thinks about where Jim might be.

It's Thursday, which means he usually gets home at 6.23 p.m. She knows this because she waits for him like an eager puppy every week, and is overwhelmingly grateful the minute he walks through the door. Jim spends three, sometimes four days a week working away in Leeds and, when Laura was her old self, back when they first met, this wasn't a big deal. Yes, she missed him. Yes, she wished he weren't away so much. But she understood he loved his job and she kept herself busy when he was away, seeing her friends and working longer hours to fill the time until he was back. When he was home, he was attentive and loving, which made the time apart bearable.

Now, though, the days when she's alone stretch on endlessly like a piece of elastic, the time between Jim leaving and returning spent waiting, counting down the hours, the minutes, until he walks back through the door at 6.23 p.m. on a Thursday evening. Debbie tells her it's no way to live but her life has been this way for so long now she has no idea if she's capable of doing anything about it. Or even if she wants to.

She turns off the taps, walks back into the bedroom to get her drink, then lowers herself into the scalding water. She ignores the scream of her skin as the water turns it from pale milk to a fiery red, keeps going until her ears are submerged, and she feels instantly cocooned, a sense of safety enveloping her as the steam spirals upwards and the tension slips away from her shoulders. The sounds of the house; the clunk of the central heating, the ticks and buzzes and hums of various domestic appliances, as well as the deadened thunk of her heart beating, are muffled through the steaming water, and she closes her eyes. Maybe when she opens them again Jim will be standing there, smiling at her. She tests it by opening one eye slightly, but there's no one there and her heart plummets to her stomach. The sense of terror that something terrible has happened to her husband is creeping closer, like a monster in a horror film.

These are the facts. One: Jim is never late. In fact he prides himself on his timekeeping, and if he is going to be late he will always let her know.

Two: Jim knows how much she needs him, how much she relies on him coming home after three days away, and would never just leave her wondering.

Three: Jim knows she's completely alone. She doesn't have any friends apart from Debbie, who lives thirty miles away with her family and can't just drop everything to come and see her, and she doesn't know any of the neighbours in the street they've lived in for the last seven months.

Four: something has happened to Jim. The certainty hits her like a hammer blow and she sits up suddenly, the water cascading off her body and splashing over the side of the enamel bath, soaking the peeling tiled floor. She stands and clambers out of the bath, wraps herself in a towel and pads, wet-footed, across the carpet, leaving a trail of damp Bigfoot prints across the landing and down the stairs.

She needs to do something.

She needs to find Jim.

She can't function without him.

She takes another gulp of her drink, then she picks up the phone.

2

THEN – SEPTEMBER 1985

For some people, the tireless pace of a kitchen was too much. But for me, usually shy and quiet and not keen on spending time with strangers, the adrenaline surge I experienced every time I stepped into the restaurant kitchen couldn't be beaten. Work consumed me, and I loved the rhythm of it; the chopping, the sizzling, the rush of heat as another dish was cooked to perfection. I felt so lucky to be Head Chef of a restaurant in the city centre at the age of just twenty-six. It was the only place I felt fully in charge, and I ran a tight ship, but I didn't like interruptions because they ruined the flow. So, when I heard someone calling me in the middle of a very busy service one night, I ignored them and assumed they'd give up and go away. But they didn't, and when I looked up again there was a figure standing beside me, right by my elbow.

I spun round, my face flushed and hot, ready to give them a dressing-down but I was stopped in my tracks by the sight of the handsome man standing beside me, smiling sheepishly. I felt the kitchen walls shift ever so slightly, and the light become a notch brighter as I took in his chiselled cheeks and long lashes.

'Oh!' I said, stupidly, my face flushing even more.

'I'm so sorry.' He shuffled his feet as I worried how terrible my hair must look beneath my chef's hat.

'What are—?'

'Could you—?' We both started to speak at the same time and laughed. Then he glanced up and smiled nervously. 'Seriously, would you mind putting that thing down?'

That was when I remembered I was holding a bloody great knife in front of me like a weapon. I dropped it onto the worktop with a clatter and his shoulders sagged in relief. 'That's better.' When he smiled his eyes twinkled.

I stuck my chin out, defiant.

'How can I help you?' I kept my voice clipped, because his handsome face didn't detract from the fact that he'd stormed into my kitchen uninvited.

'I'm really sorry to barge in like this, I can see you're busy. It's just I wanted to give my compliments to the chef and they wouldn't let me come in so I sort of – sneaked in.'

'Oh, I see.' With those words my anger fizzled out, and I noticed the anxious faces of my team watching me. I shrugged, trying for nonchalant. 'Well, you're here now. And good, I'm glad you enjoyed your meal. What did you have?'

'The duck. It was exquisite.'

I smiled. 'Thank you.'

Unsure what else to say, I turned back to my chopping board and picked up my knife. But he was still hovering expectantly. I opened my mouth to ask him to leave.

'Would you like to come out for a drink when you've finished here?' he blurted.

'Oh. I—' I stopped, completely thrown. For a moment I didn't recognise myself – I wasn't the sort of person who had men throwing themselves at me, asking me out on dates left right and centre. I felt the room tip as I tried to formulate a response.

'That would be lovely,' I found myself saying before I'd even decided I was going to say it. 'But it won't be until at least eleven, once I'm done here.' My hand was shaking and my voice wobbled but he didn't seem to notice.

'That's okay. I'll wait.'

'Well, if you're sure, then I'll see you later.'

'Great. I'm Jim, by the way.'

'Laura.'

'See you soon, Laura.'

As he made his way back into the restaurant I found a smile creeping onto my flaming face. I couldn't believe I'd agreed to a date with a man I'd never met before, just like that. What was I *doing*?

But there had been something about Jim that I'd liked the look of. Something kind, trustworthy about him.

And I was right. Later that evening he stayed behind for a drink after hours, and he was everything I'd hoped he would be, and more. We talked and talked. I found out he had a secret love of cheesy musicals, that he'd been close to his aunt Bess who had taught him to sew (although her death a few years ago had left him heartbroken), that he worked for a hotel chain, and that he hadn't believed in love at first sight until today. In return I told him about my love of cheese and Marmite toasties with brown sauce – 'And you a chef!' he'd said, laughing – the fact that I'd always wanted to be a chef, that I'd only ever kissed three boys and that I did a great impression of Margaret Thatcher. I even found myself telling him that my dad had walked out when I was young and that I missed my mum, who lived with her boyfriend, Brian, who I couldn't stand, something I rarely talked about with anyone. 'I've never believed in love at first sight before either,' I added, coyly. He held my gaze for a few seconds and I felt my body flush with heat. Then his eyes flicked to the clock.

'God, I'm sorry, it's crazily late,' he said, draining his whisky and wiping his mouth with the back of his hand. He was tantalisingly close to me, and I could make out the dark chestnut of his eyes, flecked through with gold, searching my face. I studied him back, wondering what it was about this man that made me feel as though I'd known him for months, years even.

'When can I see you again?' he said, twirling a piece of my hair with his finger. His voice was low, gruff, and I felt it in my bones.

'Tomorrow?' I said. He hesitated just a fraction of a second, then closed the gap between us and planted a gentle kiss on my lips. My whole body buzzed.

'That sounds perfect.' Then he stood and held out his hand. 'I'll make sure you get home safely.' True to his word, he found me a taxi, paid my fare upfront and waved as we drove off, leaving him on the pavement all alone. And that was that.

I finally believed in love at first sight.

3

NOW – 17-18 SEPTEMBER 1992

The police don't care. Laura has told them Jim hasn't come home but the young police officer on the other end of the phone dismissed her concerns before she'd even got to the end of her sentence.

'I'm sorry but we don't class an adult as missing until they've been gone for at least forty-eight hours,' he said.

'Yes but—'

'I'm sure he'll be home soon, Mrs Parks,' he said, cutting her off.

'Can I at least leave my details, in case?' she said quickly, twisting the phone cord round and round her fingers until they turned white. The officer sighed, and someone shouted in the background.

'As I said, Mrs—'

'Fine. Don't worry.' She hung up before she started crying, but then the tears sprang immediately, uncontrollably.

Now she doesn't know what to do with herself. It's only been two hours since Jim was expected home, which means there are almost two long days to get through before the police will listen to her, and even then it's doubtful they'll understand quite how worried she is. She's not sure how she can make them care.

She walks over to the kitchen window again and peers through the blinds, twiddling with her sapphire wedding ring, which is now too loose on her finger. The street outside is as much a mystery to her as the Sahara Desert or the Himalayas: insurmountable, distant. Terrifying. It's peaceful now, the darkness fully drawn across the sky, and she watches the branches of the willow tree in the centre of the green dance in the Wotsit-orange light from the street lamp. An empty crisp packet skitters across the road, becoming lodged in the wall of number five before finally escaping and continuing its journey. She wishes she could follow it. She knows it would be so simple to just open the front door, step outside and walk across the road to knock on the tatty plastic door of number nine, introduce herself to the people who live there, and ask for their help. Her head *knows* there's nothing to be afraid of out there.

And yet it feels like an impossible task.

Since the attack, she hasn't been outside, not once. When they left London to move here, to this lovely little commuter town half an hour outside the city, she was heavily drugged like some sort of cattle and deposited in this house so that she never even knew she'd been outside. And even though it had been her idea – she'd been insistent that a change of scenery was what she needed, that getting away from the bustle of the city would help her to get over the attack – it quickly became apparent that she'd simply brought her anxiety with her lock, stock and barrel. So that's why, since they arrived here seven months before, she hasn't left the house, not even to go out into the garden, which mocks her every day as the weeds grow taller and the flowers bloom and die.

Jim's home for half the week, and when he's here she feels as though maybe things aren't so bad after all. It matters less that she's unable to do anything for herself, because Jim does it for her. He does the food shopping, and doesn't even object to buying the vodka and wine she asks for every week. He cleans, he cooks, he pays the bills.

Plus, it's Jim who's made a home for himself here. It's Jim who has got to know the neighbours.

'I hate the thought of you being here all by yourself, I wish you'd come with me to meet some of them,' he said one day just before he was due to leave for another four days of work.

'I can't, Jim, you know that.'

'Maybe I could invite someone round, then? Make a night of it?'

'No.'

He bit his lip and turned his head away. Laura knew he found it frustrating but she couldn't help it. Every time she got anywhere near the door, visions of those eyes peering out from the black balaclava flashed before her, and she couldn't take another step. The thought of someone she barely knew coming into the house was almost as bad.

So she's stuck here all day, alone, with only the occasional visit from Debbie – not exactly Jim's greatest fan – to break the monotony. How has her life become so infinitesimal?

Now, as the daylight fades and shadows deepen in the corners of the room, everything makes her jump. Simon from across the road putting the bins out; his wife pulling into her driveway and slamming the car door; a cat dashing out from behind next door's front wall and knocking over a garden gnome. Everything makes her heart race.

And now Jim isn't home when he's meant to be, and she has no idea what to do.

* * *

In the end, she drinks, the same as she always does. She knows she really needs to eat something, but cooking has been another thing that she hasn't been able to face doing much of recently. She misses it.

Cooking has always been a part of her for as long as she can remember. When things were tough, whenever she felt sad or insecure, she cooked. The slice of a knife, the smell of roasting garlic, the sizzle of a steak – they were all things she could lose herself in whenever she felt down. But now she can hardly even bring herself to open a tin of beans or turn on the oven for a frozen lasagne. It all just feels too much.

Jim has been understanding, of course, the way he always is. But the ready meals and baked potatoes he rustles up after a long day at the office are a huge come-down from the sorts of meals she loved to cook: fragrant curries, wild mushroom risottos, grilled seabass, duck confit, the smells of the spices filling every corner of the house. Those things seem a million miles away from her now, and it makes her feel as though she's lost a part of herself.

She opens the bread bin and pulls out a half-eaten loaf of Mighty White and checks a slice for mould. It looks fine so she sticks it in the toaster and waits. When it's cooked she spreads a thin layer of butter on it, grabs her vodka bottle, and heads to bed. If she can just fall asleep, maybe things will look brighter tomorrow.

Maybe Jim will be home.

* * *

For a few seconds after she wakes up, she's forgotten everything that happened yesterday. In fact the main feeling is of a pounding headache and a nauseous feeling in her stomach, which momentarily overrides everything else. Her eyelids are stuck down and when she peels them open the light pouring round the edges of the curtains is so bright she has to close them again and hold her palms over her eyes while the blotches subside.

She rolls over onto her side and fumbles on the bedside table, trying to find a glass of water, something to quench her raging thirst. But instead her hand hits something cold and hard and the crash it makes as it hits the carpet wakes her up with a start. She peers over the edge of the bed and sees the vodka bottle she brought up with her last night, rolling around on the floor. It's empty. Ugh.

She stays still a moment longer, waiting for her head to settle, then rolls onto her back and stares up at the ceiling, trying to put her thoughts into some sort of coherent order. She drank most of a bottle of vodka last night. Debbie would be furious if she knew. Jim won't be too happy either.

Jim!

The memory of the previous evening hits her then and she pulls herself up to sitting, ignoring the spinning room, instead listening for any noises that might indicate that Jim finally came home while she was passed out, or that last night was, in fact, nothing more than a terrible nightmare. She strains her ears, listening to the sounds of this shabby house – familiar now, after seven months: the clunk of the boiler as it fires up, the drip of the broken tap in the bathroom, a low hum from next door's hoover. She hasn't even met the woman who stands just a few feet away from her on the other side of this wall, and yet she hears her daily movements all the time. What an odd existence.

As the realisation hits that she's still alone, her stomach drops. She needs to get out of bed and do something, try and work out what's happened to her husband. She swings her legs out of bed and shuffles across the carpet, concentrating on not throwing up. As she switches on the bathroom light she catches sight of herself in the mirror above the sink and groans. Her skin is almost translucent – hardly surprising as it hasn't seen the sun for more than eighteen months – and the dark circles under her eyes are black, like bruises. She turns away, not wanting to see the reality of what she's done to herself: her gaunt cheeks, her haunted look. She hovers over the loo for a few minutes to make sure she's not going to be sick, then pulls on a fresh pair of jeans – they hang off her now, so she loops a belt through them – and an old jumper and heads back down to the kitchen. Through the fug of her hangover she has the idea that she needs to try to formulate some kind of plan to find Jim.

On autopilot, she fills the kettle with water, spoons Nescafé into a mug, then takes the phone off the hook and drags it over to the kitchen table, stretching the coil of plastic until it strains to get back in its base. She grabs the notepad from yesterday, where the number for the local police station is scribbled, and redials it. She knows they're not going to do anything, but she needs to feel as though she's doing something.

'My husband is still missing,' she blurts as soon as someone answers, even though she has no idea whether it's the same prepubescent officer she spoke to the previous evening.

'I'm sorry, madam, can you tell me who's missing, please?' says a female voice.

And so Laura repeats her story about Jim not coming home last night, about how she rang and was told he hadn't been missing for long enough, but that she's worried about him.

'I see.' A silence. 'And you say he's been missing for how long?'

She glances at the clock on the cooker whose green digits tell her it's 8.36 a.m.

'Fourteen hours, as far as I know. But it could be longer. It's definitely been more than that since I spoke to him.'

'I see,' she says again, and Laura feels fury unfurl in her like a weed, stretching its leaves to the edges of her patience before the officer has even had the chance to dismiss her.

'You don't understand,' Laura yells, her voice cracking as she leaps up, the wooden chair toppling over behind her and clattering to the floor. 'He's never late. He's always home on time, and he would never just not turn up. He—' Her voice breaks. She was going to say that Jim knows she can't cope on her own, but she realises before she does how pathetic it sounds, and also how little difference it will make to anything the police do anyway.

'I totally understand, Mrs—'

'Parks,' she supplies.

'I totally understand what you're saying, Mrs Parks, and I understand why you might be worried. But the trouble is, you see, that we're not allowed to investigate missing adults for at least forty-eight hours following their disappearance.'

'Yes, I know that, but—'

'The thing is, Mrs Parks, the chances are extremely high that your husband simply stayed out for the night and forgot to let you know. Grown men tend to come home sooner rather than later and we simply don't have the resources—'

Laura has heard enough and she races across the kitchen and slams the phone down before the officer has even finished her sentence. Well, screw them if they don't want to help. But she knows her Jim, and she knows he would never abandon her after she's been on her own for almost four days straight if something terrible hadn't happened to him.

Her hands shake as she pours her coffee, taking care not to let the water splash across the worktop. The fridge reveals the milk has gone off so she tops it up with cold water and a spoonful of lumpy Coffee Mate, which turns it a weird grey colour. She knows she should probably eat some food to soak up the vodka in her bloodstream, but she feels sick to her stomach and certain anything she eats will curdle instantly. Instead she picks up the fallen chair, sits back down at the kitchen table and studies the stripes of sunlight that have been painted across the tabletop by the morning sun squeezing its way through the gaps in the half-closed blinds.

She clearly needs a better plan than relying on the police. She pulls the notepad towards her, turns to a new page, then picks up a half-chewed pencil from a nearby pot, and jots at the top of the page:

Finding Jim

She stares at the words for a while, the letters bleeding into each other, and tries to think this through logically. It doesn't matter that she *knows* Jim would never just up and leave her on her own. She needs to work out what might have happened to him, and what she's going to do about it – all without leaving the house.

Work?

She scribbles underneath. Jim works in Leeds for half the week, and has done since long before they were married. He's some sort of director – she believes, although when she really thinks about it she's never actually checked, which is odd – of a large international chain of hotels, and shortly after they moved in together he started working up north for half his working week. She didn't mind, not really, and even though she missed him when he was away, given the intensity of their relationship at first it did at least mean she had time to see other people, do other things. She asked if she could go with him once or twice, but he put her off, assuring her she'd be bored as he worked such long hours. She notes down a couple of names she's heard him mention and puts a question mark by their names.

Chris and Dev?
Dead/hurt?

She's aware this could cover any number of things, including someone hurting him and him falling ill, but, as she doesn't want to think about it too much, she just makes a note to call some of the hospitals in Leeds and London and moves on.

Friends/family?

The trouble with this, she realises instantly, is that she doesn't really know how to get hold of Jim's friends and family. He doesn't have any immediate family, and his friends all seem to be connected to his job, which means she hasn't met them either. How has she allowed this to happen? She draws a giant question mark next to this section and decides to come back to it later, if need be.

She ponders her list. It doesn't seem like much, and yet it's all she has. She's always known that she'd need to try and overcome her agoraphobia sooner or later, but since the attack Jim has always been there for her, being the frontman in their marriage and blunting the edges of any glaringly obvious gaps in her social abilities. Without him, she's lost.

4

THEN – OCTOBER 1985

The candlelight flickered between us as Jim studied the menu.

'It's always hard finding somewhere decent to take a chef,' he said, running his finger slowly down the steak list. 'But I've been here before and the food is pretty good.' He gave a goofy grin. 'Not as good as yours, obviously.'

'It looks lovely,' I agreed, even though I was trying to ignore the over-inflated prices. This wasn't the sort of place I normally came to and I couldn't help feeling a little self-conscious, not least because everyone in here – Jim included – was at least ten years older than me. 'I'm just grateful to eat something I haven't had to cook myself.'

'Well, good.'

The waiter appeared at our table and Jim put his menu down.

'We'll both have the steak, rare, and a bottle of the Pinot Noir,' he said.

'Oh, I—' I started, but Jim flashed me a smile.

'Trust me, the steak is the best thing in here.'

'Okay,' I agreed, handing my menu back.

He studied me in the dim light. His eyes shone and I noticed the fine lines radiating out from them, the hint of grey at his temples, the only obvious sign of the fourteen years between us. He was so handsome, and so much more loving and attentive than men my own age. Not that I'd had much experience. I'd only ever had two boyfriends before, and they had never been as exciting and intense as this. *This* was what romance should look like. This was how real men did it.

It had only been two weeks since Jim had burst into my kitchen and into my life. Since then we'd seen each other most days, and each time had felt more extraordinary than the one before.

'You barely know him,' Debbie had said when I'd told her I thought I was falling in love.

'But I feel as though we've known each other for years,' I'd admitted, knowing I was failing to explain the true depths of my feelings for this man. She'd frowned, as I'd known she would.

'Laura, what's going on? This isn't you. This isn't how you behave.'

'What do you mean?' My voice had been sharp and Debbie had noticed.

She'd sighed. 'I mean—' She'd shrugged. 'Nothing. I guess... I just think you should be careful. You've gone this long without giving your life up for a man, and I just worry that you've gone a bit gaga for this Jim.'

'Gaga? I thought you'd be happy for me,' I'd said, more than a little grumpily.

'I am. I will be,' she'd said. 'I just think you're taking it a bit too fast. What's the hurry?'

'How long were you with Steve before you got married?' I'd said, challenging.

'You're thinking of *marrying* this guy?'

'No! But you're missing my point. You and Steve weren't

together very long before you became serious. I just don't understand why you've got such a problem with me doing the same.'

She'd hesitated then, and studied the tabletop where our
almost-empty glasses of wine sat in puddles of water. Then she'd
looked up at me with concern in her eyes. 'Because this is so out of
character, Lau. I've always thrown myself into relationships full
pelt, you know that. But you? You don't. You're careful, more
cautious. And this is—' She'd stopped again, frowned. 'I just want
you to be careful, that's all. Promise me you will be?'

I'd softened and decided not to cause an argument. Debbie
was my oldest friend, and she was only looking out for me. Besides
our other friends had arrived then and the moment had gone.

'Promise,' I'd agreed as the others had sat down. We hadn't
said another word on the subject for the rest of the evening or, in
fact, since that night a few days before. But now, as I sat opposite
this man who'd turned my world upside down in just two short
weeks, I felt a nugget of resentment at Debbie for not being more
supportive, for trying to spoil what otherwise felt so amazing, so
new. So thrilling.

The waiter arrived with the wine and Jim and I chatted easily.
Even though we hadn't known each other long it felt easy, natural
between us.

We were on our second bottle of wine and our steak plates had
been cleared away when Jim reached across the table and took my
hands. A spark ripped through me at his touch, the way it always
did, and his gaze was intense, as though he was searching right
into my soul.

'I've got something to tell you,' he said, licking his lips
nervously. 'And it affects us.'

'What is it? What's wrong?' I said. I felt dizzy with worry.

'You know I work for a hotel chain?'

I nodded.

He looked down at the table briefly, then back up to meet my gaze. 'They want me to start working in Leeds a few days a week.'

'Oh.' I hated the thought of him being away so often, but it was such early days between us I didn't have the right to feel upset about it.

But he hadn't finished. I watched his shoulders rise and fall as he took a deep breath.

'Laura, I know we've only known each other a couple of weeks but, honestly, I feel as though I've known you for years and I hate the thought of us being apart when I'm home, in London. I—' he met my gaze now '—I want to be with you. All the time.'

I stared at him, trying to read his eyes, my heart skittering around like a balloon in the wind. 'What are you saying?'

'I want us to move in together.'

Was he being serious? Debbie's words jolted through my mind as I considered what he was saying – her warning for me to be careful, not to do anything out of character. But then I thought about the time I'd spent with Jim, how much fun we had, how happy he made me feel. How safe, and secure, in such a short space of time, and I knew I didn't want to give that up.

'I...' I hesitated, watching the shadows dance across his face, highlighting the curve of his cheekbones.

'I know it's really soon. I don't expect you to give me an answer straight away. But I've never felt like this about anyone before, and I just want to spend as much time as I can with you.' He looked back down at his hands on the tablecloth and my heart surged with love. *Love, already?* I heard Debbie's voice whisper in my ear, but I pushed her away. She didn't understand what it was like when Jim and I were together. This was like nothing I'd ever experienced before.

'Yes,' I said, my voice hoarse. I coughed and said it again, louder, as Jim looked up at me, his eyes wide. 'Yes, I'd love to move in with you.'

'Really? Do you mean it?' His voice was high, excited, and I loved that I made him feel that way.

'I do, Jim. I agree it's soon, but I also agree it feels right.' I shrugged. 'I say bugger it, let's do it.'

'Oh my God, Laura, I can't believe this.' His grip on my fingers tightened and I smiled as happiness flooded through me. So this was what it felt like to be utterly adored. I knew now that I'd never felt it before, and it felt amazing.

Two weeks later Jim and I got the keys to our own flat. I'd given a month's notice on the flat I shared with virtual strangers in Kentish Town, Jim had done the same on his soulless flat in Hammersmith, and we'd pooled our resources to rent a gorgeous two-bedroom flat in a street of Victorian terraces in East Finchley. It wasn't an area I knew well but Jim had been keen.

'This is a million miles better than my old place,' Jim said as we lugged the last of the boxes up the stairs.

'Definitely better than mine too.' I laughed as I almost dropped my box of books in the hallway.

The minute I'd seen this apartment I knew it was perfect. The high ceilings, the small fireplaces in each room, the wide, expansive windows looking out onto the street: I could instantly see myself making this place feel like home. And judging from the number of boxes I'd already moved in, it wouldn't take long to fill it up with all the things I loved. Jim, on the other hand, had barely anything, and I couldn't help wondering where all his 'stuff' was. The one time I'd stayed over at his flat it had felt cold and impersonal – almost clinical, the walls painted magnolia, the prints on the wall generic scenes of boats and fields and cottages, and barely anything personal anywhere.

'Where are all your things?' I'd asked.

He'd shrugged. 'I'm not here a lot, I don't have much,' he'd said.

'But it's so – impersonal,' I'd replied, running my finger along the mantelpiece, which had been empty apart from a single framed black and white photo of a couple. I'd picked the photo up, but before I could ask Jim anything about it he'd plucked it from my hands and put it back where it had come from.

'Sorry,' he'd said. 'I don't like anyone touching that photo. It's the only one I have of my mum and dad together before they died and – well, I can't risk anything happening to it.'

'Oh. Sorry.' I'd felt chastened.

'No, I'm the one who's sorry, Lola,' he'd said almost instantly, using the new nickname he'd decided suited me better than Laura. 'Of course you're welcome to touch whatever you like in this flat. After all, you're not just anyone, are you?'

I'd been about to ask him what had happened to his parents, realising it was odd that there was still so much I didn't know about him when we were moving in together, but he'd changed the subject and I hadn't found the right time since. I wasn't worried, we had plenty of time to get to know each other now we were going to be living together.

'Right, shall we christen the bed?' Jim said, grinning like a naughty schoolboy the minute the door closed behind us. And before I could say another word, or tell him I wanted to unpack, or do anything else at all, he'd dragged me into our brand-new bedroom and made love to me there and then on a mattress covered in nothing but a single sheet.

5

NOW – 18-19 SEPTEMBER 1992

Just before five o'clock, Laura's doorbell rings. Normally this would be enough to send her running for the safety of her bedroom, but today is different. Because today Debbie has come to help her. She scurries to the door, closes her eyes while she opens it, and lets her best friend enter. It's not until the door is closed again and Laura is wrapped in a hug that she dares open her eyes and start to relax.

'Oh, darling girl,' Debbie says. She's a good few inches taller than Laura and Laura finds it comforting to feel the press of her friend's cheek on top of her head. They stand there for a few seconds before Debbie pulls away. 'Come on, let's get away from this door.'

One of the things Laura loves best about Debbie is how she always knows exactly what she needs. They've known each other since secondary school, and while other friends came and went, Laura and Debbie always stayed strong, solid. They were together through the teenage years, when Debbie was off snogging boys while Laura stood shyly on the sidelines, and Debbie was Laura's cheerleader when she got her first job as a chef. Debbie is, and always has been, the only person Laura's ever told all her secrets to. The fact that Debbie isn't Jim's greatest fan is the only fly in the ointment, and one that's become harder to ignore over the years. 'I just think he tries to control you too much,' was all Debbie would say on the matter when Laura asked her why she didn't like her husband, and she's never wavered in her opinion. Which is why Laura is worried what Debbie is going to make of Jim going missing now.

They head straight to the kitchen at the back of the house, where Debbie unpacks the milk and teabags she's brought with her, flicks the kettle on and opens the cupboards searching for cups. It irks Laura more than it should that her best friend doesn't know where anything is in her kitchen any more. It shows how little she's seen her best friend in recent months – and it's entirely her fault.

'Have you eaten?' Debbie says as they sit down at the dining table with their drinks.

'Not really.'

'Oh, Lau. You've got to look after yourself.' She peers at her, eyes narrowed, and Laura is acutely aware of how terrible she looks. 'Have you been drinking?'

'No!' Debbie narrows her eyes.

'Last night?'

Laura hangs her head. 'Yeah,' she admits. 'Sorry.'

Debbie's fingers press against her forearm. 'Don't be sorry. I just worry about you.'

Debbie stands, opens the fridge, and places a just-in-date yogurt and a KitKat on the table. 'Eat this, and I'll make us something proper to eat in a bit.' She sits down opposite Laura. 'Now, tell me what's going on.'

Laura peels the paper wrapper off the KitKat and runs her thumbnail down the foil, snapping the chocolate in half. She takes a bite and chews slowly, then looks up at Debbie's concerned face.

'I'm so scared something's happened to him.' Her voice is wobbly and she coughs, takes another bite of her KitKat, the sugary chocolate giving her a head rush on an empty stomach. Her hands are shaking and she wraps them around her cup to warm them. The light in the kitchen at this time of the evening is dim with the blinds closed, and dust dances in the tiny stripes of light that slip between the cracks.

'I've rung all the hospitals in and around Leeds, and a few in London,' Laura says, eventually. 'I've spoken to the police but they're not interested.' She stops, aware of how sad it sounds that that's the extent of her detective work. 'I just – I don't really know how to get hold of Jim's friends since we moved. I don't even know where his address book is.' They used to have a book with all the phone numbers of friends and family on the table in the hallway in their flat in London. But she doesn't remember having seen it since they moved here – and she's only just noticed.

Debbie breathes out slowly, her forehead creased by a frown.

'You do remember that Jim's got form though, don't you, Lau?'

Laura's heart drops. Debbie's right. This isn't the first time Jim has disappeared – although last time he was home within forty-eight hours and distraught about worrying her, having been called away on urgent business without access to a phone. How could she have forgotten?

'I know,' she says, her voice hoarse. 'I just – this feels different. He knows—' She stops. Debbie knows what she's saying. She might not be keen on Jim or even quite understand why Laura loves him so much, but even she understands that Jim would never just up and leave her when she's so vulnerable.

'I know, darling,' Debbie says. 'I'm sorry. You're right, this is different. *Things* are different.' She drops her gaze to the list on the table between them, suddenly thoughtful. 'What are you most scared about, Lau?' she says eventually. 'That something terrible has happened to him, or that he's left you by choice?'

Laura listens to the silence in the room, to Debbie's gentle breathing, to the drumming of her heel on the floor as her leg jiggles up and down. 'I don't think he's left me,' she says quietly. 'I don't think he'd do that. Would he?'

'No, I don't think he would either. But what's the alternative?'

Laura's breath hitches. 'I – I can't stop thinking about him lying in a ditch somewhere. I keep wondering whether he's been attacked or hit by a car, or been beaten up...' She trails off. 'And I hate myself for thinking that would be a better alternative than him leaving me deliberately.'

There's the truth she could admit only to Debbie. That it would hurt her more to lose Jim by choice than by accident. Debbie nods in understanding.

'Well, the good news is that he's not in hospital, at least not anywhere obvious,' she says. 'Have you rung his office?'

Laura shakes her head. 'I couldn't remember anything about the company he works for,' she admits, ashamed. 'I don't know anything about his life outside these four walls any more. I'm a terrible wife, no wonder he's left me.'

'Don't be daft,' Debbie says. 'Anyway, it's a bit too late in the day to be worrying about tracking down his office now.' She stands, tying her unruly blonde hair into a high ponytail efficiently. 'I know you don't feel hungry but you need to eat. I'll cook dinner and then we're going to come up with a plan. Okay?'

Laura feels as if she might cry and swipes her hand across her face. 'I'll help.'

For the next twenty minutes they stand in companionable silence boiling water, opening tins of tomatoes, peeling and chopping some past-their-best onions they find in the back of the cupboard, and rustle up a plate of pasta and tomato sauce.

It's not until the food hits Laura's stomach that she realises how hungry she is. She wolfs the pasta down, hardly pausing for breath, then clatters her fork against her plate. Debbie is barely halfway through hers and she looks up at her knowingly.

'I think the first thing we need to do is get some food in that fridge,' she says, sucking up a piece of spaghetti and slopping sauce on her chin. She wipes it away with a piece of kitchen roll.

'I know. Jim usually does it.'

Debbie takes another mouthful. 'Do you want some of mine? I had a huge lunch so I'm not that hungry.'

Laura shakes her head. 'I think there might be some ice cream in the freezer though.' She stands. What she really wants right now is to open a bottle of wine, drink the whole thing down and pass out in bed again, oblivious. But she knows what Debbie would have to say about that. So instead she busies herself scooping ice cream into a bowl and eating it slowly.

Debbie pushes her plate away and wipes her fingers. 'Have you got any paper?'

Laura opens a drawer in the dresser and pulls out the list she started earlier. She turns over the top page to reveal a fresh sheet and hands it over.

'Right. I've been thinking about this on the way over,' Debbie says, tucking a stray hair behind her ear. 'I think we need a plan, starting with a list of people who might have some clue about where Jim could have gone.'

'There isn't anyone, I told you. And I don't know where his address book is anyway.'

Debbie holds her pen up in the air. 'I don't mean his old friends,' she says, lowering the pen onto the paper. 'Didn't you tell me that Jim has been getting to know the neighbours since you moved here?'

'Well, yes,' Laura says. 'But I don't see how that helps. We've only been here five minutes.'

Debbie sniffs. 'You moved here seven months ago, darling. I know it's felt like no time to you, but knowing Jim he will have made friends with some of your neighbours, and I reckon we could use that to our advantage.'

Laura frowns. 'But how? I don't know them at all. And I can't leave the house, so it's not as if I can knock on people's doors and ask them if they've seen my husband.'

'I'm not suggesting that. At least, not yet.'

'Ri-i-i-ight...' Laura feels panic starting in the pit of her belly and spreading out to her chest, limbs, fingers and toes until her entire body is quaking. She watches as Debbie writes a word at the top of the page and underlines it twice. Laura strains her head to read it.

Neighbours.

'Okay, what do we know about the people on this street?'

Laura shakes her head. 'Nothing. I told you, I've never met them before.'

'That doesn't mean you don't know anything about them.' She fixes Laura with a look. 'Think about it. When Jim has been out to see someone, he must have told you something?'

Laura shakes her head again. She can't do this, she just can't.

'I need a drink,' she says suddenly, standing. She opens the fridge and pulls out a bottle of Zinfandel, grabs two glasses from the cupboard and tries to ignore the look on Debbie's face as she fetches the corkscrew from the drawer. As she pours the drinks Debbie stands up. 'Wait there a sec,' she says. She leaves the room and Laura hears her walk down the hallway, past the living room, and open the front door.

Laura takes a large gulp of wine, and as the alcohol hits her bloodstream, her limbs instantly start to relax. She takes another sip, and another until the glass is empty, and she pours some more and gulps it down quickly. She glances at the door. Where *is* Debbie? The seconds tick by on the kitchen clock and she starts to wonder whether her friend has got so fed up with her that she's left as well. But just as a familiar swell of panic begins, she hears the front door close and soft footsteps approaching along the hallway. As Debbie enters the room Laura notices her friend glance at the half-empty bottle of wine on the table, but she doesn't mention it, and instead places her notebook back on the table.

'What's this?' Laura says, trying to decipher the lines, squares and squiggles Debbie has drawn.

'It's a map of your street.' She points her pen at one of the squares. 'This is your house.' She moves her pen across to the adjacent square. 'This is your next-door neighbour. These are all the other houses on the street, and this is the green with the tree in the middle.' She grins. 'I'm quite proud of that.'

Laura studies it for a moment. Debbie has marked out the rough position of every house on the cul-de-sac, and written a number in the centre of each one.

'How's this going to help?'

'We're going to collect some clues,' Debbie says, deliberately ignoring Laura's belligerent tone.

'What do you mean?'

She clears her throat. 'I don't believe for one minute that you know nothing at all about any of your neighbours. So together we're going to work out who lives where, and what little snippets of information you might have about them, buried deep in there.' She taps her index finger on her temple.

'How's that going to help me find Jim?'

'Well, once we've worked out who Jim might have got to know best over the last seven months, we're going to pay them a visit.'

Laura stares at her. 'And I assume by *we* you mean both of us?' she says.

Debbie nods sheepishly. 'I do. But—' she holds her hand up as Laura starts to object '—just listen. I'm not expecting you to do this straight away. But I really, really think that, if there's even a slim chance that your neighbours might know something about what's happened to Jim, it's got to be worth asking them. And it would be better if it was you rather than me who asks them. I *also* think that you can totally do this, Laura. With my help, of course.' She places her pen down on top of the notebook firmly, and tries to meet Laura's eye.

'But... I can't.'

Debbie prises Laura's fingers away from her empty wine glass and cradles them in her hands. 'You *can*, Laura. I promise. I'll be here, I'll help you, with all of it. And in the absence of any real help from the police or any way of getting hold of Jim's friends or colleagues, it could be your only option.'

Laura studies her friend's familiar face and sees nothing but warmth in it. She's only trying to help, Laura knows. But she also simply doesn't have the same faith as Debbie appears to have in her. She pulls her hands away and shakily pours another glass of wine.

'I know you don't want to do this, Lau, but promise me you'll at least think about it? I just think there's a chance that people who don't know Jim as well as you do could hold a clue as to where he's gone, even if they don't realise it. He was always trying to protect you from anything bad, so he'd have been unlikely to tell you if anything was troubling him. But he might have told someone else.' She stops, waiting for Laura to reply. And because Laura hates letting her friends down, she finds herself nodding, and agreeing to give it a try.

* * *

Debbie stays over in the end, promising that Steve and the kids totally understand. 'It's not as though I'm away a lot,' she says, pulling an emergency toothbrush from her bag. 'Besides, we've got work to do tomorrow, and I need to go and buy you some food.'

'Thank you,' Laura says. Although she's relieved not to be alone again, she can't help but feel a stab of panic that Debbie's presence means she can't drink herself into oblivion again. Instead, she'll have to face things head-on, something she hasn't been good at these past few months.

Bright and early the next morning and, in Laura's case at least, with much less of a hangover than usual, the pair find themselves at the dining table again, this time with more paper and some coloured pens they've dug out from a drawer. Laura has searched for Jim's address book on the off-chance it was hidden somewhere, but had no luck, while Debbie has already been to the corner shop for supplies. They munch on toast and jam and drink tea and juice, Laura's belly gurgling at the welcome sustenance.

'Okay, let's draw a bigger map, and try to work out who lives where and who might know Jim the best,' Debbie says, smoothing out a large sheet of paper with her hand. 'Then we can decide where to start.'

Laura's grateful for Debbie taking charge, and watches as she draws a circle for Willow Crescent, adding the road that comes off it heading towards the main road. She adds boxes for houses, checking them against her earlier sketch, then finishes it off with the green and the willow tree in the centre, sitting back to admire her work.

'Ta-da.'

Laura leans forward and studies it more closely. 'Now what?'

'Now you have to tell me everything you know about who lives in these houses. Names, how old they are, how well they know Jim. Their shoe size, if you know it. Anything could be useful.'

'Okay.' Laura studies the houses one by one, wracking her brains for anything Jim might have told her about the occupants.

She stabs the house immediately next door with her index finger as inspiration strikes. 'The people who live here, number one, are Mr and Mrs Loveday. She's Carol and he's...' she closes her eyes and thinks for a second '...Arthur. Carol and Arthur.'

'Great.' Debbie writes their house number and names inside the square. 'What do you know about them?

'They're retired. She likes to garden and he – actually I don't know much about him. But Jim seems to like them. They often chat in the garden, and he's been to their house a few times, I think.' She stops, disappointed she can't remember anything more, but Debbie's unperturbed, scribbling a few notes beside it and moving on.

'What about this one?' Debbie jabs the next square, the one on the other side, with her pen. 'Any ideas?'

Laura shakes her head. 'They're hardly ever there. I think he's a pilot or something, away a lot, and she works long hours. No kids, and they seem to be on holiday half the year. I don't think Jim knows them very well.'

'Okay.' Debbie scribbles

number three, away lots

and moves on.

Number four?

Laura leans forward. 'That's Ben.'

Ben?

Debbie writes the name carefully on the paper.
'I'm fairly sure he lives alone.' She searches the dark corners of
her brain for more. 'Yes, he does. Jim's been out drinking with him
a couple of times, and he's never mentioned a wife or girlfriend.
They play poker occasionally with some of Ben's local friends. Jim
seems to like him.'

Debbie jots down

single man, poker and nights out.

'I don't know anything about number five. I think a couple live
there but I hardly ever see them. Number six, though, is a woman
called Jane. She's got kids – teenagers. Abbie and Archie, Jim says.
He's helped her out a few times with odd jobs. She's a single mum,
works full time, the kids are left pretty much to themselves during
the day. Archie's always out there kicking a football around, Abbie
seems quieter, but Jim says she's an amazing artist. Good kids, I
think.'

'Great. Teens, football, art, DIY. Next?'

Laura frowns, trying to remember who lives at number
seven. 'Ah, yes, got it. Young couple, Simon and Sophie... no.
Sonja? I think that's it. They have a little girl who he looks after
while she's at work. No idea what she does but Simon and Jim
seem pretty friendly. Actually he might go to the odd poker
night too.'

Debbie nods. 'You're doing well. I honestly didn't think you'd
know as much as this.'

'Me neither.'

Debbie smiles and scratches her head with the end of her pencil. 'Right, number eight?'

'No idea. Jim's never mentioned them. But number nine is a lady called Marjorie Phillips, who lives with her daughter, Faye. I remember more about them because Marjorie never leaves the house either so we spend most of our lives staring at each other through our windows even though we've never actually spoken.'

Debbie scratches a cross through number eight and looks up. 'Tell me more.'

'As far as I can make out, Marjorie is in her sixties and disabled. I couldn't tell you what's wrong with her, but her daughter, Faye, seems to do everything for her while Marjorie spends her days watching what everyone else is doing through the living-room window.'

Debbie nods encouragingly. 'Does she know Jim?'

'I think he helps them out sometimes. Probably feels sorry for Faye, running round after her mother all the time. I think he's done the odd bit of shopping and sat with Marjorie while Faye goes out. She likes a gossip, apparently. Seems to know everything there is to know about everyone.'

'She could be useful, then.' Debbie draws a big red circle round number nine and writes

likes a gossip

beside it in big red letters. 'Maybe we should go and see them first.'

Laura peers out of the window to the other side of the street where she's certain she can make out Marjorie's outline through the gauzy net curtains, and shudders. It may only be a few metres away but it might as well be half the planet. She shakes her head. 'Not yet.'

Debbie pauses, her pencil resting on her lip. 'You're right. We'll start with the closest house and gradually move further away, but not until you're ready. Sound okay?'

Laura shrugs. The truth is, she doesn't really believe she can even get past her front door, let alone next door, no matter how much determination she can summon up. Even thinking about it makes her head spin, her palms damp and her chest feel as though someone is sitting on it. But that's a hurdle for another time. For the moment, at least, this plan is keeping her mind off the fact that Jim still isn't home. One step at a time.

'I'm afraid I don't know anyone from the last two houses, but I do know a bit about Tracy, the lady who owns the corner shop,' Laura adds. 'Jim goes there quite a lot. Seems she's lived here most of her life and knows most of the comings and goings. I reckon she might be a good one to talk to as well.'

Debbie sits back and studies the rough map she's sketched, reading the notes as she goes. She sticks her pen behind her ear and folds her arms, then jabs her finger into the box next to the one denoting Laura's house. 'We'll start here, then, with Mr and Mrs Loveday.' She looks up. 'It seems like the simplest choice, given it's the closest.'

Laura stares at the drawing for a moment, trying to imagine stepping outside the house, walking to the end of the path and turning right into her neighbours' garden, then into their house. A few short metres, nothing more between them than a hedge and a small fence. It should be easy. But it feels like an impossible obstacle.

6

THEN – MARCH 1986

I stretched my limbs and yawned as the morning light filtered through my eyelids. I opened one a slit and saw Jim silhouetted against the bright window.

'Are you off?' I mumbled sleepily.

'Not today, I'm going tomorrow, remember?'

I opened both eyes and squinted at him. 'What?'

Jim still worked away in Leeds three or four days every week and although I dreaded the days he was gone, it had become part of our routine now, and I just tried to make the most of the time he was away.

He sat down on the bed and leaned over me, his breath warm on my cheek.

'I've got that work thing, don't you remember? So I'm staying here tonight and going up to Leeds tomorrow.'

I shook my head. 'No, I don't remember that at all.'

He pressed his lips against mine. They felt cool and tasted of coffee.

'You silly sausage,' he said, pulling away and smiling at me. 'I knew you weren't listening.'

I frowned. I was certain I would have remembered if Jim had told me he was going to be here for another night, but I let it go.

'So what is this work thing?' I asked, hauling myself up to sitting. He ran his fingers down my shoulder and towards my breast and I shivered. 'Jim, stop it,' I said, giggling as I pushed him away. He grinned, and turned to tighten his tie.

'It's just a dinner, you know, boring work talk.'

'Oh, right.' I swallowed. 'No partners?'

He tipped his head to the side quizzically. 'I don't know whether some people are inviting other halves. Why?'

I shrugged, suddenly embarrassed. Why did I think he'd want to invite me along to a work thing when we'd only been together for six months? Just because it felt as though we knew each other inside out already, it didn't mean other people would understand how things were between us. 'Doesn't matter,' I said.

'Oh, darling,' he said. 'I thought you'd be at work, to be honest. But believe me, you really don't want to come to this. It will be boring as hell, and even the wives and girlfriends aren't your cup of tea.'

'It's fine,' I said, trying not to sound sulky and childish. Even though I was twenty-six and at the beginning of what I hoped would be a successful career as a chef, I still felt immature around Jim sometimes, even if he didn't mean to make me feel that way.

I couldn't help wondering, though, whether Jim had ever taken another girlfriend along with him to dos like this before. He hadn't told me much about any of his exes, preferring to keep them well in the past, which made sense, but he had told me that, although he'd never been married, he had been in a few serious relationships before. Maybe that was one of the reasons he didn't want to introduce me to his colleagues yet – perhaps they'd loved his exes and he wanted to wait a bit longer before bringing me into the picture. I hated the idea of him with someone else, so quickly pushed it out of my mind.

'Honestly, it doesn't matter. I just thought it would be nice to see you for an extra night, that's all. I get lonely here all by myself.'

'I know, and I am sorry I have to work away so much, I hate being apart too. It's not ideal but at the moment there's so much going on with work it's impossible to change it.'

'Maybe I could come with you up to Leeds one day? Just for a few days.'

'But what about your work?'

'I could take a few days off.' I shrugged, suddenly shy again. 'I don't know, I just thought it would be nice to see where you spend half of your life.'

He smiled and took hold of my hands. 'I'd love that, darling. Honestly. But I'll warn you, it's pretty tedious. I spend most of the day in the office and when I'm not there I'm schmoozing clients. You'd be just as lonely as you are here but without all your friends around you.'

'Maybe you're right. Never mind.'

He kissed my fingers one by one. 'But I tell you what. As I'm going out tonight and leaving you here all by yourself, how about you go out with your friends? My treat.'

'But I—' I stopped. I'd been about to object to him giving me money when I earned my own, but we both knew he earned a lot more than me and he'd told me several times I had to think of it as our money, not mine and his.

'Please, Lola? Let me treat you?'

'Okay,' I relented. 'That would be lovely, thank you.'

He leapt up from the bed then and disappeared. I stayed where I was for a few moments, enjoying the lie-in. It had been a late shift last night and had been almost 1 a.m. by the time I'd climbed into bed. I listened to Jim shuffling around in the kitchen, and then I heard his voice, muffled. Who was he talking to? I strained to hear but he was too far away and the bedroom door was half closed.

As I waited for him I thought about how much had changed for me in the last six months. I'd gone from being single and living in a grotty flatshare, to living with a man I adored and who made me feel special every single day. Even though we were apart half the time, when we were together, we spent every minute talking and the more I got to know him, the more I loved everything about him.

One fly in the ointment had been when he'd confessed he didn't think he was able to have children. 'It was one of the reasons me and my ex split up, because she couldn't cope with the fact I wasn't able to give her what she needed,' he told me one night. He'd looked heartbroken and my heart had melted for him. He'd looked at me, his eyes wide. 'I'm telling you this now so you can still walk away,' he'd said. And even though I had always imagined a future with children in it, now I'd met Jim I couldn't imagine a future without him in it. 'I don't want to walk away,' I'd assured him.

While he didn't like to talk about his exes any more than that, he told me everything else. I learned how his parents had both died in a car accident when he was twelve, and how he'd been brought up by his aunt, who died a few years ago, which meant he had no other family. At least it explained why making a new family with me was so important to him.

He told me how he'd worked hard to get where he was, determined to make something of himself. I was discovering all the little things too: how he only liked cream in his coffee not milk, how he preferred black and white horror films to the modern-day ones with their special effects, how he'd once tried rowing but found the competitive side of it so awful he'd quit after a month.

How he liked shepherd's pie for dinner at home but would always go for rare steak when we ate out, and preferred drinking wine but usually went for Scotch when entertaining clients. He had a small group of friends but I hadn't met any of them yet, Jim claiming that the time we had together was too precious to spend with other people. I couldn't argue because I agreed.

What it did mean, though, was that I was seeing my own friends less and less. Debbie was still a regular fixture in my diary, especially on the days when Jim was out of town, but I only ever really saw the others – Sammy, Sarah and Miranda – when Debbie organised it and made me come out. I hoped they would be free this evening for a catch-up.

'All sorted,' Jim said, interrupting my thoughts as he came back into the room. I was struck once more by how handsome he looked in his suit, how grown up and important, and I tried to imagine him being bossy and authoritative at work. I smiled.

'What's all sorted?' I said, gratefully accepting the cup of strong tea he handed me.

'Tonight.'

'What do you mean?' I took a sip of my tea but it was scalding hot, so I reached over and placed it carefully on my bedside table then turned back to face Jim. 'What's happening tonight?'

The smile on his face told me he was up to something. 'I've booked a table for you and your friends.'

'What? Where?'

'It's a secret.'

'But how am I supposed to get there if I don't know where I'm going?'

He tapped his nose. 'I've arranged for a taxi to pick you up and take you. And your friends. It's all arranged.'

'But—' I stopped as Jim gripped my hands.

'Listen, I know you don't see your friends very often and I don't like to think that's because of me. So I want to treat you. I thought it would be nice for you to have a night out.'

I dropped my gaze. He was being so kind, so generous. So thoughtful. How could I tell him that I preferred to just go to the pub with my friends where we could drink wine and laugh as hard as we wanted, rather than to some fancy restaurant where we'd have to mind our manners and limit the amount of wine we drank because we kept having to check the price of everything?

How could I tell him that, in fact, all I really wanted to do was come with him, meet some of his friends and colleagues and be part of his life, officially?

I couldn't, not when he was trying to do something nice for me.

'Thank you, Jim, that's really kind,' I said instead.

'You're welcome, sweetheart.' He kissed my knuckles, then his face turned serious. 'I'd do anything to make you happy. You know that, don't you?'

7

NOW – 23 SEPTEMBER 1992

'Right, stay there, I'm just going to open the back door. You don't have to move towards it, you don't have to do anything, okay? Just sit there, and watch me.'

Laura does as Debbie says, keeping her thighs glued to the wooden kitchen chair, her hands gripping the edges. Her palms are wet and her heart is pounding so hard it feels as though it might bruise her chest. She feels sick.

She watches, frozen, as Debbie pushes down on the handle and, inch by painful inch, pulls the door inward across the kitchen tiles. The garden reveals itself slowly: a slice of sky, a chunk of hedge, a corner of grass, the edge of the patio. The sky is a pale, hazy blue, smudged by wispy cloud, and the grass glistens with dew. Laura stares at it and inhales slowly, in through the nose, out through the mouth, filling her lungs and chest with air the way Debbie has taught her. Her heart is still hammering, and her skin prickles as though a breeze is rippling across the hairs on her arms. She shivers and closes her eyes, steadies her breathing. She can do this.

'Okay, try and open your eyes again,' Debbie says, her voice coming from a few feet away. 'Nothing bad will happen, I promise.'

Laura sits for a moment longer, takes a deep breath in and then out, then slowly prises her eyelids open, taking a few seconds to focus on the scene in front of her. The back door is still open, and Debbie is standing beside it, her face full of hope.

'Look, that's it,' she says, indicating the garden beyond the door. 'There's nothing scary there. Just grass. And trees. And sunlight.' She nods encouragingly but Laura can't bring herself to look at the benign strip of garden beyond the door. She feels as though she might topple off the seat so she grips it even more tightly.

'I'm going to open it a bit more, but not much, okay?'

Laura gives a tight nod and holds her breath as Debbie pulls the door slightly more open so that the slice of garden becomes a chunk, the lawn overgrown and unruly, the potted plants brown and dying. A chilly breeze weaves its way through the gap and across the floor.

And then Debbie opens the door fully so that Laura can see a door-sized section of the outside world. Her head is spinning and fear slithers around inside her, but she forces herself to look at it. She tries to picture herself standing up, then putting one foot in front of the other until she reaches the threshold. Then she tries to imagine stepping outside for the first time, first one foot, then the other onto the weed-strewn patio, so that her entire body is standing outside in the fresh air; breathing it through her nose until her head is filled with lightness, air, freedom.

She wishes she were the Laura who could do that without a second thought. She wishes with all her heart that she could get this over and done with and move on with trying to find Jim. But she knows it's going to take a lot of effort to emerge from this frightened shell. The question is, can she do it before it's too late?

Her legs are trembling.

'I—' She stops, her voice stuck in her throat, her mouth parched.

'Are you okay?' Debbie's voice seems like a million miles away as she stares out of the door. She watches as a single magpie hops across the lawn, dipping its beak every now and then before flapping its wings and flying away. She gives him a salute as he soars off, decades of ingrained superstition overriding her fear. She smiles at the ridiculousness of it – but it's one for sorrow, *two* for joy, and there was only one. She can't take the risk.

'I want to walk towards it but I just can't.'

'That's okay. You're doing really well.'

'I know but it's crazy. I mean, I feel as though my bottom is physically stuck to this seat, that if I stand up the chair will come with me. And even though I know that's not true, I still can't do it. I can't explain why, I just – can't.'

Debbie takes the three steps across the floor towards her and crouches down, her hand on Laura's knee. 'It doesn't matter. We can try again. We'll get there, okay?'

'Okay.' She sniffs. 'And thank you.'

Debbie stands, plants a kiss on her cheek, and closes the back door.

* * *

The back-door-opening incident has stirred a memory in Laura, one she hasn't thought about for a long time. It's of her and her father, in the kitchen at home. Her dad had been baking, his apron was covered in flour and the kitchen looked as though everything they owned had flown out of the cupboards and landed somewhere else in the room. Laura must only have been about five or six, and she loved watching her dad bake. It was such an incongruous thing for him to do; he was a real man's man, a mechanic who loved football and spent most weekends at the social club drinking pints. But at home Laura and Mum saw a different, softer side of him. Baking was his passion, and he loved whipping up something delicious in the kitchen: lemon meringue pies, chocolate brownies, fairy cakes, millionaires' shortbread, pasties. The house always smelt like a bakery, and the smell reminds Laura of home, even now.

On this day she'd walked into the kitchen to see what he was making. He'd had the back door slung wide open but it had still been boiling hot, flour particles drifting in the warm air. Laura had pulled a chair next to him and climbed up, her hands already covered in flour. Her dad had ruffled her hair, smearing the flour into her scalp as well.

'Oops.' He'd grinned, his wonky teeth on display.

'What you making, Daddy?' she'd said.

'Something special.'

'Is it a secret?'

'It is. I can tell you but you have to promise not to tell anyone, okay?'

Laura had nodded eagerly.

'I'm making a special coconut cake for Mummy. She's not feeling very well and I thought this might make her feel a bit better.' He'd put his finger to his lips, leaving a smudge of butter behind. 'But keep it secret, yes?'

She'd nodded again. 'Where is Mummy?'

'Hospital, remember?'

She'd frowned. She hadn't remembered, no. She hadn't thought anyone had actually told her that. Why was Mummy in hospital?

'Is she dying?'

'No, sweetheart, she's not dying. She'll be home tomorrow, and then we can help her eat this delicious cake, can't we?'

Laura had nodded conspiratorially. Daddy said Mummy was okay, so she must be. But that was the day that Laura realised baking for people could make them feel better. Because when her mum had come home the next day she'd looked sad, but when she'd seen Laura standing there holding the cake, her mum had smiled and been happy again.

Laura later learned that her mum had been in hospital having a hysterectomy, but all that had mattered that day was that the cake had worked, and from that day on she'd helped her dad make cakes, pastries and pies most weekends. Cooking had become her passion, the thing that made her feel content.

Now, the memory has made her feel melancholy. Not only for her parents in better times – before her dad walked out, before her mum met Brian the Bastard – but because it's made her realise how much she misses cooking. She stopped cooking after the attack and has barely been in the kitchen since. But she can't help wondering whether getting back to it might help her start to heal.

'Shall we try opening the back door again?'

Laura looks up to find Debbie holding out a steaming cup of tea. She takes it gratefully.

'Yes. Let's try.'

They walk into the kitchen and Debbie repositions the chair ever so slightly closer to the door, then whips it open so that Laura feels as though the outside has rushed inside to meet her. She gasps and takes a slow, shaky outbreath, puffing her cheeks full of air. Her hands are already starting to tremble and she sits on them to keep them under control.

'Right, are you ready to try and walk towards me? Just a little way.'

Laura nods and, on wobbly legs, the chair pressed hard against the backs of her knees, she stands. Then slowly, as though she's learning to walk again, she grips the worktop and teeters forward on one foot, then the other. The door is close now, close enough to smell the leaves huddling where they've dropped beneath the tree, to taste the slight pinch of cold on her tongue. She breathes in, trying to ignore the dampness creeping over her skin. She's tried this so many times before with Jim, she doesn't know how she's going to do it this time. Except she has more of a reason now. She needs to get out, to speak to people who might know where her husband is.

Keeping that in mind, she takes one last, long step towards the door and grips the frame as she stands, eyes closed, breathing the air deep into her lungs. Her head spins and she feels sick but she's made it! She opens her eyes and takes in the small patch of earth she calls her garden. She's missed it, just being out here in her own private world.

She feels a hand on her back, then Debbie gently holds Laura's hand. 'Do you want to try a bit further?'

She shakes her head. She's desperate to, but it feels too much all at once. 'Maybe tomorrow?'

'Are you sure? You're doing so well.'

'Yes. Yes, I've had enough now.'

Laura swivels and hurries away from the door. Seconds later she hears it click shut and feels her body deflate like a punctured balloon as she collapses onto the dining chair.

'Sorry,' she says.

'What are you sorry for? You did brilliantly. Have you ever got that far before?'

Laura shakes her head.

'Well, then. We'll try again next time, and then we'll go a bit further the time after that. Small steps, okay?'

'Thank you, Debs. I honestly don't know what I'd do without you.'

Debbie shrugs. 'You'll never have to find out, will you?' She swallows. 'Speaking of which...'

'What?'

Debbie looks sheepish. 'Don't think I'm prying, but I wondered if you're okay for money. You know, with Jim not here.'

Laura flushes. 'Oh, right. Yes, I—' She stops. 'I've got a bit in an account that Jim gave me every month. It should last a while.'

Debbie nods, satisfied. 'Okay, if you're sure. I hope you don't mind me asking.'

'Course not. Thank you.' Her voice cracks on the last word. She's more grateful than she could ever express for her friend's concern.

Debbie stands. 'Now, shall I make us some lunch?'

'I'll do it.' The words shoot out, surprising even herself. But Laura knows as soon as they're out there that she wants to do this. Something about pushing herself today has given her more courage than she's had in months.

'Are you sure?' Debbie looks worried. 'I know you haven't been so keen to cook since...' She trails off. 'You know.'

'Positive.'

As she heads into the kitchen and starts pulling ingredients from the fridge – the vegetables Debbie had bought at the corner shop, a tin of tuna, a block of cheese – Laura feels a sense of satisfaction settle over her, despite everything. For so long now she's had someone else to do everything for her, to protect her from facing the world. She thinks about her mum, and how, after Laura's dad left, Pat fell apart, unable to look after herself properly. Which was why she let Brian inveigle himself into their lives, to get his feet well and truly under the table and push Laura out.

'We're alike, you and me,' her mum had said the day Laura announced she was moving out.

'We're bloody not,' Laura had said indignantly. 'I'm *nothing* like you.' The seventeen-year-old Laura had been mortified at the idea of being as weak as her mum, as reliant on someone else – on a *man* – to look after her. But she can see now that's exactly what she's been doing these last seven years. Her mum was right after all. How she wishes she could tell her, but she doubts she'd be welcome at her old home any more – even if she could get there.

At least one good thing has come out of this. Even though Jim is still missing and she's still terrified about what might have happened to him, Laura is beginning to stand on her own two feet, and face her fears at last.

And she absolutely won't give up until she's found her husband, and brought him home.

8

THEN – DECEMBER 1986

'But you promised you'd come,' Debbie said, as if I didn't already feel guilty enough about letting her down.

'I know, but Jim said he needed to talk to me about something, so I have to wait in for him to call.'

'Isn't he home tomorrow anyway?'

'Yes but... he said it was important...' I trailed off, aware of how pathetic I sounded. The second's hesitation before Debbie spoke again told me she agreed.

'Okay,' she said, sighing. 'Whatever. I guess it must be, then.'

'I really am sorry, Debs. But at least you're not going on your own – Sarah's going as well, isn't she?'

'Yes, she is. Not quite the same though.'

The line hummed between us for a moment. I almost crumbled, told her I would go with her to watch her work colleague perform with his band, just the way I'd promised. But then I imagined how upset Jim would be if I was out when he rang, and I held my tongue.

'Have fun, then.'

'I will.'

The line went dead, and I felt a heavy weight settle in my belly. I hated letting Debbie down, but I was fully aware I was doing it more and more these days. And Debbie was right, Jim *was* due home tomorrow. I just had to hope she'd understand.

I swallowed down the pebble of doubt lodged in my throat, and switched on the TV, where a new programme called *Brush Strokes* was playing, and tried not to think about how guilty I felt for choosing a man over my friends – something we always promised we'd never do, no matter what.

The canned laughter from the TV washed over me as I thought about the number of times I'd seen my friends in the last few months. We used to go out at least once a week, for drinks or dinner, a trip to the cinema, picnics in the park. Being scattered across London meant it was important for us to make a regular arrangement to get together. But since I'd met Jim over a year ago, the times I'd actually made it to one of our catch-ups had dwindled so much that now I couldn't actually remember the last time I'd seen all of my friends together.

I told myself it was all right, that wanting to spend all my time with the person I was falling in love with was perfectly normal, and that my friends would forgive me. But the truth was, I was worried I'd already lost most of them. There were only so many times you could let someone down before they started to wonder whether you were worth fighting for.

Yet there was something about Jim that made me want to be there with him. Although at first the three or four nights he was away every week made it easier to see my friends, as time passed it became trickier, as he began ringing at awkward times in the evenings, so that, if I didn't want to miss him, I had to make sure I was at home to take his call.

'You know you will survive if you don't speak to him every

single day, don't you?' Debbie had said one day after I'd cancelled yet another night out.

'Of course I do,' I'd snapped, and luckily Debbie had left it at that. The trouble was, I knew she was right. I knew I was being pathetic and needy – and yet it seemed important to Jim, and so it was important to me.

The sound of the phone ringing made me jump and I reached over to the side table and snatched up the receiver, turning the volume down on the TV at the same time.

'Jim?'

There was a crackle, and a beep, and then a tinny recorded voice started speaking:

Hello. This is an automated message.

I slammed the phone down before it could get any further, and sat back. *Brush Strokes* had finished and *The Bill* theme tune had started. I checked my watch. It was already after eight, and Jim had said he'd ring around dinner time. I sighed, pushed myself up to standing and took my dirty plate through to the kitchen, scraping the rest of the congealed baked beans into the bin. I might be a chef, but I still hated cooking for just me and often settled for something easy. I opened the fridge and found half a bottle of Chardonnay and poured myself a large glassful, then took it back through to the living room. I sat on the sofa, and tried to concentrate on what DI Galloway was saying on the TV, but I couldn't focus so I wandered back into the kitchen and refilled my empty wine glass, then went back to wait for the phone to ring again. Where *was* Jim? Probably out with colleagues, or working late. Why else wouldn't he have rung when he said he would?

It occurred to me that Jim had never actually given me his work number. In fact, now I thought about it, I wasn't entirely sure what the company he worked for was even called. All I knew was that it was a big hotel chain, and although he'd no doubt told me once, it had never occurred to me that I'd need to know any more details. After all, he rang me every day, so it wasn't as though I actually needed to call him – as he said, he was busy working most of the time so it was easier this way.

As the minutes ticked by I found myself becoming more and more agitated. I'd stayed in tonight, let my friends down again, because he'd told me he had something important to talk to me about. Now it was almost ten o'clock and I was sitting here like a lemon, still waiting for him to ring.

I could hear laughter from the flat upstairs, and a pang of sadness bolted through me. I stood and walked to the window. For London, this street was quiet. But there were still signs of life, couples walking home arm in arm, friends laughing, people chatting.

And here I was, alone.

I refilled my glass and went to run a bath. Even though I felt cross, I took the phone off the cradle and carried it through with me, resting it on the closed toilet lid before lowering myself into the scalding-hot water. As I lay back, I shut my eyes and let my mind drift.

How had I become so isolated from the world? Apart from when I was at work, I barely saw anyone apart from Jim. I missed having someone to call when I was feeling down. Debbie was brilliant but I knew she didn't trust Jim so I tried not to talk about him too much. I thought about Mum, too. It had been months since she'd last rung me, the longest we'd ever gone without speaking. Although we'd had a strained relationship since she'd shacked up with Brian, she'd still always been there for me when I needed her. Now, though, I wasn't so sure she'd want to hear from me, and it broke my heart. I let out a long sigh.

Suddenly, the phone pealed loudly. I sat up so quickly that water and bubbles sluiced over the side of bath, soaking the bathroom floor. I quickly dried my hands on a towel, and snatched up the handset.

'Hello?' I said breathlessly.

'Hey, gorgeous, it's me.'

Jim. At last.

'Hey,' I said, reaching for a towel and quietly stepping out of the bath as I cradled the handset between my cheek and shoulder.

'What are you up to?' he said.

'I'm just out of the bath.'

'I wish I was there with you.' His voice was deep, husky.

'Me too,' I replied, feeling my face redden. Despite all the time we spent apart, I still found any vaguely sexy talk on the phone mortifyingly embarrassing. Luckily, Jim didn't take it any further, and as I padded through to the bedroom, he told me about his day, about the awful meeting he'd had, about how he was seriously thinking of looking for a new job, maybe one that meant he didn't have to be away from me so much.

This is it, I thought. This is what he's rung to tell me. He's getting a new job, based in London, so we can be together all the time. I felt my body sing with happiness as I waited for him to tell me his news.

But then he changed the subject. 'So, what have you been up to?' he said.

'I—' I stopped. 'Not much. Work. Watched some TV.' I didn't tell him about the bottle of wine I'd almost finished because I knew he didn't like me drinking alone. I cleared my throat. 'So, what was it you wanted to talk to me about?'

'What?'

'You asked me to stay in because you had something important you needed to tell me,' I reminded him.

'Oh. Right. Yes.' He sounded worried and I immediately found myself on edge. Was he about to tell me this wasn't working, that he wanted me to move out? It was always my fear, however much he reassured me that he loved me, and I tried not to picture how my life would be without him there holding me up.

'What is it, Jim? You're scaring me.'

'It's nothing serious, it's just...' He paused and my anxiety ratcheted up a level. 'I need to be away for Christmas.'

The world stilled for a moment before the words sank in.

'Again?' I thought about last Christmas when we'd only just moved in together. I'd been full of excitement about it, had pictured romantic strolls, lazy mornings lying round in our pyjamas, games of Scrabble and dinner for two during the Queen's speech. After spending the last few Christmases working because I'd had no one else to spend it with, I couldn't wait. But then Jim had admitted he'd already promised to work and that it was too late to get out of it, so I'd spent the day with Debbie and Steve and the kids instead. It had been fun, but I'd been so desperately looking forward to finally making up for it this year.

'I'm so sorry, love, I know it's a bugger but it's just the nature of the job. If something goes wrong in one of the hotels, it's me that has to sort it out.'

'Oh.' I tried not to sound so disappointed but I couldn't help it. 'How long for?'

'Just a couple of days – from Christmas Eve until the twenty-sixth, maybe the twenty-seventh?' He sighed. 'I really am sorry. I promise to make it up to you.'

'It's okay. I'll just go into the restaurant. They always need someone in.' My voice was small.

'Thank you, sweetheart. Christmas won't be the same without you. Listen, I'm sorry to dash but I've still got something to finish before I can leave to come home tomorrow morning. Sleep tight, love you.'

'Love you too.'

Then he was gone, and I was left listening to the dialling tone, shivering in my damp towel. Alone, again.

9

'Just one more step, come on, you can do it and you'll be there,' Jim urged, his voice even, calm. He was endlessly patient, and Laura was desperate to please him. If she didn't make it outside he'd be disappointed and she didn't want to let him down – again. So she lifted her foot from the doorframe and placed it carefully back down on the patio. But as she did, a burning feeling scorched up her leg until it felt as though her entire limb was on fire. She looked down and flames licked the side of her leg from her ankle up, melting her trousers into her skin. It should have hurt but she felt nothing, she was numb. She looked up at Jim, wanting him to see how well she was doing, craving his approval, but he was so far away now she couldn't see him any more.

'Jim!' she called. 'Look at me, I'm outside!' She let go of the doorframe and put her other foot in front of her and flames engulfed that too. She cackled and looked back up at the sky. Jim was falling towards her, tumbling faster and faster, and she smiled. He'd be so pleased when he saw how well she was doing. She just wanted to please him, to show him that she was the Laura he'd fallen in love with. That she wasn't broken any more, she was fixed, and he could love her again. But as he got closer she saw his face was covered with a balaclava, and piercing grey eyes stared at her through tiny round holes cut into the fabric. Terror engulfed her and she was back in that dark alley, the glint of a knife, the roar of fear in her ears. She screamed until her throat was raw.

This was what happened when she tried to leave the house. She'd told everyone but they wouldn't listen, they thought she was just being silly, that the same thing couldn't happen again. But he was here and she was fighting, fighting, adrenaline coursing through her body, kicking and biting and scratching and he had hold of her by the throat so she couldn't scream and she kicked out, hard, and he let go, just for a second, and she screamed and screamed and ran and then he was gone and she could hear Debbie's gentle voice, and she knew she was going to be okay, it was all going to be okay...

The air tickles Laura's face, and a leaf drops from the tree onto her hair. She brushes it away and watches it fall to the ground where it disappears, indistinguishable among the pile of reds, golds and purples. The leaves have turned early this year and they're stunning, their intricate lines, curves and spikes forming a beautiful carpet across the lawn. Laura lifts her head and concentrates on planting her feet firmly into the earth, feeling the softness of the grass beneath her shoes, the cool air caressing her skin through her thin jumper. She clamps her arms to her sides, unclenches her fists and inhales deeply, filling her lungs with air, then blowing it slowly back out again. As she takes another breath in she pictures the air filling her entire body with freshness, with clean thoughts, with new life. Then she exhales, trying to purge herself of all the accumulated toxins. How long would it take, how many deep breaths, to get rid of all the darkness, all the terror inside her, to be bright and clear and happy again? She breathes in once more and closes her eyes. She feels light-headed. Is she really here or is this another dream?

When she opens her eyes Debbie is standing right next to her, exactly where she said she'd be, a smile on her lips.

'You did it!' Debbie's voice is a whisper, as though saying the words too loudly will destroy the fragility of what Laura has achieved.

Laura gives a small nod. She can't think about it too much – about the fact that she's outside, in plain sight – or she'll feel terrified all over again. But she *has* done it. She's made it out of the back door and into the garden for the first time in more than eighteen months, and nothing bad has happened. The world hasn't ended, she hasn't been hurt. She's just here, in the fresh air, breathing, alive. She allows her gaze to wander, to take in the overgrown hedge, the too-big tree, the rosebush that had been a blaze of colour all summer but now has dead petals clinging to it for dear life.

The house is behind her and she slowly turns to take in the rest of the garden; the white metal bench, the mossy patio with the table and chairs still huddled together, unused and unloved since they moved here. The back of the house, that she's never actually seen before, looms over her, the upper windows dark, like inquisitive eyes, protective. The rhythm of her heart has settled, a steady but insistent thrump thrump against her ribcage, and her hands have stopped shaking. She strains her ears. She can hear a faint tweet of birds, a clipping sound like a hedge cutter, and a steady thump that might be the boy opposite kicking his football against the garage. A car door bangs somewhere and an engine starts, then the sound slowly fades into nothing. Life goes on, as it has always done. Nothing has changed.

Except her.

'I think I can do this,' she whispers.

'You can. You are doing it.' Debbie struggles to hide the excitement in her voice. She hadn't imagined Laura would get this far quite so quickly, but she's clearly under-estimated her friend's determination.

'You were right,' Laura says. 'This is the only way I'm going to be able to help Jim. I need to get out there and find him. He needs me.'

She looks around the garden, tears shining in her eyes. She's made it. She's on her way.

* * *

After Debbie has left, Laura pours herself a large glass of vodka and reflects on how far she's come in just a few days. She's never thought of herself as brave, but for the first time ever, she's beginning to feel as though she might just be brave enough to do this one thing. Jim is counting on her. It's what's getting her through it.

After the first day and the aborted attempt at getting into the garden, she was worried she might never make it. But later that evening after Debbie went home she tried again, and this time, under the cloak of darkness, she managed to stand up from her chair without falling over.

Throughout the next day she tried a few more times, and each time she got a tiny bit closer to the door until, early this morning, she finally reached the threshold. Debbie was amazed at her friend's progress when she arrived later that afternoon and they finally made it out into the garden.

'At least one good thing has come out of Jim disappearing,' Debbie said as they walked back inside. 'You're finally overcoming your agoraphobia.'

Laura didn't think much about her words at the time but now she realises that Debbie was right. Laura might constantly feel as though her whole body has been swallowed by anxiety, but not only has Jim's disappearance given her a reason to get better, it's also forced her to be stronger than she's had to be in a long, long time.

Laura allows herself to think about Jim for a moment, about their life together. When they met she was totally swept up in the romance of it. At forty to her twenty-six he was significantly older than the men she usually went for. But more than that, he was straightforward and open. Her previous boyfriend had been quiet and shy, too scared to tell her how he felt. Too similar to her, if she was honest, which meant it was destined to fail from the start.

But when she met Jim, he was so different, it felt almost like starting all over again, from scratch. Wiping the slate clean and learning the new rules.

Not that she'd had that much experience with men. She'd spent most of her teenage years without a boyfriend, until she'd started to believe she was never even going to kiss a boy, let alone find someone who liked her. And then, finally, blissfully, it had happened, at a friend's house party. It had involved alcohol of course – Cinzano swigged straight from the bottle, which had reappeared again many hours later in a bush outside – but finally, at the ripe old age of fifteen, Laura had had her very first snog.

Dating didn't come easy to her, but she tried. All her life she'd had an overwhelming need to be looked after, protected. Dad had been her hero, the person who made her fall in love with cooking and food, and when he walked out, her mum didn't have much left to give. She did her best, but she was weak, and when Brian came along with his fags tucked behind his ear and his cocky swagger, she believed he'd look after her the way Laura's dad always had. By the time it became abundantly obvious that Brian was neither a protector nor a good man, he had his feet well and truly under the table and it was made clear to Laura that she was in the way.

She left home at seventeen and moved in with Debbie. Debbie had been desperate to get away from home too, and they both started working behind the bar in their local. Debbie took to it immediately, always finding ways to chat to the men who spent their days propping up the bar, downing pint after pint of ale, without letting them put their lecherous hands anywhere near her. Meanwhile Laura begged to be allowed to work in the kitchen away from all of that, and in the end, when the cook left, the landlord reluctantly offered her the job.

'Just make sure you don't get any fancy ideas,' he said as he stubbed out his Benson & Hedges in the overflowing ashtray.

She didn't stay long, but soon after she found a job in a local restaurant where she could be more creative than just heating up frozen shepherd's pies and boil-in-the-bag slabs of gammon. She missed Debbie but at least they still saw each other at home. Even though Debbie was only six months older than Laura she'd always been wiser, savvier, and if it hadn't been for her, Laura probably wouldn't have got through those first years of living away from home.

Soon, work became Laura's focus. Creating new dishes, working her way up from kitchen assistant to junior chef and, eventually, head chef, gave her an independence she'd never experienced before so that, by the time Debbie moved out to buy a flat with her new boyfriend, Steve, Laura was doing things on her own for the first time in her life. She began to think that maybe she didn't need anyone else after all.

Then she met Jim.

After he barged into her kitchen – 'I didn't barge, I politely entered and left again until you'd finished,' he insisted – Laura felt the knot of tension in her belly slowly start to loosen as she realised that, actually, she did like having someone to look after her after all.

Jim made her feel safe, it was as simple as that. 'Just make sure you're not mistaking security for love,' Debbie warned.

But Laura knew she wasn't. Jim was like no other man she'd ever met, and in return for him looking after her, Laura made sure he was the most important person in her life too.

While Jim sorted the bills, paid the mortgage, spoke to people on the phone and helped her to blossom from a shy, slightly awkward young woman into a grown-up with friends and a social life, Laura looked after him too, in her own way. She'd spend hours whipping up special meals, learning Jim's favourites and perfecting them: toad in the hole with plenty of fiery mustard; American pancakes with blueberries and maple syrup for weekend breakfasts; scones and cream, Welsh cakes, home-made jam. She loved seeing his face when she presented him with her latest creation. He looked after her, and she looked after him. It worked perfectly, and they didn't need anyone else.

It's only now, with Jim missing, that it occurs to Laura that, by cutting herself off from everyone else in her life apart from Jim and Debbie, it means she's quite, quite alone.

* * *

The doorbell peals and Laura leaps up, her heart racing. It's gloomy now, the late-autumn shadows pushing themselves into the deepest corners of the living room, so she flicks on a lamp,

downs the rest of her vodka, and makes her way cautiously to the
front door. Even this action is a huge step and as she reaches for
the latch and pulls the door open she takes a deep breath and
averts her gaze from the outside world.

'Sorry I'm late, had a childcare nightmare,' Debbie says, stepping inside and shaking off her coat. Before Laura can close the
door, two other, smaller figures step in behind her friend and
hover uncertainly in the hallway. 'Sorry, Lau, Steve was meant to
be at home this afternoon but he had to go out last minute so I
brought the kids with me. I hope you don't mind.' She sweeps her
arm towards her two children apologetically.

'Of course not,' Laura says. She's always loved Laura's children,
Lily and James, but she hasn't seen them since the incident and
she wonders whether, at nine and six, they even remember who
she is. She crouches down. 'Hello, you two, it's lovely to see you,'
she says. Neither of them reply but Laura is rewarded with a shy
smile from Lily.

She waits while Debbie helps them out of their coats, hands
them colouring books and a small plastic tub of Lego and dishes
out strict instructions to be good.

Sorry, Debbie mouths as the kids file into Laura's living
room.

'Honestly, it's fine,' Laura says, and is surprised to find that,
actually, she's quite pleased to see them. 'I'll put the TV on for
them.'

'Say thank you to Aunty Laura,' Debbie says as the TV springs
to life.

'Thank you, Aunty Laura,' Lily choruses, while James sits
mute, watching Anthea Turner talking animatedly from a school
somewhere on *Blue Peter.*

With the children entertained, Laura and Debbie make their
way through to the kitchen.

'So what time are they due?' Debbie says, filling the kettle and finding cups.

She checks her watch. 'About half an hour.'

Debbie nods. She's tied her wild curls up in a scrunchie on the top of her head, and tendrils keep escaping, springing loose. She hands Laura a steaming mug of tea and a plate with an enormous slab of Battenburg on it.

'I stopped at the baker's on the way here, thought you might need some sustenance,' she says. 'Eat. I'll just take the kids some.'

Laura does as she's told, and sits obediently at the table. Her hands are shaking and she's desperate for a drink, but she needs to stay clear-headed because the police are coming round to see her.

Finally, nine days after Jim went missing, they've agreed to come and take some details from her. Under normal circumstances, having strangers in her home would be almost as bad as having to leave the house. But these are not normal circumstances, and with each hour that passes, and each hour that Jim is away, Laura's courage is growing.

Debbie returns and lowers herself into the chair beside Laura with her own piece of cake and takes a bite, licking the crumbs off her lips.

'So, how are you feeling?' she says.

'Terrified.'

'Course you are. But you're also braver than you think.'

'I don't feel very brave.'

Debbie doesn't speak for a moment, then says quietly: 'We will find him, you know.' She reaches for Laura's hand. Before either of them can say any more, the doorbell rings again, and they stand.

'Ready?' Debbie says.

'Ready.'

As they approach the door they can make out two silhouettes through the stippled glass. Laura's heart thumps wildly, and when

Debbie squeezes her hand she realises how clammy her palms have become. She watches Debbie's hand rise to open the latch as though it's a frame-by-frame stop-motion video, and she thinks she might throw up. And then the door is open and Laura takes a deep breath and greets the two police officers standing on the doorstep. One is tall and blond, the other shorter, with grey hair cut close to his head. He has a friendly face.

'Mrs Parks?' the shorter one says, and she nods mutely.

'I'm DS Brian McDonald and this is PC Stuart Compton.'

'Come in,' Debbie says, stepping to the side. Laura holds her breath and presses her nails into her palm as the two police officers pass. It's not until they reach the kitchen that she lets out her breath and tries to relax. She can do this.

'Can I make anyone tea or coffee?' Debbie says.

'No, thank you,' the blond officer says, and Laura waits for them to sit down before she takes a seat herself, pushing her uneaten cake to one side. She stares at a point just above the youngest officer's head and waits for them to speak, her pulse thudding in her temple.

'I understand you're concerned about your husband,' DS McDonald says.

'Yes.' Her voice cracks.

He pulls a notebook out of his pocket and clicks a biro open. It hovers over the paper, and Laura wonders what he's going to write in there before he leaves today. She imagines him rolling his eyes later, unsure what she's making such a fuss about. How can she make them both understand?

'Laura?'

She looks up and sees all three pairs of eyes watching her, waiting for her to answer a question she hasn't heard.

'I'm sorry, what?'

'I was asking whether you might tell us what's happened,' PC

Compton says, smiling kindly. 'When exactly did your husband go missing?'

She tells them everything. About how Jim works away four days a week, her agoraphobia, and why she's so worried about his disappearance.

'I'm scared something terrible has happened to him,' she says finally, her throat dry and scratchy from more talking than she's done in a long time. 'He wouldn't just disappear and leave me all on my own. He just wouldn't.'

DS McDonald leans forward. Laura can see a few notes scrawled on his pad but can't make them out. 'We'll look into it, I promise,' he says. 'Would you be able to give us an up-to-date photograph of your husband?'

'Oh, yes, of course.' Laura jumps up and pulls open a drawer. 'I'm not sure we have very many but – ah, yes, here you go.' She hands over a photo of Jim on their wedding day two years previously and it strikes her how odd it is that they hardly have any photographs of each other apart from these.

'Thank you. I think we have everything we need for now.' He glances at his colleague, who gives a nod, then they both stand. Laura follows suit.

'We'll let you know if we have any news, Mrs Parks, but please get in touch if you hear from your husband in the meantime, won't you?'

Laura is so grateful they haven't dismissed her fears she feels as though her throat is blocked. 'Of course. Thank you.'

When they've gone, Laura is so exhausted she might as well have run a marathon. But there's also a sense of underlying pride. She did it. She let people in, and she held a proper conversation with them.

'You did brilliantly,' Debbie says, wrapping her in a hug.

'Thank you,' she whispers.

'Mu-u-u-u-um!' a call comes from the living room. 'I'm hungry!'

And while Laura and Debbie fuss around making some dinner for the kids, Laura realises that today is the first time she's truly believed she might be able to finally overcome the agoraphobia that's been crippling her for so long. And she might just be able to find Jim.

10

THEN – AUGUST 1987

London was busy tonight. Well, London was always busy but this evening it felt packed to the rafters, as though you couldn't squeeze another single body into it even if you tried. There were people everywhere: shoehorned into Tube trains, funnelling along underground corridors, spilling out of pubs and restaurants and theatres. This was the sort of London I loved. Bustling, vibrant, exciting London, and the London I didn't get to see anywhere near as much as I liked these days. Best of all, I was here with Jim, ready for a night out.

It was rare that we came into town together. Usually we stuck to our local area of north London because Jim claimed it was so much nicer to be able to walk home rather than having to bother with overloaded buses and Tubes or fork out for a taxi. I went along with it, mostly, even though I'd love to come into the city centre more often, and couldn't help wondering sometimes why, with the money he earned, Jim was so against paying for a taxi when he was so generous with everything else. But here we were tonight, just the two of us, on our way to see *Starlight Express* for Jim's birthday, and I couldn't wait.

We strolled hand in hand, dodging other pedestrians as they walked towards us or swarmed around us. The sun was dropping below the buildings, leaving a residual warmth clinging to the pavements and buildings, and a wave of happiness washed over me.

'I wish we did this more often,' I said, leaning my head on Jim's shoulder. I felt his head turn towards me and I looked up at him.

'We go out all the time,' he said, his face furrowed.

'I know. But we never come into town. I love it on a night like this.'

He was silent for a moment and I wondered what was going through his mind. Did he think I was being too demanding? I was about to say something else when he gave a tight smile. 'I thought you liked it where we live?'

'I do.' I pulled away and looked at him, confused. 'I love it. I just love this too. Always have.'

He nodded curtly. 'Fair enough. I just thought because you work in central London you'd have had enough of it on your days off. Never mind.'

I could feel annoyance pulsing off him in waves so I decided not to push it and just enjoy the evening we had planned.

I'd bought these theatre tickets for Jim's birthday, and when I'd presented him with them he hadn't seemed as pleased as I'd hoped he would.

'What's the matter?' I'd said as he'd studied them, his head down. 'Have you already seen it?'

He hadn't looked up for a minute, and when he had he'd been smiling, although I hadn't been sure it reached his eyes. 'No.' He'd cleared his throat. 'No, I haven't. These are great, thank you.'

He'd put the tickets to one side and stood to pour us another drink then, and I'd been left with the distinct impression that I'd done something wrong. Was it because I'd booked the tickets as a surprise without checking with him first? But how could I have done that for a birthday gift? Or was there another reason, something I hadn't thought of, that had made him react the way he had?

He hadn't said anything else though, and when the day had finally arrived, three months later, he'd seemed happy enough about going. Now, I wondered whether I'd imagined his reaction all along, and was worrying about nothing.

As we approached the Apollo Victoria Theatre he seemed to slow, and I felt his grip tighten around my hand.

'Are you okay, love?' I said.

'What? Yes, totally fine. Why?'

'You seem tense.'

Jim looked at me, his face unreadable. 'I'm fine, really. I'm just tired, that's all. It's been a tough week at work.'

I nodded. But as we scurried the last few hundred yards to the theatre Jim still seemed on edge, and every now and then I saw him flick his gaze from side to side as though he was searching for something, or someone. I wondered whether it was the crowds that bothered him, although I'd never seen him like this before. Maybe it *was* work. Perhaps I should ask him about it more.

We reached the theatre and Jim yanked me inside so fast I almost tripped over. When we entered the compact foyer he seemed to visibly relax, and as a result so did I. We checked our tickets and were making our way to the stairs leading to the first-floor bar when I heard a shout from behind. I turned to see a man waving wildly at us. I didn't know who he was but he definitely seemed to know us, so I nudged Jim.

'Is that a friend of yours?' I said, indicating the man, who was still smiling and trying to wave us over. Jim flicked his glance over in that direction, then immediately turned away and pulled me up the stairs. When we got to the top I started walking towards the bar, but Jim steered me towards the door into the seated area.

'Don't you want a drink?'

'It's getting late, we should probably just find our seats,' he said, checking his watch.

Before I could say anything else he thrust the tickets at the usher on the door and we walked into the almost-empty theatre to locate our seats. As we settled into them, I turned to him.

'What was that all about?'

'What do you mean?'

'All that hurrying. It was as though you were trying to run away from that man.'

'What man?'

'The one waving at you.'

'Oh, no. Sorry, I just didn't know him. He must have been waving at someone else.'

There hadn't been anyone else nearby. 'I thought he called your name though. Are you sure you don't know him?'

'What is this, the Spanish Inquisition?'

'What? No. I just thought it must have been someone you know.'

'Well, it wasn't,' he snapped. 'You must have been mistaken.'

'Oh. Okay.' I turned away from him. I wasn't sure why the evening had suddenly taken such a sour turn, but I was keen to steer it back on course. Jim clearly didn't want to talk about it. And maybe he was right, maybe I *was* mistaken. I mean, why would Jim pretend not to know someone?

'Do you want a drink, then? I'm going to get one.'

He checked his watch. 'Please. I'll have a red wine.'

I stood and headed back out to the bar. I had a quick look round to see if I could see the man who I was still certain had been gesticulating at Jim, but there was no sign of him, so I went to order our drinks. When I got back inside, the row was filling up, and by the time I'd shuffled back to our seats Jim seemed in a better mood. I handed him his drink.

'Thanks, love.' He pecked me on the lips. 'Sorry about before. It's just been a tricky day at work, but I shouldn't have taken it out on you.'

'It's okay.'

'But I really didn't know that man, you know.' He laughed. 'Why would I ignore someone if I knew them, you silly sausage?'

I shrugged. 'I don't know.'

We sat and watched the show in silence, holding hands in the darkness. But I couldn't help noticing that, when it finished, Jim was in a hurry to leave before everyone else, and practically dragged me down the street away from the theatre where we almost fell into the first taxi we found. And as we roared into the late evening traffic, I was left with an unsettling feeling that I'd missed something important.

PART II

SEARCHING

11

NOW – 1 OCTOBER 1992

Number one Willow Crescent
Carol and Arthur Loveday

'Carol, get away from that window, for goodness' sake.'

Carol lets the net curtain drop back against the frame and turns to face her husband, Arthur, who's in his armchair, newspaper stretched out across his knees.

'I'm not doing any harm Arthur.' Carol's face creases into a pinch and she turns back to the window, pressing her nose against the lacy nets. 'Besides, that Laura from next door is out there, you know. Actually *in the garden.* I've never seen her out there before.'

'I know, you said.' Arthur picks his paper up and gives it a snap. 'I just don't understand why you're so surprised. It *is* her garden.'

'I'm well aware of that Arthur,' Carol says, rolling her eyes. 'But she's never out there. Never. I've never seen her *anywhere.*' She gives a small tut as punctuation.

'Right. Sorry.' Arthur returns to his paper, more interested in the racing news than the fascinating fact that some woman is walking down her own garden path. Honestly, does Carol really have nothing better to think about?

'Arthur!'

He looks up wearily, unsure whether he's ever going to find out the results of the 12.45 at Catterick Bridge. 'What, love?'

'I said I haven't seen him for ages either.'

'Who?' He tries to sneak a look at the paper, but she's watching him like a hawk.

Jim.' She points with her head in the general direction of the window as if that clears it all up. 'He's not been round for a couple of weeks, now I come to think of it.'

'So?'

'What do you mean "so"?' Her voice has risen a few octaves and Arthur squirms at the assault on his eardrums. 'I mean, first he disappears and then she's outside, just standing there, not moving.' She glances back at the garden. 'I think she's got her eyes closed now. It's weird, Arthur. Something's not right.' She pulls the net curtain aside, then lets it drop right back down again with a gasp. 'Bugger, she saw me!'

'Well, what do you expect if you stand there staring at her? You do know windows are see-through, don't you?'

'Don't be so sarcastic, Arthur, it doesn't suit you.' Carol moves away from the window and lowers herself carefully into the armchair next to her husband, her hands twitching in her lap. She picks up her knitting from the side table, puts it back down again. She stares at the TV in the corner where a newsreader is explaining something important about the AIDS epidemic, but the sound is turned so low she can hardly make out a word they're saying, so she plucks a copy of *Take a Break* from the rack and turns the pages without really seeing them.

She puts it back on the arm of the chair, stands, smooths her skirt, sits again.

Arthur sighs heavily behind his paper. 'What are you fussing around for?'

'I'm not fussing.'

'You are. You can't keep still. If you're that worried about what's going on next door, why don't you just go out there and ask her?'

'I can't do that!'

'Why not? It's the only way you're going to find anything out.'

'I can't very well march out there and ask a woman I've never met before why she's in her own front garden and what she's done with her husband, can I?'

Arthur hides his grin behind his hand. His life won't be worth living if she sees him laughing at her but he can't help it if she's so ridiculous sometimes. 'I wasn't suggesting you put it quite like that, love. But maybe you could just go out and say hello. You never know. A conversation might start.'

Carol tuts. She hates it when Arthur's right. He's always so insufferably smug about it. And if he thinks by putting his hand over his face she can't see him laughing at her, then he has another think coming.

'Okay, then, maybe I'll do just that.' She stands again and checks her reflection in the mirror. There's lipstick smudged on her teeth so she wipes it off with the sleeve of her cardigan and smooths her hair down. It springs straight back up again. She's just about to march out of the room in a decisive fashion – making sure she shuts the front door nice and firmly so that Arthur knows she's gone to do exactly what she'd said she was going to do – when the doorbell peals through the room. Carol jumps so much she almost hits her head on the standard lamp and she sees Arthur pretend not to laugh again.

'Who's that?' She checks her watch. It's midday, they never

normally have visitors at midday. Mind you, they *did* order some tea towels and a new rolling pin from the Freemans catalogue the other day, so maybe that's what it is. She just wishes these delivery drivers didn't feel the need to ring the blessed doorbell every time they delivered something, as though it needs announcing. Surely it'd be perfectly acceptable to just leave it outside? She can't be doing with answering the door every five minutes to every Tom, Dick and Harry.

'How on earth do I know? Aren't you going to get it?'

'Well, yes, of course I am.' She marches across the room and opens the front door decisively, ready to accept the package she's expecting.

'Oh!'

Carol jumps again, and the woman on the doorstep jumps too, her face white. Despite the fact Carol had been intending to go outside to speak to Jim's wife, Laura, she was still the last person she'd been expecting to find on her doorstep. Carol wouldn't have been more surprised if a delivery driver had turned up at her front door wearing a clown costume and thrown a custard tart in her face. And now Laura is staring at Carol as though she's seen a ghost, her face drained of all colour, and she's shaking like a leaf. Carol wonders if there's something wrong with her. Maybe that's why she never leaves the house and they've only ever met Jim. He'd never mentioned she was mentally impaired, although you probably wouldn't, would you?

Suddenly Laura sticks her hand out towards Carol.

'Hello, I'm Laura. From next door.'

Carol takes the warm palm in hers and shakes it limply. She can't help noticing the hand is damp. She drops it and then spots someone else standing behind Laura. Another woman with blonde hair, tall and pretty. This second woman steps forward and holds out her hand too and gives a much firmer handshake, really quite firm in fact, and says, 'I'm Debbie, Laura's best friend.' She has a lovely warm smile and Carol finds herself smiling back, slightly inanely. This is *most* unexpected.

Suddenly she remembers herself.

'Oh, you must think I'm awfully rude, please do come in.' She opens the door fully and steps aside as the two women walk into the hallway. 'Would you mind leaving your shoes just here, please?' She indicates the small shoe rack and waits while they line their trendy ankle boots up next to hers and Arthur's sensible shoes, then ushers them through to the living room where Arthur is still reading his paper. He glances up as they walk in and Carol tries to catch his eye, but he refuses to meet her gaze. He stands, his paper crumpled in one hand, and holds his other hand out and shakes both of theirs firmly as Carol flutters around in the background plumping cushions and straightening ornaments.

'Please, do sit down,' she says, gesturing towards the sofa, and they both sit, Debbie comfortably, Laura perched on the edge as though something would hurt her if she sat back properly, looking round the room nervously. For the first time, Carol sees her beloved living room through these young strangers' eyes and wonders what they make of her rose-printed wallpaper, the huge swags of curtain, the framed family photos lined up along the walls, the frilly cushions and shelves and shelves of spotless, dust-free ornaments. She smooths her skirt down again and looks round the room expectantly. It soon becomes clear it's going to be down to her to make conversation.

'Can I fetch you something to drink? Tea? Coffee? Something stronger?' She hopes they want tea; she makes excellent tea.

'Tea would be lovely, thank you,' Debbie says. Laura just smiles and Carol wonders whether she can't speak very well.

'I won't be a moment.' She bustles out of the room and fusses around laying out the teapot, milk jug, sugar pot and cups on a tray – her nicest cups, of course, for visitors – then arranges a selection of Bourbon and Rich Tea biscuits on a plate. She wishes she still had some of those nice Fox's ones left, the ones with the chocolate on them, but Arthur scoffed them all yesterday so these will have to do. She carries the whole lot through to the sitting room, wobbling slightly under the weight. As she approaches she can hear the murmur of voices and she hopes Arthur hasn't asked them lots of questions that she's missed the answers to. He's always doing things like that even though he knows it infuriates her.

She needn't have worried though as when she gets there they're only talking about the weather. She might have known Arthur wouldn't think to ask them anything important like what they're doing here.

'Right, well, please help yourselves.' She gestures towards the tray, then sits on the armchair next to Arthur, facing the two women on the sofa.

'This is an unexpected pleasure. It's very lovely to meet you at last,' she says, smiling at Laura.

'You too.' Laura's voice is quiet and Carol leans forward to hear her better.

'Only, it's been, what, a good few months since you moved there—' she tips her head to one side to indicate the house next door '—and we've only ever had the pleasure of meeting your lovely husband, Jim.'

'Carol, don't—' Arthur starts but Carol stops him with one of her stares.

'Yes, sorry, I...' Laura pauses, unsure what to say, how to explain. Carol doesn't let the hesitation stop her though.

'How *is* Jim, anyway? We haven't seen him for a while. He usually pops round every few days, doesn't he, Arthur? Lovely man, so kind.'

Debbie, the other woman, coughs and speaks next. 'Well, actually, that's what we hoped we might be able to talk to you about.'

'Oh?' Arthur says, as Carol's ears prick up. She can smell gossip a mile off and this has a *very* strong scent that something interesting is about to happen.

'Yes,' Debbie replies, and Carol feels herself leaning so far forward she's in danger of tipping off the chair and landing face-first on her flowery carpet. She doesn't want to miss a word. 'I don't know how much Jim told you about Laura?'

Carol glances at Laura, desperate to know more. 'Told us?' she says, her voice almost a squeak. 'He didn't really tell us anything, he just said you weren't very well. I didn't like to ask any more. I don't like to be nosey, you know.'

She ignores Arthur's snort, and instead watches as the two women exchange glances. Then Laura gives a tiny nod and clasps her hands in front of her. She's trembling like a bowl of jelly. She begins to speak in her timid voice and Carol holds her breath in order to catch every word.

'He's right, I haven't been well,' she says. 'I've—' She stops, looks down at the carpet. Carol can hardly bear it. 'I have something called agoraphobia. It means I'm too frightened to leave the house, or to be around other people.' She smiles weakly and flutters her hands around the room as if to indicate exactly what she's talking about.

'Gosh,' Carol says. 'I've never heard of that before. It sounds awful, you poor thing.'

'It is. It's—' She stops again, swallows. 'It's been difficult these last few months. It was why we moved here, to try and get me better.' She gives a self-deprecating laugh. 'That clearly didn't work out.'

Carol watches her for a moment, trying to decide what to say. To think, this woman has been too scared to leave her house, and yet here she is, sitting in front of Carol right now in her very own living room. This must mean something exciting has happened. But before she can ask anything more, Arthur pipes up.

'This the first time you've been out of your house, then, is it, love?'

Laura nods. 'Yes. Apart from a few practices in my garden, this is it.'

'That must have been very difficult. You're very brave.'

'Thank you.'

Carol studies Laura a bit more closely. Now she comes to think of it, Laura *does* look very pale, and she seems quite on edge, as though she's about to burst into tears. Carol does hope she's not, she's not very good with people crying, and she doesn't want to get the settee covered in snot.

'Well, is there anything we can do to help you? Now that you're better, I mean.'

Arthur shoots Carol a look and she frowns. What has she said wrong now?

'I don't think she's better, Carol. I think she's *trying* to get better. Isn't that right, love?'

Laura nods again, and this time Debbie speaks.

'It's been a slow process, but Laura's been doing brilliantly,' she explains. 'But there's a reason for this happening now, and in fact we did wonder whether you might be able to help us.'

'Oh?' Carol thinks she might burst if they don't tell her what they want soon – but she's glad she's managing to hide it well.

'The thing is, Jim's gone missing.' This is Laura again, and her voice wobbles on the last word.

'Missing?' Carol repeats, trying to contain her excitement at this turn of events. Here she'd been, wondering what the day was going to bring, and now this mystery has been brought to her actual door. Who else on the street knows about it, or is she the first?

'He left for Leeds on Sunday night, as usual, and was due to be home on Thursday, as usual. But he – he didn't come home. That was two weeks ago.'

Now this is getting good. Missing for two weeks?

'Oh no,' Carol says, her hand fluttering to her chest. 'You poor thing. We had no idea Jim had gone missing, did we, Arthur?'

'Well, of course not,' Arthur says.

'And you haven't heard from him at all?'

'No, she hasn't, Carol, that's why he's missing,' Arthur adds, and Carol wishes, not for the first time, that he were close enough for her to give him a kick in the shin. She turns back to Laura to hear more of the story, but not before throwing her husband a dirty look that she hopes he's seen.

'No, I haven't heard a thing. I've spoken to the police, who have said they'll help, but I – I don't think they're taking it very seriously. I think they assume Jim will walk in the door at any moment and everything will be fine but – well, they don't know Jim, not like I do. I know he wouldn't do this.' A single tear escapes from Laura's eye and she swipes it away with the back of her hand. Beside her, Debbie's hand reaches out and presses gently on her friend's arm, then she takes over the story.

'In a nutshell, Mr and Mrs Loveday—'

'Please call us Carol and Arthur.'

'Okay, thank you. In a nutshell, Carol and Arthur, we were hoping you might know something that could help us find Jim.'

'Oh, I see.' Carol sits back. Well, this is a turn-up for the books. Actually she can hardly believe her luck. A real-life drama is happening right in front of her eyes, in her own street, and she is one of the first to know about it!

A thought occurs to Carol then. That will have been what the police car was here for the other day. She wondered at the time, of course, only Arthur didn't seem keen to go out and try and find out more, and she couldn't because it was threatening to rain and she'd only just had her hair set at the hairdresser's that morning, and the frizz would have been unspeakable. Anyway, she's glad she's solved the mystery now. She doesn't like loose ends.

Arthur would say she watches too many soaps, of course, and that she's getting carried away with herself. But she's determined to help them. After all, doesn't this poor woman need her? She's just said as much. Ooh, it's like an episode of *The Bill*.

'Well, I'm sure we can help, can't we, Arthur?'

'Yes. Yes, I'm sure we can.' He nods and then frowns. 'Although we don't actually know where he's gone – do we?' He glances for confirmation at Carol, who tuts loudly.

'No, of course we don't actually *know*, Arthur.' She smiles at Laura and rolls her eyes, then throws a glance at her husband that says 'I'll deal with you later'. She turns back to Laura, smiling. 'No, I'm afraid Jim never told us he was going anywhere. Well, of course not, if he didn't tell you. But I'm sure we can come up with something that might help. After all, we knew him quite well, didn't we, Arthur?'

'Yes, dear.'

Laura leans forward until it looks as though she might tip off the sofa. 'I hoped you'd say that. I—' She glances at Debbie. 'We know Jim was friendly with a few of the neighbours and we thought, well, we hoped, that someone might have a clue, might remember something that could help us.' She shrugs. 'It's worth a go.'

Carol nods so vigorously she feels dizzy. She can't remember anything Jim might have said, off the top of her head, but she isn't going to tell Laura that yet. She's sure she can help her solve the mystery and find her missing husband somehow. She'll be a hero, have her picture in the local paper and everything – imagine that!

She reaches out and pats Laura's knee gently, ignoring the flinch as she does. 'Now, where shall we start?'

Laura glances at Debbie, her eyes wide.

Debbie sniffs. 'The last time you saw him, I suppose. Did he say anything unusual, or seem different that day? Can you remember?'

Carol screws up her face, her nose almost disappearing into the hollow between her eyes. The last time she'd seen Jim she had been in the garden, she was certain of it. Yes, because she'd been dead-heading the roses and he'd stopped and chatted with her on his way to the station. He'd seemed normal, she'd have said. But maybe, now she comes to think of it, there *was* something different about him that day. Yes, she's sure of it in fact, now she's given it some proper thought. She's surprised she hadn't noticed it before, actually. He seemed – sadder. That was it. Not his normal cheerful self. Preoccupied, as if he had something on his mind. She opens her mouth to share her memory, but before she can get the words out, Arthur pipes up again.

'He came round sometimes, just to say hello. Carol loved his company and they'd always sit in here and she'd show him old photos, of the kids, the grandchildren, you know. One day, we'd had a man come round and try to convince us to remortgage our house – well, you know, we're pensioners now, we don't need to release any money to go on a big cruise or anything like that. Why on earth would we want to remortgage our house? But he'd been very insistent and had been round a couple of times, pushing us more and more to sign some papers. I'd told him to leave us alone more than once but he didn't seem to take the hint. Well, Carol had been worried about it, and when she told Jim he told us not to worry, that he'd deal with it for us. He looked cross too, do you remember, Carol? I'd never seen him look like that before.'

Carol nods mutely.

'Anyway.' Arthur stops, rubs his hand over his balding head, smooths down a couple of stray strands. 'It's not that we're incapable, you know. It's just that Jim always seemed so *completely* capable, so it just seemed easier to let him deal with it. Do you know what I mean?'

Laura nods. She does. She knows exactly what he means. Jim's all-round *capability*, she realises now, is precisely the reason she hasn't tried hard enough to get over this anxiety, to get herself better. Not that she blames him, of course. But it's just that, because Jim has always been so good at sorting everything out for her, it has never felt necessary for her to try very hard.

'So what happened?'

'Oh, nothing in the end. We never saw the man again, although I don't know to this day what Jim said to him. But it worked, whatever it was.' A smile flickers across Arthur's face. 'Carol was so relieved. She'd thought she was going to be conned out of all her money and end up on *Crimewatch*.' He smiles and Carol grimaces at him.

'I did not!' She turns away from Arthur crossly. 'I was just grateful to Jim for helping us. Our boys are so far away now, one in Australia, one in Sweden, we couldn't have asked them, and I didn't think this man was going to give up very easily.' She shrugs, plucks a stray thread from her skirt and watches as it flutters to the flowered carpet. She wishes she'd hoovered; there are crumbs from Arthur's fruit cake everywhere. She hopes nobody notices.

To distract attention from the floor she picks up the plate of biscuits from the tray and offers them round. Laura takes a Bourbon and nibbles on it distractedly. The poor girl looks as if she needs a good meal, she's so pale and skinny. Maybe she can cook for her, try and fatten her up a bit.

'Would you like to stay for lunch? We're only having toad in the hole, but there's enough if you'd like some?'

Laura catches Debbie's eye. Maybe if they stay a bit longer they might get something more out of them? She gives a small nod.

'That would be lovely, if you're sure?'

'We'd be delighted.' Carol's face lights up. She stands and smooths her skirt again. 'Can you come and give me a hand, please, Arthur?'

'What? Oh, right.' He heaves himself out of his chair and smiles at the two women, then follows his wife out of the sitting room and into the kitchen. Carol is almost brimming over with excitement. She shuts the door firmly behind her, opens the fridge and pulls out a packet of pork sausages.

'This is brilliant, isn't it, Arthur?'

'You're not serious?' Arthur takes the sausages from her and starts snipping the packet open carefully. Carol turns back to the fridge to look for the milk. 'Of course I am, why not? This is a real-life drama, Arthur.'

'Carol, you do realise that this poor woman's husband has gone missing, don't you?'

'Of course I do, I'm not stupid. But I'm sure nothing serious has happened to him, and it means we can help find him, don't you see?'

Arthur shakes his head. 'Love, not everything is like it is on *Corrie*. Something bad *could* have happened to him. This might turn out to have a sad ending after all, you know.'

'Oh, don't be so dramatic. I'm sure Jim's perfectly fine.'

'Why?'

Carol stops, unused to being challenged. 'Well – I—' She lines the sausages up neatly on the baking tray with some onions and pours oil over them. 'Well, I don't know, do I? I can't imagine anything bad will have come of him. Things like that just don't *happen*, do they?'

'Course they do, love. Every day. You need to stop treating this like something fun to fill your day with, and start taking it more seriously. It's not an Enid Blyton novel, you know.'

Carol slams the oil down on the worktop.

'Yes, I'm quite aware of that, Arthur, thank you very much.'

Arthur sighs. He knows what this clipped, Queen's English voice means. It means that Carol is upset and that he is going to be punished for it, probably with a bad mood that lasts several days. He sighs again, then rubs his wife's arm gently, trying to calm her down. 'Come on, now, dear, don't be like that. We've got to concentrate on helping these two ladies, haven't we? Not bicker between us.'

Carol takes a long breath and holds it for so long Arthur is worried she's about to keel over. 'Yes, okay,' she finally relents, whooshing the held breath out along with the words.

For the next few minutes they bustle around the kitchen making batter and peeling potatoes. They don't say another word, but as the potatoes cook and the batter rises, Arthur knows there's a silent truce between them because there's no more slamming of utensils and the huffing and puffing has ceased. He is forgiven, if grudgingly.

Lunch made, they all sit down in the dining room, where Carol has placed mats, knives and forks and a basket of sliced bread and butter as well as a gravy boat on the table. Each plate is piled high with sausages wrapped in Yorkshire pudding, mashed potato and peas. Laura hasn't seen such an enormous portion for a long time, and isn't at all sure how she's going to manage it all.

'This looks lovely, thank you, Mrs Loveday,' she says.

'Carol, please. And thank you. Help yourself to gravy.'

Debbie picks up the enormous gravy boat and pours the steaming sauce over her dinner, then Laura does the same. As they chat Laura eats forkful after forkful, chewing carefully, taking her time. She can't quite believe she's sitting here, in someone else's house, eating a meal. It's as though someone else is pretending to be her while she's actually back in her own living room next door, downing a bottle of wine alone. She's come so far in the last few days it's hard to believe she's still the same person.

She just hopes Carol and Arthur can't tell how fast her heart is pounding or how sick she feels, how terrified she is about the prospect of leaving here after dinner and retracing her steps home. But she knows she'll do it, whatever it takes. And she'll do it over and over again until she gets the answers she needs if it means she can find out what's happened to Jim.

Her attention is drawn back to the conversation at the table by a nudge from Debbie.

'Laura?'

'Sorry, I was miles away. What was that?'

'Arthur was just asking whether the police have found anything yet,' Carol says, scooping a tiny forkful of mashed potato into her mouth.

'No, not really. They've promised to keep me posted but – well, it seems as though he's just disappeared into thin air. That's why I'm so scared that he's never coming back...' She tails off, her words clinging to the Yorkshire pudding she's just chewed that's now blocking her throat.

'The thing is, Jim has always been such a stickler for timekeeping,' Debbie adds. 'He's – reliable. So this isn't just anyone going missing. This is *Jim*. We can't understand it.' She pushes some peas onto her fork. 'We think someone somewhere must have a clue as to what's happened to him. A person doesn't simply disappear.'

Carol nods. 'No, no, of course they don't.' She turns to Laura. 'But if the police haven't found anything then nothing too bad can have happened, can it? I mean, they'd have found something, wouldn't they?'

Laura shrugs. 'Not if he didn't want them to.'

A silence hangs in the air as everyone lets the words sink in.

'So you think he's left you deliberately, then, do you?' Carol struggles to contain her glee at this new development, choosing to ignore the eye roll Arthur gives her across the table.

Laura nods. 'Yes. At least that's what I'm hoping. Because the alternative doesn't bear thinking about.'

'Oh dear.' Carol's hand shoots out and rests on Laura's arm. She pulls it away when Laura flinches. 'I'm sure he'll turn up.'

Laura puts her fork down. She doesn't normally spill her guts to virtual strangers, but if she wants their help, she has to offer them something in return. She takes a deep breath, which makes her feel dizzy. Her knife is clutched so tightly in her right hand her knuckles have turned white.

'I don't know how much Jim told you about me?'

Carol shakes her head. 'He didn't tell us anything.' Her eyes are round, like a child waiting for an ice cream.

'Well, it's a long story. About eighteen months ago I was attacked, and since then I haven't been able to leave the house. It's why we moved here, because I – we – thought it would help me, to move away from where it had happened.' She sighs. 'As you've probably guessed it hasn't helped at all, and things are just as bad. In fact things are worse for Jim because, not only has he got me to look after, but he's nowhere near his friends any more, so he never sees them. That's probably why he's made such an effort to get to know so many people here. It's been tough, and I knew he was struggling but – well, I suppose I've been so self-absorbed I hadn't noticed how hard things had got for him too.' She wipes a tear from her cheek, the reality hitting home all over again. She's been over and over it in her mind so many times, but, somehow, saying it out loud to Carol and Arthur in such plain terms has made her see how selfish she's been.

'Oh, my dear.' Carol reaches out and places her hand firmly on Laura's forearm and this time she doesn't move it away.

'Sorry.' She looks up at the faces watching her round the table.

'You've got nothing to be sorry for.' Carol rubs her arm and removes her hand, linking her fingers together on the table in front of her. 'What an awful thing to have gone through. I just wish we'd have known, maybe we could have helped.'

Laura nods. 'I guess Jim had his reasons for not telling anyone about me. He must have thought it was private and he probably wanted to meet new people without that hanging over his head.'

Carol looks at Arthur, who has his head buried in his dinner, scooping peas frantically with his fork so he doesn't have to catch her eye.

'Well, thank you for telling us.' Carol stands. 'Has everyone finished eating?'

Surprised by the sudden change of subject, Laura nods and Carol quickly removes her plate, a splash of gravy dripping onto the white tablecloth. 'I'll just take these through to the kitchen. Will you help me, Arthur, please?'

'What? Oh, right, yes.' He stands quickly, relieved to have something to do, and the pair of them shuffle through to the kitchen again, this time laden down with plates.

'Well, this is a turn-up for the books, don't you think?' The door is barely shut before the words are out of Carol's mouth in a loud, urgent whisper. 'Sounds like Jim really has disappeared on purpose.' She nods and rubs her chin as though trying to solve a mystery. Arthur piles the plates in the sink and turns on the tap.

'It could still be serious though, love.'

'I know.'

'And she's very brave to come here and ask for our help. You've got to remember that. She's not just gossip fodder.'

'Arthur Loveday, how could you even think that about me?'

Arthur hides a smirk and runs the plates under the hot water, steam rising up round his cheeks. 'You know what I mean. We've got to really try and help her. I mean *really*.'

'Of course we will. Although I'm not sure I know what we can do, in all honesty.' She pauses to open the fridge. 'Do you think they'll mind if we only have yogurts for afters?'

'No, love I'm sure they're full anyway.'

She pulls strawberry yogurts from the fridge then digs out a tin of peaches from the back of the cupboard. 'Maybe these as well.' As she divides the peaches between four bowls she carries on. 'I just can't think of anything Jim might have said that could give us a clue as to where he might have gone. Can you?'

There's a second's silence. 'Arthur!'

'I was thinking, love. I can't pluck something clean from my head just like that.' He dries his hands on a tea towel and hangs it over the oven door handle. 'But no, I can't either right now. But maybe something will come to us, in time.'

She nods.

'Unless...' Arthur pauses, a bowl of peaches in each hand.

'What, love?'

He shrugs. 'Well, unless that man who was trying to sell us a new mortgage came back and did him in?'

'Now who's been watching too much TV?'

'Well, we don't actually know what Jim said or did to him, do we?'

'Arthur, this isn't the blooming *Sweeney*, this is Willow Crescent. Jim hasn't been done in. He's just disappeared for a bit, but he'll come back, I'm certain of it. We just have to try and help Laura to find him.'

Arthur nods. 'You're probably right, love.' Then he pushes the door open with his toe and walks into the dining room.

'Right, peaches!' He places them unceremoniously in front of Debbie and Laura and walks back for the rest, Carol hot on his heels.

'I'm sorry we can't offer you something better for afters, dears, it's just we weren't expecting visitors and I hadn't had time this morning to make anything.'

'It's fine, peaches are lovely, thank you.' Debbie plucks her spoon from the table and stabs a peach, which slips out of the side of the bowl and shoots across the table, leaving a trail of sticky syrup in its wake.

'Oh, my goodness, I'm so sorry!'

'No, no, don't fuss, it's no bother.' Carol rubs furiously at the stains on the cloth as Debbie scoops up the offending peach and lifts it back into her bowl.

'Carol, love, stop fussing, we'll just wash the cloth later.'

Carol stops, mid-rub, and sits down. 'You're right, sorry. I just didn't want it to stain.'

'I really am sorry,' Debbie says, her cheeks flushed.

'Really, it doesn't matter.' Carol picks up her spoon and turns towards Laura. 'What does matter is finding this young man of yours.' As she turns to Laura she bites into the peach and some syrup slides slowly down her chin. 'Me and Arthur have been talking, haven't we, Arthur?'

'Yes.' He shoves half a peach in his mouth so he doesn't have to say anything further.

'Anyway, we've been thinking and we're sure we can help you. I mean, we can't think of anything in particular Jim said, but we're sure something will come to us, and in the meantime we can help you investigate.'

'That sounds lovely, thank you.' Laura tries to hide the disappointment in her voice.

'I mean, he really helped us out with the mortgage man,' she continues. 'And Jim's always been so kind. We'll do whatever we can.'

With nothing more to say they all concentrate on finishing their bowls of sticky fruit. As soon as the last mouthful is swallowed Carol leaps up again.

'Would anyone like some tea?'

'No, thank you.' That was the most Laura has eaten for months, and she's not sure she'll even be able to move off the chair. Tea would push her over the edge.

'Coffee?'

'No, thank you. In fact, I think we should probably be getting back.'

'Oh, really, so soon?' Carol's crestfallen face makes Laura feel guilty but she nods anyway.

'I think Debbie needs to get home…'

Debbie checks her watch. 'Yes, I really should be getting back or my husband will think I've left the country.' She smiles, then stands and starts gathering bowls.

'No, no, no, I'll do that, you two better be getting going.' Carol takes the bowls from Debbie's hands and shoos her away. Arthur pushes some wayward strands of hair from his face, smoothing them down across the top of his head as they all start moving as one towards the front door.

When they get there Laura turns to Carol, trying not to notice the looming spectre of the front door. She takes a deep breath and sticks her hand out, ignoring the tremor in it. 'Thank you so much for lunch.' Carol takes Laura's hand and clasps it between hers.

'You're very welcome. We're so thrilled to have met you at last. And we promise we'll do everything we can to help you find that husband of yours.'

'Thank you. You've been so kind.'

As Laura walks out of the door, Debbie clutching her hand, she tries to pay no mind to the spinning garden, the hammering of her heart and the shaking of her body and concentrates on putting one foot in front of the other, again and again and again until she finds herself stumbling through her own front door, desperately trying to catch her breath.

Suddenly she's being squeezed, Debbie's arms tight around her shoulders. 'You did it, you made it!' Her voice is high and excitable and Laura can't help smiling. She *has* done it. Not only had she made it out of her house – which, now she's back in it, she realises is more oppressively silent than peaceful and quiet – but she made it into somebody else's house and spent at least two hours there, talking to them, making conversation, eating their food, getting to know them. She's behaved like a normal person. She isn't sure how she's done it, but that doesn't matter for now.

Debbie lets her go and she shivers. 'I did, didn't I?'

She nods. 'This is just the beginning, Laura. We're going to get round all these houses—' she sweeps her arm in the general direction of the crescent '—and we're going to find out what's happened to Jim, whatever it takes.'

'And if we don't?'

Debbie shrugs. 'We will. But if we don't – well, then you'll have made some new friends and made it out of the house, won't you?'

'I will.' And that, in itself, is nothing short of a miracle.

* * *

It's almost dark when a banging on the door wakes Laura up from where she was dozing on the sofa. She glances at the clock, bleary-eyed. It's gone six, and it takes a second for her to work out where she is. Slowly it comes back to her. When she got back from Carol and Arthur's, Debbie had to go home, and Laura, exhausted from the sheer mental effort it took to get out of the house, opened a bottle of wine. She peers down at the floor now and sees the empty bottle tipped on its side and groans as a wave of nausea rushes over her.

The pounding starts again and her heart begins hammering, a delayed reaction. Who on earth can be calling round if it isn't Debbie?

She stands up gingerly, waiting for the room to stop spinning, then creeps along the hallway towards the front door. When she's almost halfway there the letterbox flaps open and a pair of eyes appears in the slit.

'Oh, you are in, I was beginning to think you'd disappeared as well,' a familiar voice says. When Laura doesn't reply, the voices continues. 'Laura, it's me. Carol. From next door?' she adds helpfully.

Realising Carol can see her standing there staring at her through the letterbox, Laura hurries along the hallway and opens the door.

'Hello, dear,' Carol says, smiling.

'Um, could you come in so I can shut the door, please?' Laura says, trying not to look out into the creeping darkness of the garden.

'Oh, yes, of course, how silly of me not to realise,' Carol says, stepping inside gleefully and looking around with barely veiled interest at the pictures on the hall wall. Without speaking Laura turns and walks into the kitchen, Carol following close behind, then turns to face her neighbour, leaning heavily on the worktop for support.

'Is everything all right?' Laura says, waiting for Carol to speak, but the older woman is too busy taking in the dated kitchen cupboards and piles of rubbish dumped by the back door. Laura feels suddenly self-conscious about the state of the place that she'd assumed nobody other than her best friend would see and picks up a dishcloth and swipes ineffectually at a surface for something to do.

Eventually Carol realises Laura is waiting for her to say something. 'I hope you don't mind me popping round unannounced, it's just, Arthur and me were talking after you left, trying to work out if there was anything Jim might have said before he – you know, disappeared. Any clues.'

Laura waits for her to carry on.

'You see, the thing is, I couldn't think of anything at first and neither could Arthur. Not that he ever notices anything anyway. I mean, Jim could have walked in with three heads and he probably still wouldn't have twigged something was wrong. But then that's men for you, isn't it, all worrying about the racing results but utterly oblivious when something obvious is staring them in the face?' She stops and sees Laura staring at her, waiting for her to get to the point. 'Ahem. Yes, well. Anyway. So Arthur and me were talking and then something suddenly occurred to me, something I hadn't thought much of at the time. But the thing is, the last time Jim came round, I noticed a photo on his keyring.'

'A photo?'

Carol nods excitedly, warming up to the idea. 'Well, two photos, truth be told.'

Laura sighs, trying not to feel exasperated at the slow, dramatic reveal. 'Who were the photos of, Mrs Loveday?'

'Carol, please.' She smiles happily and leans towards Laura. 'They were of two children.'

'Children?' That was *not* what Laura had been expecting.

Mrs Loveday – Carol – nods enthusiastically. 'A boy and a girl.'

'Right.' Laura's heart is thumping.

'Well, of course, I asked him who they were.'

'And?' Laura is trying not to shout.

'He said they were his niece and nephew.'

Laura's blood runs cold. 'Are – are you sure that's what he said? His niece and nephew?'

Carols looks at her as though she's completely stupid and nods. 'Of course I'm sure. I asked him their names but he just changed the subject and put the keys back in his pocket. At the time, of course, I didn't think there was anything odd about it, just that he was in a hurry and didn't have time to chit-chat. But it was only when I was thinking about it again after you left that it occurred to me his behaviour might have been construed as being a bit odd.' She stops, and looks at Laura expectantly, but Laura can't speak. She feels as though she might fall over so she pulls out a chair from the kitchen table and slumps into it, her heart thumping erratically, her legs feeling like jelly.

'Are you all right, dear?' Carol sits next to her and rubs her back gently, and Laura doesn't even have the energy to pull away from her touch.

'I—' she starts, and feels tears welling in her eyes again.

'Oh, no, dear, I didn't mean to upset you, I am sorry,' Carol says. She stands and heads over to the kettle. 'Let me make you a nice up of tea, to calm your nerves,' she says, and starts bustling around looking for cups and teabags and milk. Minutes later she plops a mug of tea in front of Laura, who takes it gratefully, then turns to look at her neighbour.

'Jim doesn't have a niece and nephew,' she says, her voice shaky. 'He's an only child.'

Carol tries to hide her surprise, and places her hand gently on Laura's arm. She doesn't pull it away this time.

'Oh, dear, I am sorry to throw this at you like this. I mean, I could have been mistaken—' she knows she isn't '—but I'm sure there's a perfectly reasonable explanation.'

Laura shakes her head. 'But why would he have said that?'

'Perhaps he just didn't want a nosey old biddy like me asking questions,' Carol says, smiling kindly.

Laura nods. 'Maybe. But it still doesn't explain why he had a keyring with photos of children on. I've never seen him with a keyring like that.'

'Perhaps they were someone else's keys, dear. Maybe he was looking after them or picked them up by accident and just didn't feel the need to explain himself.' She sighed. 'As I say, I just thought it might be useful. You know, a trail of clues to follow, like breadcrumbs. But it could be nothing at all.'

'You're probably right. But thank you for letting me know.'

A few minutes later Carol leaves, and Laura is all alone again. And although she feels certain there must be a reasonable explanation about this keyring, she writes it down on the edge of the map Debbie has drawn, and underlines it twice. Just in case.

12

THEN – OCTOBER 1989

The phone was ringing as I walked up the stairs to the flat.

'All right, all right,' I said, kicking my shoes off before snatching up the receiver. I was breathless so it took me a few seconds to realise that nobody had said anything on the other end of the line.

'Hello?' I said, again.

Still nothing.

I strained my ears, trying to make out any sound at all over the hum of the phone line. Was that someone breathing, or was I imagining it? I waited a couple of beats, then yelled, 'Stop ringing me,' and slammed the phone down with a shaking hand.

I stood for a moment in the cool quiet of the hallway, staring at the phone as though it were culpable for letting a crank call through, and tried to slow my racing heartbeat. Then I walked slowly through to the living room where the curtains were still wide open and yanked them closed, my arms weak with fear. I peeked through the tiny gap I'd left and out into the darkness of the street below. It was quiet tonight, not a person to be seen. Yet all I could imagine was someone lurking in the shadows, watching me. The thought that they could see me but I couldn't see them sent me into a panic all over again and I pulled my face from the gap in the curtains and tugged them fully closed, then switched on the side lamp and curled up on the sofa, my legs tucked under me, and tried to take some long, deep breaths.

That was my night ruined. The restaurant had been quieter than usual so I'd finished slightly early and hurried home, hoping for a glass of wine or two to wind down before bed. But now I was rattled, and I couldn't settle at all.

I stood again, agitated, and stalked through to the kitchen and opened a new bottle of wine. I poured myself an enormous glass and downed the lot in one go. My head spun, and I held onto the kitchen worktop to steady myself, then poured another glass and took that and the bottle back through to the living room, my hands still shaking.

This wasn't the first time I'd had a call like this, but this was the first time it had happened late at night. The first call had come one morning a couple of weeks ago, just after Jim had left to drive up to Leeds. We'd said goodbye and I'd been about to step into the shower when the phone had started ringing. I'd hurried to answer it in my towel, but hadn't quite got there in time. But just as I'd headed back towards the shower it had begun again – only once again, whoever was there hadn't said a word before hanging up. At the time I'd been so irritated at being disturbed I hadn't given it much thought, assuming it was just a wrong number. But since then it had happened on a further two mornings. Now, though, the call had come late at night, and I was scared.

Why was someone trying to spook me? Why did they keep ringing and hanging up without saying anything? Was someone following me? After all, they always seemed to ring when I was on my own, as if they knew Jim wasn't here. I took another huge gulp of wine to try and steady my nerves.

I longed to tell someone my fears, so that they could reassure me that there was nothing to worry about, that it was just my imagination running overtime. But even as I thought it, I realised there was nobody I *could* confide in.

It couldn't be Jim because I didn't have a number to call him on when he was in Leeds – he always rang me. It had been months since I'd last heard from Mum and apart from Debbie, who I refused to call *again* for fear she'd get fed up with me, I hadn't seen any of my friends for months. I didn't know what they were up to, or who they were seeing and, I realised with a jolt, it was entirely my own doing because I spent most of my time either with Jim or waiting around for him to ring.

I was entirely alone.

Desperate to blot it out, I finished off the second glass of wine, poured another, and took it through to my bedroom. Two thirds of a bottle of wine on an empty stomach in half an hour had made my legs wobbly, and I was glad to collapse into bed, fully clothed. I sat for a minute, propped up on pillows, listening for any sounds in the flat – a handle squeaking, a floorboard creaking, a window being opened. Nothing. But I knew the only way I would get to sleep now was to pass out, so I finished the wine, and lay my head back on the pillow and waited for oblivion.

* * *

When I woke the next morning, the sun streamed through the open curtains and my mouth felt as dry as a desert-worn sandal. When I sat up my head spun so I took it slowly, squinting against the bright light. The empty wine bottle on the bedside table reminded me what I'd done the previous night, which brought memories of the mystery phone calls flooding back, and I swallowed down a feeling of nausea.

Who *was* ringing me, and what did they want?

I glanced at the clock. It was only 7 a.m. Jim wouldn't ring me for hours. Besides, I hadn't told him about the previous calls because I hadn't been particularly worried. But something about the call last night – the breathing, the late hour – had tipped me over the edge and now it was all I could think about. I knew I could see if Debbie was awake, but I was too ashamed that I'd drunk myself into a stupor rather than deal with the problem head-on, the way she would have done.

I climbed out of bed, ignoring the queasiness, and made my way to the living room. I opened the curtains, half expecting to see someone watching me from the other side of the road like in some TV thriller, but there was no one there apart from a young guy putting his bins out and a middle-aged woman jogging past, her ponytail swinging from side to side. I cast my gaze up and down, but it was all clear.

I walked into the kitchen and downed a pint of water while standing at the sink, rivulets cascading from the glass down the sides of my chin and into the sink. I gulped as though I hadn't drunk anything for a week, then refilled my glass and downed that too. I slammed it down on the counter, angry all of a sudden. What was wrong with me? Why couldn't I deal with things like a normal person? Why did I always have to panic, and drink to forget?

Determined to think about something else, I decided to get outside for a walk. It was still early but the sun felt warm through the windows and maybe a brisk walk would clear my head, help me see things more clearly. Besides, Jim would be back tonight, and I didn't want him to see me scared or hungover. He wasn't here enough as it was, I wasn't about to waste the time we did have together.

Pulling on some clothes, I raced down the stairs and out into the warm London sunshine. There was a stiff breeze and I shivered as I made my way down the garden path and onto the street. I turned right and headed towards the shops, which would then lead towards Cherry Tree Wood. I swung my arms and marched quickly and tried to let my mind drift, away from thoughts of the previous night, and instead focus on Jim's return later that evening. Perhaps I'd buy something nice for dinner, a steak or a lovely piece of cod, cook him something special, something I'd make for customers but that I rarely bothered with at home. Yes, that was what I'd do. Forget about the phone calls, put them behind me and concentrate on me and Jim.

As I rounded the corner at the end of my street something caught my eye. A flash of black, a sudden movement, and I whipped my head around and squinted at the house opposite. There was nothing there. Heart hammering despite no obvious danger, I kept walking, slower now, my eyes on the hedge where I thought I'd seen someone. Was I going mad? Maybe too much alcohol and not enough sleep had made me conjure things that weren't there. But I was convinced I'd seen something, or someone, lurking in my peripheral vision.

And then there it was again. A sudden movement, then a figure emerged from behind the low wall of a house and sprinted off down the road. I stood, frozen to the spot for a few seconds, and then, before I could think about it too much, I set off after them, crossing the road, my low-heeled boots a hindrance to my progress.

'Hey, wait,' I yelled, ignoring the strange looks from passers-by as I barrelled after the figure, who glanced over their shoulder once before upping their pace, arms pumping at their sides. They were small and clearly much fitter than me and getting further away and my lungs were burning, so, as it became clear I was fighting a losing battle, I stopped, breathing heavily, last night's wine threatening to show itself once more, and watched helplessly as they disappeared out of sight.

I stood still in the shadow of a shop window for a few minutes, my whole body trembling. I now knew without a doubt that I wasn't being paranoid after all. Someone had been watching me, and following me, and if it wasn't the same person who had made those crank phone calls over the last two weeks I'd be surprised.

But what I couldn't work out was who it was, and why anyone would feel the need to spook me. I didn't really see anyone, apart from Jim and Debbie and my colleagues at work, and I couldn't imagine it being any of them. Had someone from the restaurant had a bad meal, a disgruntled customer trying to get their revenge? No, that was ridiculous. It must be more than that.

And yet, I was at a complete loss.

I'd lost my desire to go for a walk now and, even though my stalker – if I could call them that – was long gone, I felt nervy, on edge, and just wanted to be back at home in the safety of my flat. I checked my watch. Jim would be home in a few hours, and I didn't have work tonight, so I'd go home and wait for him and make something to eat with whatever we had in the freezer. He wouldn't mind.

It wasn't until later, as I was preparing a piece of salmon I'd found, that it hit me again just how insular my life had become. The only people I ever confided in were Jim and Debbie, and the more time that passed since the episode this morning, the more I realised I was probably being paranoid, and didn't want to tell them about it. But there was no one else. No one I could just pick up the phone to, maybe laugh it off, explain it away, without concerning them about the state of my mind. Jim would think I was being paranoid, and I worried Debbie would tell me the same. But I also knew she would tell me I needed to get out more, that my life was becoming so reduced that I saw big problems in minute things. In other words, she'd think I imagined it, because I was lonely, even though she wouldn't say it in so many words. The trouble was, she was right. My life *had* become too small, and I'd never even seen it happening.

13

NOW – 3 OCTOBER 1992

Number four Willow Crescent
Ben Adams

Rain pummels the window so hard it sounds like nails smacking against the glass. Every now and then the sound stops and the room is peaceful again, until the wind changes direction and it starts all over again. Laura pulls open the curtains and the room hardly lightens at all. The sky is so leaden it feels as though it's bearing down on the house, the street, the houses across the road. She presses her face closer to the glass and can just about make out the smudged outline of the trees, which a few days before were loaded with the reds, yellows and oranges of autumn, parading their colours in the breeze like models sashaying down a catwalk; now all that's left are spindly bare branches shivering in the breeze, leaves dumped carelessly on the ground like clothes shed on a bathroom floor. Everything is smothered in a heavy blanket of grey.

Jim has been missing for two weeks and two days. To Laura, it feels like a lifetime of worrying – but at least she has a plan today, rather than the endless cycle of days drifting round the house trying to plug the gaps of time with pointless activities.

She hovers a moment longer, wondering what secrets are hiding just outside her bedroom window waiting for her to discover them like a twisted game of hide and seek. There has to be something, otherwise Jim might never come home. That isn't something she even wants to contemplate. It is inconceivable.

She turns and dresses hurriedly. She can't stop thinking about what Carol told her last week about the mystery photos on Jim's keyring. She's told Debbie about it, of course, and together they've tried to work out what it might mean.

'I'm sure Carol must have been mistaken,' Debbie reassured her. 'At worst Jim probably just picked up someone else's keys from the office.'

'But why would she say it?'

'Some people like to try and be useful,' Debbie said carefully. 'It happens all the time. People sometimes… misremember things. Things they're absolutely certain took place, but when the evidence comes in, they never actually happened. It's – our minds sometimes trick us into believing something we really want to be true.'

'So you're saying you think Mrs Loveday made it up?'

'I'm not quite saying that. I'm just saying we need to treat what she said with caution and not jump to any conclusions.'

'I guess you're right.'

Laura pretended she was reassured by Debbie's words, but the truth is she's still rattled by Carol's revelation. It keeps nagging away at the back of her mind, no matter how hard she tries to push it away.

Now, to make matters worse, Debbie has had to cancel coming

round to help her pay a visit to the next neighbour on the list, Ben Adams, today.

'I'm really sorry, Laura, but the kids have both got parties to go to and Steve's been called into work,' Debbie told her last night. 'Can we make it another day?'

Laura had considered it for a minute. She hadn't left the safety of her own front garden by herself yet. Getting out of the garden and onto the pavement and walking two doors down was asking a lot, even with Debbie there. But she didn't want to wait either. Time was ticking and she needed to get on with her plan to find Jim and bring him home.

'I'll go on my own.'

A hesitation. 'Laura. You can't.' She listened to the click of Debbie's tongue against her teeth. 'This is huge. You're doing well but are you sure you're up to this?'

'Not in the slightest.'

'Well then, wait. I'll come tomorrow I'll make sure I'm there.'

It was tempting, and she nearly accepted, the thought of staying inside and drinking her way through a bottle of wine instead much more appealing. But that would only waste time, and Jim needed her. She had to be strong.

'I'm going to go.'

A rush of breath. 'Okay, darling. Ring me if you need me, promise?'

'Promise.'

'And remember. Breathe. Don't panic. Nothing bad is going to happen. Okay?'

'Okay.'

And so she is going to do it alone. At least, she's going to try.

* * *

The rain isn't showing any signs of easing, and all the procrastination in the world won't change the fact that she's dreading this. It's now or never.

She pulls on her trainers and yanks on the squeaky arms of her raincoat, which hangs by the front door despite the fact she hasn't worn it once since they've lived in this house. Jim obviously hung it here in the hope that she'd need it one day, and the thought makes her both happy and sad at the same time.

She opens the door and the wind almost knocks her over, bringing a blast of cold air and pellet-like raindrops with it. She pulls her hood up and holds it on with one hand, then takes her first tentative steps onto the front step. Whenever she's been outside before she's taken it slowly, one step at a time, looking round at everything before taking another step forward. And even that has been a struggle. But today the weather is so vile she doesn't have the luxury of taking it slowly. It's head-down-and-run-for-it kind of weather, and she isn't sure if she's up to it. But then she thinks again of Jim, and knows she has to try, so, taking one last glance round, she slams the door behind her and sprints to the front gate. All she can see is the path beneath her feet, grey and stony and soaking wet. She ignores her peripheral vision, trying to pretend it isn't there, that it's just her feet on the concrete and nothing else. She quickly pulls open the gate, her heart beating so fast it bruises the inside of her ribcage, and concentrates on putting one foot in front of the other, over and over, black foot on grey concrete time and time again until she risks glancing up and realises she's reached number four without even noticing. Without stopping to wait at the gate she runs to the front door and steps underneath the overhanging porch with relief. Her feet are soaked through and water drips from her coat, down her legs and soaks into her jeans. After a grand total of ninety seconds she resembles a drowned rat. Not the ideal scenario for meeting one of her new(ish) neighbours. But she is here now, and she is going to see this through if it kills her.

She presses on the doorbell before she loses her nerve and hears it ring somewhere inside the house. A glance at her watch shows her it's only eight o'clock in the morning and she feels a pang of guilt at disturbing someone so early, but she wanted to get it over and done with. Besides, it's too late to worry about that now.

Through the bevelled glass panel in the door she sees a figure approach, then the door is open and she's staring into the piercing blue eyes of a man about the same age as her.

'Hello?'

She raises her head and pushes her hood down and sticks her hand out. 'Hello, I'm Laura. Jim's wife.'

His face smooths and his eyes widen as he takes her hand and shakes it warmly. 'Oh, Laura, hello!' He glances outside. 'God, come in, it's bloody awful out there. You must be drenched.' Then he moves aside and she steps inside his house, the second stranger's house in just a few days. She's done it.

* * *

When the doorbell goes, Ben is irritated. He's only just got out of bed and is about to go for a run. What idiot rings at people's doors this early in the morning?

He drains the dregs of his coffee, switches off the dulcet tones of Gary Davies' breakfast show, gives his still-sleeping golden retriever, Rocky, a quick tickle on the head as he passes, eliciting a half-hearted woof and a tail-thump, and goes to answer it, hoping to get rid of whoever it is quickly.

He doesn't recognise the figure hunched on the doorstep, dripping wet, even when she pulls her hood down to reveal a pinched, worried face and a head full of dark curls. He's preparing for his 'no thank you I'm not interested in anything you have to say' speech when she speaks first, and he wouldn't have been more surprised to hear her say she was Jim's wife than if she'd been wearing Mickey Mouse ears and doing a tap dance on his doorstep. She's at least fifteen years younger than he'd expected her to be, and much prettier, despite the bedraggled look.

'Oh, Laura, hello!' He glances outside. The weather is getting worse, perhaps now isn't such a good time for a run after all. Then he notices just how wet she is and pulls the door right open. 'God, come in, it's bloody awful out there you must be drenched.'

Now here she is, dripping all over the carpet in his hallway, looking lost and scared. He isn't quite sure what to say or do.

He holds out his hand. 'Here, give me your coat, I'll hang it up to dry.' She shrugs out of her jacket and hands it to him and he stands for a moment, unsure what to do with it. Drops of rain splash onto the carpet as Laura continues to stand there, arms clasped tight against her waist, shivering. The poor woman looks terrified.

'Right, er, shall we go into the kitchen? Perhaps I can make you a coffee, warm you up a bit?' Ben says, finally hanging the sopping wet coat over the bottom rung of the banister.

Laura gives a small nod and follows him into the kitchen where she carries on dripping all over the floor, her shoes squeaking across the tiles. 'Sorry.' Her face is blotchy and red as she bends down to pull her trainers off with shaking hands. Ben frowns. He's got to know Jim pretty well over the last seven months since he and Laura moved to Willow Crescent, but he's never met Laura. He knows she exists, of course, but he's only ever seen shadowy images of her through darkened windows, a silhouette on a dark night, a face at the window. He isn't the most observant of people but even he knew something wasn't right there, but it was equally obvious that Jim didn't want to talk about it, so he didn't push it. He assumed though that there was something seriously wrong, some dark, sinister secret his wife must have been hiding, otherwise why else would he have kept her a secret? Watching her now, though, a small, huddled figure with a stricken look on her face, staring at an invisible spot on the floor between them, hands clenched so tightly in front of her that her knuckles have turned white, it's almost impossible to believe.

He is, however, terrified he is about to find out what *is* wrong with her, because he doesn't handle emotion and feelings very well these days. He's had enough of them to last a lifetime.

Aware he should probably speak, he says, 'So, coffee?'

'Only if you're making one.' Her voice is quiet, tremulous, and she coughs to clear her throat. It seems strange that someone as confident as Jim would be married to someone as quiet and mouse-like as this woman in front of him.

'Instant okay?'

Laura nods.

Relieved to have something to do, Ben fills the kettle and spoons coffee into mugs. 'I won't be a minute and we can go and sit down. I should probably get some more stools in here but – well, there's only me, really.' God, get a grip, Ben, you sound like a fool, waffling on.

Laura's eyes pass briefly over the single stool that sits at the breakfast bar. The kitchen is the same size as hers but where hers is homely, old-fashioned – not her taste, but not offensive either – this one is stark, hardly a sign that anyone even lives here. If it weren't for a few crumbs scattered round the toaster and the kettle on the side, it would look abandoned.

She shuffles her feet on the tiles beneath her wet socks. She's starting to get cold. She knew Ben lives alone – at least she always assumed so. But other than the fact that he plays poker and went out with Jim for a few drinks from time to time she knows very little else about this man, and she suddenly feels nervous. Only Debbie knows she's here, and she's busy with the kids all day. An image shoots into her mind again: a hidden alley, dark grey eyes, being unable to breathe... Oh God, she can't do this. She's made a terrible mistake coming here. She has to leave, now.

She turns and skids slightly as her socks slip on the tiled floor, but she rights herself and sprints from the kitchen, grabbing her coat from the bottom of the stairs and slinging the door open. By the time she reaches the bottom of the path her breath is coming in frantic gasps and she feels dizzy, the world spinning around her like a merry-go-round. She can hardly see where she's going with the rain in her eyes and her hair plastered to her head, a cold wind in her face. Her breathing is shallow and she thinks she might pass out, and then suddenly – sweet relief! – she's at her front door and her hand is fumbling, shaking, trying to get the key in the lock and then finally the door opens and she collapses onto the floor, water dripping from her clothes, sticking to her skin, her breathing sharp, staccato, the door blowing back and forth in the wind behind her, tapping on the wall insistently. But she's home, she's safe, and nobody can get her now.

A few minutes pass before she can drag herself into a sitting position, and she gives the door a hard shove with her foot to close it. She sits for a moment, legs crossed, hands resting on her knees and tries to remember the breathing techniques Debbie taught her. Slowly, slowly, her vision starts to come back, and her breathing returns to normal. She's okay. Nothing has happened, and nothing is going to happen to her. Not in here.

She doesn't dare think about how she must have looked to Ben, running out like that. He must think she's mad. Perhaps she is, she thinks, as she stretches her legs out in front of her and realises she isn't wearing any shoes and her socks are wet through and muddy. She thinks back to her mad dash back to the safety of her house and doesn't remember stopping to pick up her shoes at any point. Oh God, she's left them there. She'll have to send Debbie round later to get them back for her, and apologise.

Maybe this whole thing isn't such a good idea after all. Maybe she isn't as ready as she thought she was.

* * *

There's a squeak behind him, then the sound of footsteps, and by the time he's turned round, Laura has gone, banging the front door behind her. Ben stands, mug in hand, mouth gaping slightly open, and thinks, *What the fuck?* Then he looks down at the patch of floor where she was standing and sees her trainers. She's left without her shoes. Why was she so desperate to get away from him that she'd leave her shoes behind? What on earth just happened?

With a sigh he puts the kettle back down on the worktop and bends to pick up Laura's discarded shoes. He really, really doesn't want to get involved, if he's honest. But he can't help feeling worried about Laura. And, now he comes to think about it, he hasn't seen Jim for a few weeks either. Not even a quick 'all right?' as Jim left for work or a chat on the way to the shop. It's a bit odd.

Besides, Laura is going to need her shoes back, and after that dramatic exit he doesn't expect to see her on his doorstep any time soon.

He shoves his coat on and walks to the door. Just as he goes to pull the door open he hears a rhythmic thumping and Rocky appears at the top of the stairs, holding his head on one side expectantly.

'Not now, buddy, sorry,' he says, and the dog sits down, his tail wagging enthusiastically on the carpeted floor. 'Later, promise.'

It's still chucking it down outside, and Ben wonders how long it took Laura to notice she was walking along the pavement in just her socks. Her feet must have been freezing. He closes the door behind him, locks up and walks briskly past next door to Laura and Jim's house. It seems odd that, after several months of friendship, he's never actually set foot inside this house before.

He rings the bell and waits. A few seconds pass and no one comes. He presses the doorbell again, holding it down for longer this time. Again, nothing. He's about to leave the trainers hanging on the door handle and hope she finds them later when there's a scraping sound, and then Laura's dishevelled face appears through a tiny crack in the door. Her face reddens instantly when she sees who it is and her eyes lower to the ground.

He holds out her shoes. 'You left these.'

She looks at the trainers and, realising she needs to take them, opens the door a bit more and sticks her hand out, hooking the laces with her finger.

'Thank you.'

She hovers a moment longer, the shoes dangling from her hand, and neither of them speaks. Ben wishes he were good at this sort of thing, but he never has been. When there is a silence to fill, his mind just goes blank.

Fortunately Laura speaks first. 'I'm sorry about before.' A drop of water escapes from her ponytail and sneaks its way slowly down her forehead towards her eye. He watches as it reaches her eyebrow and splashes onto the floor. She wipes her head with the back of her hand and looks up. Her eyes are wide and, he notices, a gorgeous shade of dark brown. 'I didn't mean—'

'It's okay—' They both start speaking at the same time and he stops. 'Go on.'

'I was just going to say I didn't mean to be rude, before. I just got a bit spooked.'

'Well, I am pretty scary.' Ben shrugs, not sure what else to say.

Laura just nods sadly and he worries he's said completely the wrong thing.

'Thanks for bringing my shoes back.' She points her toe out of the door. 'My socks are a bit of a state.'

'Yes.' Oh God, why can't he just say something less moronic? 'Listen, is everything okay?' Yes, of course it is, Ben, that's why she just ran out of your house without her shoes on because she was so desperate to get away from you. Idiot. 'I just got the impression you came to ask me something.'

Laura shakes her head. A gust of wind sends the rain horizontally, smacking Ben side-on in the face. He staggers sideways. He should be going, this isn't helping anyone. But as he turns to leave, Laura speaks.

'Jim's gone missing.'

Three words, but they stop him in his tracks. 'What?'

'Jim's disappeared.'

'Oh...' This explains a lot. 'Since when?'

'Two weeks. And two days.' Her face is white and she looks so lost. 'I was just wondering whether – whether he might have said anything to you. About anything?'

Ben stands for a moment in the pouring rain, his mind racing. *Did* Jim say anything? He can't say for sure. He's usually pretty oblivious to even the most obvious of things. But he finds he really wants to help this woman.

'I'm not sure.' He takes a step forward and she flinches. He holds his hands up and steps back again. 'Sorry.'

Laura shakes her head. 'No, I'm sorry. I'm being ridiculous.' She opens the door fully. 'Do you want to come in? I promise not to run away this time.'

'Are you sure?'

'Yes. Mainly because it's my house and there's nowhere else to go.' She tries a weak smile at her own joke.

He hesitates. He really does want to go in. Partly because he wants to find out what's happened to his friend, and partly – or perhaps mainly – because there's something about this woman that intrigues him. Making a split-second decision, he steps inside. Laura slams the door behind them, cutting the howling wind off in its tracks and leaving the hallway feeling deathly quiet as he drips water all over her floor. He kicks off his shoes, hangs his sodden jacket at the bottom of the stairs, then follows Laura into the kitchen, which, although the same size as his, is much more homely. Which isn't hard, if he's honest. Things have kind of fallen apart a bit in the last couple of years since... He stops. This is not the time to think about that.

Laura gestures for him to sit at the table and he does, obediently. 'Do you want that coffee you never got?'

'That would be great, thanks.'

While she makes it he looks around. He knows Jim and Laura haven't lived here long so this probably isn't to their taste, but it still feels welcoming. Mugs of different sizes line the shelves and pans hang from hooks above the worktop. There's a photo stuck to the fridge of a younger Laura and a much younger-looking Jim grinning into the camera outside a black and white building and he wonders idly where they were.

Laura plonks a coffee cup on the table and sits opposite him, clutching her own mug like a security blanket. He hopes she isn't about to start telling him something terrible; he isn't sure he can cope. He realises he's holding his breath and lets it out slowly so she doesn't hear.

'I really am sorry about before. I feel I owe you an explanation,' she starts.

'You don't have to—'

'I do. I...' Laura pauses, clearly trying to form the words. 'I suffer from agoraphobia.'

Ben looks up, surprised. That isn't what he was expecting. 'You mean, like, you can't leave the house?'

'Yes and no. I can't leave the house because every time I even think about it I feel sick and panicky, and terrified something terrible is going to happen to me. I can't have people in the house either, and I struggle to concentrate on one thing at a time. I've stopped caring about anything. I'm in a constant state of anxiety. And so I stay here, inside these four walls, stuck, like some sort of tragic Miss Faversham, destined to rot away and never see the light of day again.' She stops and takes a sip of coffee while he processes what she's just said. 'Jim's been brilliant, he looks after me, but – well. He's gone, and now I don't know what to do.'

'Wow.' It isn't enough but it's all he has, for now.

'I know. I'm sorry, it's a lot to put on someone I've only just met, but – well, I did just run practically screaming from your house with absolutely no explanation. So there you are. That's why. It was also... the agoraphobia was triggered after I was attacked, outside my own flat. And I just thought – well, I panicked, when I realised I was in someone else's house and that nobody knew where I was.'

Ben nods. 'You were scared of me.'

'I'm scared of everything.' She smiles weakly and he smiles back. She looks pretty when she smiles, little dimples forming in her cheeks and her eyes crinkling at the edges.

He places his hands flat on the table and studies his nails. 'So tell me about Jim. What's happened?'

'That's what I'm trying to find out. Two weeks and two days ago, he left the house. As far as I know he went to work, but he never came home. Now I have no idea where he is or what's happened to him. Neither does anyone else, it seems.' Her voice wavers but there's no sign of tears.

'Oh, my goodness. Have you spoken to the police?'

'Yes. They're looking into it. But there's nothing so far. No money taken from his account. He's just – gone. And I'm scared, Ben.'

It's the first time she's said his name and it sounds strange on her lips.

'So you're trying to find him yourself?'

She gives a mirthless laugh. 'I've got to do something. Things have been pretty tough recently. For him. For us. We've left London, and our friends – well, his mainly – and I'm stuck in here, going mad day after day, and he's taken the brunt. He just wants to get on with his life but he can't because he's trapped here looking after me. Me, work, me, work, and nothing else. So quite honestly I can't blame him if he has left me, but I just need to find him. I need to know he's okay.' She wipes her face with her hands and rubs her eyes. 'God, it's a bloody mess.'

They both sit and drink their coffee for a while.

'I promise I'll try and think whether Jim said anything to me, but I have to be honest, he never told me any of this. It feels like he might have been protecting you from – pity, I suppose. So I only knew your name and that you were his wife, and then he never spoke about you, and I – I never asked anything else.' He shrugs. 'It's just blokes, I guess. But it does seem unlikely that he'd ever have told me anything about your problems or about wanting to leave you. It's just not what we talked about. I'm really sorry, I know that's not what you need to hear.'

Laura shakes her head. 'Don't worry. I'm not expecting it to be that easy. Chances are I won't find anything at all. But I just feel like someone, somewhere, must hold a clue. He must have said *something* to somebody that might give us an idea about where he's gone. And even if that clue doesn't exist, I've got to at least *try* and find it. I owe him that.'

Ben pauses. 'Am I the first person you've come to see? On the street, I mean.'

'You're the second. I went to see Mr and Mrs Loveday first – sorry, Carol and Arthur – next door.' She pauses. 'It was closer.'

Ben nods in understanding. 'Did they have anything that might help? Jim knows them, doesn't he?'

She hesitates. What Carol told her about the photos on the keyring has rattled her, and she still hasn't worked out what it could mean. She's not sure if she wants to share it with anyone else, in case it makes it feel more sinister. But if she doesn't, what's the point of doing this in the first place?

'I'm sure there's a perfectly reasonable explanation,' Ben says carefully as she finishes explaining what Carol claimed to have seen.

'That's what my best friend, Debbie, said. She says we need to take it with a pinch of salt.'

'But you think there's something in it?'

She sighs. 'I really don't know. I hope there isn't, and that Debbie's right. But I'm scared this is just the tiny tip of an enormous iceberg, and if I start looking into that then I might find even more stuff that I don't want to know.' It isn't until she's said the words out loud that she realises they're true. What if Carol was right, and Jim did have photos of children on a keyring that he didn't mean her to see? What would be the implications for them? She looks at Ben, who seems deep in thought.

'You know Jim better than I do. Obviously,' he says eventually. 'But I just don't see it. I mean, I just can't see that he'd have any sinister secrets.'

'Yeah, I know.' She does know that. At least, she always has done. But there's a small but growing part of her that can't help wondering whether it might mean *something*. Whether there might be some connection between the photos on Jim's keyring and the person who used to hang around her flat in London, or the silent phone calls she used to receive, or even the fact that she doesn't really know anything about her husband's life when he's away from her. Her head feels muddled and she pushes the thoughts away.

The room has brightened, and outside the window the rain has eased a little, the hammering becoming more of a gentle tap. Ben is suddenly struck by the idea that he needs to get out of there. Jim might not have told him anything about Laura, but Ben definitely told Jim about himself, and he has no idea how much, if anything, Laura knows about it. He really doesn't feel like talking about it, not right now. He needs to go.

He stands suddenly and Laura jumps.

'Are you going?'

'Yes, sorry. I was – I've got to get some work done and – well, the rain's stopping so...' He trails off, aware he's being rude. His shoulders slump. 'Sorry, Laura. I will have a think, and I'll let you know if I remember anything, okay?'

'Okay. Thank you.'

'Right, thanks for the coffee. I'll see myself out.' Then he leaves the room and a few seconds later closes the door firmly behind him.

As he hurries home he tries to process everything he's just learned. His friend has disappeared, and either he really doesn't want to be found or someone is making sure he isn't found. Neither of those suggestions sound good. And Jim's wife, Laura. Well, at least he knows what's wrong with her now. It isn't what he expected, but it is awful. But worst of all, worse than any of this, is that Laura has stirred something in him. She's weak and vulnerable and trying to find her missing husband, and he was attracted to her. What kind of man does that make him?

Trying to block out all thoughts of the morning he's just had, he turns away from his house, ups his pace and runs until his lungs burn and his legs are close to collapse. Only then can he forget.

* * *

It has been two and a half years. Two and a half long years that Ben has been on his own. For the first six months people were sympathetic. They'd ask him how he felt, bring beers round, invite him for nights out. But that seemed to be the official limit on grief. Some unexplained deadline he never received the memo for. It seemed that, six months after watching your wife die from ovarian cancer, you were supposed to be starting to feel better. To be 'getting over it' and 'starting to move on'. Except he didn't feel like doing any of those things, and he stubbornly continued to grieve. Slowly, his friends stopped ringing or calling round to see if he wanted to go out. Invitations dried up. And even the people he did see stopped treating him with kid gloves and started pretending nothing had happened. Life, for them, went on.

But not for him it didn't. Not by a long shot.

Helen's death broke him, and he still can't see any way of getting fixed. Whenever he thinks about her, about them, he tries to picture when they first met, or when they bought their first flat together, or when they got married. He forces the image to the front of his mind and tries to hold it there. Usually he succeeds. But sometimes the darker memories creep in, worming their way round the edges of the barrier he's constructed in his mind, and he can only think of her at the end. Images of his precious, beautiful Helen in bed; in pain, her hair long gone, exhaustion written across her skeletal face. She tried so hard to stay upbeat, to keep a smile on her face. But in the end, it got her. She was beaten.

And so was he.

Their home holds so many memories that at first he could hardly bear to be in it. He'd drift around it like a ghost, from room to room, the memories of Helen so painful it was like being stabbed in the heart. He thought he would have to move, to get away from the place where his heart had been broken, make a fresh start. But slowly he began to realise that he didn't want to leave. He wanted to live through this pain, because it meant he'd loved her as much as he'd always believed, as if this were proving it, showing the world he had meant every word.

And to his amazement, slowly, slowly, being in the house became a little less painful. When he walked into the bedroom where he'd nursed her for the last few weeks, he stopped seeing the equipment used to administer her pain relief, the piles of pills on the bedside table, the cardboard bowl in case she needed to be sick, the crumpled, sweaty sheets. Instead he started remembering better days, happier days. The day they first moved in, with hardly a stick of furniture to their names except a bed, a wardrobe and a couple of ancient dining-room chairs after years of living in furnished accommodation. They'd eaten beans on toast by the light of the bare bulb swinging from the living-room ceiling rose and drunk red wine until their mouths were a deep shade of purple and their words were slurred. Helen had danced in front of the bedroom window in her bra and knickers, laughing hysterically. 'Come away from there, we've got no curtains, the neighbours will see everything!' he'd said, giggling along with her. But she hadn't cared and had carried on dancing, head thrown back, arms in the air, until he'd pulled her onto the unmade mattress and they'd christened their new home.

He thought of the Christmases they'd spent there, her obsession with wrestling the biggest tree they could find into the living room so that it bent over at the top; the dinner parties they'd thrown, the room they'd planned to turn into a nursery one day but had run out of time until that became an impossibility.

So he'd stayed, and here he still is, almost three years later, living alone, working all the hours he can from his office round the corner, and hardly seeing anyone apart from a few friends in the village from time to time. And Jim, of course. He was pleased when Jim moved in. A new friend, someone to enjoy a drink and a chat with, as well as the odd game of poker. He told Jim all about Helen, about the last few years. He didn't realise until now that it was completely one-sided, and that Jim hardly revealed anything about himself or Laura, or the reason they'd moved here in the first place.

He wonders whether that was his fault for never asking.

Maybe it's a sign of his heart finally beginning to heal that he can even think about someone else's needs, or maybe it's something else, but he finds that he really wants to help Laura. He must be able to think of something that could give her a clue about what's happened to Jim. He thinks back to the nights he's spent with Jim, the games of poker they've played, the things Jim *has* told him. He tries to dredge up something, anything, even a tiny crumb of detail that might help in any small way. He thinks about what Laura told him about the keyring, and wracks his brain for something that might shed some light on it. *Could* it be significant? Could it really be a clue as to Jim's whereabouts? He just can't see how.

His lungs are starting to burn and he slows his pace as he completes his circuit, and the end of Willow Crescent is in sight. He slows to a walk as he passes the corner shop, and by the time he gets back to his front door he's sweaty and exhausted. His watch reveals he's run at a much faster pace than usual, and he wonders what he was running away from. His inappropriate feelings for Jim's wife perhaps? He shakes the thought from his head.

It's not until he's letting himself in his front door that something occurs to him. It was something and nothing, and he probably would never have remembered it if he hadn't spoken to Laura today. But now it sits there, in his memory, shining like a diamond, and he examines it from all angles to see if it's something he should tell Laura. Whether it could be useful in tracking Jim down, or whether it would just upset or confuse her more.

A month or so ago, during one of their poker nights, they all drank more than normal, him, Jim, Simon and a couple of the others, and they gave up pretending to play cards. Ben could hardly see what he was holding in front of him, so the memory is fuzzy round the edges. But he remembers Jim talking, telling him about his wife, and he remembers something that jarred at the time, only he couldn't have said why. It's only now he's met Laura that it's slotted into place. He called his wife something else. Another name. what was it? He sifts through the debris of his mind to find it. Cheryl? No, not that. Kerry? No, more unusual. It's the only reason he remembers it, because it wasn't a common name, and he recalls noticing it at the time. He can't quite grasp it now, but the actual name isn't important. What is important is whether he should tell Laura about it. Jim denied it at the time, and in his drunken state Ben accepted his denial. Even now, looking back, he can't be 100 per cent certain he didn't imagine it.

But he should tell Laura. He should. No matter whether it's significant to her investigation, he owes it to her to tell her what he (half) remembers, in case the half-remembered name means something to her. After all, it could just be someone from the family, someone she recognises, and she can laugh it off.

But if it isn't, then it might just be another cog in her search for her husband, and he can't deny her that. He picks up the phone and calls Jim's – and Laura's – number.

14

THEN – OCTOBER 1989

I heard the key in the lock and felt pathetically grateful that Jim was home. Since the stalker incident earlier that day I'd felt nervous, on edge, jumping at my own shadow. Just having someone else in the flat instantly made me relax. When had I become so reliant on someone else to make me feel safe and happy?

I reached the hallway before Jim noticed me. He was fiddling with something on the side table.

'You're home!' I said, walking towards him with my arms outstretched.

As he looked up, a flash of something I couldn't read flickered across his face before he smiled, slipping his keys into his pocket.

'What a day,' he said, pulling me into a tight hug, and I breathed in his familiar scent, the smell I always missed so much when he was away. I leaned away slightly and looked up at him.

'What happened?'

He rested his chin on my head and let out a long sigh. His body felt warm against me. 'Oh, just boring work stuff. People being difficult. Deals going wrong. And a terrible journey – the train was packed and I had to stand all the way from Peterborough.'

'Oh, you poor thing.' I stepped away and headed towards the kitchen. 'Glass of wine?'

'Love one,' he said. 'I'm just going to jump in the shower and I'll be there.'

He headed into the bathroom and I opened a bottle of Merlot, glugged it into glasses and took a long sip. What had Jim been doing when I'd walked into the hallway? What had he been trying to hide?

Before I could think about what I was doing, I slipped into the bedroom where Jim had discarded his suit on the bed. The shower was still running so I snatched up his suit jacket and dipped my hand into the pocket where I'd seen him put his keys. I pulled them out and studied them. They were just his keys, with his front door key, his office key and his usual BMW keyring. I put my hand back into the pocket and searched around but there was nothing else in there.

I shoved the keys back into the pocket and threw the jacket on the bed just as Jim walked in with his towel wrapped around his waist. He was still in good shape and I felt a surge of desire as he walked across the room and kissed me deeply. 'What are you up to in here?' he said, grinning.

'Nothing, I was just going to put your suit away.'

He looked at where his suit was lying crumpled on the bed. 'Don't be daft, I'll do that. Anyway it needs dry-cleaning, I spilt some wine on it last night.'

'Oh, were you out?'

'Yeah, it was a work thing. You know, always having to network in this blooming job.'

I nodded and smiled. But as Jim got dressed and I headed back to the kitchen to grab our glasses of wine, I felt a stab of envy at these people who got to spend all this time with the man I loved four days a week, while I sat at home on my own, missing him. As time had passed I'd seen other people less and less, and I felt lonely and isolated, living here. I rarely went out – the odd cinema trip or meal with Debbie was the extent of it, my other friends having drifted away after endless cancellations by me. One of them might ring me for a chat from time to time but, far from cheering me up, it usually left me feeling more depressed at how stilted our friendship had become.

I only had myself to blame.

Jim sat down next to me and I snuggled into his side and tried to put everything out of my mind. Besides, I had something more pressing to tell him.

'You seem on edge, is everything okay?' he said, taking a sip of his wine.

'I'm fine.' I wanted to have a chance to have dinner first, talk about normal things before I told him about what had happened. If all I did was cling to him in fear every time he walked through the door, how long would it take for him to get fed up with me?

He pulled away and peered down at me and I met his gaze.

'Come on, Lola,' he said, 'you can't fool me. What's happened?'

I sighed, and sat up, tucking my feet beneath me.

'I think someone is following me,' I said.

'Following you? What do you mean?'

I took a deep breath and told him about the encounter in the street earlier that afternoon.

'And you're sure whoever it was, was following you?'

I nodded. 'It wasn't just that.'

'What? What else happened? Has someone hurt you, threatened you?'

I shook my head. 'No, nothing like that. But the night before, when I got home from work, I had a weird phone call.'

'Weird how?'

'I answered and whoever it was didn't say anything but – I could hear them breathing.'

'Perhaps it was just a wrong number.'

I let out a whoosh of air. This was exactly why I hadn't wanted to tell anyone about the phone calls. On the surface of it, they sounded innocuous, nothing to worry about. A wrong number, an automated phone call from a sales company: easily explained away. But I felt certain there was more to it, and the more time that passed and the more I ruminated on it, the more certain I became.

'It wasn't the first time,' I said. 'It happened a few days ago too.'

He shuffled his body round and studied me intently. Then he reached over and tilted my chin up so that I was looking right into his face.

'Why didn't you tell me?' His voice was gentle, caring, and I felt tears fill my eyes.

'I didn't want you to worry,' I said, choosing not to tell him I was more concerned that he wouldn't believe me.

He leaned over and planted a gentle kiss on my lips. 'I'm sure it's nothing, but I'm here now so there's nothing to worry about.'

'Thank you,' I said.

'Now come here and give me a kiss.' Then he wrapped his arms around me and I tried to let myself forget.

* * *

It had been a long, hot shift at the restaurant, and I was ready to flop. I usually tried to arrange the nights I worked round the days Jim was away, but I couldn't get away with it every weekend, and this Saturday night had been particularly busy. I just wanted to get home, have a shower and go to bed.

But as I walked out of the restaurant and towards my car, I saw a figure hovering beside it and I froze. Trying to control my breathing, I glanced up and down the road to see if anyone else was around, but it was silent, not even the buzz of a motorbike cutting its way along the empty street. I dug my hand into my bag and wrapped my fingers round my car key, leaving the point sticking out between my fingers. It was hardly going to defend me against an attacker, but it made me feel a little bit safer. I stood frozen for a minute more, then started creeping towards my car. As I got closer I could see in the orange glow from the nearby street light that the figure was facing away from me, head down. I wondered whether it was the person I'd seen running away from me a few days before, but they'd been slight, almost waif-like beneath baggy clothes, whereas this person was bigger, with broad shoulders, and cropped hair. I stepped closer and something must have alerted them to my presence because they turned around. And as they did, and I made out the familiar jawline, the long straight nose, the pale glow of cropped blonde-grey hair, the tension whooshed out of me instantly.

'Jim?' I said, stepping closer, and he whipped his head round to face me.

'You're done,' he said, smiling.

'I am.' My body was still shaking from the adrenaline surge, and he must have seen the look on my face. 'What's wrong?'

'You terrified me, standing there like that in the dark.'

He looked down at himself, then back up at me. 'Oh God, I'm so sorry, Laura. I thought I'd meet you from work so you didn't have to feel scared on your way home. But I've gone and terrified you even more by hanging round like some mad stalker, haven't I?'

'Well, yes. There isn't normally a strange man hanging round my car at—' I checked my watch '—gone midnight.'

He shook his head and stepped towards me, arms outstretched. 'I'm so sorry, darling. I didn't think. I was just trying to protect you.' He wrapped his arms around me and gave me a squeeze. 'Forgive me?'

'Course I do.' My heart was slowly going back to normal and I looked up at him, his skin glowing orange on one side, the other half of his face in shadow. 'But what made you come all the way down here?'

'I was thinking about what you said, about someone following you, and I didn't like the thought of you leaving the restaurant all by yourself with some weirdo hanging around. So I thought I'd come and pick you up.'

'But you can't do that every night. I've – I've got to learn to get on with things.'

'I know.' He turned to face the car. 'Listen, let's get going, shall we? It's getting chilly. Want me to drive?'

Despite myself, I couldn't think of anything better than being driven home. I threw him the keys and climbed into the passenger seat.

As we set off through the streets of north London, I let my eyes close and my body relax. Jim might have given me a fright, but I was actually touched by his concern. His voice beside me made me jump.

'Sorry, what?' I said, rubbing my eyes. Jim was smiling at me.

'I said I changed our phone number today.' He looked pleased with himself.

'What? Why?' I said, properly awake now.

'I thought it was wise, given the phone calls you've been receiving.'

'Oh.' I wasn't sure what to say. I knew Jim had only done it to be kind, but I couldn't help thinking it would make me even more isolated. I didn't hear from people much as it was, but when I did, the phone was my lifeline.

'I thought you'd be pleased.'

'I am. I was just – I didn't know you were going to do it, that's all.'

'Well, no. That's because I didn't tell you. But listen, Laura, someone has to look out for you, make sure you're safe, because you're not doing a very good job of it yourself.'

'What do you mean?'

'I mean like parking in dark, secluded car parks late at night, like chasing after people you think are following you, like not telling me you were receiving worrying phone calls.' I watched him as he concentrated, his brow furrowed as a van cut him up and he swore under his breath. He glanced at me quickly then back at the road. His hand landed on my thigh, the warmth radiating through my trousers. 'I just want you to be safe, love.'

I pressed my palm against the back of his hand and threaded his fingers through mine. 'Thank you,' I said, my voice a whisper.

We didn't speak for the rest of the journey, and I let my eyes close and my mind drift off and tried to forget about everything that had happened and allow myself to feel safe. Because I was, wasn't I? I had Jim to look after me.

15

NOW – 6 OCTOBER 1992

Number six Willow Crescent
Jane Hardwick and children, Abbie and Archie

The morning dawns bright and sunny, warmer than it has been for most of the summer, with fluffy white clouds in a blue sky and the branches of the willow tree swaying in a gentle breeze. Laura stands at her bedroom window watching the world go by. Her neighbours' routines have become almost as familiar to her as her own. Ben goes out for a run most mornings and is gone for around forty-five minutes, then comes home and takes his dog for a walk; Jane slams the door behind her about half an hour before her kids leave for school and returns about four o'clock, often with arms full of carrier bags from the local Safeway. Sonja from over the road is always out of the house early, and Laura usually only ever sees her return, while her husband, Simon, is out at irregular times, pushing a buggy or bundling their daughter into her car seat. Marjorie opposite, like her, never leaves the house unless her daughter, Faye, is pushing her in her wheelchair, while Carol and Arthur next door are always pottering about in the garden, or knocking on neighbours' doors – at least Carol is. Arthur occasionally has a chat with someone by the garden wall, and every Friday night he leaves the house at exactly 7.25 p.m., dressed in his flat cap and tweed jacket, presumably to meet friends for a pint in the pub a few streets away. He's usually gone a good three hours before he returns, weaving up the front path, a crooked grin on his face. It's comforting for Laura, to see that people's lives are carrying on as normal.

Today, Simon is standing outside his front door smoking a surreptitious fag, blowing smoke into the warm air in puffs. He leans against the porch, his arms folded. She wonders if he can see her. He looks deep in thought. Jane's driveway is already empty and Archie is outside, playing keepie-uppies with his football as he always does before school. The tap, tap, tap of the ball against his foot, occasionally bouncing on the tarmac, is rhythmic.

She remembers a few years ago, when she and Jim were still living in the flat in London, when she started seeing the figure outside their flat, watching her; remembers the silent phone calls that had scared her so much, and for the first time she feels grateful to be here dealing with Jim's disappearance, in the safety of this cul de sac, rather than there, where she'd spent so much time feeling watched, exposed.

She steps away from the window and studies herself in the mirror above the dressing table, where her make-up sits gathering dust. Her skin is pale from lack of sunshine, her curly hair flattened against her head like a crumpled wig. She leans forwards, runs her fingers along her lips. They're dry, and her skin appears flaky and grey under the harsh sunlight pouring in through the window. Her eyes are tired-looking, a dark rim beneath them, the lines around them deeper than usual. Hardly surprising given she drank her way through most of a bottle of vodka last night. Her medicine, even though she knows it's killing her. She really needs to start wearing make-up again; the make-up was a mask, before, gave her confidence. Now, though, she sees that without any at all she looks pale and ill.

She goes to lie down on her bed and stares up at the patterns dancing on the ceiling, a fly buzzing lazily around the window frame. Her vision blurs slightly and she closes her eyes tight, screwing them up and pressing the palms of her hands into them until lights dance in her vision. If she lies here, completely still, perhaps she'll wake up and everything will be back to normal. Perhaps everything that has happened in the last eighteen months will turn out to be a horrible nightmare, and she and Jim will be happy again.

But she knows it's hopeless and, before she can stop it, the one thing she's been trying not to think about since Ben's phone call slams back into her mind without warning. The name Ben struggled to remember; the name Jim had drunkenly referred to her as by accident one night a few weeks before. She thinks about the conversation now, replaying it over in her mind.

When the phone rang her heart leapt with hope, the way it always did, as she wondered whether it was Jim, or news of Jim. The only other person who would be calling this number was Debbie, so when she picked up the phone and heard Ben's voice on the other end she was surprised, and a little bit pleased. He sounded nervous, and when he explained what he'd remembered, about the name Jim had used for her – Cheryl, or Kerry, or something like that – she didn't think much of it. She simply added it to her list of potential clues and hoped that, eventually, something would leap out at her, something to really give her a push towards working out what had happened to her husband.

But the more she thought about it afterwards, the more she

wondered whether it *was* significant. It wasn't as though the name were anything like hers, and she began torturing herself with thoughts of who this mystery Cheryl or Kerry might be. Could Jim have a hidden past that she knows nothing about? Or is she over-dramatising, making more of this than is actually there? She just can't imagine Jim hiding something like that from her. Besides, why would he?

Her thoughts are interrupted by the shrill ring of the telephone. After a frantic search she finds the handset lying on the bed.

'Hello?'

'Is this Mrs Parks?'

'Yes, it is.'

'My name is Jonathon. I'm your police liaison officer.'

Laura's heart stops, and she sits up, her head spinning. Her throat thickens, the words getting stuck.

'Mrs Parks?'

'Is there bad news?'

'No, no. Nothing to worry about. In fact – well, I'm afraid there isn't much news at all, not yet.'

'You're not – giving up, are you?'

'Certainly not. We will continue to actively look for your husband, Mrs Parks, but...'

'What?'

'Well, if he doesn't want to be found, then it is going to be extremely difficult.'

Laura swallows hard. Her throat feels blocked. 'Is that—?' She coughs. 'Is that what you think has happened? That he doesn't want to be found? That he's hiding from me?'

'Not exactly hiding. But there are no signs yet that anything untoward has happened, so all other conclusions point towards him having chosen to disappear. But as I say, we're keeping all lines of investigation open. I'm sorry we don't have anything more positive to tell you yet.'

'Okay. Thank you.' Her voice feels small.

When she ends the call Laura lies back on her bed. She wanted to cry and shout and rail against the police officer for failing to find Jim, for assuming he'd left on purpose. But the truth is, she's beginning to come to exactly the same conclusion. And it makes her feel both terrified and furious at the same time.

Yes, things have been tough recently. Yes, she's been pretty much oblivious to Jim's needs. But how could he just up and leave her? Why would he do that, knowing she's ill?

The only thing she can do is carry on looking, carry on asking questions, and hope that someone holds the key to his disappearance. It's increasingly becoming her only hope.

Only then will she get any answers.

* * *

Debbie is due about two o'clock, so when the doorbell peals as she's scraping the remains of her sandwich in the bin just after one o'clock she's surprised. Debbie's late more often than she is early.

She pulls the door open and takes a quick step back. 'Oh!'

Ben is on her doorstep, looking sheepish. He has a bottle of wine in his hand and she finds her mood lifting at the sight of him.

'Hello, Laura. Sorry to come round out of the blue but I've been feeling bad about what happened the other day and I wanted to say sorry.' He holds out the bottle. 'I also wanted to say that if you need any help looking for Jim, I'd like to. Help, that is.'

Laura stands still a few seconds, numb with surprise. Surely she's the one who should be apologising to Ben, not the other way round? Yet she can't deny she felt a little shiver of pleasure when she opened the door to him.

'Oh, well, thank you.' Should she invite him in? She was planning to leave soon. She's due to try and pay a visit to the next neighbour on the list, Jane, and her children, Archie and Abbie, and she's just waiting for Debbie to come and accompany her.

'So, is there anything I can do?'

'I—' She stops as a thought occurs to her. 'I don't suppose you know Jane, do you? From across the road?' She points vaguely in the direction of Jane's house.

'Jane Hardwick? With Abbie and Archie?'

'Yes.'

'Yes, I know her quite well. She was friends with – with my wife. She's lovely. They all are, actually. Why?'

'I was thinking of trying to go over there later. See if she knows anything.'

He glances over, then back at her. 'Would you like me to come with you?'

'I – my friend Debbie is coming.'

'Oh, okay. No worries.' He looks crestfallen.

'Maybe you could come too? As you know her? It might help.'

She doesn't know what makes her say it, but it's out now and she can hardly take it back. Ben's face lights up.

'Yes, I could do that.'

'Okay.' Laura inhales deeply, aware she's being stand-offish. 'Sorry, would you like to come in? We'll be going over there as soon as Debbie gets here.'

'Thank you.'

Laura watches as he bends down to remove his shoes, and her face flushes as she remembers the manner in which she left his house a couple of days before, in her socks. As she leads him into the kitchen, her belly is in knots. Is it simply the presence of someone else in her sanctuary? Or is it because, for the first time in years, she's actually considering letting someone new into her life?

'Can I get you a drink?'

'We could open this, if you like?' Ben points at the wine in his hand. 'If you don't think it's too early?'

'A man after my own heart,' she says, trying to hide her flushed face as she takes the bottle from him.

Why is Ben making her feel so jittery? She feels like a nervous schoolgirl trying to impress a boy. She pours the wine and they settle at the kitchen table.

'So, how are you getting on with your investigations?' Ben says, twirling his glass round on the tabletop.

Laura shakes her head. 'There's nothing new. The police just rang and they have nothing new either, which means the only clues I have are what you told me, which could be something or nothing, and the keyring that Carol mentioned.' She sighs. 'It could be that he has a secret past he hasn't told me about but I just —' She stops. 'Truthfully it's simply beginning to look as if...' She trails off, not wanting to say it out loud.

'He's gone on purpose?'

She nods. 'I wouldn't have said it a few weeks ago. I never would have thought Jim could do something like this. I mean, you know what he's like. Kind, reliable. But...' She runs her hands through her hair. 'Well, it appears he was more unhappy than I ever knew. It's just a shame I didn't notice.'

'You can't blame yourself. It's not your fault you're stuck in here.'

'No. But it wasn't his either and he did everything he could to help me. I just threw it all back in his face.'

Ben doesn't know what else to say. Jim didn't tell him any of this and, although his friend seemed quieter the last few times he saw him, there was nothing that made him concerned. Nothing he could specifically say had changed. He wishes he could tell Laura more but it seems he didn't know what was going on in his friend's life at all. He sighs.

'You never know, Jane might be more help.'

Laura gives a small nod. 'She might. But nobody has known anything so far. They didn't even know I was ill.'

Ben looks sheepish. 'I guess Jim was just trying to protect you.'

She shrugs. 'I know. But it's so frustrating.'

Silence presses in the space between them and Laura takes a gulp of her wine. She can feel it blurring the edges of her anxiety the moment it hits her mouth. She notices Ben hasn't drunk any of his yet.

'I...' She tails off.

'What?' Ben says, his forehead creasing.

'I – I hope you don't mind me asking, but what happened with your wife?'

Ben feels his heart somersault and almost drops his glass onto the table. 'Oh, I—' He's so unused to meeting people who don't know about Helen, who don't see him as the tragic widower, that he's forgotten how to talk about it.

'Sorry, I shouldn't have asked.'

'No,' Ben says. 'It's just – well, I haven't talked about her for ages. Not since I told Jim a few months ago actually.' He wipes his hand over his chin where a dark shadow has already started to form, then meets Laura's gaze. 'She died.'

'Oh, Ben, I'm so sorry.'

'It's fine. Well, it's not but – well. It was a while ago.' He looks down at the table and tells her about watching Helen die, how utterly broken he was, and how lonely he's felt ever since. Once he's finished the silence hums between them. Laura watches his hand, resting on the table, and wishes she knew him well enough to reach out and cover it with her own, to offer some physical comfort.

'I'm so sorry,' she says again instead, aware of how meagre her sympathy must sound. Ben shakes his head. 'Thank you. It's – it's been hard. But I'm getting there.' And he is. He is finally able to talk about Helen without feeling as though he has a stone lodged in his throat. He can think about her without feeling as though his world is about to end.

Before Laura can say anything further the phone rings.

'Hang on, I'd better get this,' she says, jumping up to answer.

As Laura speaks to whoever is calling, Ben takes the opportunity to study her more closely. She's small, her tiny frame swamped by the too-big clothes she's wrapped herself in. But it's her posture that makes her seem almost childlike, sitting curled in on herself as though she's trying to take up as little space in the world as possible. Her curls lie flat against her head as though they've run out of energy and tiny lines fan away from her eyes. She looks exhausted. He jumps as she turns and notices him watching her, a line appearing between her brows, and he looks away quickly, his face flushing. He studies his feet as she ends the call.

'That was Debbie. She can't come, James is poorly. Her son.'

'Oh.'

Laura looks even more lost than usual. 'I guess that's that, then.' After what happened last time she tried to go out on her own she isn't going to risk doing it again. She'll just have to wait.

'We could go without her, just me and you?'

Laura looks up, her eyes wide. 'I—' She stops. Can she risk having a panic attack in front of this virtual stranger – again? He'll think she's completely mad. But then again, he has just opened up to her about his wife, and she really does need to get on with her search, so...

'If you have time that would be great, thank you.' She sucks in air through her lips and nods her head furiously as though trying to convince herself.

Ben jumps down from his stool. 'Shall we go, then?'

'Now?' Her head spins, and she's not sure it's the wine.

'There's no reason to put it off, is there? Unless...' He wants to say 'unless you're too frightened', but he doesn't want to remind her, so he bites his tongue.

She stands too, her hand still on her wine glass. 'You're right. We should just get on with it.' She takes one last sip and turns, a look of determination on her face. Together they walk to the front door, put on their shoes and stand facing the glass panels in the door. Sunlight pours through them, sketching asymmetrical patterns on her jumper and across her hands. Laura is acutely aware that the light is outside, and in a minute she'll be standing out there in full daylight, instead of in here, in the semi-dark. It's a lot to get her head around.

She takes some deep breaths in and exhales loudly, trying to calm her racing pulse. Next to her Ben shuffles his feet, waiting for her to finish. Finally she turns to face him, her face filled with fear.

'Let's go.'

She pulls the door open with more determination than she feels and takes a step forward. Almost immediately she stops and Ben nearly crashes into her back. The air is crisp and cool. Fallen leaves race each other across the pavement in front of her. Carol isn't in her front garden, and Archie isn't kicking his football around any more. There's a buzz of a chainsaw, someone giving their hedges one last trim before winter sets in, and a young child crying, but she can't see anyone. The crescent is surprisingly quiet and she's relieved. No doubt Mrs Phillips across the road is watching them through her net curtains but Laura doesn't dare look.

She trains her gaze on the path in front of her, the short stretch from her front door to her gate. She's done this before; once when she went next door to see Carol and Arthur, and once when she went to see Ben, although she hardly remembers that journey. She can do it again.

'Do you want me to help?' Ben appears at her side and she jumps. 'Sorry, I didn't mean to scare you.'

'It's okay. This is the worst bit. I just need to get to the end of the path. I don't suppose you could hold my hand, could you?'

'Of course.' He reaches down and takes her fingers in his. They feel warm and slightly clammy, and he holds them gently at first, the feeling of connection with someone other than Helen after so long a little overwhelming. 'Is this okay?' She nods silently. He concentrates on not thinking too much about the feeling of her hand in his, her skin soft against his own drier palm.

Laura takes a tentative step forward and her grip on his hand tightens. She takes another, and another, slowly at first and then faster, each time her hold on his fingers tightening until they feel as though they're being crushed in a vice. He doesn't say anything, just holds his breath and carries on walking beside her, watching the focus on her face.

Finally they reach the gate and she removes her hand and rests it on top of the iron railing. Her eyes are closed and he studies her again, her face turned up to the sun. Her skin is so pale it's almost translucent, and she seems to shine in the pale afternoon sunlight as though lit from within. She opens her eyes, turns to him and he looks away quickly.

'Thank you.'

'No problem.' He still holds the memory of her hand in his. 'Are you ready to carry on?'

'I think so.'

Together they walk through the gate and across the road, not holding hands this time, but the tops of their arms touching on every other step. Ben tries not to notice.

It's only a few metres across the street to Jane's house, but it may as well be a hundred miles away. Laura's whole body shakes and her brain feels as though it's too big for her head. Her skin prickles and the light dances in her eyes. Her breath comes in short, ragged puffs, and the road feels so unsure beneath her feet it could be made from marshmallow.

And yet, at last, they make it. Jane's small front garden stretches in front of them, the front door only a few metres away.

'I hope she's in after all this.' Her grin looks more like a grimace and Ben smiles back.

'Come on, let's get it over with.' He grabs her hand again and almost drags her up the path to the front door before she can change her mind, and knocks loudly. Silence hums in the air for a few brief moments as Laura stands with her eyes closed, and then the door swings open.

'Hello, Ben.' Jane's gaze passes quizzically to Laura, who snaps her eyes open.

'Hi, Jane. This is Laura.' He pauses. 'Jim's wife. She wanted to come and speak to you, and I said I'd introduce you.'

Jane's mouth stretches into an enormous grin and she sticks out her hand and shakes Laura's vigorously. 'Oh, Laura, it's really lovely to meet you. Although—' She looks over Laura's shoulder into the street behind. 'Aren't you – did you—?' She stops, suddenly awkward.

'You knew?' Ben sounds surprised.

'About Laura's agoraphobia? Yes, Jim told me.' Jane looks back at Laura apologetically. 'I hope that was all right?'

Laura nods briefly, strangely comforted at not having to explain herself as Jane ushers her inside. 'Come in, come in, you shouldn't be standing out there on the doorstep.' The pair bustle through the door and relief floods through Laura. It might be a stranger's house but it's still better than being out in the big wide world. And at least she's doing this; she's conquering it, and it will get easier. She hopes.

A few minutes later, installed in Jane's sparse living room with a mug of strong milky tea in her hands, Laura starts telling Jane about Jim's disappearance. Jane likes Laura instantly and can see why Jim loves her so much.

'So you think you might find a clue, if you go and speak to everyone in the street?' Jane takes a sip from her mug and flinches, the hot liquid scalding her tongue.

Laura shrugs. 'That's the plan. I know it sounds a bit desperate.'

'God, no, it really doesn't. I think it's a brilliant idea. And really brave.'

Laura smiles. 'Thank you. Actually it makes it a bit easier, that you already know about my – condition. It turns out Jim didn't tell many people. I wonder why he told you.'

'Oh, I don't know. People always seem to tell me everything. I must have a friendly face.' A smile splits her face and lights up her eyes.

Laura laughs. 'Maybe that's it.'

'Seriously though, the other day I was minding my own business queuing at the checkout in the supermarket when the woman behind me started telling me all about her divorce and why her husband was such a bastard.' She grins. 'I'd only popped in for some bread and milk and ended up counselling her for half a chuffin' hour.'

Laura smiles. She could listen to Jane's sing-song Scouse accent all day, and she can see why people might feel they could open up to her. She can see why Jim might have done too.

Jane leans forward, her elbows on her knees. 'To be honest,

though, it was a bit different with Jim.' She looks behind her as though checking no one is listening. 'Sorry, don't want the kids to hear this. Jim was helping me, with me divorce.'

'Oh?'

'Yeah. The thing is, Robbie – my ex – was a total bastard, truth be told. He treated me terribly, beat me black and blue, sometimes even in front of the kids, but he was clever. Tried to keep it private. Got the shock of his life when I left him. Just packed me stuff while he was at work, and left with the kids. Nothing he could do about it. We came down here, rented this place, far away from him, to finally get properly away. The kids miss him, but he never bothers with them. Was all "you can't take my kids away from me, I've got rights" at first but the novelty soon wore off. Besides, he's buggered off now, left the country, gone to work in Spain. Good riddance, I say. The further away, the better.' She turns to Ben. 'Sorry, Ben, I know you've heard all this before, but I just wanted to explain it to Laura.'

'No, it's fine. You carry on.' He sits back and sips his coffee thoughtfully.

But Laura is confused. 'But Jim isn't a lawyer. He works for a hotel chain. What does he know about divorce law?'

Jane shoots Ben a look and Ben shrugs. She looks back at Laura. 'It wasn't really divorce law, to be honest. He just said he might be able to help me. I – I s'pose I just assumed it had something to do with his ex-wife.'

Laura turns cold. 'His *what*?'

'His...' Jane starts, her eyes flitting back and forth in confusion.

'Jim's never been married before,' Laura says, slowly.

'Hasn't he? God, I'm so sorry, Laura.' Jane looks horrified.

'What made you think he had been?'

Jane shrugs, clearly uncomfortable. 'I must have just assumed.' She reaches out and presses her well-manicured hand against

Laura's arm. 'Honestly, please ignore me. It was probably just that Jim saw I was struggling and wanted to help me. I must have misunderstood.' She sighs heavily. 'I'm so sorry, I didn't mean to cause more problems than I solve.'

Laura shakes her head. 'It's fine. I just...' She just what? Doesn't trust her husband? Of course she does. Jim hasn't been married before, he's told her that.

So why is she feeling so shaken?

'Well, anyway,' Jane says, 'I don't suppose any of that has a thing to do with Jim's disappearance, but after I told him all the gory details of my disastrous marriage I suppose he felt more like he could talk to me about his.' She claps her hand over her mouth. 'Oh God, not that I was saying your marriage was a disaster. He never said that, I just meant—'

'It's okay. Really. I know what you meant.'

Jane shakes her head, her face red. 'I really am sorry. I'm not doing very well today, am I? I didn't mean it how it sounded at all. It's just that Jim felt he could talk to me, or maybe he felt he *should* talk to me, tell me something about himself, because I'd told him so much about me.' She drags her hand through her hair. 'Anyway, I tried to help, but I don't really know much about agoraphobia so I doubt I was much use. But he was great to me. Really great...' She tails off.

Laura feels stunned. She knew she and Jim had grown apart a bit recently, but it seems as though Jim had an entire life separate from her, where he knew all these people, played an important part in their lives, helped them out with dodgy mortgage advisors, played poker games and gave free divorce advice. Who else does he know in this street? What other secrets has he found out about the people living here? And will any of it be any use to her in finding him?

'I'm sorry, this must all be a huge shock to you,' Jane says. She shakes her head. 'I can't believe I know so much about you, but we've only just met. You're much younger than I'd expected. Well, he told me you were younger, but you look – much younger, I suppose. You know what I mean.'

'I do. He's fourteen years older than me, but he's the one who has the energy for both of us. At least, I thought he did.'

Jane nods. 'The thing is, Jim's helped me loads, so if he's gone missing and you need anything, then I'm all yours, sweetheart. I'll do anything to help you find him. He's been bloody good to me.'

'Thank you. I just – I guess I don't really know where to start.'

'You've found nothing in his things, then?'

'His things?'

Jane frowns. 'You've looked through all his things, right? His clothes, his papers, his pant drawer? Never know what you might find in a pant drawer.' She grins but then stops when she sees the look on Laura's face.

'No. I haven't done any of that. It never really occurred to me.'

'Blimey. First thing I did when I started thinking about leaving Robbie was search through all his stuff. I was positive he was having an affair. Turned out he probably wasn't, he was just a knob.'

Laughter bursts out of Laura like a bullet, unexpectedly.

'I suppose I've never really had a reason not to trust him before. But I do need to, you're right.'

'Good. So what else can we do to help?'

'Well, I was kind of wondering if there was anything he said that might give us a clue about where he's gone. I know it sounds unlikely, but you never know. Did he seem different to you, in the last few weeks?'

Jane shakes her head. 'You know what, I wouldn't have said so. But now you mention it there were a few things.'

Laura's ears prick up and her heart patters harder against her chest. 'Really? Like what?'

'Well, he stopped coming over as often. I assumed it was because he had more work on, or because we'd nearly come to the end of the things he could help me with, so I didn't give it much thought at the time – that's probably why I hadn't really twigged that I hadn't seen him for a couple of weeks. But it was a change.' She stops, thinks some more. 'There was something else too. One day he was talking about you, telling me about how hard it was to see you like this, how he'd do anything to help you get better. He talked about you quite a lot, but this time he kept saying he felt like he'd failed you, that you'd be better off without him. It was strange, but I assumed he'd just had a tough day and was feeling exhausted. I told him he was doing a brilliant job, of course I did, but it didn't make any difference. He just didn't seem to believe in himself. I even offered to come over and meet you, see if I could help, but he said no. He told me you couldn't have people in the house, that you were scared of your own shadow and it was killing him that he couldn't make you better.'

Jane pauses and takes a breath. She hopes she hasn't said too much, but it's all coming back to her now, the look on his face as he sat at her kitchen table, as though the weight of the world had crushed him. He was a 2-D version of himself that day. It had passed by the time she saw him the following week, but remembering it now she feels bad for not pushing him, for not trying to find out more. Perhaps it was a cry for help. Perhaps she could have stopped him leaving.

She clears her throat. This isn't about her, it's about Jim, and Jim is a good man. And it's also about his wife, Laura, who's made it over to her house despite being terrified of going outside her front door. She needs to do whatever she can to help her find Jim.

Laura looks like a confused child, the tea gone cold in the cup in her hand, her head down. She seems utterly lost and she watches as Ben reaches over and places his hand on her knee. 'Are you okay?'

Laura looks up. She seems surprised to realise where she is, and she nods. She looks down at the hand on her knee and moves away slightly. Ben's face flushes. Jane watches all of this with interest, and realises one thing. Ben has a crush on Laura. She stifles a smile. If the circumstances weren't so awful, she would be pleased. Ben has been through such a tough time since Helen died, and it's the first time she's seen him even so much as look at another woman. But this is neither the time nor the place.

She coughs loudly and they both look up.

'Right, so I think the next thing to do is look through Jim's things. What do you think?'

Laura nods.

'Do you want me to help? I'm quite good at it. Had plenty of practice.'

Laura shakes her head. 'No. No, I think I should do this bit on my own. But thank you, Jane. You've been very kind.'

'Oh, don't be silly. I just feel bad I can't help you any more.' She sits forward. 'The day I told you about, when Jim was feeling down. He didn't say anything about leaving, or wanting to get out. I honestly didn't feel like that was what he was getting at. It felt more that he just needed someone to talk to, someone who already knew his circumstances – your circumstances. But I will have a think, see if there's anything else I can remember, and I'll let you know as soon as I do.'

The front door slams and a few seconds later a face appears at the door.

'Hi, Mum.' A teenage girl looks round at the room, her face scrunched into a frown.

'Hi, love. This is Laura, Jim's wife. And Ben, from next door, obviously. Laura, this is my daughter, Abbie.'

'Oh, right. Hi.' Abbie gives a little wave and steps back awkwardly. 'I'm just getting something to eat. See you later.'

She leaves, and Laura stands and brushes her jeans down over her thighs.

'I'd better be going.'

Ben stands too.

'Do you want me to walk you back?'

Laura looks at him gratefully. 'Would you mind?'

'Course not.' His smile is warm.

'Thank you so much, Jane. It's been really great to meet you.' Laura holds out her hand but Jane pulls her into a hug and holds her for a brief moment. 'It's brilliant to finally meet you too, Laura. Jim's a good man. I hope we find him soon and get him home.' She looks at Ben but he refuses to meet her eye.

Then they leave, making their slow, steady way across the crescent towards Laura and Jim's house, Ben holding Laura's elbow firmly. Jane watches them until they close Laura's front door behind them, then she goes to find her daughter.

* * *

'What do you think it means, that Jane thought Jim has been married before?' Laura asks Debbie, the minute Ben has said goodbye and gone back to his own home. The thought has been playing on her mind since Jane told her about Jim helping her with her divorce, and now the question has exploded out of her like a firework, without warning.

On the other end of the phone Debbie clicks her tongue, and Laura waits. 'I don't know, Lau,' she says slowly, in that way she has of considering her words before she speaks. 'What do *you* think it means?'

Laura huffs. She loves Debbie but she can be infuriating sometimes, always trying to be diplomatic.

'I don't know, Debbie, that's why I'm asking you!' She stops, breathless for a moment. 'You think this means something, don't you?'

'I didn't say that.' Debbie pauses again. 'I just wonder – could there be something about Jim, about his past, that you don't know? That he's kept from you?'

'I know you've never really liked Jim but surely you don't really think he's got some dark, sinister past?'

'I didn't say dark or sinister, and I never said I didn't like Jim. I just wondered whether there could be something he hasn't told you, for whatever reason. It doesn't mean he has a terrible secret to hide, just that – I don't know. He was trying to protect you or something.'

'Protect me?'

'You know, the way he always does. The big, strong protector who wraps you in cotton wool as though you're made of glass.'

There's a pause as she takes in her best friend's words. 'Is it – is that really what you think of me?'

'No, Laura, it's not what I think of you. I don't think you need protecting, I never have, despite what your mum told you. I think you're strong and incredible. I think that *Jim* has always thought you needed it, and it's something we've disagreed on before. You know this.'

Debbie is right. They have disagreed on it plenty of times, but over the last few months, when Laura really felt as though she did need protecting – from attackers, from the darkness, from the outside, from her own mind – Jim really stepped up and was what she needed, and any criticism of his overprotectiveness from

Debbie either stopped or simply washed over her completely, so lost was she in her own terrified mind.

Now, Laura doesn't know what to say. Is there a chance that Jim has been through a divorce he's never told her about? But why would he have thought she couldn't handle the truth? He was forty years old when they met, it's not as though she expected him to be baggage-free. And yet he had been, relatively. There were no messy ex, no children, no awful family in the background. No nothing.

'I just don't see why he would do something like that,' Laura says now, her voice quiet.

Debbie takes a deep breath. 'I know, darling. And I love you for that. But the truth is, your husband has gone missing with no explanation whatsoever. So far there's no sign of foul play, so it looks as though he's gone by choice, and you know very little about his past.'

'I know lots about his past.'

'Only what he's told you.'

'Well, of course. That's normal, isn't it?'

'It's – unusual, Lau.' She hesitates. 'Most people learn about their partners from more than one source. From friends, family, colleagues. They build up a picture of them, what they're like when they're with other people, see how they react to situations outside the home, how they interact with strangers. That then builds up a full, rounded picture of the person they love. But with you and Jim it's – it's always been different.'

Laura doesn't speak because her heart is pounding too fast for her to catch her breath.

'You know what I mean, Laura. You and Jim. Since you met it's always been about you and him, and no one else was allowed to penetrate that tight bubble. I forced myself in, of course, but everyone else – well, everyone else was pushed further and further away until they could no longer reach you. Including your mum.'

Laura's heart flips at the thought of her mum. She wants so much to ring her and tell her what's happening, but the fact is Debbie is right. She has pushed her away so much that she doesn't feel as though she can just pick up the phone and ask her for help, even though she's certain her mum would welcome her with open arms.

'But it's not just about your friends and family,' Debbie continues. 'It's Jim's.'

'What about them?'

'Well, what do you know about them? Who do you know, who have you met in the last seven years?'

'You know perfectly well his parents are dead,' she says, her voice sharp.

'Yes, I know that's what he's told you. But even if that is true – which I'm sure it is,' she adds before Laura can object, 'then what about uncles, aunts, cousins, all the other family members people have in their lives, even if it's just in the background?'

As she waits for an answer Laura feels her body shaking. But not because she's angry. Because she's scared that Debbie's right.

She really doesn't know anything about Jim's life apart from what he's told her. She's never had any reason to question whether it's the whole truth, but now she's not so sure. After all, he's left, so it's clear she doesn't know him as well as she thought.

The room starts closing in around her, and she feels her throat tighten, her airway constricted as though something is blocking it. Her head is spinning and she feels as if she might faint... but then through the fog she can hear Debbie speaking to her, her voice urgent.

'Laura!'

She forces herself to focus on the voice on the other end of the phone, but her throat is so dry she can't get any words out. She places the receiver on the table, dashes to the sink and gulps down huge mouthfuls of water from the tap. Finally, her thirst sated, she picks the receiver back up.

'Sorry,' she rasps.

'Oh, thank God, I thought something had happened to you,' Debbie says. 'I'm so sorry, Lau, I didn't mean to upset you. I shouldn't have said that.'

'No,' she says, and swallows to clear the lump from her throat. 'You're right. You've always been right.'

'Not completely—' she begins, but Laura cuts her off.

'You are, Debs. You knew from the very beginning there was something strange about mine and Jim's relationship, but I never wanted to listen. But there it is. You were right. I don't know his friends, his family, or even anything about where he actually works. In the seven years we've been together we've only spent two Christmases together as he always seems to have to work. That's —' She stops, her voice caught again. 'That's not normal.' She chokes the last words out in a sob.

'Oh, darling, I'm so sorry. I – I wish I could be there with you. I'm worried about you.'

Laura doesn't answer for a while, letting the sobs subside into hiccups.

'I'm going to go,' Laura says, suddenly desperate to be alone with her thoughts.

'Are you sure? You don't want to talk a bit longer?' Laura knows Debbie is worried she'll drink herself into a stupor, and she can't even face lying to her about it.

'Positive,' she says. 'I'll ring you tomorrow.'

Then before Debbie can say anything else Laura cuts off the call, lays the receiver down on the table so she can't ring back, and opens a brand-new bottle of vodka.

16

THEN – MARCH 1990

I checked the answerphone for the umpteenth time, trying not to let the panic overwhelm me. No messages, no missed calls. Nothing.

I paced across the living room and peered out of the window again, down at the street below, hoping to see a shadow emerge from the darkness, a familiar figure stride towards the flat.

But seconds passed, and no one came.

Jim was late. Only a couple of hours late, but I hadn't heard a word from him since yesterday and in anticipation of his return I'd made steak for dinner, which was currently drying out in a warm oven. I felt my stomach tighten as I continued to peer along the street, my vision blurring. A sudden movement across the road made me jump and I pressed my face close to the glass, my breath clouding it so I had to rub it clear. What was that? Was that someone in the hedge by the house opposite? I squinted but couldn't make out any distinct shapes, anything that had been there now melted into the shadows. Rattled, and trying not to think about the figure I'd seen hanging around outside the flat and outside the restaurant a number of times over the last few months,

I yanked the curtains shut and flicked the side-table lamp on. I perched on the edge of the sofa and tried to steady my breath, so I could think clearly.

Jim was rarely late – he knew how much I missed him when he was away, and although he kept promising he'd look for a job that didn't take him up north at least three days a week, he was still there and didn't show any signs of changing anything. But he did at least always make sure he got home when he said he would.

Except today.

I stood suddenly, a thought occurring to me. I was sure I'd written a phone number for his office in the back page of my address book one day. I'd been insistent, promising him I wouldn't call unless it was urgent because he said it was frowned upon to receive personal calls in the office. Besides, I knew he was often out on site, visiting the company's hotels round the area, so most of the time it was pointless anyway. But two hours late felt pretty urgent, so I didn't think he'd mind.

I pulled open the drawer of my bedside table where I'd always kept my address book and stopped. It wasn't there. I moved a couple of things to see if it had slipped underneath them but there was nothing there either. Confused, I checked Jim's side. Nothing. Weird.

I headed to the kitchen and checked the drawers in there; the cupboard in the living room; the bookshelves in the spare room. But it was nowhere to be found. I knew I hadn't put it anywhere else, so where was it?

I felt bereft suddenly. That address book, with all my friends' numbers carefully scribed inside, was my lifeline. But now it was gone.

The only numbers I knew off by heart were Debbie's, and my mum's.

I carefully dialled Debbie's number, and when she answered I blurted, 'Jim's not home.'

'What do you mean not home?' She was chewing something and I heard her swallow.

'He was due home two hours ago, and he's not here and he hasn't rung and I don't know what to do.' I felt breathless.

'Hey, hey, hey, don't get upset, sweetheart.'

'Sorry.'

'It's fine. I just – I don't think two hours is anything to panic about.'

'But Jim's never late.'

'I know. But think about it. He could be caught up in a meeting, or on the train, or he might just have lost track of time. There are all kinds of explanations other than the ones I know you're thinking.'

Despite myself I smiled. Thank God for Debbie, who knew me so well. I honestly didn't know what I'd do without her.

'Listen, give it another hour or so and if he isn't back then you can come round here, okay? I would come there but James has started waking up in the night again and I'm exhausted.'

At the mention of Debbie's youngest son, who was only three, I was wracked with guilt. She had so much on her plate, working part-time at a primary school and with two young children, and here I was, bothering her with my pathetic neuroses.

'Thanks,' I said weakly.

When I hung up I sat for a minute, wondering what to do next. How had I got to the stage where I not only had no one else to turn to, but I didn't know how to get in touch with my husband or any of his friends or colleagues? How had I let myself become so cut off?

Maybe there was something I could do. Maybe Jim had an address book somewhere. Even though I hadn't seen it while

searching for mine, there must be some places still left to look. I
retraced my steps and rummaged carefully through the cupboards
and drawers again, looking for any phone numbers on scraps of
paper that might be useful.

Twenty minutes later and I was back to square one, with no
address book, and no hope. I headed to the fridge and poured
myself a large glass of vodka and knocked it back. As it hit my
bloodstream I felt my heart rate slowing down and my head begin
to fizz. I closed my eyes, and tried to order my thoughts.

I was yanked back to reality by the phone ringing. Heart
hammering, I ran across the room and almost ripped the receiver
off the wall.

'Jim?'

Silence. A hum. Gentle breathing. Then before I could say
anything, the dial tone.

'Fuck you!' I screamed, throwing the phone against the wall. It
smashed in two and skittered across the kitchen floor. I poured
another vodka and drank it down, then stood, hands on the worktop, and tried to breathe.

I was trapped. There was no way I was going to bother Debbie
tonight. I was being totally selfish even thinking about it. Instead, I
picked up the vodka bottle, stomped into our bedroom, and drank
until I passed out, with a vague hope that, when I woke up, Jim
would be home.

* * *

He wasn't home. My eyes were slits against the harsh sunlight
pouring through the open curtains, and my mouth felt dry. I sat up
and the world spun before righting itself, and I swallowed down a
lump in my throat.

Beside me the emptiness of Jim's side of the bed taunted me, and a wave of terror washed over me, mixing with my hangover and making my stomach roll over. Why had I drunk so much when I needed a clear head to deal with Jim's disappearance?

I padded through to the kitchen and saw the fragments of the phone scattered across the floor. Stepping over them, I filled the kettle and made a strong coffee, hoping to tamp down the nausea. I popped some bread in the toaster and forced it down with a thin scraping of butter. Afterwards, I felt less sick, but the terror was still there.

Despite the broken telephone handset I noticed there was a light flashing on the receiver, and I leapt up and almost ran through to the living room where the unbroken phone was. I snatched up the handset and dialled in to listen to my messages.

Hi lovely, it's Debbie. I thought you were coming over. I hope you're okay. Ring me.

My heart sank. Not Jim.

Hand shaking, I hung up and walked over to the window and pulled the curtains open. The street outside looked the same as ever, and I wondered how everything could carry on as normal when everything in my world had tipped on its head.

It was almost forty-eight hours later when Jim finally walked through the door, and by then I'd convinced myself he was dead. I'd called in sick to work and refused to leave the house just in case Jim was trying to ring me, cradling the only phone that still worked and even taking the handset into the bathroom with me when I went to the loo. I'd floated round our flat like a ghost, only coming to life when the phone rang or I heard footsteps in the communal hallway outside. I barely ate, I drank endless coffee interspersed with vodka and wine so that I was in a constant state of vague drunkenness.

And then, at the end of day two, just as I was about to give in and call the police, I heard Jim's key in the lock and he burst through the door. I was standing in the doorway of our bedroom before he'd even had a chance to call my name, and I threw myself into his arms, any anger I'd felt extinguished by the instant relief that he was home, he was here, and he was safe.

The feeling of his strong arms around me felt so good I didn't want to pull away, but eventually I had to, and I looked up at his face and realised I'd soaked his shirt with my tears.

'I'm so, so sorry, darling,' he said, his voice low.

'I thought you were dead.'

He kissed the top of my head. 'I'm not dead. I'm just an idiot.'

I pressed my cheek into his chest and felt his warmth radiate into me. My body felt exhausted and I hadn't realised how much tension I'd been holding.

'Where have you been?' I mumbled.

He pulled away and grabbed my hand. 'Let's go and sit down and I'll explain.'

I let myself be led into the living room, where we both sank onto the sofa. Jim pulled me into his side and spoke. 'Firstly, I'm so sorry I didn't ring you. You must have been going out of your mind.'

I nodded but didn't speak.

'I got called away to an emergency in one of our hotels in the Middle East, and I didn't have a chance to ring you before I left – I asked my colleague to let you know what had happened and that I'd be a couple of days, but clearly he didn't do it.'

I stared at him. He looked tired and stressed, the lines radiating out from his eyes and around his mouth deeper than usual.

'You've been to the Middle *East*?' I said, my mind working over-time to process this revelation. He glanced down at me, an apolo-getic smile on his face.

'I know, mad, isn't it?'

'But—' I stopped, unsure. 'You told me you hate flying.' It was the reason we'd never been on a holiday abroad, sticking instead to short breaks in the UK.

'I do,' he said, shaking his head. 'But I work in the hotel busi-ness, Lola, and we have hotels all over the world. I only fly when I absolutely have to, and even then I have to be heavily sedated.' He frowned. 'Don't you believe me?'

'Of course I do,' I said.

'Good.' He reached for my hands. 'I truly am sorry though. I promise not to disappear like that ever again. Forgive me?'

'I forgive you.'

He looked round the room then, seemingly taking in his surroundings for the first time. His eyes landed on the half-empty bottle of vodka on the coffee table.

'Oh, Lola, have you been drinking again?'

I felt myself stiffen. 'Don't.'

He pressed his hand against my thigh and I stared at the carpet. 'I just worry about you, here all by yourself, drinking too much.'

I snapped my head round to look at him. 'You disappeared, Jim,' I said.

He nodded. 'I know.' He tucked a strand of hair behind my ear. 'I just wish you wouldn't drink so much.' He smiled and reached out for the bottle. 'Perhaps I should get rid of this.' He began to stand.

'No!' I shouted, surprising even myself. Jim stood in front of me, vodka bottle in his hand. 'Don't. I won't drink it,' I said. 'Not now you're home.'

He studied me for a moment. 'Okay,' he relented. 'But I am hiding it from you from now on.'

I felt my heart sink. If only he knew how much I relied on it to cope. But I didn't dare let him know what a crutch it had become on the days when I was alone.

As he walked towards the kitchen, taking my lifeline with him, it occurred to me that he hadn't really explained why he hadn't called me himself to let me know what had happened. Something about his story felt off, and I couldn't shake the feeling that there was something he wasn't telling me.

17

NOW – 7 OCTOBER 1992

The afternoon stretches in front of Laura like a cat sleeping in the sun. Before Jim went missing she filled her days with a monotonous routine of daytime television, housework, drinking and sleeping: anything to make the time pass until Jim returned. She was always in a state of high alert, waiting for something to set her heart racing, and the only way she could calm that anxiety was with alcohol.

Now, she could kill for a glass of vodka, but she's determined to hold off a bit longer, to wait until it's at least vaguely evening. Somehow, since she's started getting herself out of the house, opening up her world again, however little the steps, her normal routine just doesn't seem enough.

Besides, she has so much to think about, she needs to keep a clear head. She pulls out the street map Debbie drew a couple of weeks ago, and studies the list she's scribbled down the side. These are the clues she's gathered so far, and the little snippets she's picked up keep bouncing round her head like balls in a pinball machine as she struggles to make connections between them. What did Jim mean when he told Jane that Laura would be better off without him? And why did Jane think Jim had been married before? *Was* he simply being kind by helping her with her divorce papers, or is there something he hasn't told Laura, as Debbie believes? What about the keyring with the mystery children on it?

She rubs her head. The tension is building and she feels as though her skull might just crack open if she doesn't get some answers soon.

She stands suddenly. She needs something to keep her busy, and she knows just the thing. She's going to take Jane's advice and search through Jim's stuff. She's never felt the need before, and would have felt guilty doing it, but it's becoming more and more obvious that Jim has been keeping things from her, and if she wants to stand any chance of seeing him ever again she really doesn't have any choice.

She heads up the stairs and into their bedroom and pulls open the wardrobe door. An overwhelming scent of Jim hits her and she feels her legs buckle beneath her. She wasn't prepared for that and she crouches for a moment, trying to steady herself. She inhales deeply and returns to the wardrobe. Where to start?

She pulls a jacket out and sticks her hands into the pockets. A memory of doing this before, when she thought she'd seen Jim slipping something into his pocket one evening, slides into her mind. She hasn't thought about that day for ages, and feels sad at her old self, the more confident, self-assured Laura who could get on with life, could leave the house, go to work. Was she really as confident as she remembers, or has time simply blunted the memory of how things were back then?

The pocket is empty, so she moves on to the next jacket, and the next, but there's nothing. Not an old tissue, or a receipt from a train journey. Damn Jim and his obsessive tidiness. Her pockets would be full of old boiled sweets covered with fluff, ancient cinema tickets, odd slips of paper, half-used lip balms. Not that they would be useful clues, but at least it would give some hint of the person she was.

She spends the next hour pulling out jackets, trousers, even rummaging through Jim's sock drawer to see if there might be any clue whatsoever. She doesn't know what she's expecting to find – it's not as though something is going to jump out at her and hit her between the eyes with a huge sign on it marked 'clue' – but she's both hoping she will find something, and praying she won't.

She pulls jumpers, T-shirts, socks and pants from drawers, runs her hand round the back of cupboards; she yanks boxes from under the bed and tips the contents onto the floor, sorting through piles of blankets, well-thumbed cookery books, an old fancy-dress costume, a spare set of chef's whites, yellowed now and covered in dust – all her old stuff, from her old life, hidden away from sight.

She haphazardly shoves it all back under the bed and stands, brushing dust from her trousers, and casts her gaze around the room. Where should she look next? Where is Jim most likely to have left something useful, something that might lead her to him?

She heads out of the bedroom and turns towards the front of the house, and the smallest of the three bedrooms that Jim quickly commandeered for his own when they moved in. She's hardly been in here, never really felt the need, but it strikes her now that this would have been the most obvious place to start, and that by not doing so she has been trying to pretend that she isn't really snooping at all.

All pretence now dropped, she pushes open the bedroom door and steps inside. Unlike the rooms she uses, this one is as neat as a pin, not a thing out of place. Even the pen pot and the telephone on the desk in the corner are lined up perfectly, although covered in a thin, two-week-old layer of dust. It's almost as though this room is never actually used, but that someone just comes in and cleans it every now and then, like a shrine. She stands in the middle of the carpet and looks round, wondering where to start.

There's a small desk in the corner, and a filing cabinet behind it. She heads towards it and tests one of the drawers. It's locked. She frowns. Why would Jim feel the need to lock things away in his own home? She searches the desk to see if she can find a key, pulling open the drawers and peering into pen pots, but there's nothing. There's barely anything at all in these drawers bar a calculator, a small, blank notebook, and a new packet of pens. She closes them again and spins round, trying to think where he might keep a key. Perhaps he keeps it on his keyring. In fact, the more she thinks about it, the more likely that seems. If he's going to lock a cabinet, he must have something to hide, and he knows she's unlikely to notice an extra key on his keyring.

Just in case, she searches the bookshelves, looking in between books, running her fingers along the top and bottom of them just to make sure there's nothing hidden anywhere. She checks behind the curtains, along the skirting board and under the chair. Finally, satisfied there's no filing-cabinet key hidden in here, she slumps onto the leather-backed chair and closes her eyes, trying to decide what to do next. Even though she began this search half-heartedly, feeling guilty that she was even contemplating snooping on her husband, now she's found the locked filing cabinet she feels determined to get into it, even if only to prove that there's nothing significant to find.

That's when it hits her – Jim's things reveal absolutely nothing about him whatsoever. His suits hanging in the wardrobe, his neat sock drawer, his half-empty drawers, his tidy lines of books on the shelves. Nothing in this room or anywhere else in the house would give you a clue about Jim's personality – about his love of black and white horror films, or his short-lived career as a rower, or his love of good red wine and eating out in fancy restaurants. It's as though it's her home that Jim simply stays in from time to time, leaving a few essential items while the rest of his life is elsewhere. She can't believe she's never noticed it before. What does it mean? Is it just the way he is – neat, precise, minimalist – or is there something more to it?

Suddenly galvanised into action, she hurries downstairs and finds a toolbox balanced on a high shelf in the garage. She takes it back upstairs, takes out a screwdriver and a hammer and begins to tap around the filing-cabinet lock. Nothing happens, so she tries sticking a small screwdriver into the lock, but it stops halfway. Rummaging through the toolbox, she tries to think what else might work, but the truth is what does she know about picking locks? Maybe she should speak to Debbie, see if she has any bright ideas.

She sits at Jim's desk and picks up the phone and dials Debbie's number. As it rings she studies the framed photo on the desk. It's of her and Jim from a few years ago, before the attack. She looks happy, relaxed, although she can remember that day, when they went to the Isle of Wight for a long weekend, one of the only holidays they've ever had together, and she remembers feeling on edge all weekend because Jim seemed distant, distracted, and disappeared several times to make calls to the office from the phone box round the corner.

There's no answer, and Laura hangs up despondently. Who else can she ask for help with this? Arthur next door might know how to break a lock, but she doesn't feel comfortable asking him. She's fairly certain Jane would be willing to help, given it was her idea, but she doesn't know her well enough yet to ask. Which leaves only one other person who might help her. She runs downstairs to grab the piece of paper with everyone's details on, and rings the number printed neatly in the corner. Her heart hammers as it rings; she's half-hoping there won't be any answer...

'Hello?' Ben is out of breath and she imagines him just back from a run, his skin glistening.

'It's Laura.'

'Laura, hi. Everything okay?'

'Yes, yes. Sorry, are you in the middle of something?'

'No, it's fine. Has something happened?'

'Not really. I just wondered if you have any idea how to pick a lock.'

'Oh, that's not what I expected you to say.' She can hear his smile down the line.

'Well, no. I'm doing what Jane suggested and I've found a locked drawer in Jim's study that I want to open.'

'I see.'

'Can you help?' She knows she sounds impatient.

'Well, I'm not famous for breaking and entering, but I can give it a go.'

'Thank you.'

'I'll just have a quick shower and I'll be over.'

Ben arrives half an hour later, his hair damp and wearing a dark blue shirt that makes his eyes shine. Laura tries not to notice how handsome he looks as he steps inside and removes his shoes. Instead she takes another sip of her second glass of wine and smiles at him.

'Would you like a glass of wine before we start?'

'Please.'

Ben follows her through to the kitchen, which Laura has made a half-hearted attempt to clean since he was last there. She's been sitting here since she rang Ben, going over her worries in her mind. She thinks about the things that have begun to occur to her as strange: the fact Jim never wanted to go on holiday for longer than a few days; that she never knew where he actually worked, or met any of his colleagues; and now the fact that he has a locked filing cabinet in the house. Is it all pointing towards a dark hidden secret, or is she just a victim of an overactive imagination?

Laura hands Ben a glass of wine. Their fingers brush and he snatches his hand away quickly.

'Shall we go straight up?'

'Sure.'

They walk towards the stairs and up to the study. At the top she pushes the door open and gestures vaguely in the direction of the desk.

'So you never come in here?' Ben says, hovering in the doorway.

'Not really. I mean, there was never any need.' She feels foolish even admitting it out loud. After all, her world has been confined to these four walls since they moved here, how could she have willingly made it even smaller?

Ben walks across the room and stands in front of the desk. 'You've checked all these drawers?'

'Yes. They're almost empty.'

Ben nods, then sticks his hand in his pocket and pulls something out. 'These could be our secret weapons,' he says triumphantly, and Laura watches as Ben takes a paper clip and straightens out one end of it, leaving the other end curved round.

'What are you going to do with that?'

'I'm not convinced it's going to work, but someone once told me that this is an easy way to pick a lock,' he says, gripping it between his thumb and finger. 'Apparently you can find the mechanism if you wiggle it around a bit.' He frowns, and turns towards the cabinet. Laura moves to stand next to him, holding her breath.

'Right, here goes.' Ben sticks the thin piece of metal into the lock and moves it around, back and forth. Laura holds her breath as Ben continues to move the paper clip gently backwards and forwards, listening carefully. His tongues sticks out of the side of his mouth and his brow is deeply furrowed.

'If I can just... make... it... move... ' he says, pressing his ear against the cool metal.

'Shall I have a go?' Laura says.

'Just a sec.' He gives it one final twist and there's a gentle 'click', the lock turns anticlockwise and the drawer unlocks. Ben widens his eyes disbelief. 'No way,' he whispers. 'I didn't actually expect that to *work*.'

'Well done,' Laura says. Her palms are clammy.

Slowly, Ben eases the drawer open and they peer inside. Laura isn't sure what she was expecting to see, but she's surprised and a little let down by how little it contains after all that effort. She reaches inside and pulls out a bundle of paper folders from the bottom and heads towards the desk and sits down. Ben stands behind her, watching over her shoulder. She can hear him breathing gently.

'Here goes nothing,' she says, and feels the press of Ben's hand on her shoulder as she opens the first folder. She's not sure how she feels about another man touching her, even innocently, and she tries not to flinch.

She pulls the papers out and lays them across the desk. As she skims her eyes across the first few sheafs she feels disappointment spread through her.

'Bills,' she says, flicking through the rest of the bundle of gas, electricity and phone bills.

'Try the next one,' Ben says, flicking the flap open. Laura pulls those papers out to find more of the same.

'Why the hell were these locked away?' she says.

'Who knows? Maybe Jim didn't even realise he'd locked it?'

'Maybe.'

'I know it's not what you hoped for, but it's probably a good thing,' Ben says as Laura opens the next folder down and pulls out yet more papers. 'I mean, you didn't *really* want to find out something terrible about your husband, did you?'

'No...' Laura says. 'But I had hoped to find something that might help me find him.'

All she needs is another clue, something to point her in the right direction, and she pinned all her hopes on this drawer.

She's about to shove the papers back inside the folder and back into the drawer when something catches her eye – there's a single piece of paper in the bottom of the drawer. She bends down and picks it up.

'What's this?' She turns it over. It's a generic card with a picture of a puppy and *Happy 30th Birthday* embossed in gold scroll. Laura opens it, reads the few words scrawled inside, and almost drops the card on the floor. She feels breathless, and the walls close in around her...

'Laura, what is it? What does it say?' Ben gently prises the card from Laura's hands and reads the words too.

'Oh.'

Laura can't speak. The words keep scrolling in front of her vision as if taunting her.

Dear Jim.
Happy 30th Birthday son.
Always thinking of you,
Dad x

'It's from his dad,' Laura says, her voice barely more than a whisper. 'But his dad is dead.' She feels her body start to shake. Ben longs to comfort her but is unsure how welcome a hug would be from him right now, so holds back.

'But this is from when he was younger,' he says. 'It's not recent.'

Laura shakes her head. 'He said—' She stops, clears her throat. 'His parents died when he was twelve. He was brought up by his aunt, who he doesn't speak to any more.' Even as the words come out of her mouth she realises how ridiculous it is that she doesn't know any more details than that. Seven years she and Jim have been together, and she has barely asked him a single question about himself.

Or is it more that he deflected any questions she did ask him, until she stopped asking him anything?

Her head feels muddled, as though all the things she thought she knew were turning to liquid and dripping through her fingers. She can't pin anything down in her mind. Is that what he told her, that his parents died when he was twelve? Or has she got confused? Her mind has been so entirely focused on herself and her own problems that she hasn't paid any attention to Jim.

And yet this is one thing she was fairly sure of. Jim's parents died when he was twelve. He was brought up by his aunt, whose name she doesn't think she's ever known, although the name Bess is hovering at the edges of her mind. Why would she think all this if it wasn't true? And if it is true, how can his dad have sent him a card for his thirtieth birthday – and what was it doing locked away in this drawer? She can only assume Jim had no idea it was here.

'I don't know what to do,' she whispers, her voice cracking. Without hesitation this time, Ben's arms are around her and she's sobbing into the shoulder of this man she's only just met, and feeling comforted and devastated all at the same time.

18

THEN – SEPTEMBER 1990

I gawped at the one-storey black and white building as our car came to a stop in front of it, and tried to get my brain to work out what was happening.

'Well?' Jim said, beside me.

Unclipping my seat belt, I climbed out of the passenger seat and walked closer to read the sign hanging above the door. 'Gretna Green. Famous Blacksmiths Shop.'

'Oh!' I gasped, turning to face Jim, who was now out of the car too and standing just behind me. 'I...'

He stepped towards me and took my hand, then lowered himself down onto his knee. The world seemed to slow as he dug around in his pocket with his other hand, and pulled out a small, bottle-green box and flicked it open with his thumb. There, nestled among the dark-green satin, was a sparkling sapphire ring.

'Laura Coleman, I've loved you since the very first day I met you. You mean everything to me, and I want to prove it to you. Will you marry me?'

My head spun as I tried to take in the fact that any doubts I'd ever had about Jim loving me enough were so obviously a figment of my imagination. Because here he was, asking me to marry him. I knew without a second's doubt what I was going to say.

'Yes!'

'Oh, thank goodness for that,' Jim said, slipping the ring onto my finger and standing up to wrap me in a hug. 'I don't think my knees could have coped with being down there for much longer.'

I grinned and pulled away from him, planting a soft kiss on his lips. 'You silly thing. You didn't really think I might say no, did you?'

'Well, of course not, who could resist this?' he said, holding his arms out and giving me a goofy grin.

'You idiot,' I said, slapping his arm. 'What happens now? Do we just walk in and get married?'

He shook his head. 'I applied for our licence last week, and we're booked in for three o'clock this afternoon.'

'You were confident,' I said.

He shrugged, sheepish. 'Just hedging my bets.' He turned and walked back to the car. 'Come on, let's go to the hotel and get changed.'

I followed him and as we drove I sat and studied my ring, turning it one way and then the other and marvelling at the sparkle that shone from it.

'I can't believe you organised all of this without me knowing anything about it,' I said.

'Oh, you'd be surprised at how sneaky I can be sometimes,' he said.

I shot him a glance. 'Not too sneaky, I hope.'

He flicked his eyes away from the road to meet mine briefly. 'Of course not.'

'But seriously. What made you decide to do it?'

Beside me, Jim shrugged, keeping his eyes on the road. 'I knew it was important to you and I didn't want to lose you.'

I shipped my head round to look at him again. 'You thought you'd lose me?'

'Yes.'

'What made you think that?'

'You more or less said so.'

'What?' What on earth was he talking about? I watched as several different emotions flickered across his face before he answered.

'You said you thought being married would feel really different to just being together.'

I frowned, confused. 'Did I? When?'

'Are you serious? You said it when we watched that film a while back, *Steel Magnolias*, and they were getting married.'

I didn't reply. I remembered the film but I didn't remember saying that. But I also didn't want to cause a row, not today of all days. This was meant to be the happiest day of my life, and I didn't want to spoil it after Jim had gone to so much effort. So I just reached for his hand and squeezed it, and held it until we arrived at our hotel.

As we let ourselves into our room I felt momentarily disappointed at how ordinary it looked, and chastised myself immediately for being such a spoilt brat. It might not be a fancy honeymoon suite, but that wasn't what getting married to the person you loved was all about. Still, I thought, as we carried our bags over the threshold, a girl only gets married once.

I didn't have long to dwell, because Jim was like an excited puppy beside me, bouncing around from one thing to the next, barely able to settle.

'What on earth is wrong with you?' I said, grinning at him indulgently as he fiddled with the kettle, opened a packet of shortbread, picked up one of the pillows from the bed. He threw the pillow down, picked up his small holdall, and unzipped it.

'I've got a surprise for you,' he said, rummaging inside his bag.

'Another one?' I wasn't sure I could take any more surprises today.

'This is part of the same one really.' He pulled something wrapped in plastic out of his bag and held it in the air triumphantly. 'Ta-da! Your wedding dress!'

'Oh!' I stepped forward to look at it more closely. 'It's…'

'You don't like it.' He sounded like a heartbroken little boy.

'No, I do, it's lovely. It's just – I hadn't expected it.' I took the dress from him and held it up in front of me and turned to face the mirror. It was pale blue, floor-length with short puffed sleeves. It was so far away from what I would ever have chosen I wanted to cry, but I didn't want to upset Jim so I plastered a smile on my face. 'Thank you, Jim, it's beautiful,' I said.

He wrapped his arms around me from behind and looked over my shoulder at us both in the mirror. 'Do you really like it? I wanted you to have something special to wear.'

I turned my head and kissed him. 'I do, thank you. I love you.'

'I love you too, wife-to-be.'

19

NOW – 8 OCTOBER 1992

Number seven Willow Crescent
Simon and Sonja Harrison and baby Amelie

'Come on, chop-chop.' Laura groans as she squints through half-closed eyes to find Debbie perched on the edge of her bed.

'What are you doing here?' she mumbles, her mouth dry.

'Ben let me in.'

Laura rubs her eyes to try and clear her mind. What on earth is Debbie talking about? Why is Ben here?

Slowly, her mind fog clears and fragments of the previous evening float into her mind. The birthday card she'd found locked away in Jim's office... crying on Ben's shoulder... drinking too much wine... and what had happened after that? Had Ben *stayed*?

'Ben?' she says, the only word she can manage.

'When you rang me last night you were in such a state I asked him to stay with you to make sure you were okay. He slept on the sofa.'

'Oh God...' Laura groans, shame flooding her body.

'It's fine. It was just a precaution. He didn't seem to mind.'

'Where is he now?'

'Downstairs, making coffee.'

'Right.' She can't think about the fool she must have made of herself in front of this man she's only known for five minutes.

'Anyway, you need to get going,' Debbie says. 'We've got things to do, people to see. You can't just sit festering in your pit all day.'

Laura groans. She feels as though she's only had about five minutes' sleep. She climbs out of bed and heads to the bathroom. 'I'll just have a shower, then I'll be there.'

As she lets the water pummel her, she thinks about how far she's come, as well as everything they've discovered over the last few days. She's decided not to jump to conclusions about what she found in Jim's filing cabinet. She's watched enough episodes of *Columbo* to know that, just because something looks a certain way, it doesn't necessarily mean it's not a red herring. Chances are there's a perfectly reasonable explanation for the card – if it was anything to worry about why on earth would he have risked keeping it here? What that explanation might be, however, she has no idea.

Stepping out of the shower, she hurriedly gets dressed and heads down to the kitchen where Debbie and Ben are sitting at the kitchen table, studying something. They both look up as Laura enters.

'Feeling better?'

'Yes, thanks,' Laura replies sheepishly. She's ashamed of herself, and vows to try and cut back on how much she's using alcohol as a crutch. 'What are you doing?'

'Just looking at what we've got so far.'

Laura leans closer to look over Debbie's shoulder and sees the map of the cul-de-sac with the list of clues scribbled down the side. Underneath it Debbie has added.

Jim's dad not dead?

Seeing it written down makes Laura shiver despite her promise to herself.

'I've made some toast,' Ben says, pushing a plate towards her, and she's overwhelmed with gratitude for these two people. One, her best friend of twenty years, the other a man she's only known for a few days but who is already starting to feel important to her.

'Thank you, you two,' she says. 'I'm so embarrassed about last night, but I honestly don't know what I'd do without you.'

She picks up a slice of toast. Food is the last thing she fancies, but she knows she has to eat. Even she can see how thin she's got, how deep the hollows in her cheeks have become, how loose her clothes are.

'So, are you ready for this morning?' Debbie says. They've planned to go and speak to Simon and Sonja, who live at number seven.

Laura swallows and shrugs. 'Not really.'

Debbie reaches for her hands and Laura welcomes the comfort she gets from her friend's touch. 'You'll be fine, Lau. You're doing brilliantly. I'm so proud of you.'

Tears prick Laura's eyes. How can Debbie be proud of her, when she isn't even proud of herself? 'Thank you.'

Debbie pushes the sheet of paper closer. 'So, this is what we know about the people at number seven so far,' Debbie says. Laura peers at the scrawled notes.

Simon and Sonja. Young couple, little girl. She works, he's at home. Plays poker?

'This doesn't tell us much,' Debbie says. 'Is this all you know?'

'I think so. I've never actually met them.'

'How about you, Ben? Do you know Simon and Sonja well?'

Ben swallows the piece of toast he's chewing and shakes his head. 'Not really. I've known Simon for years but we mainly see each other at poker nights or for the occasional beer at the pub. And since baby Amelie was born he's hardly been out at all so...' He tails off apologetically. 'Sorry, I know that's not much help.'

'It's fine.' Debbie refolds the map and holds her arm out for Laura to take. 'We might as well get going. Ready?'

Laura nods and stands, clutching Debbie's hand. 'Ish.'

'That'll do me.'

'I'm sorry, guys, I've got a meeting in an hour, do you mind if I...?' Ben indicates the door.

'God, course not. I—' Laura stops, embarrassed. 'I'm so sorry about last night. I – I really appreciate you staying.'

'It's fine, really,' Ben says, his face flushing. 'Good luck.'

Ben scurries out and seconds later they hear the door slam, then Debbie takes Laura's elbow and they head in the same direction. Even though she's done it several times now, Laura's heart rate still accelerates with every step closer they get towards the outside world. She inhales slowly, drawing air deep into her lungs. She'll be fine, there's nothing to be scared of; she's already proven that. Perhaps if she tells herself that enough times she'll eventually believe it. She shrugs her coat on and squeezes Debbie's hand.

The door swings open, and a cold wind blows squally rain under the porch and through the front door, soaking the carpet. They step outside, Laura's grip on Debbie tightening. She pulls her hood up and takes in the garden, the grass flattened by rain, the leaves on the ground heavy with water. The sky is a furious grey, and the wind blows in all directions, taking the raindrops with it, through the bare branches of the trees that have finally given up the last of their leaves to the late-autumn weather.

'God, it's hideous. Shall we do this quickly, like ripping off a plaster?'

Laura gives a small nod, then looks out across the street past Jane's house, to Simon and Sonja's. The door is closed but there's a car on the driveway and a light shines in the window. It looks a long way off, but she's done it before, she can do it again.

'Right, let's go.'

They hurry to the end of the path, heads down, through the gate and onto the pavement. They step onto the road, soaked leaves half blocking the drain. Laura lifts her gaze from the ground and her head spins, the grey sky seeming to stretch on forever. A twig snaps beneath her foot and she jumps, looking quickly behind her. No one. Nothing. It's just her and Debbie, there's no one following them. They're fine.

They keep moving forward one step at a time, and Laura keeps her eyes trained ahead, focusing on the solidity of the bricks, the wooden door, the sturdy maple tree in the garden. The world swims in front of her eyes and she struggles to hold her gaze steady. The walls of the house bulge, the tree tips, the letterbox on the door stretches into an ugly mouth, a mirthless laugh. She stops suddenly and drops to a crouch, cradling her head between her hands. She feels Debbie's hand on her back as water drips down her hair and into her eyes. 'Come on, Laura, you can do this. We're nearly there.'

Laura sucks air in through her nose and out through her mouth, in through her nose, out through her mouth, over and over until her head stops spinning and she thinks she'll be okay to look up again. When she does manage to lift her head, she can see Debbie's face is etched with concern.

'What happened?'

'I don't know. I panicked.' She stands carefully, holding Debbie's hand again. Everything seems to have returned to normal. Debbie was right, she *can* do this. 'I'm okay. Let's go.'

Even though only a few moments have passed by the time they arrive at the Harrisons' house, to Laura it feels like hours since she left the safety of her front door. But she's done it, and she feels ridiculously pleased with herself.

Debbie's hand hovers at the door. 'Ready?'

Laura nods weakly.

A sharp rap on the door, and a few seconds later it swings open and a tall woman stands there, a harassed look on her face. A child screams in the background.

'Hello?' She looks from one to the other with a frown.

Debbie sticks her hand out and smiles and, yet again, Laura is grateful she has someone else to take charge. 'I'm really sorry to bother you but we wondered if you could help us.'

The woman gives a tight smile, ignoring Debbie's outstretched hand, and waits for them to continue.

'I'm Debbie, and this is Laura. She's Jim's wife. From across the road?' Debbie waves in the general direction of the street and Laura watches as the woman's face softens and a small smile replaces the previously stern look.

'Ahh, Laura, I'm Sonja. I've been expecting you to come round.' Her voice has a slight burr, more than a hint of a Scandinavian accent.

'You have?'

She nods. 'Yes, Carol told me about Jim and said you'd prob- ably come and speak to us.' She stops, a stricken look on her face. 'Oh my, she told me you don't like being outside too, and it's pouring with rain. Please, come in, come in.' She steps back to let them in. The baby is still screaming in the background.

'Sorry about Amelie. She's got an ear infection and it seems to have turned her into the crossest child in the world, which is why I haven't left for work yet. I feel bad, leaving her, you know?'

Laura nodded. 'Do you need to go and see to her?'

'No, no, Simon's with her. I expect he'll be down in a minute.' She leads them into the kitchen where the rain hammers down on the flat roof of the extension and drowns out some of the sound of crying.

'Please, sit.'

They sit obediently on the stools indicated. As welcoming as she is, there is something formidable about this woman that makes you do as you're told.

'Let me make some coffee.' They don't argue and, besides, it will probably do Laura good to have another coffee to clear her head. The vodka followed by the panic attack has left her feeling woozy and light-headed.

'So, Carol tells me Jim's disappeared?'

Laura nods.

'Three weeks ago, huh?'

Laura nods again.

'Wow.' Sonja pours strong coffee into mugs and passes them round, then leans forward with her elbows on the counter, facing them. Her face is a picture of concentration.

'That's very strange.'

Laura feels a flutter of something, maybe excitement, in her stomach. She waits, hardly daring to breathe while Sonja clicks her tongue over her teeth. Finally she speaks again.

'Yes. It's strange because I thought I saw him the other day.'

Laura snaps her head up. 'What? When?' She grips her hands tightly round her coffee cup to anchor herself.

'I was in London, in Hyde Park, one day last week. Wednesday it might have been. Yes, I think it was. I was cutting through the park to go to a meeting, needed some fresh air. It was a bit, how do you say – drizzly – and I had my hood up so my hair didn't go frizzy.'

Come on, come on! Laura thinks. *I don't care about your hair, tell me about Jim!*

'Anyway, I was walking past the Serpentine café and there was a man there, sitting at one of the tables with a drink. He was throwing scraps of sandwich to a duck.'

She pauses and it's all Laura can do not to scream at her to carry on.

'What happened then? Did you speak to him?'

'Yes. I realised it was Jim so I called out to say hello. But when he saw me he just stood up and walked away. I assumed I must have got it wrong at the time, but of course I didn't know he was missing then, so it didn't seem too strange.'

A silence hangs in the air as her words settle.

Could it really have been Jim that Sonja saw – and if it was, what would that mean?

'But you think now that it definitely was Jim?' Debbie asks the question that Laura dare not.

Sonja considers it for a moment, then gives a small nod. 'Perhaps. Although I could also have been mistaken. I was in a hurry, so I only saw him very briefly.'

Laura feels the hope draining out of her again. 'So it was just the once you saw him, was it?' she asks.

'Yes. I haven't seen him again, although I haven't been that way since that day.' She looks at Laura. 'I am sorry, Laura. If I had known he was missing I would have come over to tell you about it sooner.'

Laura's distress must show on her face because Sonja moves towards her and presses her palm on her arm. 'I don't mean to get your hopes up, I just thought it might help. But I think I might be wrong, no?'

Laura shakes her head. 'No. No, I'm really grateful you told me.' Her voice quivers. She looks at Debbie and the confused look on her face reflects her own.

They all turn at the sound of the door opening.

'Oh. Hello.' Simon looks awkward at the sight of so many people in his kitchen. He has a cigarette packet in his hand and a frown scratched into his forehead.

'Simon, this is Jim's wife, Laura, and her friend, Debbie.'

'Oh, hello. I'm so sorry to hear about Jim.' He looks from one woman to the other and then back again. 'He's not – nothing's happened, has it?'

'No. I was just telling Laura and Debbie about when I thought I saw Jim last week.'

Simon looks flustered. 'I'm not sure that's very helpful, Sonja. You said yourself you didn't know if it was definitely him, and—' He pauses. 'It might be false hope, is all I'm saying.'

'Better than no hope, no?'

'Not necessarily.'

Silence hangs in the air for a moment and Laura and Debbie shuffle uncomfortably. Then Simon turns to Laura with his hand stuck out.

'Anyway, it's lovely to meet you.'

'You too,' she says, shaking his hand warmly.

'I'm sorry we haven't been over to see you about all this. We only found out about it a few nights ago when Carol came over.' He smiles. 'She likes to keep us all informed of what's going on round here.' He clears his throat. 'She also told us about your – you know. Agoraphobia. I had no idea. Jim never mentioned it. He didn't really talk about you at all, he always seemed to change the subject if I ever asked.' He shrugs. 'Sorry, that sounds terrible. I just mean he didn't like to talk about you. I guess now I know why.'

'It's okay. It seems he didn't tell most people about me. I'm beginning to wonder what on earth people must have thought was wrong with me.'

Simon doesn't react. 'So how did you get over here today? You know, if you can't leave the house?'

'Simon!'

'What? It's a perfectly reasonable question.'

'It's fine. I – well, since Jim left I've been trying to get out of the house to go and speak to people on the street who knew him. I suppose I hoped I might come across some clue as to what's happened to him. I feel like Hansel and Gretel chasing bread-crumbs though, to be honest.'

Simon nods thoughtfully. 'It's a good idea.' He rubs his chin. 'I wish I could help, but ever since Carol came over I've been trying to work out if there was anything he might have said that might be helpful. But there's nothing. I saw him for a poker game a while back, with Ben and a couple of friends from the pub, and he seemed normal. You know. Chatting, drinking beer, having a laugh.'

'Come off it, you're hardly going to notice if he was feeling a bit sad, are you?' Sonja cuts across him. 'You lot just go out and drink and smoke too much and never actually ask anyone anything of any importance.' She rolls her eyes. 'You're such *men*.'

Simon holds his hands out. 'She has a point. We didn't really talk about stuff like that. I probably wouldn't have noticed if Jim had cut his head off unless it affected our night out. Sorry.'

Laura isn't desperately surprised. Sonja's possible sighting, on the other hand, however slim the possibility that it was him, is nagging away at her. She turns to Sonja.

'Would you mind telling the police about seeing Jim?'

Sonja's face flushes. 'Yes, of course. Although I wouldn't want to give them any false leads. Or you any false hope.'

'No, it's fine. I'm grateful for any kind of hope at the moment. Until now there's been literally nothing.'

Sonja nods, her eyes filled with sympathy. 'Okay, yes, I'll tell them.' She heads towards the hallway. 'In fact I'll ring them now.'

'Thank you.'

She leaves the room and Simon sinks into a chair. 'God, I hope he turns up. He's a great guy. I really like him a lot.'

'Thank you. Me too.'

'I'm happy to help you look for him, you know. I'm pretty cooped up here with the little one all day and – well, to be honest it would be good to have something to occupy my brain. It's only been just over a year but I feel like it's turned to mush. Sonja goes out to work every day and I'm stuck at home in a never-ending cycle of nappies, plastic toys and nursery rhymes.' He sighs. 'Sorry, I know it's not about me. But just let me know if I can do anything.'

'Thank you.'

Sonja comes back in. 'I've told them. They said they will add it to the file.' She shrugs. 'Maybe I'll walk past the same spot tomorrow and see if he's there again.'

'Would you?' Laura feels excitement rising in her chest again.

'Why not? It has to be worth a go, right?'

'Thank you.' Laura wishes with all her heart she could take the train with her, walk through Hyde Park and see all the children playing, people strolling, eating their lunch on benches. But it feels like another world.

A low wailing sound floats down the stairs. 'That'll be Amelie again. Well, that was short-lived.' Sonja shakes both of their hands efficiently. 'Lovely to meet you both.' She turns to Simon. 'I'll see to her, you see these ladies out.'

Dismissed, they walk to the front door and moments later

they're heading home. Somehow, moving back towards her house doesn't feel as terrifying as going the other way. The street seems benign, unthreatening now. Maybe this is progress.

For the first time in a long time, Laura feels hopeful. It might only be a tiny glimmer of hope, but it's something.

20

THEN – MAY 1991

The branches of the straggly magnolia tree in the garden behind ours had exploded with blossom, which was already scattering like snowflakes across the scruffy patch of shared garden. It had been just over two months since I'd last set foot outside this flat, and the changing seasons told me everything I needed to know about how quickly time was marching on without me.

'Can't you even try and go to work?' Debbie begged. 'You love your job.' She was right. Cooking had always been the thing I turned to whenever I felt low, not to mention how hard I'd worked to get where I was. How could I throw it all away because of one man in a dark alley?

And yet I just couldn't do it.

I struggled to describe the terror I felt, the all-consuming dread that, if I left the safety of my flat, something or someone would be waiting for me, ready to pounce. It took over my mind, my body, paralysing me every time I even considered setting foot outside.

I wasn't sleeping either; how could I let myself be so vulnerable? The worst times were when Jim was away. Those long, sleepless nights were when the terror crowded in and left me shaking and sweating, tangled in my sheets every morning and feeling more tired than I had when I'd gone to bed.

Jim begged me to speak to my doctor, to ask for something to blunt the sharp blades of my fear. But I refused that too, having some confused idea that I needed to remain alert at all times. And yet at the same time I was drinking more and more to forget. I'd tried limiting it at first because Jim disapproved of me drinking so much and I didn't want to keep asking him to buy it for me. But then I convinced Mr O'Neill from the shop three streets away to deliver a box of six bottles to me and leave it on my doorstep, so I stopped keeping track of how many I was getting through.

So that was where I was, two months after the attack. Stuck indoors, alone half the time, and making my husband's life a misery the other half. I swung violently between abject terror and utter boredom, but at least I felt safe cocooned inside my little flat, so that was where I stayed. Jim had recently brought home a VCR to try and keep me occupied and I spent days in my pyjamas watching the same films over and over again: *Steel Magnolias*, *Indiana Jones*, *Romancing the Stone*, *Heathers*.

But Jim was coming home today, so I'd made an effort to wash my hair, get dressed and plan a meal for this evening – although even then I'd have to send Jim out to the supermarket to buy the ingredients before I could cook it for him. God, how utterly helpless I was. It was a wonder he was still with me, the stress I put him through.

I turned away from the back garden and sat down on my bed. I was so exhausted all I felt like doing was lying down, closing my eyes and going to sleep. But I knew it wouldn't be as easy as that, and I also wanted to at least try and do some cleaning before Jim got home. It took all the energy I had to haul myself to my feet and wade through to the kitchen to dig out the cleaning products. I was just reaching for a new cloth when a clatter outside the back door made me jump so much I clonked my head on the edge of the cupboard and almost knocked myself out.

What the fuck was that?

Despite the throbbing in my head, I peered down the stairs towards the back door. The stippled glass was clear, no shadowy figure lurking. But that didn't mean the coast was clear. I pulled myself to my feet and stumbled closer, creeping down the stairs step by step, trying not to make any noise. My heart pounded and my legs shook with terror, but I was determined to carry on. Finally, I reached the bottom step, and stretched my hand out to push down the handle. But halfway there it stopped, hovering in mid-air as though on a paused video.

I couldn't do it.

I couldn't open the back door.

I stood for a moment, frozen, unable to move either forward or backwards. Then the world rushed into my brain again, and I turned and sprinted back up the stairs, through the kitchen, along the hallway and all the way to the living room at the front of the house. The curtains were always closed in here, so I threw myself onto the sofa, buried my face in a cushion and curled myself into a ball.

The next thing I knew, there was a hand on my arm, and I was being shaken gently. I snapped my eyes open and looked up.

'Jim!' I lunged into his arms and clung to him, and he lowered himself onto the sofa and held me. Eventually, he pulled away.

'What's happened, darling?' he said.

I closed my eyes. 'There was a noise outside and I thought... I thought...' I gulped in air.

'Hey, hey, hey, what is it?' He rubbed my upper arms and I felt the tension slowly drop away. I hung my head. 'I thought there was someone there. I thought they were trying to get in.'

'Oh, Lola,' he said, pulling me to him. I sat for moment, safely cocooned in his arms. It wasn't until a few minutes later I realised it was already dark outside.

'What time is it?' I said, squinting to make out the glowing green figures on the VCR. My vision swam, my eyes red raw from crying.

'It's seven o'clock,' he said.

'Oh God, I was going to make you dinner,' I said, horrified.

'It doesn't matter, darling, I'll make something.'

'No!' I leapt up, brushed myself down, aware suddenly of how awful I must look. So much for making an effort, for wanting Jim to see the old Laura, the Laura he fell in love with rather than the scared, cowering creature I seemed to have become. 'I wanted to make you something special, I made a list, only...' I trailed off, aware that he was unlikely to want to traipse round looking for an open shop at this time of the evening. I let my arms drop to my sides, suddenly exhausted with feeling like this all the time.

'It doesn't matter,' he said. 'Really. I'm just glad to be home. I don't need anything fancy to eat.'

I dropped my head, then looked back up at him. I studied this kind, handsome face I'd loved from the moment I first set eyes on it, and tried to smile. He still loved me despite everything. I didn't need to prove anything to him. Everything was going to be fine.

'I love you, Jim,' I whispered.

'I love you too.' He kissed my nose gently, then stepped away. 'Now, why don't you go and see if there's something in the freezer we can rustle up for dinner, and I'll make sure there's nothing untoward going on outside?'

I nodded, and we made our way to the kitchen, where I found the cleaning products I'd pulled out earlier still scattered across the floor. I hadn't even got round to doing that, and it struck me then what a mess the place looked, with piles of dishes in the sink and empty drinking glasses along the side, dust on every surface and washing piling up. The whole place needed a damn good clean, and with me not being at work and Jim working all the hours he could, I knew he always hoped I'd at least have the place looking half decent when he got home. I also knew that, given the state of me when he walked in just now, he wouldn't say anything about it.

But for me, that was worse. I felt a like schoolgirl with a black mark against her name, and I could feel the disappointment in him because I felt it myself.

While Jim went down the back stairs to investigate what the bang had been, I set about cleaning the kitchen. I kept my back turned to the open door even though it was all the way down a flight of stairs, and ignored the cool breeze that trickled through the open doorway into the kitchen. I didn't relax until I heard the back door slam, and Jim's footsteps heading back up towards the kitchen again. I turned to face him.

'The bin had fallen over, there was rubbish scattered all over the garden,' he said, heading to the sink to wash his hands. 'It was probably a fox, although they don't usually come out during the day.' He lathered soap all over his hands. 'Maybe it was just the wind. Anyway, it's all sorted now, the rubbish is all back in the bin, and there are no terrifying creatures waiting to murder us all.'

I froze. I knew it was a joke to Jim, but it wasn't to me. He must have seen the look on my face because he quickly dried his hands and wrapped his arms around me. 'Sorry, Lola, I wasn't thinking. There's nothing there. There's absolutely nothing to worry about.'

We stood for a few minutes, then I pulled away.

'I'll make a start on dinner.' I turned toward the freezer.

'Thanks, love. I'm just going to get changed out of my work clothes, then why don't you go and have a soak in the bath, let me finish off here?'

I turned to look at him. 'Are you sure?' There was nothing I wanted more right now than to have a leisurely soak. Even thinking about it, I could feel the tension dropping from my shoulders.

'Positive. Give me a sec.'

He disappeared into the bedroom and I heated the oven up and tipped chips and chicken Kievs onto a baking tray. It wasn't exactly high-end cooking but it was quick and easy and it was more nutrition than I'd managed for the rest of the week.

'I've started the bath running for you, put loads of bubbles in just the way you like it,' he said, reappearing. He'd dumped his suit and was dressed in a green polo shirt and straight-legged jeans, similar to the way my dad used to dress.

'Thanks, Jim. These need about twenty-five minutes and—'

'I'm quite capable of cooking some food,' he said. 'Now go!'

I didn't need telling twice.

As I lay back in the bath, letting the scalding water warm my skin and soothe my aching muscles, I closed my eyes. For the first time since Jim had left four days before, I wasn't a ball of tension, thrumming with fear. Just knowing Jim was here, and I was safe, made me relax. I felt a wave of shame wash over me. I knew this was bad for me, but what must it be like for Jim, coming home to me? Did he ever wish he could stay where he was and not come home at all? I wouldn't blame him if he did.

Distantly I heard the phone ring, but I felt so sleepy I barely registered it. My head was swimming with heat, so I woozily climbed out, dried off and pulled on the clothes I'd been wearing before. I padded back through to the kitchen, where Jim was pulling something out of the oven.

'Ah, perfect timing,' he said, smiling as I entered.

'Sorry it's not something better,' I said, reaching for a couple of plates.

'Don't be daft, it's fine.' He divided the chips between the plates, placed a Kiev on each, and drained the peas, steam rising up round his face.

'Bon appetit!' he said, placing it down on the table with a flourish and sitting down beside me.

'Thanks, Jim. Seriously. I appreciate it.'

'It's no problem, love, really. You seemed like you needed it.'

'I really did.' I longed to tell him exactly how terrified I'd been this week, how I'd been so on edge that every little noise had made me almost jump out of my skin, but I didn't want to worry him any more than I already had. Instead, I asked him about his week.

'Oh, you know. The usual. It's stressful but not something you'd want to hear about.'

'I wouldn't mind. You never tell me anything about your job. I don't even know exactly *where* you work.'

He shoved a forkful of peas into his mouth and grimaced. I waited while he chewed, then he smiled.

'You know what I do. But I don't want to waste the precious time when I'm with you talking about work, or the people I work with. It's fine. It's a job, it's busy and it pays the bills.' He shrugged.

I felt a pang of disappointment that he'd done what he always did when I asked about anything outside the life he had with me, and refused to open up. I assumed it was because he genuinely didn't want to talk about it when he was away from there, which I knew I should feel pleased about – that he wanted to focus on us. But a small part of me still longed to be thrown just a few nuggets of information, a few details I could treasure in his absence that would put some flesh on the bones of his working life. After all, it took him away for 50 per cent of our marriage.

'Oh, who was on the phone?'

'The phone?' He frowned.

'Just now, when I was in the bath. I heard it ring.' My heart stopped. 'It wasn't another silent call, was it...?' We hadn't had one since Jim had changed the number but it didn't mean I didn't think about it.

'Oh no, sorry, I forgot it even rang. It was just Debbie.'

'Debbie? Did she say what she wanted?'

'No, I just told her you were in the bath and we were about to have dinner and that she should call back tomorrow.'

'Oh. Right.'

He frowned. 'Was that the wrong thing to say?'

I pushed my peas round my plate. 'I just – I would have liked to speak to her, that's all. She's so busy and she was out last night so I haven't spoken to her for a couple of days.'

Jim chuckled. 'Honestly, Lola, you rely on that woman too much. It's not healthy.'

'That woman? She's my best friend!' I could feel heat rising in my chest even though the last thing I wanted was to be fighting with Jim.

'I know she is, but you know what I mean. She does an awful lot for you, and she's got a family of her own. Besides, I'm home now.'

I could feel tears threatening, the telltale burning sensation at the back of my eyes, and I blinked them back furiously. Because Jim had hit a nerve. I was aware that I demanded a lot from Debbie, and that I should probably be giving her some space to be with Steve, Lily and James. But with Jim away so much, I needed her, it was as simple as that. I couldn't understand why Jim didn't get that. I was about to say as much when Jim spoke again.

'Besides, I thought we might be busy after dinner,' he said, sliding his hand across the table and cupping mine in his.

'Busy?'

'Yes. You know. In bed.'

'Oh!' I felt my face flame. 'I – I—' I stopped, unsure what to say.

Since the attack Jim had been patient about the fact I hadn't wanted to have sex with him. In fact at first I hadn't wanted him anywhere near me, as if my body was in such shock that just the thought of my husband touching me repelled me. Slowly, I'd let him near me again, and we'd been close – but only to an extent. I still didn't want him to touch me intimately, and I had to close my eyes every time he kissed me in case I saw the eyes of my attacker instead of Jim's. But I knew I needed to get over it, that it wasn't fair to make him wait forever.

'Yes, of course,' I said, trying for a smile. I leaned over and gave him a kiss, trying to lose myself in the familiarity of him. He responded hungrily, as though starved of affection, and pulled me onto his lap and ran his hand from waist to my breast, pushing my bra aside. I tensed, but he didn't stop, and I made myself carry on, desperate to make him happy. After all, if I couldn't even give him this, what *was* he getting from me? I let him push his tongue inside my mouth, then tried to relax as he ran his lips down my neck, onto my exposed breast. I tried to respond the way I always had, pulling his head even closer to heighten the sensation, but then he ran his free hand up between my legs and pushed my knickers aside and I leapt up, leaving him sitting there staring at me, completely confused.

'I'm sorry, I—' I stuttered, tugging my top down self-consciously.

'I'm sorry, Lola, I thought you were ready. You seemed... you seemed like you were enjoying it.'

'I was, I am, I...' I was gabbling. I took a deep breath, desperate for air in my lungs. 'I'm sorry. I really am. I just – I need a bit more time.'

He reached out for my hand and pulled me gently towards him so I was looking down at him. He kissed my hand tenderly. 'It's okay, really. I understand. I just wish that *bastard* hadn't hurt you, then none of this would be happening.' He reached up and stroked my cheek. 'I just want my Lola back.'

'Me too,' I said, choking back a sob.

* * *

In the end Jim extended his stay for an extra day. 'I've told my boss my wife needs me,' he announced on Sunday night, the night before he was due to leave again.

'And doesn't he mind?'

'He hasn't got much choice really,' he replied.

But it was now Tuesday morning and all Jim staying longer had done was make it harder when he did leave. We'd had a lovely weekend, just the two of us, despite me not wanting to go anywhere. Jim had taken the phone off the hook so nobody could disturb us – I didn't have the heart to tell him I wanted to speak to Debbie – and we ordered takeaways and watched films that Jim rented from Blockbuster every night. I knew he'd been hoping for some intimacy, but I wasn't quite there yet. How long would he be willing to wait?

I spent the morning trying to clear the backlog of housework that had built up over the last few weeks, but every task felt like a mammoth effort. And after a weekend with Jim drinking nothing but wine, I was also desperate for some vodka to numb the terror that slowly clawed its way back in with every passing minute alone.

I went to the cupboard and pulled a bottle out. There was only an inch or so left in the bottom. I leaned down to find another bottle but there was nothing there. The rest of the cupboard was empty. Where was my vodka?

Feeling panic rising in my throat, I dropped to my hands and knees and scrabbled round in the cupboard, pulling out tins and bottles. But it wasn't there.

Heart hammering, I opened another cupboard, and another, slamming them shut as I went. I was frantic now, the urge for a drink taking me over. I crept to the front window and peered out into the street, trying to decide if I was desperate enough to try and get to the corner shop. But when I pictured the walk there, along three busy streets, panic overwhelmed me and I had to sit down and take some deep breaths and calm myself down again.

There had to be another solution. I glanced at the clock. I couldn't call Debbie because she was at work, and Mr O'Neill had only delivered a case of six bottles two days before Jim got home. What would he think if I rang for another one? Did I care?

I marched to the phone, deciding that ringing Mr O'Neill was my only course of action, the thought of a day without vodka too much to bear. But then a memory flashed into my mind of me moving bottles before Jim got home. I flew into the spare bedroom, and yanked open the wardrobe doors where, like some sort of mirage, there they were: my box of bottles, with four still remaining. Kneeling down, I grabbed one like a starving child handed a piece of bread, screwed the lid off and tipped it down my throat, ignoring the burn as it hit my windpipe and swirled into my stomach. I felt myself relax, my limbs becoming heavy, my mind softening. I took another deep swig and sank to the floor, lying down like a starfish, my back pressed into the carpet, my head swimming.

What would people think if they could see me now, before midday, lying on the floor, downing vodka like water? I sat up slowly, trying to stop my head spinning, then stood, and walked carefully through to the kitchen. I should at least get a glass. As I entered the kitchen I saw the phone handset on the table. I picked it up and returned it to its cradle, and was just reaching for a glass when it rang, making me jump so much I almost dropped the bottle on the kitchen floor.

I stared at the phone for a few seconds. Should I answer it? What if it was the silent caller again, back to taunt me?

But what if it was Jim, or Debbie? Would they panic if I didn't answer? They both knew I didn't go anywhere. I snatched the receiver up and held it to my ear.

'Hello?'

'It's me.'

Debbie. My body sagged with relief and I sat down before I collapsed.

'Thank God,' I whispered, my throat raw.

'What's the matter? What's happened?'

'Nothing. Nothing, I'm fine.' My voice was stronger now. I wanted her to hear I was okay, but it obviously hadn't worked.

'What's going on, Lau? Why do you sound weird?'

'I don't sound weird. I was just glad it was you and not someone scary.' I took a swig from my bottle and slammed it down on the table. It took me a few seconds to realise Debbie hadn't replied. 'Are you still there?'

'I am.'

'Good.'

'Laura, are you drunk?'

'What? Of course not! I'm just pleased to hear from you.' I tried to enunciate my words very clearly.

'You are, aren't you? Your words are all slurry.' She sighed heavily. 'Oh, Lau, what's happened? Why are you drinking at this time of the day?'

I knew there was no use denying it. 'I'm sorry, Debs. Jim just left and I was lonely and scared and...' I trailed off, aware how pathetic I sounded.

'Please stop drinking. It'll only make you feel worse.'

I didn't reply. 'Come on, Laura. You can't sit there feeling sorry for yourself about having nobody to talk to when you don't even call people back when they ring you over and over again.'

'What do you mean?'

'I mean this weekend. I rang a few times but apart from the first time when Jim said you didn't want to speak to me—'

'He said what?'

'He told me you were in the bath and that you had a nice evening planned and I probably shouldn't ring again for a few days. I tried a few more times but it was engaged all weekend. I assumed you'd left it off the hook deliberately.'

'Jim did.'

'He did tell you I popped round, didn't he?'

I felt a bubble of worry float up. 'No, he didn't. When?'

'Yesterday morning before I went to work, when I assumed Jim had left. He said you didn't want to see anyone.'

'He stayed home an extra day. But he didn't tell me you'd come round...'

'So you were there?'

'Of course I was, I never go anywhere!'

The silence hummed loudly. 'Debs?'

'I'm here. I was just trying to work out why Jim would do that. I would have thought he'd be pleased to know I'm looking out for you when he's away so much.'

I had no idea either. 'I'll talk to him. I'm sure he didn't mean anything,' I said. 'Will you still come round later?'

She paused. 'Do you promise to stop drinking? Because I don't want to have to come over and stage a rescue mission.'

'You have my word.'

21

NOW – 11 OCTOBER 1992

Number nine Willow Crescent
Marjorie and Faye Phillips

Marjorie feels grumpy today, and the only thing that makes her feel better on days like this is biscuits. Just as well Faye has bought some more, she thinks, popping a chocolate Bourbon into her mouth and brushing away the crumbs that have fallen into her lap as she chews. Faye can hoover them up later. She's a good girl.

'You're not eating biscuits right before dinner again, are you, Mum?' Faye says, her voice making Marjorie jump.

'Why do you always creep up on me like that? Trying to catch me out all the time?'

Faye sighs. 'I'm not creeping up on you, you just didn't hear me. Anyway, if you weren't doing anything wrong there wouldn't be anything to catch you out about, would there?'

'Humph.' The sound, through biscuits, is muffled and Faye

rolls her eyes. Her mother is obviously in a mood again and she has a feeling she knows why.

'Been watching your soap, Mum?'

Marjorie swallows down a huge lump of chewed biscuit. 'Might have been. Why?'

'Because you're always so moody afterwards. Don't know why you watch it if it makes you so angry.'

'Because I love Jim Robinson, that's why. He's so dishy.'

'Dishy! Mum, you are funny.'

'I am not funny. I'm just saying, he's worth getting angry for, that's all. Anyway. That's not all that's made me annoyed.'

'Go on, what else has annoyed you, then?' Faye suspects she's going to be blamed somewhere in this.

Her mother sighs dramatically. 'That blooming boy.' She nods towards the net curtains as though they're hiding someone behind it.

'Which boy?'

'That Hardwick boy. Always banging that football around as though he's Gary Linny-thing. It gets right on my nerves.'

'I think you mean Gary Lineker, Mum.' Faye squashes down a smile, afraid of making her mother even more tetchy. 'He's not doing you any harm though is he?'

'Not *physically* dear, no. But the noise. It goes right through me, that constant thump, thump, thump, it jangles my bones. Why can't he take the ball somewhere else, to a park or something, or better still go inside and do something quiet?'

'He's all right, Mum, don't fuss. It could be a lot worse.'

'Humph.' It's a source of constant amusement to Faye that her mother actually does make a *humph* sound when she has nothing further to say on a subject, like a closing statement boiled down into one short, grumpy noise. She changes the subject.

'Do you need anything, Mum? I was thinking of popping to the shop.'

'What? Oh, you're going out again?'

Faye sighs and rolls her eyes. The way her mother goes on you'd think she is always out, gallivanting around, when the sad truth is that here she is, a forty-five-year-old woman, living with her mother, no family of her own, and stuck in the house at least twenty hours a day. Her only escape is the odd trip to the corner shop or, if she's feeling really daring, a drive down the A road to Safeway. Sometimes she stops for a cup of tea when she's finished her shopping and even that makes her feel guilty because her mum hates being left on her own.

Faye suspects that her mother is far more capable than she lets on. But she's been mainly wheelchair-bound for three years now since her hip operation, and so Faye has become even more trapped.

'I'm only going to get a few things. We need more teabags and bread and I thought I might get a nice cake for tea.'

Marjorie shrugs. 'Well, if do you insist on going then some carrot cake would be nice. And maybe some of those marshmallow things, the round ones, what are they called?'

'Tunnock's tea cakes?'

'That's them. Good to have them in just in case.'

In case of what exactly? An invasion of aliens who are allergic to marshmallow? Faye bites her tongue and just says, 'Okay,' then shrugs her coat on. 'Right, I won't be long. Will you be all right? Have you got everything you need?'

'Yes, I'll be fine, don't fuss, dear. But do try and get back before it's dark, won't you?'

'Yes, Mum.' Faye kisses her mother on the head and is almost at the front door when Marjorie shouts out. 'Faye, Faye, quick, come here!'

Heart racing, Faye runs back to make sure her mother hasn't hurt herself. But rather than the catastrophe she imagined, Marjorie is simply staring out of the window, her face pressed up against the net curtain, peering over the glasses perched on the end of her nose.

'What's the matter?'

Marjorie looks up briefly, her face bright with excitement. She points to where she was staring.

'Look.'

Faye glances out of the window but can't see anything out of the ordinary.

'What am I meant to be looking at?'

'Her.' Her mother's voice has gone all wobbly and Faye turns to look again, puzzled. She can make out two women walking across the street, one slightly behind the other. She doesn't think she knows either of them.

'Who?'

'It's *her*, the woman from across the street.'

Faye must still look confused because Marjorie gives an over-dramatic sigh. *'Jim's* wife. The one that never leaves the house. Except now she has. *Look!'* Her finger points towards the street again and Faye realises that the two women are making their way towards their house.

'Oooh, she's coming here, I knew it! Carol said she would. I've seen her going into a couple of the other houses and I wondered if she'd come here too.' Marjorie is almost shaking with excitement. She loves nothing more than a good bit of gossip, and this is certainly more than a bit. Faye remembers now, Carol coming round the other day. She sat in with Marjorie for ages, and they talked non-stop about this chap, Jim, who lives across the road, having gone missing, and about his wife who has some sort of weird condition that means she never leaves the house – but who, despite all of that, is apparently now going round talking to all the neighbours.

'She'll be over to see you soon, I should think,' Carol said. 'She wants us all to help her.'

Faye barely listened either at the time or afterwards, when her mother harped on endlessly about it. It didn't seem like that big a deal. It wasn't as if she knew anyone involved. But then what does someone like her know about the important things in life? It's not as though she has anyone to care whether she goes missing or not. Well, apart from her mother, of course, but that's only because she needs someone to buy her Malted Milks, make her endless supplies of tea and help her in and out of the bath. Apart from that, Faye has no one. She sighs. She'll probably have to delay her shopping trip now until she's seen off these women. Her mother doesn't need excitement like this. It makes her heart funny and she feels faint for hours afterwards. No, she'll make sure they don't come in and disturb them.

Faye starts to make her way to the front door to pre-empt the doorbell. Her mother's screech stops her in her tracks.

'Don't you dare stop them from coming in, young lady!'

Faye turns to find her mother twisting her wheelchair away from the window and straining to push it across the thick carpet.

'Mum, what on earth are you doing?' Faye races across the room to help but Marjorie bats her away. 'There's no way you're getting rid of them, Faye.' Her voice holds a hint of threat and Faye knows there's no arguing with her. 'I've been waiting for her to come round for *days*. Don't you dare spoil it for me now.'

Faye takes a step back, her hands held up in surrender.

'Okay, okay, I'll let them in.' She peers out of the front window. 'But I'll at least let them ring the doorbell first, shall I?'

At that exact moment the doorbell peals through the house.

'Well, go on, go and let them in, then.' Marjorie shoos her

daughter away and Faye huffs heavily as she makes her way to the front door, sweltering in her winter coat. She pulls open the door to be faced with an attractive woman with blonde hair pulled back into a high ponytail and a smaller, skinnier woman with a grey face and dark curly hair puffing up round her sunken cheeks. They both look surprised, probably because she opened the door about two seconds after they'd rung the bell.

'Hello.' Faye offers what she hopes is a friendly smile. The taller, fair-haired woman steps forward and holds out her hand. 'Hello, I'm Debbie, and this is my friend Laura. She lives over there.' She gestures behind her. 'We wondered whether we could ask you some questions.'

Faye gives a curt nod and steps back to let them in. She knows she comes across as unfriendly but the truth is that women like this – confident, outspoken, brave – make her feel her shortcomings even more acutely, and she retreats into herself until she can hardly remember who she is any more. She knows they'll see her as a quiet, mousey, downtrodden woman and in many ways they'll be right. She just wishes she knew how to show them there's more to Faye Phillips than meets the eye.

She waits impatiently while they remove their shoes and coats, then shows them into the living room where her mother sits, regally, in her wheelchair, smiling at them serenely.

'Mum, this is Debbie, and Laura.' She waves her hand at her mother. 'This is Marjorie.'

Marjorie's face breaks into a huge smile and she sticks out her hand. 'Oh, ladies, it's lovely to see you, it really is. Do come in and sit down. I've been waiting for you for ages.'

Faye sees the look of confusion on their faces as they perch on the sofa and steps forward to explain. 'Carol came round the other day and told Mum you'd been over to see her, so Mum thought you might come here too.'

They both nod as realisation dawns. Faye watches them take in the scruffy living room. The shelves cluttered with ornaments, the well-worn rug on the floor, the tie-dye throw hanging from the wall, sagging in the middle where the pin fell out months ago. Studying their living room through fresh eyes, with its hippy rugs and throws, Buddhas lined up along the shelf and books about tarot reading, she wonders what they must make of it. Of them. She flushes with shame.

'Can you make these ladies a cup of tea now, Faye?'

'Yes, Mum.' She looks at them both and smiles without it reaching her eyes. 'Tea or coffee?'

'Tea would be lovely, please,' says curly hair – she was Laura, wasn't she?

'Tea for me too, please. Thank you.' Debbie's smile is warm.

She gives a small nod and turns on her heel.

As she bustles about the kitchen preparing the tea she's glad to be away from the prying eyes of these strangers. She hates herself for feeling so inferior in their presence, but it's the way she's been since she was a little girl. There's no point pretending she's ever going to change now.

Tea made, she walks slowly back through to the living room, balancing everything precariously on a cheap plastic tray. When she enters the room again her mother is leaning forward in her chair talking animatedly.

'And so you think he might have done a runner, then, do you?'

'Mum!'

Marjorie's head whips round. 'What? It's what she's just been saying, isn't it, Laura?'

Laura nods her head miserably and despite herself Faye can't help feeling a bit sorry for the woman, being verbally assaulted by her mother like that. She knows she's a bit much if you've never met her before. 'It is beginning to look more and more like that, yes.'

Marjorie is clearly in her element. 'Listen to this, Faye,' she says. 'Jim's gone missing and Laura here is trying to find out what's happened to him, and thinks we might have some clues to help her find him. What do you think to that, then?' She stops and plucks another Bourbon from the tray that Faye has placed on the coffee table and takes a bite, crumbs attaching themselves to the light sprinkling of hair on her chin like Klingons. She chews and takes a breath. 'I was saying, love, that we know Jim quite well, don't we?'

Faye studies her mother's face. She doesn't really know Jim at all, to be honest, only that he popped round a couple of times to see Marjorie. Faye has hardly spoken more than a few words to him. But her mother loves a bit of drama, and adores being the centre of attention, so of course she's playing it up as much as she possibly can. Faye has to stop herself rolling her eyes.

'You do, Mum. I'm not sure I can be much help.'

Marjorie gives her daughter a look that suggests she will deal with her later, then turns back to the two women sitting on the sofa opposite.

'Well, anyway.' She swipes yet another biscuit, a custard cream this time. 'Do help yourselves, won't you? You look as though you need a bit of feeding up.' She wipes her mouth and leans forward so far it seems as though she's about to tip right forward and land face-first on the swirly carpet. Faye isn't sure she'd feel that inclined to help her up. 'Listen. I have an idea.'

Laura shifts to hear better. The poor woman is clearly desperate for any information they can give her, and Faye feels even more sorry for her. The trouble is, Faye also knows exactly what her mother is about to suggest, and she isn't entirely convinced it's what Laura has in mind.

'How would you feel about me doing a tarot reading for you?'

Faye watches as Laura's face passes from interest to surprise to confusion to – what is that now? Pleasure? She's *happy* about her mother's suggestion? Surely not.

'Oh.' Laura glances at Debbie next to her, who shrugs. 'I don't suppose it can do any harm, can it?'

'Exactly!' Marjorie claps her hands in glee. 'I'm sure we'll be able to find out *something*.' She turns to Faye. 'Pass me my cards, will you, love?'

Faye plucks the silk-wrapped pack from the shelf and hands it reluctantly to her mother.

'Now, let's clear this table.' Marjorie pushes the tray to one side and sweeps the crumbs off with the back of her hand onto the carpet. *I guess I'll be hoovering that up later, then,* Faye thinks uncharitably. Marjorie shakes the cards from the pack and hands them to Laura.

'Now, give these a shuffle, love, and then, when you're ready, split them into three piles and lay them down here.'

Laura does as she's told and lays down three separate piles. 'Right you are. Now, think about what question you want to ask the cards. Maybe it's about whether Jim will come home, something like that. Whatever you want. Then, when you've got your question, choose whichever pile of cards you feel most drawn to. Then let me know.'

There is a moment of silence, then Laura places her hand on top of the middle pile. 'This one.'

'Okey dokey.' Marjorie picks up the middle pile and puts the other two back inside the pack. Then slowly she starts to spread the cards out on the table in front of her, from the top of the pile. Faye has seen this so many times before, even learnt to do it herself when she was younger. But even though she doesn't read cards herself any more, she still loves watching her mother at work. It's instinctive for her, almost as though she knows what card is coming before she's even turned it over. Faye watches Laura's face as she studies the – to most people – indecipherable pictures on the brightly coloured cards in front of her. It's clear Laura has no idea what she's looking at and, again like most people, her face reveals a mix of fear and hope in equal measures.

Her mother stabs at the first card with her forefinger. This card is all about the present, so she isn't expecting it to be great news. It depicts a devil, and a man and woman chained to a post beneath him. The devil, Faye knows, is a terrifying image for most people to see.

'This here is about breaking free from your dark side, and having the courage to express your true feelings,' Marjorie explains, her fingers tapping lightly on the card as she speaks, marking out her words like a metronome, or an incantation. A frown lightly creases her forehead and she looks up at Laura, who meets her eye uncertainly. 'It means you should let go of your inhibitions, and express your true emotions.'

Laura gives a small nod, but says nothing. Marjorie's finger slides over to the next card. Faye watches as Laura's eyes widen at the Death card, with its depiction of Death riding a horse, wearing black armour. Most people panic about this card too, but it's never about someone dying. She hopes Laura understands what it's trying to tell her.

'Now there's no need to worry, my dear. The Death card doesn't mean what you think it means.' Marjorie closes her eyes, deep in thought. 'It doesn't mean someone has died, or someone is going to die. It represents the death of an idea, or a plan.' Her eyes flick open again to take in Laura's reaction as she says her next words. 'Or the death of a relationship.' She lets her hand linger slightly longer as she watches Laura take in her words. 'It means, my dear, you shouldn't feel afraid to free yourself from a past that no longer serves you well, and to proceed towards a new future.'

Faye watches as Laura swallows, her face pale. Her eyes dart towards Debbie, but Debbie is watching the cards, deep in thought herself. There is just one significant card left, and Faye holds her breath as her mother explains what it means.

'This one, my dear, is the Lovers card. This represents the challenges and difficulties of finding the right partner, the right person to be with in life.' She pauses for effect. 'It means you need to consider your long-term interests and, if you can't make two potential relationships work together, then you should let one of them go.'

Her words hang in the air for a moment, like so many tiny fragments of paper being suspended before dropping messily to the ground. Then, with a huge sigh, Marjorie sits back in her chair and wipes the back of her hand across her forehead dramatically. She's good at this, but by God does she love the drama of it all as well. If they didn't have the same nose, Faye would sometimes wonder whether she's actually Marjorie's daughter at all, they're so unalike.

'Well, I hope that's shed some light, dear?'

Laura nods but says nothing. She looks even more pale than when she arrived, and she doesn't seem to know what to say. Luckily Debbie comes to her rescue.

'Wow, that was great, thank you so much, Mrs Phillips.'

'Oh, please do call me Marjorie. Mrs Phillips sounds so formal.'

'Well, thank you, Marjorie. It's been very – enlightening.' Faye can detect a hint of displeasure in Debbie's voice and wonders what her problem is. Her mother has just given Laura a really good reading, and it all sounded pretty positive to her. The end of an era must be about her and Jim as they were, and maybe even about her agoraphobia. The new beginning – well, that could be Laura and Jim in their new life when he comes back. Unless Laura has met someone else in the meantime, of course, which is entirely possible. It all seems so obvious to Faye, but, she supposes, it can all be a bit confusing and overwhelming for someone who has never had a reading before.

'Mum, you look exhausted, do you think you should take a nap before dinner?'

'Oh, don't fuss, I'm fine.' Marjorie turns to Laura and Debbie. 'I hope it's been of some use, at least,' she says, reaching forward and gripping Laura's hand between her own chubby ones. 'These things are not always crystal clear immediately. Sometimes the cards tell us things we weren't expecting or give us messages which are a little hidden and it can take a while to work out their true meanings. But they're rarely wrong. Rarely. I'd say you've got a pretty good reading there and everything's going to turn out okay. Wouldn't you agree, Faye dear?'

'Yes, Mum. It sounded great.' She stands woodenly. 'Anyone want more tea?'

'Oh no. Thank you.' Laura looks shell-shocked and stands abruptly. 'Thank you so much, Mrs Phillips – Marjorie – but I think we've really got to dash.' She glances out of the window where the sky is an ominous grey again through the heavy net curtains.

'Oh yes, you don't want to get wet, do you?' Marjorie gathers up her cards and places them carefully back in the pack. 'Well, it's been really lovely to meet you and thank you for popping over.'

'And thank you for doing this – reading for me.'

Marjorie nods. 'You're very welcome, dear. Jim loved the couple of readings I did for him.'

'You – you did tarot card readings for Jim?' The surprise is clear on Laura's face.

'Why yes, it's why he came over. I think he was looking for answers. I did two for him – or was it three, Faye dear?'

'I'm not sure, Mum.'

'Oh well, anyway. I don't know what he was hoping for, but he always seemed happy with the result.'

'Oh. I see.' Laura looks even more shaken and Debbie takes her elbow as they turn to leave.

'Thank you for the tea, Faye.'

Then, after a quick goodbye, they're gone. Faye is relieved they didn't stay longer. The peace and quiet can sometimes get to her, but at the end of the day this is where she's most comfortable, in her own home, just her and her mother. Why else would she still be here otherwise?

She scurries back through to the living room where Marjorie is munching on yet another biscuit. 'Mum, stop eating biscuits before dinner!'

'Well, you put them there,' she says, popping the rest in her mouth and giving a satisfied smack of her lips.

'For our guests.'

'Humph. Well, anyway. They both seemed lovely, didn't they?'

'Yeah.'

Marjorie looks at her. 'Oh, Faye, what's wrong? You never seem to like anyone.'

Faye shrugs. 'I do. I like lots of people. I just – I don't know. They made me feel uncomfortable.'

'Well, I thought they were nice. And I thought the reading went pretty well, didn't you?'

Faye shrugs again. 'Yes, Mum.' She clears the cups from the table and walks towards the kitchen. 'Anyway, I'm going to the shop now. I'll see you later.'

And before her mother can object, she closes the door behind her, ignoring the muffled cries for her not to leave her on her own.

* * *

It takes at least ten minutes for Laura to feel like speaking once she gets back to the safety of her own home. Debbie plonks a mug of over-strong tea in front of her and sits opposite her at the kitchen table.

'What do you make of all that, then?' Debbie says, slurping her tea noisily.

Laura rubs her eye and cups her hands round her mug. 'I—' She swallows. 'Honestly, I have no idea. I mean, Jim had a *tarot* reading? Twice? I can't...' She stops, lost for words.

Debbie nods. 'That's exactly what I thought too. It doesn't strike me as a very Jim thing to do.'

'It isn't. I've never known him to take any interest in things like that. Not ever. It's – it's really odd.'

'Maybe he was desperate.'

Laura flinches. 'Desperate? What about?'

Debbie pulls the sheet of paper with the map and the notes they've made on it and taps it gently. 'So far, the picture we're building up of Jim's state of mind isn't looking too promising, is it?' She jabs the biro onto next door. 'Let's assume for a minute, for the sake of argument, that everything each person on this street has told you is fact.'

Laura nods weakly.

'Well, in that case, Jim has a keyring with photos of some mystery children. A keyring that you've never seen, by the way.' She takes a sip of tea and moves the pen on. 'He referred to you by the wrong name when he was drunk.' She jabs the next house. 'Jane seemed to think he'd been married before, he's been spotted in London and pretended not to know Sonja, and he's been to Marjorie's to ask for a tarot reading on more than one occasion. Not to mention the birthday card from the dad you were told was dead...' She looks up at Laura's face. 'If we assume that all of these things are fact – which, of course, they might not be – then it seems as though Jim almost definitely had something to hide.'

Laura buries her face in her hands. Debbie's right. Of course she is. She's been so desperate to believe that Jim would never lie to her, or hurt her, that she's ignored all these alarm bells. But she can see by looking at it now, objectively, that even the way their marriage worked before Jim went missing was unconventional. How many couples have no contact with other people apart from work colleagues? How many wives know literally nothing about their husband's jobs – and have never thought to push for answers? Has she really been in denial for all these years?

'You're right,' she says. 'But what the hell do I do about it?'

'Well, we definitely can't give up now. It feels as though we're about to have a breakthrough.'

'Do you think? I don't see how.'

'We've still got to find out from Sonja whether she managed to find Jim again – or the man she believes to be Jim.' She looks up at her friend, and reaches for her hands across the table. 'We could tell the police what we've found?'

Laura shrugs. 'I doubt they'd take much notice. They haven't so far.'

Debbie shakes her head. 'You're probably right.'

Laura feels her heart dropping, her head filling with cotton wool. There's so much to take in. What has happened to the man she thought she knew – and if he isn't the person she married, who *is* he?

22

THEN – SEPTEMBER 1991

'I can't stay here.' I'd been trying to say the words for days, but just couldn't seem to get them out. But now, the night before Jim was due to go back to Leeds, they'd burst out of me like air from a pressure cooker.

Jim stopped his packing, a folded white shirt hovering in mid-air.

'What do you mean?'

I sighed, my breath shaky. I wasn't sure how to explain it to him. How could I convey the constant terror I felt every time I was alone in the flat? Or explain the ball of anxiety that sat in the pit of my belly like a stone, or the fact that I couldn't ever look out onto the street at the front of my own home in case I saw a shadowy figure lurking there again, watching me, waiting. Jim knew I was terrified my attacker would strike again, or that my stalker would return, but there was something else.

'The phone calls have started again.'

He paled; his eyes widened.

'When?'

'Last week. And twice the week before.'

He dropped the shirt into the top of his case. I couldn't read the expression on his face, but when he spoke again his voice was tight, guarded. 'But I changed the number. Are you certain? Could it not just have been a wrong number or a dodgy sales call?' He reached for my hands and threaded his fingers through mine. 'Because you know how much your imagination works overtime, love.'

I shook my head. As I'd stood in the darkness of the hallway listening to the person on the other end breathing, I'd been filled with terror, but now, with Jim here and in the cold light of day, I did have my doubts. Perhaps it had just been a wrong number and my brain had filled in the rest.

I stared at our hands, entwined on my lap, and shrugged. 'I was certain.' I looked up at him. 'But you're right, how would they know our new number?'

He smiled then and pulled me to him, enveloped me in a tight hug. I pressed my cheek into his chest and listened to his heartbeat thrum-thrum next to my ear.

At moments like these, when Jim was here and he was holding me, I felt as though I was being ridiculous. Of course you can get through a few days on your own, I'd tell myself, you're being daft. And often it worked. Until Jim actually left, and then the demons would come rushing straight back in again. I needed to remind myself of this now and try and get him to understand that it was about more than just the phone calls.

I pulled away from him and clasped my hands in my lap. I stared at my fingers and listened to my raggedy breathing.

'I still don't want to be here any more.' My voice was shaky. Beside me, Jim said nothing. 'I want to move somewhere else. Somewhere safe.'

'Somewhere out of London?'

I nodded.

'But nowhere is completely safe, Lola. What do you think is going to happen if we live somewhere else? Do you think you'll be happy and relaxed again?'

'I don't know, Jim. But I do know I have to try.' A sob escaped me and I ran my hand up and down my arm. My skin was pale and covered in goosebumps.

'Hey, hey, Lola, don't get upset. You just sprang this on me, that's all.'

I looked at him. 'Will you at least think about it?'

He hesitated a moment and my heart stopped. Then he nodded, snapped his suitcase shut and said, 'I'll give it some thought.'

* * *

Over the next few days while Jim was away I tried my best to ignore the gnawing anxiety about being alone, and spent hour upon hour trawling through the Yellow Pages and ringing estate agents in towns and villages all across the Home Counties. Jim hadn't actually agreed to move, but he had agreed to think about it, and I knew that if I could find somewhere not too far outside London he was more likely to agree to it. I'd suggested we move to Leeds but he'd seemed absolutely adamant he didn't want to live there.

'But it would make life a lot easier and would mean we can be together all the time,' I'd said.

'My life is here, with you,' he'd replied. 'I don't have any connections with Leeds, it's just a place to work for me, and I prefer to keep my work and my home life separate. Besides, you'd still be alone when I was in London.'

So I'd agreed to look closer to home. More than anything it was good to have something to occupy my mind – and it definitely meant I drank a lot less – and by the time Jim got back four days later I had a pile of house details to show him.

'You really are serious about this, aren't you?'

'I am.' Just the thought of being in a place where terror didn't lurk round every corner or down every shadowy street, somewhere people looked out for each other, was already making me feel happier, more relaxed. I was convinced that, if we moved to the right place, I'd get better. I just needed to convince Jim.

Over the next few days we arranged to see a few houses. 'Do you think you'll be able to come and see them with me?' Jim asked me.

I felt my stomach roll over. In my enthusiasm for finding a new home I hadn't even considered the fact that I'd have to leave the flat to go and look at it. I shook my head sadly. 'Can you go on your own?'

Jim sighed. 'Oh, Lola. Are you sure this is going to work?'

'It will, I'm sure of it. I just need a bit more time.'

'All right. But I'm still not convinced that running away from your problems is the solution.'

'I don't know what else to try.'

Jim paused then, and looked sheepish.

'What? What's wrong?'

He coughed. 'I've arranged for someone to come and check up on you while I'm not here.'

I froze. 'What?'

'I worry about you here all alone while I'm away, so someone is going to come and check up on you, get some food in for you, that sort of thing, on the days I'm not here. A woman, of course.'

I felt as though my words were stuck in my throat like a sharp piece of flint. 'I—' I didn't know what to say. How could Jim have done this without even asking me? 'I can't have someone here.'

'But I'm here, and Debbie comes round sometimes, doesn't

she?'

'But this is different, Jim!'

'How? How is it different?'

I wanted to scream. 'Because it is!' I was shaking, and could feel my palms become sticky with a sheen of sweat. I sat down and put my head between my knees and took some long, deep breaths and slowly I felt my breathing return to normal. I raised my head and Jim was sitting opposite me, waiting. He hadn't moved to comfort me as he usually did and I assumed it was because he was so angry.

'I'm sorry. I just – the thought of a stranger coming in here is almost as bad as the idea of leaving the flat on my own. I can't explain it. It's like my body goes into flight mode, and I can't think straight.' I looked at him pleadingly. 'Please can you cancel it?'

He nodded stiffly. 'Okay.'

He wouldn't look me in the eye, and I walked round to him, wriggled myself in between the table and his chest and squeezed myself onto his knee. Then I pulled his chin round to face me and planted a kiss on his lips. 'I'm sorry, Jim. I love you.'

His eyes were filled with tears and I realised it was the first time I'd ever seen him cry. 'Oh, darling, what have I done to you?'

'I'm sorry, love. I just...' He rubbed his face. 'I'm just finding this all so hard to navigate.' He looked me right in the eye. 'I love you so much, I just want to see you happy. I want us to be happy again.'

'We are happy, aren't we?'

He shook his head and my heart felt as if it had been sliced in half. 'No, we're not. We're just surviving.'

I dropped my head onto his chest and we sat like that for a while, holding each other. Eventually, Jim spoke. 'I'll cancel it. But we'd better hope that this move changes something, because I don't know what else to do.'

23

NOW – 12 OCTOBER 1992

Corner Shop
Tracy Atkinson

The wind shakes the tree in the middle of the cul-de-sac so hard it's a wonder any of the leaves have the strength to cling on. Laura stands by her front door, stiff-limbed, watching as they detach themselves from their branches and dance and swirl towards the ground, distributing themselves among neighbouring gardens.

She inhales deeply, letting the cool air fill her lungs, and releases it slowly, puffing out her cheeks and letting her shoulders relax.

She's decided to try and leave the house on her own again today. Debbie is working and Ben no doubt is too. Besides, she doesn't feel she can keep asking him for help given that she hardly knows him, even though she's fairly certain he would have agreed. Jim's words from more than a year ago keep repeating themselves in her mind – *running away from your problems isn't the solution* –

and she knows that, even though he appears not to have taken his own advice, he is probably right. She needs to face this head-on if she's going to get anywhere.

Besides, she desperately needs food – and vodka – so she has no choice but to face the world and try to make it to the corner shop.

She can do this.

She pulls on her coat and boots and grabs her bag. List in pocket, she takes a deep breath and prepares to leave the safety of, not only her home, but her street for the first time in more than eight months.

The wind is blowing wildly outside and, as it's a week day, there is nobody about. She glances around the cul-de-sac at the houses that are no longer such a mystery to her and feels an unexpected rush of warmth. The occupants are a real mish-mash of characters but they've all been so kind and welcoming in the last couple of weeks. And although she hasn't yet got any closer to finding Jim, she has discovered some things about her husband that she hadn't previously known. Even more importantly, she truly believes these people could become her friends, and friends are something she definitely needs right now.

Maybe this really could be a new beginning, whether Jim comes back or not.

She shuts the front door firmly behind her and steps into the garden with a renewed sense of resolve. For the first time in a long time the world doesn't seem to tip as she looks up at the sky. There's no sense of impending doom, no panic attack, no feeling that she's about to black out. Her hands still shake with nerves and it's taking all her strength to put one foot in front of the other, but she's doing it, and she's doing it alone.

This is progress.

At the gate she turns right and inches slowly along the path, trailing her fingertips along her garden wall. She doesn't look back or up, but keeps her eyes trained on the ground, the flip-flip-flip of her shoes mesmerising, keeping her grounded. The wall underneath her hand changes and she realises she's reached the end of her own garden and is now walking past Carol and Arthur's house, her hand resting lightly on their neat wooden fence. She wonders whether anyone is watching her and if they are what they're thinking, but she doesn't dare look up in case she loses her nerve. So she continues, slowly, slowly, until the fence runs out and she realises with a jolt that she's at the end of the street. She's made it!

Directly ahead of her is Hawthorn Road, and to her right Evergreen Close spirals off. This is the one she needs to take. She isn't entirely sure how far along the road the shop is, but she's got this far, she can make it now.

She turns right and, with nothing else to hold onto, she clutches her bags tightly in front of her. The wind whips hair around her face and she wishes she'd brought a hat, but she ploughs on, pushing strands from her face as she watches her feet, one, two, one, two, one, two.

She passes nobody and when, finally, she looks up she's amazed to see the shop in front of her. It's only small, and banners along the front window advertise the fact they sell the local newspaper, ice creams and lots of different types of beer and wine. There's a small ads display selling sofas, motorbikes and guitar lessons, and a stack of newspapers, half covered with a sheet of plastic that flaps about in the wind. She stands outside for a moment and imagines walking inside, making small talk with the woman behind the counter, then leaving and walking home with her goodies in a carrier bag. It's so ordinary and yet she hasn't done something like it for so long it feels like an impossible hurdle.

She steps forward and pushes the door open and a bell

above her head tinkles, announcing her arrival. A woman has her back to her and is chatting with another woman behind the counter – probably Tracy, she realises – but they don't turn round, and just carry on as though she isn't there. Relieved, she makes her way along the left aisle, picking up a loaf of bread, some beans, a packet of pasta, a small cake, some eggs and tomato sauce. She marvels at how it feels so alien, yet so familiar at the same time.

She grabs a few more things and then hovers for a while in the spirit aisle. She really wants to buy several bottles to last her. But she also doesn't want anyone to know she has a problem. Because, well, she doesn't, does she? She just needs this, for now, to get through a tricky time. It's like medicine.

As a compromise she picks up three one-litre bottles of vodka and puts them in her basket, which is now overflowing and heavy. The women are still chatting but their voices are low and she can't make out what they're saying.

Painting a smile on her face, she walks up to the counter and heaves her basket on it.

'Oh, hello, Laura!' Laura looks up to see Jane smiling at her warmly.

'Oh, hi,' she says, returning the smile. To her surprise she finds she really is pleased to see her. 'Not at work today?'

Jane reaches out and squeezes the top of Laura's arm. 'I'm on my way. It's *so* good to see you out and about,' she says. She turns to the woman behind the counter. 'Tracy, this is Laura. Jim's wife.'

Tracy's eyebrows lift from her forehead and her wrinkled face almost folds in on itself as she smiles. 'Oh, hello, Laura, I've heard lots about you. It's wonderful to meet you at last.' Her face crumples. 'Oh, but Jane's just been telling me about Jim. I thought it was strange that I hadn't seen him in a while. I'm so sorry. Is there any news?'

Laura shakes her head. 'Not yet. The police haven't been in touch for a while.'

'It's such a shame, it really is. I do hope he comes back soon.'

'Actually, you might be able to help, mightn't she, Laura?' Jane says, turning back to Tracy.

'Oh, really, how?' Tracy leans her elbows on the counter and rests her chin in her hands. Jane nods at Laura to take over.

'Oh, right, yes,' she says. 'We – I, I mean...' She stops, her words getting tangled round each other. Seeing her distress, Jane takes over.

'Laura is trying to find out whether any of us know anything about Jim's disappearance,' she says.

'What do you mean?'

'Well, you know, whether we saw Jim behaving any differently before he went missing, or whether he ever said anything that, looking back, might seem odd.' She looks at Laura. 'I told Laura he'd been helping me with me divorce papers, and there had been a few other things, so she's trying to piece together what might have happened. That's right, isn't it?'

Laura nods. 'Yes, in a nutshell.'

Tracy nods slowly. 'I see. And how are you getting on?'

Laura hesitates. She is starting to piece together a jigsaw in her mind about what might have led Jim to up and leave, but she's not ready to share it yet. After all, it all points to the fact that she didn't really know her husband at all – and what sort of wife does that make her? 'I'm getting there,' she says.

Jane turns back to Tracy. 'Do you remember Jim acting differently just before he disappeared, Trace?'

Tracy ponders for a moment, then shakes her head.

'No, he didn't say anything to me, love.' She frowns, deep in thought. 'Although...'

Laura freezes, her heart caught in her throat. 'What? Have you thought of something?'

Tracy shakes her head again slowly. 'I'm not sure. It was a long time before Jim went missing, a few months ago, so it's probably nothing. Only—'

Laura waits, holding her breath. Could this be the final piece of the puzzle that she needs?

'A young girl came in here, asking for you.'

'For me? Are you sure?'

'Yes, I'm fairly sure it was you. She described you, although of course that meant nothing to me at the time. But she said Laura, and she mentioned Jim. Anyway, I said I couldn't help her because – well, you never know who someone is or what they might want, do you? So you can't go giving out people's details to any Tom, Dick or Harry.'

Come on, come on, Laura willed.

'Anyway, I mentioned it to Jim when he next came in and he looked confused and said I must have been mistaken, that she must have been looking for someone else.' She shrugs. 'So I put it out of me mind, like. I hadn't thought about it at all since then, and it's only now you've come round asking that I've thought of it again.'

Laura doesn't know what to say. It isn't the huge revelation she was hoping for, although she isn't sure what that would have been. But it isn't nothing either.

'What did she look like, this girl?'

'Really young, about nineteen I fink, small slip of a thing. Long dark hair, all over her eyes, baggy trousers, lots of make-up. She seemed nervous, and I didn't take much notice of her, to be honest.'

Laura can't think of anyone who fits that description, although... *Could* it have been the person she saw hanging around her flat in London that time, the one she chased down the street? That person was small, possibly a young girl. But – what on earth would they want with her? And, more to the point, how on earth would they have known she's here? Nobody apart from Debbie knows she's even moved, as far as she is aware.

No, sadly, although this seemed promising at first, the chances are it's just another red herring. As Jim said, Tracy must have misunderstood. Disappointment seeps into her.

'Thank you. I'll keep it in mind,' Laura says, pushing her basket forwards. 'Can I pay for these?'

'Course love.' Tracy begins ringing the items up and loading them into a thick white carrier bag. She doesn't flinch at the three vodka bottles and Laura is relieved.

'That's twenty-five pound thirty pence please love,' Tracy says, and Laura hands over two twenty-pound notes. As she counts out her change Jane speaks.

'Oh, I meant to ask how you got on with Jim's things.'

'Oh, I—' Laura stops, unsure how much to reveal to this woman she's only met once. She's never been one for gossip, likes to keep her own business to herself. But then again, she likes Jane, and if she wants people to help her, she needs to learn to be a little more trusting. 'I found a birthday card from his dad.'

'Right...' Jane sounds uncertain. 'I told Laura she had to search through Jim's stuff,' Jane explains to Tracy. 'Remember what I found in Robbie's piles of crap?'

'God yes.' Tracy hands Laura a ten-pound note and some coins, which she slips into her purse. 'And what did this card say?'

'It wasn't what it said. It's – Jim told me his dad died when he was twelve. This was a thirtieth birthday card.'

'And you're absolutely sure it was for your Jim?'

Laura shakes her head. 'Not completely sure, no. But I don't know who else it could have been for.' She stops. Is she being paranoid? The truth is she can't be certain of anything. All the 'clues' she's collected so far are nothing more than a collection of ifs and buts. If she really is going to find Jim, she's going to need something more concrete.

'Oh, love,' Jane says. 'I'm so sorry. Listen, maybe Jim does have nowt to hide. I mean, I always thought he was a pretty good guy, and I'm the biggest cynic there is.'

Laura nods miserably. 'Maybe. But then again, he's gone, hasn't he, and left me all on my own?'

'That's true.'

All three women stand for a moment, unsure what to say next. Then the silence is broken by the tinkle of the bell over the door and they turn in unison to see Ben. He stops dead. 'Oh, hello.' He scans their faces, then his face breaks into a huge grin. 'Laura! You made it all the way here!'

'I did.' She smiles back shyly and behind her Jane and Tracy exchange a look.

'Hello, Ben, love, everything all right?' Tracy says and he tears his eyes away from Laura to meet her gaze.

'Yes, great, thanks, Trace.'

'What can I get you?'

'Just this paper, please,' he says, waving it in front of his face awkwardly.

She rings it up and he looks at Laura again as he hands over the correct change. 'I'm not being a sexist pig or anything, but those bags look heavy – would you like me to give you a hand?'

Laura glances down at the carrier bags cutting into her hand and nods gratefully. 'Would you mind? Thanks so much.'

He takes a bag from her and then they leave with another tinkle of the bell, calling out their goodbyes as they go.

'Well, well, well,' Tracy says as soon as they're out of earshot.

'I told you.'

'I think you're right. But I don't think it's just him, you know.'

'No. Quite.' Jane grins. 'Oh, I know it's not the right time to be matchmaking but – you know, if Jim doesn't come home, wouldn't they make a cute couple?'

'They would. And who wouldn't like him? He's such a lovely man. In fact if I were thirty years younger I'd be making a play for him myself.' Tracy chuckles wickedly.

'Well, let's see,' Jane says, smiling to herself.

* * *

'Thank you so much,' Laura says as they head back towards Willow Crescent. Between them, Rocky tugs on his lead, sniffing the ground. Laura is surprised how pleased she is to see Ben.

'It's no problem,' he says.

They walk along in silence for a moment. Laura feels unexpectedly calm, out here on the street with cars passing by, when she's walking beside Ben. There's something about him that soothes her.

Ben, on the other hand, is in turmoil. He's been trying not to see Laura too much over the last few days because he's become increasingly aware that whenever he spends time with her, he likes her a little bit more. And there is absolutely nothing less appropriate than developing feelings for a married woman searching for her missing husband. Staying away has seemed the easier option: that, and hoping that his feelings might diminish if he ignores them.

But now here she is, and his feelings haven't dissipated in the slightest. In fact, if anything, he likes Laura even more. There's just something about her that makes his stomach do a little flutter when he sees her. He knows that Tracy noticed his reaction too, which was why he couldn't get away fast enough. The last thing he needs is for someone else to point out how wrong his burgeoning feelings are.

They turn into Willow Crescent and a few steps later turn into Laura's front garden. 'Would you like to come in for a cup of tea?' she says. 'I've got some cake too.' She holds up her carrier bag awkwardly.

Ben wants to scream, YES, YES, YES! But instead he smiles and says, 'Are you sure?'

'Absolutely. It would be nice to have some company.' *Your company* she doesn't say.

'I'd love to – if you don't mind Rocky coming too?'

'Course not.' She bends and ruffles the top of the dog's soft head.

Ben doesn't dare look round as he walks up Laura's path and enters her house, because he doesn't want to know who might be watching them.

Over the next half an hour they drink tea and talk while Rocky snores gently at their feet. Ben tells Laura about Helen and how hard it was when she died; he tells her about his love of cycling, and how he used to play football semi-professionally before he realised he was never going to make it and his father told him to find a proper job; he tells her about setting up his own architectural firm and how many hours he had to work for the first few years, and how when Helen died he regretted those hours spent away from her. He tells her about how Rocky has become his lifeline since he's been on his own.

In return Laura finds herself opening up in a way she hasn't for a long time to anyone other than Debbie. She tells him about her love of cooking; how she used to spend time baking with her dad, how she misses her mum and keeps imagining picking up the phone and speaking to her, asking for her help. She tells him about meeting Jim, and about their wedding in Gretna Green and how it wasn't the day she'd always dreamed of. And she tells him about the night she was attacked.

'I always thought that was the day that mine and Jim's marriage started to fall apart,' she says. 'But now I'm not sure it was ever right in the first place.'

The words hover in the air between them for a moment, Laura wondering why she's said them out loud, Ben wondering whether he should acknowledge them.

Laura meets Ben's eye and it takes everything he has not to turn away. He wonders whether she can tell how confused he is, how much he's fighting his feelings.

As Laura looks at Ben, her mind is in just as much turmoil. She didn't mean to say those words, but now she has she can see that they're true. She and Jim were never right together. He's always had control over the marriage, and she's starting to wonder whether she's mistaken a feeling of security for love.

Debbie was right: what sort of marriage is it when she doesn't know anything about the man she's married to? It's just a shame it's taken Jim walking out on her to make her realise there was something awry all along.

'I'm sorry, I shouldn't have said that,' Laura says eventually. She looks away.

'It's fine.' What else can he say? He stands, suddenly aware he probably shouldn't be here any more, alone with this woman. 'I should be going,' he says, clipping Rocky's lead on. The dog wags his tail half-heartedly.

Laura stands too and they turn towards the door at the same time, bumping into each other as they do. They both stop dead. There's barely more than an inch between them and the air hums with tension. Ben isn't breathing, while Laura feels her breath coming in short gasps as they both wonder what's going to happen next. It's been a long time since Laura wanted a man to be this close to her, even Jim, and yet she can't ignore the fact that she's hoping for more. Then Rocky barks and breaks the moment, and Ben leaps away and opens the door, his face burning.

'Thanks for the tea,' he mumbles, looking down at his shoes.

'Thank you for walking me home and – and listening.' Then she leans forward, presses her lips to his cheek and closes the door, leaving them both wondering what on earth just happened.

24

THEN – FEBRUARY 1992

My eyelids felt heavy but I forced them open and the room slowly came into focus. I didn't recognise where I was, and my chest began to tighten.

'Hello, love.' Jim's voice was close by and I turned my head to see where he was. I found him sitting in an armchair – our old armchair – by a window, watching me. I pushed myself up to sitting and felt my head swim with the effort.

'Are we here?'

He nodded. 'We arrived about three hours ago but the tranquillisers the doctor gave you must have been strong because you've been knocked out for ages.'

I rubbed my eyes and took in my surroundings. I'd seen this room on the estate agent's details many times, but it looked smaller in real life. This was the living room, which I remembered was at the front of the house. The flowery wallpaper was old-fashioned, and the paintwork was chipped, but none of that mattered, because we were here, and I no longer had to be terrified of my own shadow. Heavy net curtains hung at the window so I couldn't see the street outside, but I wondered whether I'd be able to manage it. I stood slowly and wobbled my way over to where Jim was sitting, and he stood to take my elbow.

'Take it easy, you've only just woken up.'

'I want to see out of the window.'

'Come on, then.' He steered me the last few steps and I held my breath as he pulled the net curtain aside. I leapt back as if I'd been electrocuted, and turned away.

'It's okay, it's closed,' Jim said, squeezing my shoulders. I turned to face him. Worry lined his face and guilt pierced me.

'I'm sorry. I'm just not quite ready. I'm sure it'll be fine though.' I didn't dare tell him that the feeling I'd had when I'd looked outside just then was exactly the same as it had been from out of the London flat. I'd begged him to move here, and he'd agreed despite his reluctance. I owed it to him to try as hard as I could to make this work.

'You sit down and I'll make us something to eat,' he said.

* * *

Even though I was glad Jim had taken two whole weeks off to be with me while we settled into the house, I couldn't help feeling resentful whenever he went out. Each time he did he came back with news of somewhere else he'd discovered, a shop he'd found, or a neighbour he'd chatted to. It seemed as if Jim was settling in really well, and, although I should have been pleased, I just felt jealous and even more cut off from everything than I had before.

'Come with me, love,' he suggested time and time again, but just the thought of stepping outside the front door left me so crippled with panic I couldn't move.

In fact it soon became clear that, far from helping me to overcome my agoraphobia, the move had only made it worse, because now I didn't even live close to Debbie, the only other person I still saw.

As the day approached for Jim to return to work, I could feel my anxiety levels rising at the thought of being left alone, so when he was late back from a supermarket shop one evening and the doorbell went I actually screamed. I clapped my hand over my mouth and listened to my pulse thump in my temples, a pain shoot across my neck. Since we'd arrived nobody had rung the doorbell, and Jim would have taken a key. I had no idea how long I'd been sitting there, frozen in terror, balled up on the edge of the sofa, by the time I heard Jim's key turn in the lock and the whoosh of cold air rush in with him, but that was where he found me.

He flicked on the light and I squinted up at him.

'What's going on? Has something happened?' he said, stalking across the room and crouching down next to me.

'I—' I started. 'There was someone at the door.' It sounded pathetic even to my own ears.

'It was probably just Carol from next door.' He held up a casserole dish I hadn't noticed in his hands. 'I found it on the doorstep with a note.'

I sat up and took the note from him.

Dear Jim and Laura.

Welcome to the neighbourhood. We hope you'll be very happy here. Please enjoy this shepherd's pie.

From Carol and Arthur at no 1

'Oh.' Shame washed over me.

Jim shuffled onto the sofa beside me and pressed his hand against my cheek. 'What are we going to do with you, love?' he said, his voice soft. 'Are you going to be all right with me gone tomorrow?'

I nodded, determined to show him I was trying. That he hadn't made a mistake marrying me, staying with me.

'I'll be fine. I just panicked, that's all.'

He looked at me for a moment longer, then stood. 'Right, well, I'd better get this shopping in from the car otherwise you'll have nothing to eat all week.'

I followed him into the hallway and waited while he unloaded the bags, then helped unpack the shopping in the kitchen. As we put food away in the freezer and filled the cupboards with tins, I noticed there wasn't much booze.

'Did you get the wine and vodka I put on the list?' I said, trying not to make myself sound too desperate.

'I got you a couple of bottles of Chardonnay,' Jim said curtly.

'Is that all?'

'Yes, Laura, that is all.' I was aware that he was no longer unpacking the shopping and was watching me instead. 'You have to stop drinking as much. It's going to kill you.'

'I don't drink that much.' My face flamed. Jim knew as well as I did that was a bare-faced lie. He said nothing more about it, just gave a nod and turned back to the bags, but I knew he was furious.

For the rest of that evening, as well as the last couple of days before he went back to work, there was a brittleness to Jim that I'd never seen before. The dark circles beneath his eyes suggested he wasn't sleeping, and for the first time ever I got the feeling that my husband would rather be anywhere other than at home with me.

25

NOW – 14 OCTOBER 1992

'Thank you so much for coming round, I'm not sure I could have done this on my own,' Laura says, smiling nervously.

Ben smiles back. 'It's a pleasure.'

The police rang that morning and said they had an update, and could they come round this afternoon. Even though she begged them to tell her over the phone, they insisted on doing it their way, which means she's been in a heightened state of anxiety all morning. Has Jim's body been found? Have they found him alive, but with amnesia? Or is it something less dramatic than that? She can't stand the suspense. So when Ben called to see if she needed anything, she asked if he'd come round and stay with her while she waited for the police to arrive. She was surprised by how much she hoped he'd say yes.

'Aren't you meant to be working?' Laura says now, sliding a draughts piece across the board.

'Yep. But there have to be some perks to being your own boss.' Ben hops his piece across three of Laura's and gathers them all up sheepishly. 'Sorry.'

She studies the board for a moment. She suggested a game of

draughts to distract her from the worry of waiting for the police, but in fact she's finding Ben himself quite a distraction – which is probably why she's losing so badly.

'I surrender,' she says, pushing the board away in defeat.

'Oh—' Ben starts, but before he can get any further there's a knock at the door. Laura freezes.

'Do you want me to answer it?' Ben stands.

'Do you mind?'

Ben strides to the front door and Laura listens to the mumbled introductions, then the front door closes, there are footsteps along the hallway and three people appear in her kitchen – Ben, and two male police officers. She recognises one from before – PC Compton, she thinks he is called – but the other is older and more senior-looking. She wonders whether this is a bad sign. Her legs feel odd and she stays seated.

'Mrs Parks, I'm DI Baker and this is PC Compton.' The older officer, who is tall with the physique of a runner bean, introduces himself. 'Lovely to meet you.' He holds out his hand, which Laura shakes weakly. 'Mind if we sit down?'

'No, course.'

'Tea?' Ben asks, and they all nod.

DI Baker doesn't beat about the bush. 'Mrs Parks, as we mentioned this morning we have an update for you on the search for your husband, Jim Parks.' Laura focuses on the smattering of dandruff on the officer's collar. 'I don't know whether you were informed but last week we put out a call in the London area asking for anyone who sees someone matching your husband's description to come forward. We used the photo you gave us.'

'No, I didn't know.'

'Right, sorry about that, you should have been informed. Anyway, as I said, we hoped it might give us some new leads.'

Laura nods as Ben places mugs of tea in front of everyone.

'Sugar's here,' he says, ducking out of the way and taking a seat next to Laura. She has an urge to hold his hand – just for a bit of comfort, although she knows that would be entirely inappropriate, so she reaches for her mug instead and wraps her hands round it to steady them.

The officer starts speaking again and she listens hopefully.

'We had all the usual jokers trying it on, of course, sending in mistaken sightings or quite frankly ridiculous ones, and for a while we weren't hopeful.' He pauses to take a sip of his scalding-hot tea.

Come on, come on, Laura wants to scream.

'But then yesterday we received a call that seemed to be genuine, and we have reason to believe it could be a sighting of your husband.'

Laura feels as though she might fall off the chair, and grips the sides of it to steady herself. Her head is swimming and the faces of the officers in front of her are blurred.

'Laura, are you all right?' Ben's voice sounds as though it's coming from miles away. She turns to face him, and realises he has his hand on her arm. She doesn't pull away but her skin fizzes beneath his touch.

'Sorry, I—' She swallows down the lump in her throat. 'I – where? Where was this sighting?'

PC Compton consults his notes. 'Putney. South-west London,' he adds, when she doesn't respond.

She frowns in confusion. 'What makes you think this is definitely Jim?'

PC Compton shuffles uncomfortably in his seat and glances at his superior, who gives him a nod.

'There was actually more than one report, all in the space of a few hours,' he admits, his eyes darting between Laura and Ben. 'One of them took this.' He picks up a pink folder that Laura didn't notice before and produces a grainy photocopy, which he slides over to Laura. She picks it up and studies it.

The photo shows a shadowy image of a figure walking along a high street. It's terrible quality, and the person has their back turned to the camera, head turned slightly to the left so you can make out one cheek and half an eye. The nose is a blur as though they were moving when the photo was taken. Whoever it is, is wearing a dark jacket with the collar pulled up. Laura looks up.

'What's this?'

'We have reason to believe this might be your husband, Mrs Parks.'

Laura looks back at the photo, her heart thumping, and pulls it closer to her face, but the image blurs even more. 'You think this is Jim?'

'We were hoping you might be able to confirm that to us,' the officer says.

Laura doesn't know what to say. She thought the police were coming here with some concrete evidence about Jim's whereabouts, one way or the other. Instead all they've brought is this grainy picture that's almost impossible to make out.

'Is this it?' She feels anger rising in her. All the days and weeks since Jim's disappearance, and all the months and years before that when she was trapped in her own home, barely living a life, come bubbling to the surface and it's all she can do not to rage and throw things around, to scream at them to get out.

Instead, she closes her eyes, takes a few slow, deep breaths.

'Mrs Parks?'

She opens her eyes but doesn't speak.

'Do you think this photo is of your husband, Jim Parks?'

'How on earth am I supposed to know? It's just a blur.'

The officer has the grace to look shame-faced. His superior takes over.

'I know it's hard, Mrs Parks, but unfortunately the person who took this photograph tried to take it without your husband – if that's who it is – noticing. He did say from the photo we shared that he was fairly certain it was him, but without confirmation from you there's very little we're able to do about following it up, unfortunately.'

Laura picks up the photo again and looks at it more closely. It's almost impossible to tell who this is a photo of. It has obviously been taken from a distance, and there are no distinctive clothes she recognises. Jim only really wore suits or dark clothing, jumpers, T-shirts in a variation of greys, blues and blacks. How is she ever supposed to be certain this is him?

But then again, if she wants them to follow it up, she's going to have to give them something.

She sets the photo back on the table and smooths it down with her palm. 'I think it could be him.'

Ben's whips his head round to look at her. 'Do you?'

She passes him the photo and turns back to the officers. 'I do. I can't be 100 per cent sure, but there's something about the way he's holding his head that makes me think it could be him.'

Ben hands the photo back but doesn't speak. He's fairly sure Laura has no idea whether this is a photo of Jim, but he understands why she's claiming it is. Wouldn't he do the same? And wouldn't it be great if it is, and they are one step closer to finding Jim and bringing him home?

So why does he have a lump of disappointment in the very pit of his belly?

'Thank you, Mrs Parks, that's what we were hoping you would say.'

'So, what happens now?'

'Now we need to get back in touch with the witness to gather a few more details and see if we can follow up any more leads.' He coughs. 'There is one more thing though.'

Laura's heart stops. 'What?'

'We called Mr Parks's place of work.'

'In Leeds?' Laura wonders how they found out the name of Jim's company, although she supposes that is their job.

He glances at his colleague. 'Well, that's the thing.'

'Wh–what do you mean?'

The officer shuffles in his seat and steeples his fingers together beneath his chin. 'The thing is, Mrs Parks, that your husband doesn't work in Leeds. Never has.'

For a moment the ground beneath Laura seems to tilt. 'But he does! He leaves here every Monday morning and comes back on a Thursday night. He – he's been doing it since just after we met.'

Laura isn't sure whether she wants to hear any more, but she knows she has no choice. That whatever revelation comes next is coming whether she likes it or not.

'I'm afraid he hasn't, Mrs Parks.'

Laura glances at Ben, but she can't read his expression.

'So where – where does he work, then?'

'That's just it. We're not sure.' He looks down at his paperwork. 'We're still looking for him, but one thing we are sure about is that a Mr Parks has never worked for any hotel chain based in Leeds – because there is no hotel chain based in Leeds. I'm very sorry.'

Laura can't speak, her throat has dried up and she longs to throw her arms round Ben and find some comfort from him, but instead she sits rigid on her chair, her hands tucked beneath her thighs, and watches as the police officer shuffles some papers and returns them to his pink folder. He stands, and PC Compton follows suit.

'I'm very sorry, Mrs Parks. Please rest assured that we're doing everything we can to find out what has happened to your husband, but you must remember that a missing man can't always take priority.' He ducks his head. 'Thank you for the tea. We won't keep you any longer.' They start to make their way towards the front door and, as Ben sees them out, Laura stares at the tabletop, tracing the lines of wood with her finger. She has no idea what any of this means, but she knows she needs to speak to Sonja to find out whether she ever saw Jim again.

She needs to track her husband down – no matter what happens once she finds him.

26

THEN – APRIL 1992

'Jim, come quickly!' I threw myself down on the bed, and seconds later Jim was at the bedroom door, out of breath from taking the stairs two at a time.

'What is it? What's happened?'

I was breathless too, not from exertion, but from sheer terror. I lifted my shaky arm and pointed at the blinds. 'Out there.' My voice was a croak.

Jim stalked across the room and yanked the cord of the blinds so they shot up. I shrieked. 'Jim, no, they'll see us! Put the blind down!'

He continued peering up and down the cul-de-sac, squinting into the semi-darkness. I cowered on the bed, head against my knees, eyes closed. Only when I heard the sound of the blinds being lowered again and the curtains being closed did I dare to look up. When I did it was to find Jim watching me, an unreadable expression on his face.

'Did you see them?'

Jim shook his head slowly and lowered himself onto the bed

beside me. Our thighs and upper arms were touching but he didn't move to comfort me.

'I don't know what you think you saw but there's no one out there, Laura. Again.'

'There might not be now but there was. Right in the middle of the crescent, under the big willow tree. I—'

'How did you see them?'

'Wh–what do you mean?'

Jim let out a huge sigh. 'I mean, how did you see them if you had the blinds closed?'

'I—' I stopped. 'You don't believe me,' I said, sadly.

He still didn't look at me. 'It's just hard, Lola. It's not that I think you're lying, more that your mind is playing tricks on you, which isn't healthy either.'

'But it happened before, in London, before all this, before the attack,' I said, the words falling over themselves in their scramble to be heard. 'I thought there was someone watching me and then there was, and I chased them down the street, you know I did, I told you and—' I stopped when I saw the look on Jim's face. 'You didn't believe me then either.' I felt like a child whose parents had been humouring them.

Jim rubbed his face, clasped his hands in his lap, and finally, he looked at me. 'It's not that I don't believe you *think* you saw someone there.' He paused, shook his head. 'The thing is, even if there had been someone watching you all those months ago, how do you think they would have found you again, here, now?'

'I—'

'It's not's possible, love,' he said, taking my hands and holding them gently. 'Nobody knows where we live, so there's no way anyone who meant you harm would have been able to track you down.'

I looked down at where our hands were joined and wondered whether what he was saying was true. *Could* I have been imagining it, even back then? But I know I saw someone, and I chased them down the street. And this person I saw just now – who I *think* I saw just now – why would I imagine them if they weren't there? Why would my mind do that to me?

But of course it would. My stupid mind wouldn't even let me leave my own house. It could do anything it liked.

'You're right,' I said, my voice small.

'Look at me,' Jim said, cupping my chin so I was forced to look right at him. I couldn't read the expression in his eyes. 'You can't keep doing this to yourself. I've got to go back to work tomorrow and I can't bear the thought of you here alone, terrified at the slightest noise, or imagining things that aren't there.' He let out a sigh, his cheeks puffing out. 'I've been trying to ask you this for a while, but will you consider seeing someone? A psychiatrist, or a counsellor of some sort?'

'You think I've gone mad?'

'No, I don't. But I do think you've had a terrible trauma and I want to help you. You can't go on like this. We can't go on like this.'

My heart thudded and bile rose in my throat. 'You'd *leave* me?'

A flicker of something crossed his face then disappeared before I could read it. 'No. But if you won't get help then at least get some drugs, some Prozac or tranquillisers, something so that these *episodes* can stop. Because something has to give. That's all I'm saying.' He stood abruptly and I looked up at him and there was so much I wanted to say – how I loved him, *needed* him, how I wanted him to stop working away and stay with me all the time – but it all seemed to be stuck in my throat. Then he moved away, and the moment had passed. At the doorway he turned and looked back at me. 'Promise me you'll at least think about it?'

I gave a small nod. 'Promise.'

* * *

After dinner, when Jim had gone to sleep and the house was quiet, I crept downstairs to the front room and stood peering through the tiny gap in the blinds.

Was Jim right? Was I going mad? Did I really need drugs to get me through this?

A movement caught the corner of my eye and I froze, my body on high alert. I stood watching, breath held, but there was no more movement, no more sound. The street was empty, the way it always was at this time of the night.

I walked through to the kitchen and poured a glass of water, downed it. My hands still shook. I knelt down and reached to the back of the cupboard under the sink and pulled out a bottle of vodka I kept hidden there, screwed the lid off and tipped my head back, letting the burning sensation fill my mouth, my throat, my stomach... I took another swig, and another, then almost smashed the bottle off the worktop with a clang. I stood still for a moment, waiting to see whether Jim had heard, whether he would come down to investigate and find me standing drinking vodka in the middle of the night like some desperate alcoholic. No wonder Jim didn't want to live like this any more, no wonder he was so desperate for me to do something, *anything* to get better, to get back the Laura I was when we met.

Who'd want this version of me? Even I didn't like her.

I felt totally and utterly alone. This wasn't something I could talk to Jim about, and although Debbie loved me, I didn't want to burden her any more than I already had. I'd alienated everyone else.

I was suddenly struck with an overwhelming urge to ring my mum. But I knew I couldn't. I was far too ashamed after all this time to ask her for help.

I'd never felt so utterly alone. And it was all my fault.

27

NOW – 17 OCTOBER 1992

Laura hovers at the entrance to Carol and Arthur's house and takes a deep breath.

'You've done this before,' Debbie says, pressing her palm into her friend's back.

'Not with this many people at the same time.'

'It'll be fine.' Debbie smiles reassuringly.

Carol has decided to call a meeting – what she grandiosely called an 'Emergency Street Meeting' when she came round to tell them about it the day before. Although the last thing Laura feels like doing is being in a room full of people she doesn't know very well, she didn't have the heart to refuse when Carol was being so kind. Besides, with Debbie and Ben by her side, she should be fine.

'Ready?' Ben reaches up to ring the doorbell. But before Laura can reply, the door swings open.

'You made it!' Carol says, clapping her hands together as they step inside.

Carol and Arthur's living room is packed, a hubbub of voices rising towards the ceiling, spilling out through the open window.

Laura's legs feel like matchsticks, all strength gone, but as she takes in the room and sees Jane smiling at her encouragingly, her nerves start to subside. The furniture has been rearranged, and Marjorie, Faye and Jane are lined up along the sofa, while Arthur sits beside them in his favourite armchair. Tracy has taken the other armchair, while Simon and Sonja are squeezed into the corner behind the living-room door, baby Amelie fast asleep in Sonja's arms. Debbie and Laura make their way towards the last two empty wooden chairs in the far corner, which have been brought through from the dining room, and Ben follows them, planning to sit on the floor beside Laura.

'Come and sit beside me, dear,' Marjorie calls to Ben, patting the arm of the sofa.

'Yes, you go there, it will be much more comfortable than the floor,' Carol agrees before he can object, so he settles reluctantly beside Marjorie.

Carol takes her place at the front of the room. Beside her is a small coffee table, a cork pinboard on the wall behind, while a foldable table down one wall groans with plates of sausage rolls, a quiche, cheese straws, some cheese and pineapple sticks and an enormous chocolate cake.

'You could have just stuck some Wotsits in a bowl and nobody would have cared,' Arthur said, looking up from his crossword as she bustled in and out all day.

'I know I could, Arthur, but this is important. It's got to be just right. I have standards.'

Fortunately for Arthur she didn't see his eyeroll or he would have received a clip round the ear with the damp tea towel slung over Carol's shoulder.

Carol claps again, loudly this time, and everyone stops talking and looks in her direction. She's in her element.

'Right, everyone, thank you for coming at such short notice.'

Someone coughs and an ancient ginger cat slinks its way round people's ankles. 'Shoo, Garfield, out.' After a shuffle of bodies while Arthur ejects the wayward cat, Carol clears her throat and resumes. 'As you all know, our friend and neighbour, Jim Parks, has now been missing for a month. And although the police are looking for him, they have found nothing yet. Which means it falls to us, Jim's friends and neighbours – and his wife, Laura, of course – to do whatever we can to find out what's happened to him.'

She pauses for effect. Nobody speaks.

'Right. Well, I know Laura has been to speak to all of you, but I thought it might be a good idea if we put together a trail of evidence and see if we might be able to work it out.'

She pulls out a large sheet of card from behind the sofa. In the middle she's written 'Jim' in huge red letters. The rest is blank.

'This is my evidence board. I thought we could all write on it the things we know about Jim's disappearance.'

All right, Juliet Bravo, Arthur thinks, smirking behind his hand. But Laura is touched that Carol has gone to so much effort.

'So, first, we have Laura,' Carol continues, turning her back to the room and writing in her neat handwriting. 'Laura suffers from agoraphobia. Jim becomes her carer. Hard work?'

She turns back to the room with a look of triumph. 'This is point number one.' She looks at Laura. 'Is there anything else I should add to this bit?' she says, uncertainly.

'No, that's fine, thank you, Carol.' Laura smiles encouragingly.

'Good. Well, the next point on the list is mine and Arthur's clue,' she says, writing

Carol and Arthur Loveday

on the board. 'We remembered that one day Jim had a keyring with photographs of two children on it, which he claimed were his niece and nephew. But according to Laura, Jim doesn't even have any siblings.' She adds

keyring, photos, niece and nephew?

below their names.

'Although we also decided we might have been mistaken,' Arthur pipes up. Carol throws him a dagger look.

'Yes, of course, dear, but at the moment we're just trying to collate the evidence.'

'But—'

'So, what's next?' Carol says, cutting off any further objections.

'We haven't seen Jim much at poker nights,' Ben offers. 'And there was the night he called Laura the wrong name.'

'Of course, that's an excellent clue,' Carol says. 'Can you tell the others while I write it on the board?'

'It's hard to remember because we'd all had quite a lot to drink —' he gives Laura an apologetic glance '—but when he was telling me about his wife he called her something like Kerry, or Cheryl. Something like that.' He runs his hand through his hair uncertainly.

The room is silent for a moment as everyone takes in this new piece of evidence and Carol finishes writing it on her board.

Jim called Laura Kerry or Cheryl.

'Okay, next on the list we must add Sonja, who believes she saw Jim a couple of weeks ago in Hyde Park, isn't that right, Sonja?' Carol says, barely able to control her excitement.

'Yes, that is correct,' Sonja says, her accent stronger than usual, her vowels clipped. 'I thought I saw him, but he didn't seem to recognise me when I spoke to him.' She turns to Laura. 'I've been meaning to come and tell you that I've been back several times since we spoke but I'm afraid I haven't seen him again,' she says, her pale face distraught. 'I'm so sorry, I really hoped I would.'

'It's fine. Thank you for trying.' Laura swallows down her disappointment.

'I won't give up though, I promise.'

Before Laura can reply, Carol is speaking again. She has already added:

Sonja, Jim sighting, Hyde Park

to her list and has now moved on to Jane. 'Jim was helping you with your divorce, isn't that right?' she asks as she prints.

Jane, divorce, Jim helped.

Jane nods and glances over at Laura. 'He offered to help me, and I assumed it was because he knew a bit about it because he'd been married before, but Laura says he hasn't.' *Sorry,* she mouths at Laura, who smiles to show her it's fine. And it really is. This whole process is helping to put some order to her chaotic thoughts, and she's more grateful than she thought she would be.

'Okay,' Carol says, her eyes shining. Arthur shuffles in his chair and reaches for a cheese straw as Carol turns towards Tracy.

Tracy tells us that a young woman came into the shop asking after Laura some time ago.

She writes it down on the board.

'We're not exactly sure that's linked,' Tracy clarifies. 'I told Jim about it and he said he had no idea who it might have been. She never came in again so it must have been a misunderstanding.'

'Be that as it may, I've added it to the board just in case,' Carol says officiously. 'We don't want to miss any vital evidence.' Carol turns to look at what she's written so far. 'Have I missed anything, or has anyone thought of anything new since we last spoke?'

There's a shuffling and a bit of mumbling, then Marjorie pipes up. 'I did a tarot reading for Laura, and the cards revealed that she needs to express her true emotions, stop clinging to a past that doesn't serve her well and find the right person to be with.'

Laura feels her face flame as everyone turns to look at her. She can hardly bring herself to look at Ben.

'Well, that doesn't mean anything, does it?' Carol blusters, and Laura has never been so grateful for Carol's lack of tact.

'Of course it means something,' Marjorie says, her voice louder, and Faye lays her hand on her mother's arm. 'I also told Laura that Jim liked a reading sometimes too, and *he* didn't think they were a load of old nonsense.'

Laura clears her throat. 'Yes, Mrs Phillips did say that—'

'Marjorie.'

'Marjorie did tell me that,' Laura corrects herself, 'and I was very grateful that she took the time to do it. Maybe we could add it to the board anyway?'

'Yes, we wouldn't want to miss any *vital evidence*,' Marjorie says, smiling with satisfaction as Carol huffs and writes down

tarot reading

at the bottom of her list.

'Anything else?' Carol says crossly, looking round the room and very deliberately avoiding Marjorie's gaze.

'I have something to add,' Debbie says.

'Do you?' Carol says.

Debbie looks at Laura, who takes over. 'Ben and I—' she

flushes at mentioning his name, aware that Jane will be interested in the fact they've spent time together '—we broke into a locked drawer in Jim's office at home and found – well, we found a card from Jim's dad for his thirtieth birthday.' She pauses and looks up. 'Jim told me his Dad died when he was twelve.'

Marjorie gasps. 'See, a past that doesn't serve her well,' she says to Faye, who holds her finger to her lips to shush her. Carol can barely contain her glee at this development.

'So, what do we think it means?' she says.

'I don't think Laura's sure,' Ben says. 'We wondered whether there might have been someone else called Jim in the family that she doesn't know about.'

Carol considers it for a moment, her pen to her lips. 'Does that seem likely, Laura?'

'Well—' She stops, unsure how much to reveal. 'Jim doesn't really have any family that I've known about. He told me his parents died when he was younger and I've never met anyone else. He's always said there's no one else around but I... I think we might be wise to add this to the list just in case.'

Carol adds

Jim's father still alive?

to the board and tries not to look too pleased about the situation. 'Right, I think that's everything, isn't it?' she says, looking round the room like an officious school marm.

'Actually there are a couple more things,' Laura says, and Carol stops in her tracks.

'Oh?'

'The police came to speak to me a couple of days ago and said there has been a possible sighting of Jim in London.'

'Really?'

'Well, that's marvellous.' Carol and Arthur both speak at the same time.

'Where was this?' Sonja says. 'Was it near to where I saw him?'

Laura shakes her head. 'It was in Putney. South-west London,' she adds.

'So are they trying to find him?' Carol's words are tripping over themselves in her excitement at this new lead. Oh, she knew she'd make a good detective, she always guesses the endings before Arthur does on *The Bill*.

'Someone claims to have seen him and they managed to take a photo,' Laura explains. 'So police are trying to find out more.' She doesn't mention the fact that she wasn't – and still isn't – entirely convinced that the blurry photo they showed her was actually of Jim. She needs to cling to any tiny shred of information they do have.

'That's amazing,' Carol says, eyes wide, and adds

Jim seen in Putney?

in big capital letters to the bottom of the board, underlining it twice. She takes a step back to admire her handiwork.

'And what's the other thing, dear?'

Laura takes a deep breath. 'It's something – well, I don't quite know what to make of it.' Her stomach roils with nerves. 'The police told me that Jim doesn't work for a hotel chain based in Leeds.'

'What?' Simon has spoken this time. 'But isn't that where he spends half his week?'

Laura nods miserably. 'That's what he's always told me, yes. But it can't be true because—' She stops, feeling foolish. 'There isn't a hotel chain based in Leeds.'

A silence descends on the room, the roar of the electric fire and the distant hum of cars on the road nearby the only sounds. Debbie speaks first.

'Of course, there could just be a simple misunderstanding. But – well, we're starting to think there might be something more sinister going on. Aren't we, Lau?'

Laura looks so dejected Carol feels quite sorry for her. Although she wouldn't have missed holding this meeting for the world, she can clearly see that it isn't looking very promising for Laura. She turns to face her audience. 'So this is what we have so far,' she announces. Her cheeks are pink and a stray chunk of hair has sprung loose from its bind of hairspray and bobs around every time she moves. She rolls up the sleeves of her cardigan, digs a tissue from her pocket and dabs delicately around her mouth. The room is stifling. 'I think it's safe to say that there are a number of questions here...'

Laura fixes her eyes on the photo of Charles and Diana's wedding on top of the TV and drifts off, letting Carol's words soothe her like a warm bath. While she's convinced this meeting will shed no new light on Jim's whereabouts, she has realised one thing, at least. She's no longer the weak woman she always assumed herself to be. She has proven to herself, not only that she can take matters into her own hands to make things happen, but that, in fact, there are people who care about her, and want to help her. You only have to look at everyone sardined into this room to realise that.

She's realised something else too: she's been so engrossed in this meeting that she's barely had time to worry about her anxiety, or about being scared of being outside her own home. Which means that, no matter what happens now, she's made huge progress.

This is the start of a new beginning for her – with Jim, or without him.

* * *

Laura and Debbie are the last to leave, and there's so much food left that Carol insists they take it home with them, all bundled up into Tupperware boxes.

'You look as if you need a bit of decent food inside you,' she says, handing them three enormous Sainsbury's carrier bags stuffed to the brim. 'Just make sure you put the sausage rolls into an air-tight container and pop the quiche in the fridge.'

'Thank you, Carol, you really don't need to do this,' Debbie says as they hover on the doorstep.

'It's my pleasure, really.'

It's dark now and the wind has got up, sharp shards of icy rain pelting them as they bundle down the front path, through the gate and back up Laura's path. After the heat of Carol and Arthur's house the cool stillness of Laura's hallway is a welcome relief and they kick off their boots and hang their coats on the rack, then make their way through to the kitchen. The ancient strip light stutters as it comes to life, filling the room with a harsh white glare.

'Well, what did you make of that?' Debbie says, slinging open the fridge door and piling a few of the boxes of food inside.

Laura doesn't answer at first and Debbie slams the door shut and spins round. 'What's wrong?'

Laura shakes her head. 'Sorry, nothing.' She stops and rubs her hand through her hair. 'It was quite a lot to take in.'

Debbie grins and the sight of it makes Laura grin too. Then Laura can feel her shoulders begin to shake and the mirth bubbles up inside her, rising from her very depths up through her chest and bursting out of her mouth. The sound is so unexpected it makes her laugh even harder, and soon both of them are doubled over, barely able to breathe, the tension from the last few hours, days, weeks, months frothing over and spilling out onto the kitchen floor in gasps of laughter and shrieks of hysteria. Slowly, Laura gets herself back under control, wipes the tears from her mascara-stained cheeks and lowers herself into a chair. Debbie follows suit, the hilarity simmering now, just the occasional bubble of mirth bursting out unexpectedly.

'God, I needed that,' Laura says, a smile still tugging at the corners of her mouth, and the action feels unfamiliar, but welcome.

'Me too.' Debbie reaches over and grabs her friend's hand, suddenly serious. 'I can't tell you how brilliant it is to see you smiling again,' she says. 'It's been so long.'

Laura nods. 'I know. I – I don't know what came over me.'

'What were you even laughing about?'

Laura shrugs. What *did* she find so funny? Was it Carol's overly officious tone as she conducted her meeting, the piles and piles of food they forced on her, or something else, something deeper, more primal than that? 'I think I just realised I'm not sure I even care where Jim is any more.'

Debbie sits up, suddenly serious. 'You don't mean that.'

Laura sighs. 'Probably not. I just – I can't help thinking that if he really loved me he would never have upped and left. And given all the evidence mounting up that he's been lying to me for a long time about something, I'm beginning to wonder if I even want him to come back now anyway.' She stares at the bag of food in front of her and refuses to meet Debbie's eye.

'What's brought this on? I mean, you've been going out of your mind with worry. You *love* Jim.'

'I—' Laura stops, unsure how to properly explain it. When Jim first went missing she was devastated. The shock was almost too much to bear. How could she even go on without him, how could she function every day? But as she sat in Carol and Arthur's living room this afternoon she realised something. 'I'm stronger without him.' The words erupted out of her almost of their own accord.

Debbie stares at her friend for a moment, studying the face she knows so well. 'You know I agree with you.'

'I do.'

'It's just a shame it's taken Jim going missing for you to realise it.'

Laura twists her hands together. She's desperate for a drink but doesn't want Debbie to see how much she craves it. 'I always thought I needed him, for everything. That I needed *someone*. My mum, you, Jim. But I need to stop cutting myself off from the rest of the world and start trusting people again.' She looks up at Debbie. 'I need to be free, and I can't do that when Jim's here.'

Debbie doesn't reply for a few moments and Laura wonders what she's thinking, whether she's gone too far. But then Debbie stands, opens the fridge, pulls out a half-empty bottle of wine and pours them two huge glasses. They both down them without saying a word and as she puts her glass down and wipes her mouth on her sleeve, Laura can feel the seed of hope that planted itself in her earlier begin to unfurl, trying to reach the furthest corners of her body, her mind.

'Can I ask you something?' Debbie is rummaging around in the cupboard where Laura keeps her secret stash of booze – not so secret, Laura now realises as Debbie triumphantly produces an unopened bottle of vodka.

'Sure.' She stands and takes tumblers from the cupboard, the old ones her mum used to collect tokens for from the Esso garage, and waits while Debbie pours an inch of liquid into the bottom of each.

Debbie sits down opposite her again and leans forward, waiting for Laura to meet her gaze. 'Does this have anything to do with Ben?'

'What?' Laura feels her face grow hot, and she's not sure if it's a sudden rush from the vodka she's just tipped down her throat or the shock of her best friend's words. She grips her glass tightly and tries to steady herself. 'What's Ben got to do with anything?' Her voice is an octave too high.

Debbie drains her vodka too and bangs the glass down harder than she means to. 'Come on, Lau, I've seen the way he looks at you. You must have noticed.'

Laura can't speak. Because the truth of Debbie's words has seared through her, slicing open her heart like a hot knife, exposing her feelings, not just to the world, but to her too.

'I—' she blusters. Debbie tips more vodka into their glasses and Laura deflates. 'I have noticed, yes.'

'And?' Debbie sips her drink this time and flinches at the harsh taste.

'And nothing. My husband is missing, I haven't got time to be thinking about anything or anyone else.'

Debbie doesn't speak, so Laura fills the silence. 'How can I, Debs? How can I be even starting to think about someone else when the man I love has gone missing?'

'Because you're beginning to realise he's not the man you thought he was? Because he's left you and not given a single thought to how his disappearance might have affected you? Because he's clearly keeping something big from you? Because you've admitted yourself that you're doing better without him here?'

A silence hovers for a moment, a moment when the future could go either way, depending on Laura's next words.

'There is nothing and will never be anything between me and Ben,' she says, but the wobble in her voice gives away her uncertainty. 'He just wants to help me, the same as everyone else at the meeting today.'

'Uh-huh.'

'It's true. Just because he's a handsome man does not automatically mean I'm going to cheat on Jim.'

'How long though?'

Laura tilts her head, confused. 'How long what?'

'How long do you think it's acceptable to wait for someone who's abandoned you before you start to think about moving on?' Her words are slurring a little.

'More than a month!'

'How long, then? Six months? Twelve? Three years? A decade?' Debbie closes her eyes and when she opens them she sees Laura staring into her empty glass, her knuckles white from gripping it so hard. Then Laura shakes her head. 'I don't think we should be talking about this.'

'Okay,' Debbie agrees. 'But only for now. There will come a point when you have to start thinking about yourself, Lau.' She mimes zipping her lips shut. 'Now I promise not to talk about it any more.'

Laura gives a nod and is just splashing some more vodka into their glasses when the sound of the doorbell breaks their truce. They both look up, startled.

Could it be... *Jim?* Laura mouths.

Then the doorbell goes again and she springs up, almost knocking her glass off the table, and wobbles out of the room, down the hallway and towards the front door. She can make out the silhouette of someone on the other side of the frosted glass but it's impossible to tell whether it's Jim or someone else. The alcohol has numbed her thought processes and all her blood seems to have rushed to her ears. She takes a deep breath, opens the door, and jumps back with a gasp.

'Sorry, is this a bad time?' The light bulb above Ben creates a halo round his head while his features are thrown into shadow.

'Oh, no. Course not.' She doesn't dare acknowledge that she's not only relieved it's not Jim, but pleased to see Ben. 'Do you want to come in?'

'Are you sure?'

'Yes, but quickly so I can close the door?'

'Sorry.' Ben ducks inside and Laura shuts the door behind him. 'This way,' she says as Ben slips off his shoes and follows her into the kitchen.

'Who wa—? Oh.' Debbie smiles and raises her eyebrows as Ben walks into the kitchen directly behind Laura.

'Hi,' Ben says, hovering in the doorway. He takes in the open vodka bottle and Carol's investigation board, which has been propped up against the back door, and smiles uncertainly. 'Sorry if I'm interrupting something.'

'No, no, it's fine, come in.' Debbie gestures expansively. Ben takes a seat at the table while Laura pours him a tumbler of vodka, placing it in front of him without asking. 'We were just talking about you,' Debbie continues.

'Were you?' Ben sounds nervous.

Laura wants to kick Debbie under the table but she can't do it without Ben noticing so instead she smiles serenely and takes a drink. 'We were just saying how kind it is of everyone to be doing so much to help me find Jim,' she says.

'Oh, right. Well, of course. We all liked – like Jim. I – we... well, we want to help as much as we can.' He pauses, his face flushed, and tips the vodka down his throat. 'Good God,' he says, spluttering, his throat on fire and his eyes watering. 'Have you been drinking this since you got back?'

'Yep.' Debbie grins, taking another sip. 'Although s'probablee not a good idea.' She leans forward and rests her elbows on the table. Her eyes glimmer with mischief. 'So, what brings you round here?'

Laura can feel her face burning and she lets her hair hang across her face, which only makes it worse.

'I just wanted to come and see how you are,' he says, turning to Laura. 'I know Carol can be a bit much and I'd already told her I didn't think it was a good idea to spring something like that on you, but she insisted, said she was only trying to help. I—' he stopped. 'I hope you didn't find it too hard?'

'No, it was fine'. It really was all right, nowhere near as terrifying as she thought it was going to be. 'It's kind of you to come and check up on me though.'

Across the table Debbie coughs loudly and Laura shoots her daggers.

'Honestly, you wouldn't believe how far Lau's come since Jim left,' Debbie says, ignoring Laura. 'She couldn't even peek outside the window before, and now look at her.' She sways slightly in her seat and Laura remembers why she hates drinking with her friend – it's not just that Debbie worries about her, it's also that since she had kids, Debbie can't hold her drink at all. She slides Debbie's drink away from her in the hope she'll forget about it for a while. Sadly it doesn't deter her from finishing her little speech. 'We were just wondering what would happen if Jim never comes home.' She waves her hands in the air. 'What if he never comes home and is never found?' She turns to face Ben head-on. 'How long would you say is a reasonable amount of time to wait for someone to come home before you think about moving on, Ben?'

Ben looks round helplessly, but Laura is staring at somewhere behind his head.

'I, er...' He shrugs in defeat. 'I honestly have no idea, but I'd say there's still time for Jim to come home.'

'Time? It's been more than four weeks and he hasn't even thought to let Laura know he's still alive!' Debbie's face is outraged, her hair wild round her face.

'Four weeks isn't that long.'

'How long should she wait, then? Forever, become a born-again virgin, live alone for the rest of her life, just in case?'

Ben feels his face flame. He can't think about Laura leaving Jim, he just can't, it's completely wrong. He takes another sip of vodka and grimaces. 'I honestly don't know. I mean—'

'It was different for you,' Debbie says suddenly, waving her glass in the air. 'Your wife was ill, then she died.'

'Debbie!' Despite the drink, Laura is shocked.

'What?' Her voice is indignant. 'I don't mean it like that. I don't mean it was a good thing, I just mean – Ben knows what I mean, don't you?'

Ben nods weakly. He didn't know that the things he told Laura about his wife would become common knowledge. But it is no secret, he supposes. Debbie ploughs on. 'I juss mean – well, she was gone, and you could say goodbye and move on. But Laura can't do any of that and it makes me so angry. How dare Jim leave her in limbo like this? At least if he's still alive he could have the bloody decency to let us know!'

A silence descends, and Laura can feel her head spinning. She listens to the wind brushing against the kitchen window, and tries not to look at Ben as he sits staring at his glass, his leg jiggling up and down in time to the clock above the back door. What must he think of them, of her? Will he make his excuses and leave soon? She wouldn't blame him.

'Actually, I had an idea,' Ben says then, out of the blue. Laura whips her head round and Debbie looks up too.

'What about?'

'Well, you were saying you're feeling so much better? More able to get out and do things without being overwhelmed.' Laura nods. 'How would you feel about going into London?'

'London?' she repeats, dumbly.

Ben leans forward and picks up Carol's investigation board and props it on the empty chair next to him. He points to the list of clues.

'Two of these are about possible sightings of Jim in London, right?'

The women nod.

'They're different parts of London, but not that far apart, a few miles at most. Didn't the police also say they had a few other unconfirmed sightings but only one who had a photo of the person they thought was Jim?'

'Yes, but they couldn't be sure whether any of them were actually him,' Laura says.

'I know. But what if they were? What if both this one—' he indicates the sighting reported to the police '—and this sighting by Sonja were both Jim?' He looks from Laura to Debbie and back again. Laura struggles to work out what he's getting at through the fog of vodka. When it becomes clear neither of them are going to answer, Ben carries on. 'I know it's a big city, but if you could get to London and concentrate on the areas Jim has been spotted, ask around a bit, you never know. You might just get somewhere.'

Laura thinks about it for a minute. She tries to imagine herself walking to the railway station, getting on a train, walking around a busy London street. All things she used to do without a second thought but hasn't even been able to contemplate for almost two years. *Could* she do this? Could she really take such a huge step?

'I'm not sure,' she says. Her voice is small and she clears her throat. 'It's—'

'We'll be there too,' Debbie interrupts. 'Won't we, Ben?'

Ben would love to go with them, but he didn't dare be so presumptuous as to suggest it. 'Of course. If you'd like me to.'

Laura looks at them both – her oldest friend and this man who she's only known for a few weeks but feels a real warmth for – and pictures herself doing this with them by her side.

'Okay, I'll give it a go.'

'Yesss!' Debbie punches the air. Beside her, Ben smiles. Laura watches him over the top of her glass and when he notices her looking, he looks away. She coughs. 'Anyway, enough of that tonight. I think we should sod it and get drunk. What do you say, Benjamin?'

He grins. 'I think you two might already be there.'

'Whever. You gonna join us?'

He has to catch up with some work tomorrow and he really needs to go for a run before that. He should go home, have an early night, eat some dinner. He should. But then again, maybe he should start being a bit more spontaneous, start living again. It's what Jim always told him, in fact. That he needs to let himself go a bit, learn to have fun again. Maybe he was right. And maybe this is his chance to start.

'Why the bloody hell not?' He downs the rest of his glass. 'I can't drink this shit all night though. Got any wine?'

'Loads.'

As Laura stands to open the fridge, Debbie stands too. 'I'm going for a wee.' Then she leaves the room and they listen as she stumbles to the end of the hallway and up the stairs. Laura turns, a new bottle of Chardonnay in her hand. 'This okay?'

He nods, suddenly awkward alone with Laura, drunk. His heart is thump-thumping wildly and all he can think about is closing the gap between him and Laura.

Stop it, Ben.

But then Laura steps closer and leans towards him and his heart almost stops. He can smell her scent, a musky, vanilla-y scent, and he's overwhelmed with emotion all of a sudden and he stands, pushes his chair back with a scrape, unsure whether he's recoiling from Laura or from himself.

'You okay?' Laura says, straightening up and handing him a glass.

A glass. Of course. She was getting him a glass.

He sits back down again, his legs feeling like jelly. What is wrong with him? 'Sure. Sorry.'

She studies him for a moment and he looks up and meets her gaze, takes in her chocolate-brown eyes, her pale, creamy skin. She's so delicate and he finds it impossible to imagine her with Jim. He's holding his breath and wondering what Laura is thinking. Is she wondering why he's staring at her or is she taking him in too, the way he's looking at her? The whole room stops, suspended, and Ben knows his next action could mean everything or nothing. She licks her lips and he moves an inch closer; he can see the rise and fall of her chest, and the slight reddening of her cheeks. It would only take a split second to press his lips against hers, and—

'Right, are we going to get pissed, then?' Debbie's voice shatters the moment and they both jump as though they've been electrocuted.

'Sure,' Laura says, holding out her glass as Debbie opens the wine bottle and glugs it in. Ben can see that Laura's hand is shaking, and he feels as though he can't catch his breath.

What the hell just happened there?

He can't think about it, hasn't got room for it in his head. But he can't leave either, he doesn't want to leave, so he accepts the glass of wine Debbie offers him and stays where he is.

Ben might not be able to read Laura, but Debbie can, and even through her drunken haze she can see something happened between these two when she was out of the room. What, she doesn't know, but she can see the desire in Ben's face, and the guilt written all across Laura's. She just wishes she could tell her friend she has nothing to feel guilty about. Jim is the one who's left her with a trail of lies behind him. Ben, however, has been nothing but a gentleman since the moment they met him.

She can only hope that, if they do succeed in finding Jim, Laura will come to realise the same.

PART III

FOUND

28

NOW – 24 OCTOBER 1992

'Right, ready?' Laura can feel Debbie hovering to her right and nods. To her left, she's very aware of Ben's proximity, his hand brushing against her elbow. She tries to focus on the open door in front of her and all its possibilities. Then, before she has a chance to change her mind, the two of them are propelling her along the last few steps of the hallway, away from the safety of her four walls, out onto her front step and into the garden. She waits while Debbie locks the door behind them and drops the key into her handbag, and Ben squeezes her arm.

'Okay?' he whispers, and she nods stiffly. Being in the garden is one thing, but the thought of setting foot outside this street, this town, is occupying all of her mind at the moment, and her chest feels tight, her palms clammy. She rubs them on her jeans and forces a smile.

The police haven't been back in touch either about the possible sighting of Jim or with any more news about Jim's work, and Laura isn't keen on ringing them every day, knowing it won't make the slightest bit of difference anyway. Instead, she's tried to concentrate on this trip into London, focusing on how it might feel to walk along a crowded pavement, being jostled on every side by bags, elbows, people. Will she still search for strangers in every face, jump with fear at every movement in the shadows?

She can't even begin to think about actually finding Jim. It's all too much.

'Right, let's get in,' Debbie says as they close her gate behind them. Ben's VW Golf sits by the kerb and she's so grateful that he offered to drive. The thought of the train was a step too far.

'You go up front, I'll sit in the back,' Debbie says. 'If you think you'll be okay?'

'I have no idea,' Laura admits. She hasn't even tried to imagine the thousands of cars on the motorway, the people crammed into these thousands of cars; the wide open sky, the towering buildings... She shivers, closes her eyes, and climbs into the passenger seat. She slams the door closed and instantly feels calmer, the cool, static air of the car's interior soothing her. She can do this.

She jumps as Ben climbs in the other side and his hand brushes against hers as he reaches for the gearstick. He seems to flinch and when she looks at him his cheeks are pink and he's staring straight out of the front of the car as if nothing has happened. *Perhaps it hasn't*, Laura thinks.

The journey into London is about forty minutes, and as they rumble along the motorway Laura closes her eyes and lets the sound of the road soothe her. It's not until the car comes to a complete standstill that she jerks awake and looks round, sleepily. A red brick wall looms in front of her, cars on either side. She looks to her right to find Ben watching her. 'We're here,' he says softly.

'Are you okay, sleepy head?' Debbie says from the back.

'Sorry,' Laura says sheepishly.

'It's fine. We thought it was best to let you doze.'

She twists round to look out of the back window. 'Where are we?'

'Putney,' Ben says.

They're here already. This is the place where the stranger took the photo the police believe to be Jim, so they decided it was a good place to start. Laura doesn't like to admit it, but she really isn't holding out much hope for this trip. London is a city of seven million people and she knows the chances of finding Jim among them are minuscule. She has agreed to it for two reasons – one because she knows Ben and Debbie are really trying to help and she doesn't want to let them down. But two, because she wants the challenge. She's made such progress over the last few weeks, and this feels like a good chance to show herself how well she is doing. Although right now she's not so sure that is a good idea after all.

There's something else tugging at her too, angling for attention like a bored child. A strange, anxious feeling, as though her stomach has tied itself into an impenetrable knot and is tightening with every step closer they take to finding Jim. Something she's not even sure she's admitted to herself until now.

Is she worried they won't find Jim – or that they will?

It takes fifteen minutes to get out of the car park and onto the street, but now they're here, Laura is determined. She stands in the shadow of a doorway at one end of Putney High Street and clutches her bag to her chest. She takes a deep breath in and reminds herself what they're here to achieve, then breathes out and tries to forget what happened the last time she was on a London street, in the dark shadows of a night almost two years ago.

'Okay, what's the plan?'

'Ben and I thought we should start by handing out these,' Debbie says, and shoves a piece of paper into Laura's hand. She squints at it in the stark late autumn sunlight. On it is the photo of Jim that Laura gave to the police, and below it in thick black capital letters are the words 'Do you know this man?' She looks up at Debbie questioningly.

'When did you get these made?'

'I made them yesterday,' Ben says.

'Oh, right.' Laura feels a bit blindsided. She didn't realise the pair of them were making plans behind her back. But then she's been so preoccupied with the thought of physically getting into London that she hasn't had time to think about what she might do once she got here. She's grateful they've taken matters into their own hands.

'Thank you.' She looks up at the rows of shops, chains such as Our Price and WHSmith, the odd smattering of newsagents and shoe shops, a Wimpy in the distance. 'Where should we start?'

Ben peers along the road. 'I guess we just start by going into every shop?'

'The bigger ones are no good,' Debbie says, taking charge. 'They'll have different staff in every day. But we can go into the smaller ones, like that off-licence over there, and that clothes shops next to it. And then I think we should head off the main road and try some of the side streets. See if there are any pubs, restaurants, maybe put some through people's doors?'

It seems a bit scattergun, but Laura can't think of any better plan so she nods. 'You'll do the talking though, right?'

'Course I will.' Debbie hooks her arm through Laura's. 'It's all under control.'

* * *

Although they started just before lunch, by the time they've been into most of the shops on Putney High Street and found a few pubs hidden away too, it's mid-afternoon and already starting to get dark. Although their feet ache and they're soaked through from the sudden downpour that started around two o'clock and has been on and off ever since, it's not physical exhaustion Laura feels. Mentally, she feels as though her head might explode if she has to smile at or speak to one more stranger today. And she's not sure how many more times she can hear someone tell them that they hope she finds Jim, but that, sorry, they don't know him.

Around half past three they decide to stop for a drink and find a little Italian café just off the main stretch of road. The air inside is steamy and as they remove their damp coats, Laura feels as though she could just curl into a ball and go to sleep.

'I'll go and order,' Debbie says as Laura and Ben sit down. Laura watches her friend march up to the counter, then turns her attention to Ben. He looks bedraggled, his dark hair slick against his head, and she's reminded of the first time she saw him, on that rainy day when she ran away from his house and he brought her shoes back. Was that really only three weeks ago? She feels as though she's known him forever.

'It feels strange that I've never seen you and Jim together,' Ben says, as though he's reading her mind.

'What do you mean?' She wipes a drip of rain from her forehead with her sleeve.

'It feels as though I've known you so long, but it's only been since Jim went missing.' He shrugs, suddenly shy. 'Sorry, that probably sounds weird.'

She shakes her head. 'No, I agree.' She twiddles a sachet of sugar in her fingers.

'I hope you don't mind me coming with you today?'

Laura looks up sharply. 'Why would I mind?'

'Because it's such a personal thing,' Ben says, unsure. 'I mean, you're looking for your missing husband. It would have been totally understandable if you hadn't wanted a virtual stranger tagging along. It's just, I really like Jim, and I – well, I really like you too.'

Laura doesn't know what to say. What she wants to say is that she likes him too, and that he's not a virtual stranger, that he's become important to her, in so many ways. Only, she can't even quite untangle her feelings herself – how *does* she see Ben? Does she really see him only as a friend, as she's told Debbie so insistently? Or is it more than that? Does she feel as though, if Jim weren't in the equation, there might be more between them?

She shakes the treacherous thought away. But Jim *is* involved, and he's her husband, and that's what today is about.

She's saved from having to reply by Debbie's return. 'I've ordered us tea and a piece of chocolate cake each, hope that's okay,' she says, collapsing into the spare chair. Laura moves over slightly to give her space and finds her leg brushing against Ben's. She pulls it away quickly.

Debbie isn't fooled though.

'What's wrong with you two? I've only been gone two minutes.'

'What? Nothing?'

Debbie looks from Laura to Ben and back again, but neither of them give anything away. She leans forward. 'We haven't got very far, have we?' She taps her fingernails against the cheap plastic tabletop.

'No, but we can't give up yet. There's still quite a few shops to go, and we can wander round the back streets a bit more,' Ben says, glad to be focusing on their search again.

Laura glances out of the steamed-up window of the café. 'It'll be dark within the hour. I'm not sure we can keep going much longer.'

Debbie reaches over and covers Laura's hand with hers. 'We're not giving up, Lau, I promise. If we don't find anything today, then we'll come back another day, and another one, and we'll keep coming until either we find him, or the police do.'

Laura doesn't reply and Debbie searches her friend's face. 'What's wrong?'

Laura shrugs, blinking back tears that threaten to fall. 'I don't know. I just – I feel so guilty.'

'Guilty? What on earth for?'

Laura stares at the tabletop, the scratches and stains that have gently marked it over the years, and tries to work out how to explain it. 'I—' She stops, gathers herself. 'I just don't know what the hell I'm going to say if we do find Jim.' She swallows and shakes her head, trying to clear it, to find her way through the fog. 'I mean – things have changed. Since he's been gone. For me.' The sentences are coming out in stutters and jerks, but she's warming up to it, trying to express the feeling deep in her belly, to drag it out into the open, to study it so she can work out what it really is. 'I've changed. I've become – me again. At least, I'm getting there.' She deflates, exhausted.

Suddenly Debbie's arms are round her and Laura is sobbing into her friend's shoulder in the middle of the café. She wonders what Ben must think of her and pulls back, sniffling. 'I'm sorry,' she says, dabbing her eyes with a scratchy napkin.

'You've got nothing to be sorry for,' Debbie says. 'Does she, Ben?'

'Absolutely not.'

'I just—' Laura sniffs '—I don't know. What sort of woman isn't sure whether she even wants her missing husband to turn up again?'

'The sort of woman who feels as though she's been oppressed by her husband for years?'

Oppressed. It's a big word, with dark connotations. Has she been oppressed, or has she just been glad to let Jim look after her? Wasn't it what she wanted, when she met him?

Maybe. But is it what she needs now? Is it what she *wants*?

The waitress appears suddenly, hovering awkwardly. 'Tea and cake?' she says.

'Yes, thank you,' Debbie says, taking the cups and teapots and plates of oozing, sticky cake from her tray. The waitress looks as though she can't wait to get away, but just as she turns to go, Debbie says, 'Actually, can I ask you something?'

The waitress – Dawn, her name tag says – nods uncertainly. 'Sure.'

Debbie rummages in her bag and produces the leaflet with Jim's face on it. 'I don't suppose you recognise this man, do you?'

Dawn takes the photo and pulls it closer to her face. 'Oh, yes, I do!'

Laura feels as though the world has momentarily stopped turning; as though everything has decelerated, each freeze-frame stopping and slowing until she can hardly see any movement at all... This is the first person they've come across today who recognises Jim.

'You do?' Debbie's voice is higher than usual, excited. Ben leans forward to hear her better.

'Yes. I mean... well, I think I do.' Dawn looks up. 'He usually comes in here a few times a week. He buys a coffee to take away, and sometimes a pastry.'

'What time of day?'

'Morning. Although I've seen him a couple of evenings too. He usually buys a couple of slices of cake then.' She looks at the three faces watching her, and crinkles her nose. 'Why? Has he done something wrong?'

There is far too much to explain, but Laura wants to give this woman something, so she says, 'He's my husband.'

'Oh, is he?' She looks surprised.

'Yes. Only, he disappeared a few weeks ago and I haven't seen him since.'

Dawn reddens then, shuffles her feet awkwardly. 'Oh Christ. I – I haven't said something I shouldn't, have I? I mean, I don't know much about him and I don't wanna get anyone in trouble...' She looks bewildered.

'No, it's fine. We just want to know where he is,' Debbie soothes. 'I don't suppose you know where he lives, do you?'

Dawn shakes her head and Laura feels her stomach drop with disappointment. She might not be certain she wants Jim back, but she does want to know what's happened to him and she felt as if she was getting so close for a moment there.

'I don't think it's far away though,' Dawn adds.

'What makes you say that?'

'I dunno. I always had the impression this was a local place for him, and then the other day – Wednesday last week, it might have been – I remember he came in and while I made his drink he said he'd left something at home and he'd be back in a few minutes.' She pauses. 'He was back before I'd even put the lid on his coffee, so he can't have gone far.'

Laura, Debbie and Ben sit in silence for a moment, taking in this news. It's Debbie who speaks first.

'And you're sure it's him, are you?'

Dawn glances at the photo again. 'As sure as I can be, yeah. It definitely looks like him.'

Debbie folds the photo up. 'Thank you so much. That's really helpful.'

'No worries.' Dawn heads back towards the kitchen and

Debbie turns back to the table excitedly. 'Oh my God!' she says, her eyes shining with excitement. 'We're getting somewhere!'

Laura takes a sip of her tea. Her hands are shaking. 'But what if it is him? Do we have to come back every morning and wait for him to come in?'

Debbie shakes her head impatiently. 'No, we're going to go now.'

'Now?' Ben has a piece of cake on a fork halfway to his mouth and stops.

'Yep.' Debbie grabs her coat. 'We're going to finish this—' she indicates the table '—then we're going to get back out there.'

Ben and Laura glance towards the window again. Rain is still pattering gently against the glass, but it's softer now, easing. A shaft of orange light spreads across the shiny pavement, a sign that the late evening sun is trying to beat a path through the gloom.

'See, even the weather wants us to get back out there,' Debbie says, tipping her head back and draining her mug.

Laura's not so sure this is a good idea. Searching for Jim during the day has been fine. She can cope with a bustling high street in the daytime better than she thought she'd be able to. But quiet side streets in the dark? She's transported instantly back to that night in the alleyway by her former home; the glinting knife, the blank, grey-eyed stare through the balaclava.

'I'm not sure I can do it,' she says. Debbie stops her plate clearing and looks at her.

'What's wrong, Lau?' she says, her face pulled into a frown.

'I'm not sure I can be outside in the dark.'

'Oh, darling,' Debbie says, rubbing her arm. 'I know this is going to be hard. But me and Ben will be there to protect you, won't we, Ben?'

Ben nods. 'Absolutely. I won't let anything happen to you, I promise.'

Laura knows this, and yet it still feels like an impossible ask. She swallows, gathers her courage.

'Okay. Let's do this.' She downs her drink. 'But let's do it now before I lose my nerve.'

The sky is kettle-grey, and although the rain has stopped, a damp mist still hangs in the air. Laura shivers, and tries not to let her eyes wander down every alleyway, into every dark corner. She stops, suddenly, in the middle of the pavement, halted by a scurrying sound and a crash of dustbins falling over. A fox dashes across the pavement in front of her and she lets out a breath, her heart racing.

It's not until she starts walking again that she realises she's holding Debbie's hand on one side and Ben's on the other. She snatches her hand away and instantly misses the warmth of his grip.

'Do you think it's time we called it a day?'

'I think you're probably right,' Ben says. 'I can't see a bloody thing.'

Debbie sighs. 'Yeah, I think so too.' She glances up at the illuminated windows of the Edwardian houses. 'Shame though. I really felt like something was about to happen.'

The three of them trudge towards the car park, their footsteps tapping rhythmically, shoes splashing through the occasional puddle. The orange glow of the street lights highlights the crowns of their heads every few steps as though they're stepping into the spotlight on stage, and then back into darkness again, light, dark, light, dark. Laura keeps her eyes down, not wanting to think too much about where she is. But she knows that later, back at home, she'll feel proud of herself for the progress she's made today in overcoming her fear.

They turn a corner and the street is busy again, people plunging into brightly lit shops or emerging with hands full of carrier bags, the world continuing as before. She's hardly had time to form these thoughts when Debbie suddenly stops dead, and her hand tightens round Laura's. Laura stops, and then Ben does too. Debbie's eyes are wide and Laura follows her gaze to see what's made her stop in her tracks. But there's no one there.

'What?' she says. 'What happened?'

'It's him,' Debbie hisses, through clenched teeth. She yanks her hand out of Laura's and points towards the Tube station. 'Jim.'

Heart thudding, Laura peers through the gloom towards the open mouth of the station, where there are a few people milling around, and a couple walk inside hand in hand. But she can't see any men alone, and definitely not a man who looks anything like Jim.

'Where?'

'There.' Ben points in the same direction as Debbie, and that's when Laura sees him too. He's almost at the corner by the Horse-shoe pub, and just seconds after she spots him, he's swallowed up into the shadows. She feels untethered, as if she could float away at any moment, rising above the rain-soaked street.

'Do – do you think it really was him?'

'There's only one way to find out.' Laura's arm is almost tugged free from her shoulder as Debbie pulls her towards the space where the-man-who-might-be-Jim was a moment before. They hurry, pushing past pedestrians in their haste, eyes focused on the spot where the man was last seen. There's an urgency to their scur-ried footsteps, and when they round the corner a peace cloaks them, the noise from the high street receding. They stop, almost concertinaing into each other, and peer ahead where small spots of light from the lamp posts punctuate the deepening navy blue.

'There!' Ben shouts, making all three of them jump as they look towards where he's pointing. A figure hurries along, head down, dark collar pulled high, short grey hair appearing, disappearing and reappearing as it passes below each light. It's almost impossible to tell from this distance, in this light, whether it's Jim. But, Laura thinks, there is a definite familiarity to his gait; an almost imperceptible lean to the left as he walks, the way his arms swing slightly too much. They set off again, stealthy this time, eager to catch up but keen not to be spotted, at least not yet. It's not clear to any of them what they might say or do once they get close enough to see whether it is Jim. Will they follow him all the way to his destination? What happens if he turns round and sees them before they get there? Will he run away? So many questions, and yet they press on.

Laura's pulse thumps in her throat and she tries to stay focused on the man in front of her. The gap between them is closing, but she doesn't want to get too close, not yet. What if it isn't Jim? Is it all over then? Do they give up, assume that the person who reported the sighting to the police was mistaken the same way they have been?

But what if it is?

Laura doesn't know. None of them do.

The figure stops, rummages in his jacket pocket. He's between lamp posts in the semi-darkness and they can't make out what he's doing, so they hang back behind a parked car, watching, waiting for his next move. His face is still in darkness. Then he opens a gate to his right, and walks confidently up the path to the house. They watch as he produces a key, inserts it into the lock, and the door swings open. Laura holds her breath, waiting to see whether he will turn round, whether she will be able to see if this man is her husband before he disappears into the house...

And then he does turn, and the security lamp flicks on at the same time, flooding his face with light. Laura can see, clearer than she's ever seen anything before, what she's both dreaded and hoped for.

It's Jim.

29

NOW – 24 OCTOBER 1992

Laura stands, frozen for a moment, staring at the closed front door Jim disappeared through just a few seconds ago. Her fingers stiffen into twigs, her arms branches, her body as motionless as a tree trunk. Only her heart is alive and restless, jabbering and clattering inside her chest wall like a rat trapped in a box. Beside her she can feel Ben and Debbie watching her, waiting for her to confirm what they both already know.

'It's him, isn't it?' Debbie's voice is subdued, even though there's no chance of Jim hearing them through the walls and doors of this house.

Laura gives a tense nod, her mind racing, trying to catch up with what's happening. If this is Jim – and she knows it is – then why is he here? What is his connection with this house, this street in south-west London? He seems familiar with it, comfortable, as though he's walked these streets many times before.

She turns her head to look at Debbie and Ben, and their faces reflect everything she's just been thinking. Something isn't right.

'What do we do?' Debbie says.

Laura shrugs, not yet able to form a coherent thought, let alone a sentence.

'I could go over there, if you like?' Ben says, casting a glance towards the house Jim just entered.

'I—' Laura stops, swallows. She meets Ben's gaze. His eyes flicker and glitter under the lights, deep blue, warm eyes. Kind eyes. In another time, another place, she'd want to get lost in them. But right here, right now, is neither the time nor the place. She needs to make a decision.

'I think I should go,' she says. 'But I'd really like it if you could both come with me. I'm not sure I can do this alone.'

Debbie squeezes her hand and it reassures her she's said the right thing. 'Of course we will, won't we, Ben?'

'Of course, whatever you want,' he says, his eyes glancing down to his feet and back up to Laura's face. She's pale, and the shadows cast by the angle of the street lamps make her look even more gaunt than usual.

She lifts her head defiantly. 'Fuck it. Let's go.'

She's already holding Debbie's hand but she grabs Ben's too and starts to march across the empty street. But halfway across, Laura's eyes catch a movement in an upstairs window and she stops dead.

'What's wrong?' Debbie whispers.

Laura nods her head towards the darkened square. 'Up there, in that small window, the one above the door.'

Ben and Debbie turn to look but can't see anything. Then a pale moon appears in the grey smudge, hovering between the curtains. Laura squints her eyes to try and make out what – or who – it is, but it's too dark. Then the moon shape moves closer to the window and becomes a face. A young face, pale, eyes knitted together, lips an angry smudge. It watches them, before it disappears out of sight.

'Who was that?' Ben says.

'I'm not sure,' Laura whispers. She's still standing in the middle of the street, staring at the empty window, so Debbie pulls her off the road and onto the pavement. But before they can go any further the front door opens quietly and a figure slips outside into the small front garden. Seconds later, she's standing right in front of Laura, the look on her face one of defiance.

'Don't you dare come any closer,' she says, her voice high and strong. She can't be more than late teens, with dark hair and pale skin, her lips painted a furious red and thick black eyeliner circling her eyes. She's taller than Laura and just as slight, but with her arms drawn across her chest she looks formidable.

'Wh—?' Laura stutters.

'Who are you?' Debbie moves protectively forward but the girl doesn't take a step back, doesn't cower away.

'I'm Evie,' she says, as if they should know her name. 'Jim's daughter.'

The world sways and Laura feels as though she might fall over. She feels someone holding her arm, and she takes a few deep breaths before she allows herself to speak again.

'Jim?' she says, her voice a rasp. 'My Jim?'

Evie gives a sort of nod, an angry jerk of her head, and lets out a bark of laughter. 'I guess you would call him that. Although he's not *your* Jim. He's mine. And my brother's. And my mum's.'

Laura's world explodes then; an earthquake splitting open the ground beneath her feet, the sky rupturing in a flash of devastating lightning.

'I don't know what's going on here, but I think you need to stop this right now,' Ben says, stepping forward to form a barrier between Laura and Evie.

Evie stands defiant.

'I can't let you go in there,' Laura hears Evie say. 'My mum will kill her. It'll finish her off.' Her words are challenging, but some of the venom has dropped from them now, and when Laura looks up again she can see that Evie has deflated, crumpled into herself, and it takes a moment for her to realise the girl is crying, great heaving sobs that wrack her whole body. Without thinking she steps round Ben, scoops Evie into her arms and holds her. Miraculously, Evie lets her. Time seems to stand still as Ben and Debbie stand by, unsure what to do.

Then the moment is broken by a loud shout, a door banging, and footsteps pounding towards them.

'Get off her!' the voice screeches, then hands pull them apart roughly, and Laura stumbles into Ben, her hands pressing into his shoulders, her face brushing against his as she rights herself. Ben realises his hands are round Laura's waist and once he's sure she's safely upright he pulls them away self-consciously.

'Get away from my daughter, get away from my house and get away from my husband,' the woman screeches. Despite her manic appearance, Laura can see the similarity between this woman and Evie – the same straight nose, the same slight build, the same fierce, flashing eyes, and there's no doubt that this woman is Evie's mother. Laura takes a step back.

'I'm not... I haven't,' she says, unsure which accusation to start with.

'I don't know who you think this is, but Laura is married to Jim,' Debbie says calmly, trying to wrest back some control of the situation. 'So, if that's who you're hiding inside this house, then she has every right to be here.'

'Married to Jim? I don't think so,' the woman spits. 'Because I am.'

A stunned silence falls across the group and for a moment no one moves. Laura's mind is in freefall, her synapses struggling to make the connections. But before she has the chance to say anything, the front door of the house swings open again and a figure appears.

It's Jim.

The look on his face is hard to read as he strides towards them, his gaze fixed on Laura. If he's surprised to see her here, he doesn't show it. Laura takes in the familiar contours of his face, the darkness of his eyes, the breadth of his shoulders, and remembers the first time she set eyes on him, the day he came into her kitchen and swept her off her feet, and wonders when she stopped feeling that same lurch of love for him as she had that day. Was it gradual, or had it only been since he'd left that she'd stopped feeling attracted to him in that primal, passionate way?

He reaches out and touches the woman's shoulder. She shakes it off angrily.

'Cherry, take Evie inside. I'll deal with this.'

Cherry. A penny drops in Laura's mind as she thinks about the name Jim accidentally called her to Ben. *Kerry, or Cheryl, or something like that.*

Laura feels the rage building up inside her, bubbling up like lava.

'What the fuck is going on here, Jim?' she says, her words erupting from her, scorching across the pavement.

'Yes, Jim, I'd like to know too,' Cherry says. Her voice is icy, calm.

Jim looks from one woman to the other and back again. But before he has a chance to speak, Evie does.

'Dad's been cheating on you, Mum. For years.'

Cherry looks bewildered for a moment, like a lost little girl. Then she takes in Laura, who's still huddled next to Ben. 'With *her*?'

'Cherry, it's not—'

'Don't you *dare* speak!' Cherry screams in Jim's face, then she turns back to her daughter. 'What's going on, Evie? How do you know who this woman is?'

Evie puts her arm round her mum's shoulders and pulls her in tight, then fixes a stern gaze on Jim.

'I've known for ages,' she says, her voice small now.

'Darling, you're mistaken,' Jim starts again, but Evie keeps talking. No one can take their eyes off her.

'I found out about five years ago,' she says. 'I got home early from school one day and Dad was in his study. He hadn't heard me come in and I was about to go and say hello when something made me stop outside the door. It was Dad's voice, and he was telling someone he loved her and that he'd be home soon. He told whoever it was to have fun that night, and that he'd be back in bed with her the next night. He – he said some other things that I don't want to repeat but – anyway, it was obvious to me that he was having an affair with whoever was on the other end of the phone.'

'Why didn't you tell me?' Cherry says, sobbing.

'I wanted to, Mum. But I was scared that Dad would leave, and that our family would fall apart.' She looks down at her feet. 'I thought if I could find this woman and warn her off, tell her Dad already had a family and that she was going to ruin everything, she might back off and you wouldn't ever need to know.' She looks at Jim again. 'My friend Lucy, her – her mum had just found out her dad had been cheating and had thrown him out, and she said she felt like her life was over and I – I didn't want that for me. For us.' Her voice breaks and Cherry puts her arms around her daughter. Jim steps forward to do the same but Cherry stands in his way. 'Oh, no, you don't.'

Chastened, Jim steps away.

'Anyway, I didn't know what to do, so one Thursday night when Dad left to go to Leeds, I followed him. I was sure he was going to see me, or that I was going to have to travel all the way up to Leeds with him to find anything out, and I had no idea if I would even get away with that. But I – I didn't need to.'

'Evie, really, you don't have to do this. Let me explain.' Jim sounds defeated, desperate.

'Let her speak, Jim. You've done enough damage.' Cherry's voice is flint.

'I want to hear it too,' Laura says. Even though she's dreading hearing what Evie has to say next, she knows she needs to hear it before Jim has a chance to twist anything, to make excuses. She needs to hear the whole truth about the lie her life has been for the last seven years.

Evie carries on. 'Dad didn't go to Leeds. He didn't even go to the station.' She looks at her mum. 'You know all those days he said he was working away, that he really wanted to change jobs and find something that meant he wasn't away half the time?'

Cherry nods, and Laura holds her breath, recognising the words Jim had told her, too.

'He wasn't working in Leeds. He was with her.' She looks at Laura as she says this, and Laura feels herself shrinking backwards as though she might make herself disappear.

'I – I thought he was working in Leeds too,' Laura says, her voice shaky. 'He told me the same thing.'

'Well, he was never in Leeds. Because he was living in London. In East Finchley.' Evie looks at her mum again. 'Mum, Dad has two lives.'

A silence falls then as everyone takes in what Evie has told them. A part of Laura is hoping that Jim will speak now, that there will be some obvious explanation that they've all missed, that they will be laughing at this in a few minutes.

But she knows it's not coming. Because what other explanation is there?

Something occurs to her then.

'It was you, wasn't it? Who was watching me?'

Evie nods. 'I didn't mean to scare you. I just – I wanted to see who you were. Who this woman was who was taking my dad away from me. And I suppose I thought I might try and talk to you, tell you to leave him alone. But then one day you saw me and I got scared and I—'

'You ran away.' Laura sees clearly in her mind the figure racing away from her down the street, standing outside her flat, making her terrified to even look out of the window. And she remembers Jim denying it, telling her there was no one there, that she must be imagining it. Did he know it was his daughter all along?

'Was it you outside my house too, when we moved?' Laura says.

Evie nods miserably. 'I stopped coming to watch you at the flat in the end because I knew I'd never be brave enough to actually approach you. Then Dad said he had to stay away for two weeks and I knew something had happened. But by the time I went back again, you'd gone.'

'How did you find us – me – again?'

Evie looks down at her hands. 'I broke into Dad's study and looked through his stuff. I found an old diary and saw the name of a village mentioned in it a few times so I decided to go there one day. I don't think I really expected to find you. But then I did.'

Laura thinks of the locked drawers in Jim's study at home, of all the secrets he's no doubt hidden that she hasn't even found, and can't even grasp the enormity of the lies he's told. Not just to her, but to Cherry, and Evie, and his son. Who even *was* the man she thought was her husband?

She finds herself staring at him now as he realises all eyes are turned towards him. He stands, not knowing where to look, and seeing him so defeated, like a rabbit caught in the headlights, makes Laura see him differently.

She always thought of Jim as so strong. Her protector. But he's nothing more than a coward, spinning a web of lies to cover his tracks, never owning up to his mistakes. And now he's been caught? He still can't even admit to what he's done.

'Jim?' Cherry's voice is smaller, cowed, and Laura wants to tell her not to be, to tell him what she really thinks of him. But she can see this is as much of a shock to Cherry as it is to her. More, probably, as she didn't know anything was wrong at all.

Jim steps towards Cherry and Evie and they both flinch and take a step away from him. 'Can you take Evie inside? Please?'

Cherry looks at him, her face like stone, then clearly decides her daughter is more important, and turns, guiding Evie inside. She throws a look over her shoulder before she steps into the house and Laura doesn't think she's ever seen anyone look as hurt, as broken, as Cherry does right now. Except herself, in the mirror.

Jim turns back to the three people who remain. 'I—' he starts.

'What the *fuck* have you done?' Debbie's words fly out like bullets and Jim physically recoils from them. 'How the hell have you got away with this... this charade for so bloody long? I knew there was something wrong between you and Laura, but I never expected *this*.'

'Debbie.' Laura calls her friend's name and she looks round. 'Please. Don't.'

Debbie pauses, then nods in understanding. Jim seizes his opportunity to speak.

'Laura, I think we need to get you somewhere inside, to talk. It's no good for you being out here.'

'I'm fine,' Laura says, stepping away from him. 'It's not being out here that's the problem.' For the first time in months, she actually forgot to be afraid of the outside world. 'But we do need to talk.'

Jim nods, his face revealing nothing. 'We can't go in there—' he indicates the house into which his wife and daughter just disappeared '—but there's a pub round the corner that's usually quiet at this time of the evening. Shall we go there?'

'Yes, fine.'

'Do you want us to come with you?' Ben says. Jim whips his head round as if he's only just noticed his friend's presence.

'What are *you* doing here?' Jim says.

'He's helping me,' Laura says. 'I asked him to come.'

Jim studies them both as though trying to work something out, then seems to give up. Laura shakes her head and speaks to Ben. 'No, thank you. I think this is something me and Jim need to do alone.'

* * *

Jim was right, the pub is quiet when they enter. It feels like a good place to be. Neutral territory.

As they seek out a table, Laura takes in the bar, the rows of bottles lined up behind it, the handful of people at tables scattered throughout the front room, and wonders how long it's been since she was last in a place like this. She's amazed at how calm she feels, as if everything else that has happened has stripped away her defences and made her realise there are bigger things to worry about than simply setting foot outside her home.

While Jim goes to the bar, she thinks about what's just happened, and she's in absolutely no doubt that everything Evie told her is completely true. It explains everything. It explains Jim's overprotectiveness and the fact he never wanted to go anywhere with her. It explains the lack of holidays, the fact she never really knew where he worked and was never allowed to ring him but had to wait for him to call her. It explains why she never met any of his colleagues, and hardly any of his friends. Did he even lie about his family being dead, so he didn't have to introduce her to them? Could that explain the birthday card she'd found? Could he really have been that callous?

Her stomach drops to her feet as the true scale of his deception hits her.

'I got you a double,' Jim says, putting a glass of gin and tonic in front of her and sitting opposite her with his pint.

She doesn't thank him, but waits for him to start explaining himself. He looks old in this light, the lines in his face deeper than the last time she saw him, his hair more grey, his chin speckled with unfamiliar stubble even though it's only been a few weeks. He looks as if he's lost weight too. But she doesn't comment on any of that, just waits for him to speak.

'So,' he starts, 'you're out of the house. How have you done it?'

She takes a gulp of her drink and keeps her fingers gripped round the glass, then shakes her head. 'No, sorry, Jim. You don't get to ask me anything. Not yet. Not until you've told me exactly what's going on here. I think I deserve that at least, don't I?'

He pauses, surprised at how forthright she was in her reply. Then he lowers his head and says, 'You're right.'

Then, he begins.

30

Jim

From the moment I set eyes on Laura I knew I was in trouble.

I'd only gone into the kitchen to compliment the chef – it was something I often did when a meal was particularly good. But when I spotted Laura as I hovered in the doorway, I was hit by something unexpected.

I literally couldn't take my eyes off her. Not just because it was so unusual to see a female head chef back then – although it was, especially in the top restaurants – but because she was the most beautiful creature I'd ever seen. Behind a bubbling pot on the stove from which steam rose in pale wisps, I watched her face as she concentrated on chopping whatever was on the bench in front of her. She hadn't seen me so I took a few seconds to take her in: her dark hair, which was held back in a net, and her face, pale and porcelain-like, as though she might break if you touched her. There was a bead of sweat on her temple, a line of concentration on her brow, but other than that she might have been a doll, she was so perfect.

I made my way towards her in a trance and, even though one of the waiters had shouted for her, I was at her elbow before she noticed me. She spun round, her face flushed, a huge knife in her hand.

'Oh!' she said, growing pinker.

'I'm so sorry,' I said.

'What are—?'

'Could you—?' We both started to speak at the same time and laughed. But the knife was making me nervous so I said, 'Seriously, would you mind putting that thing down?' She looked at it and her face cleared as she dropped the knife onto the worktop. 'That's better.' I said, smiling at her at last.

She didn't smile back. She didn't seem very pleased to see me standing there at all, so I told her what I'd come to say – that the food was exquisite. To my relief she smiled back, and blushed. 'Thank you,' she said. Then she turned back to her chopping.

'Would you like to come out for a drink when you've finished here?' I blurted before I lost my nerve.

She seemed surprised, and for an awful moment I thought she was going to say no. I wouldn't have blamed her – after all, she didn't know me from Adam. But after what felt like the longest pause in history, she agreed to a drink when she'd finished work.

Thrilled, I went back to my colleagues at the table, but I couldn't concentrate on what they were saying. Later, as I waited for Laura to finish, I thought about whether this was a good idea or not. I'd only been separated from my wife, Cherry, for a couple of weeks, although things hadn't been right between us for a while. But our children, Evie and Oliver, were still only young, eleven and eight, and I hadn't wanted to unsettle them. In the end, though, I'd told her I thought we should have a break and, understandably furious, she'd thrown me out. Currently I was living in a terrible, soulless flat not far from our family home, and was trying to work out where we went from here.

Meeting another woman for a drink under these circumstances wasn't ideal. But then again, how much harm could one drink really do?

* * *

I never meant for things to go so far with Laura, but there was just something about her I couldn't resist. She was intoxicating. Guileless, loyal, kind. I fell in love with her almost instantly, and I was fairly certain she felt the same way about me.

But then a couple of weeks later Cherry asked to see me, and begged me to go home. Oliver was getting into trouble at school, playing up, and he'd finally confessed it was because he hated me living away all the time. I couldn't bear to see him so grief-stricken. I had no choice but to agree.

I was heartbroken, knowing I had to end it with Laura. Because however I felt about her, my kids came first.

Except when it came to it, I couldn't do it. Instead I did the exact opposite. I asked Laura to move in with me. Honestly, I don't know what I was thinking. I just knew I couldn't let her go.

Yes, I know.

But there you have it. That's what got me into this mess and, the longer it went on, the deeper I got, the more impossible it became to find a way out of it.

Who was I kidding? I didn't want to get out of it. I wanted to be with Laura.

And that was when the lies, out of necessity, started to get bigger.

I lied about my job – I told them both I had to start working in

Leeds for half the week so I could split my time between them. It didn't occur to Cherry to check up on me, she was too busy with the kids, her part-time job at school and her friends. And Laura was so trusting she believed me when I told her it was too difficult for me to speak at work, that she would have to wait for me to ring her.

I lied about my family too. I told Laura my parents were dead, that they'd died when I was young. It wasn't as though I could let her meet them, and I had to tell her something. It seemed easier, at the time. God knows how that birthday card from my Dad ended up at the wrong house. I was always so meticulously careful about things like that. I had to be.

The whole thing was like a house of cards, teetering precariously, one lie on top of another, which one false move, one tiny mistake, could bring crashing to the ground.

It was destroying me.

It soon became clear that Laura was vulnerable. She had no one else apart from her best friend, Debbie, who was wary of me from the start. I couldn't blame her. At first I tried to win her round, but in the end it started to become easier just to encourage Laura to spend less time with her so she didn't ask so many questions. I'm not proud of myself for that. And apart from Debbie, Laura didn't have any other close friends – a few colleagues who she saw less and less of as we spent more time together, and her mum, who she already had a fractured relationship with, which all served to make my deception easier.

Laura liked it being just the two of us. Keeping Cherry and Laura apart was easier than I'd anticipated. They – we – lived on different sides of London, and Laura rarely went into central London apart from to the restaurant and back.

Then there was that evening when Laura and I went to the theatre. She'd bought tickets for my birthday and although I was reluctant to go, I thought it would be fine, just this once. Of course, that was the night my bloody colleague Nick had gone to see the same show, wasn't it? And when he called my name across the theatre I could have died right there on the spot. I couldn't let Laura meet him, and I didn't want him to see Laura too closely either in case he realised she wasn't my wife. I panicked, and I know Laura thought I was being odd that night. But what else could I have done?

Then there was the time I was two days late coming home to Laura. When I finally got home she was so distressed that I made up some story about having to fly to the Middle East, and that my colleague was supposed to have rung to let her know. But the truth was, Oliver had been rushed to hospital with suspected appendicitis so I couldn't just up and leave.

Apart from the odd incident like that, though, it wasn't as difficult as you'd imagine to lead two lives and, as the months passed, I began to relax.

I never really had a plan. I hadn't decided to become a cheat, but as the web began to weave itself tighter and tighter, I couldn't see any way of escape.

Leaving Cherry would have let my kids down.

Leaving Laura would have let her down.

I didn't know Evie had found out about Laura, of course. I can't believe she didn't say anything to me. When Laura told me someone was watching her, and that she was terrified she had a stalker, it didn't occur to me it could be true. She was often nervy by then, and I assumed she was imagining it. It wasn't until we moved and someone came to ask for me and Laura in the shop that I realised it was real – and who it might be.

The biggest mistake I made, though, was marrying Laura. In all honesty I don't know what made me think it was a good idea. Laura had been struggling for a while with loneliness, and I knew she was starting to wonder why I hadn't asked her to marry me. It was just little comments here and there, but the thought of losing her was out of the question. It might have been exhausting, juggling two families, but I couldn't abandon Cherry and the kids – and I didn't want to abandon Laura either. So I booked our wedding in Gretna Green. I knew it was against the law to lie about not being married, but I couldn't see another way out of it.

When Laura was attacked, everything changed. In fact that was when things really started to unravel. I took two weeks off to be with her because she was broken by her ordeal. I told Cherry I was being made to go away for two weeks with work. The one plus side to Laura's subsequent agoraphobia was that there was now no chance at all that she and Cherry would meet by chance.

Then Laura said she wanted to move out of London. How could I move, when my other family was still in the city? It would make life a lot harder. But in the end she begged and I didn't know how to say no without tying myself into even more knots, so I reluctantly agreed.

Moving outside London was, in the end, the straw that broke the camel's back.

Because Laura didn't get better. Far from it. She became even more scared, even more clingy. There was a fragility to her that I didn't feel able to fix. She needed me more than ever and it started to become almost impossible to leave her alone for days at a time.

I tried getting to know the neighbours in the hope that, by making friends there, Laura would see that we could settle there, and eventually she could get to know them as well.

But it didn't work and I didn't know what to do about it. The pressure was building and I felt like a man on the brink of a disaster.

And then one day, Evie told me she knew about Laura, and that if I didn't leave her, she would tell her mum and Oliver everything. It wasn't so much Cherry I was worried about, we both knew we hadn't been in love with each other for years. It was my boy I needed to protect.

So that was that.

My work, everything I'd built in order to protect each family from the other, crumbled, shattering on the ground around me.

It was over.

I had no choice but to leave.

If there had been any other way, believe me, I would have tried it. But it felt as though there was nowhere else to go. Something had to give – and it had to be Laura.

So I left, and hoped that, somehow, Laura would be all right. Walking out on her that morning was the hardest thing I've ever done, and I don't think I'll ever forget the look on her face as I said goodbye, knowing that I wasn't coming back.

Now, here she is, and the whole thing is out. Exposed.

It's over.

I'm over.

Why did I ever think I'd get away with it?

But I loved Laura. I still do. I don't love Cherry, not in the same way, but I do love my children. And that's all there is to it.

Love conquers everything.

Love ruins everything.

31

NOW – 24 OCTOBER 1992

Laura
The aftermath

Debbie and Ben have waited for her, and as she walks Bambi-legged into the small Italian restaurant on Putney High Street where they said they would be, Laura has never been so grateful to see anyone in her whole life. She feels beaten, bruised, as though she's done ten rounds with Frank Bruno.

Ben sees her first and leaps up, cupping her elbow gently in the palm of his hand and guiding her to a chair where she collapses, gratefully. Debbie pours her a large glass of red wine and Laura necks half of it, swiping her mouth with the back of her hand.

'Fuck.'

Ben wonders whether he ought to make himself scarce and is about to ask if they want some privacy when Laura speaks again.

'I can't believe it,' she says. She's trying for angry but her voice comes out weak, tremulous, and she hates herself for it.

'I assume he's told you everything?' Debbie says, taking a sip from her own glass. A drop spills onto the white napkin and spreads slowly out into the fabric and Laura watches it.

'Yes.'

'And?'

She shakes her head, trying to order her thoughts in her own mind. But it all sounds so surreal, like a bad film script. How can this have happened to her? How did she let it happen?

'Lau?'

She looks up at her friends, their kind faces, waiting. Then she takes a deep breath and tells them everything. It comes out in fits and starts, the timeline jumbled, the details muddled, but when she's finished she feels purged, cleansed. And utterly spent.

'I feel like such a fool.'

Ben shuffles in his seat awkwardly, twiddles his glass back and forth with his fingertips. He's outraged, but doesn't know how to express it, doesn't want to say too much, at least not before Laura has had a chance to process things. Debbie, however, doesn't have any such qualms.

'Don't you dare say that,' she says, her face turning pink, a vein pulsing in her temple. 'This is all about Jim Parks, and his selfish, cheating, lying, manipulative ways.'

'But you told me. You warned me there was something not quite right about him. About the way we were. And I – I dismissed you.' Laura wishes with all her heart that she could travel back in time to tell that Laura, the stupid, needy Laura from five years before, to listen to her best friend. That, actually, cutting everyone out of your life for a man isn't normal. But it's all too late now.

'No, I won't have it.' Debbie slams her hand onto the tablecloth harder than she intended and Laura is aware of other diners turning their heads to see what's going on. She slumps down further in her seat and tries to hide her face.

'Don't, please,' she whispers.

'Sorry, Lau,' Debbie says, leaning forward and taking Laura's hand that hangs limply by her side. Her voice is soft now, apologetic. 'But this isn't about *I told you so* or anything you've done wrong. This is entirely down to Jim.'

Laura nods miserably and a tear trickles down her face and splashes onto the tablecloth. She looks up at Debbie, then at Ben, their faces shining in the dim glow from the lamp in the middle of the table. 'Thank you. Both of you. I don't know what I'd do without you right now.'

'I haven't really done anything,' Ben says, his cheeks flushing. He wishes he could reach over and wrap his arms around Laura and let her know that everything is going to be all right, that he's here, and that, if she wants him to be, he will always be here. But he's painfully aware that, not only would this be entirely inappropriate right now, but also she might not welcome it at all. Then where would he be? So he stays where he is, with one hand clasped round his wine glass, the other lying flat on the table.

'You've both been brilliant,' Laura says. 'I just wish I knew what the hell I'm going to do now.'

'I tell you what I think we should do right this minute,' Debbie says.

'What?'

'Get some food, go home, and get some sleep.' She squeezes Laura's hand. 'Everything will seem better in the morning.'

'Will it?'

Debbie thinks for a moment. 'Fuck knows. But it's worth a go, right?'

Laura smiles despite her misery. 'You're right. And do you know what? I don't care if I never see Jim Parks again.'

32

NOW – 14 NOVEMBER 1992

The doorbell rings and Laura jumps, but only because she was concentrating on sticking masking tape along the skirting board and didn't hear anyone coming up the path. It's nice, she realises for the umpteenth time as she makes her way towards the front door, not to be petrified of her own shadow any more, not to jump with terror every single time the doorbell rings. She's still got a way to go before she's completely comfortable with leaving the house on her own or being in crowded places, but the last few weeks have changed her profoundly, and she's beginning to like the new Laura that's emerging.

In the immediate aftermath of the showdown with Jim, Laura didn't want to leave the house much. Partly because she was still licking her wounds, and partly because she couldn't face the shame of telling everyone the truth about what had really happened. What would these people, who had been so kind to her even though they hardly even knew her, really think when they discovered the truth? Would they see her as weak, gullible? Pathetic? She's tried to imagine how she would feel if it were someone else, but it's impossible.

Slowly, though, she began to realise that her new friends are all on her side. They were all taken in by Jim's charm too, and are as horrified as she is that he was living a double life all this time, and none of them had the faintest idea.

Laura told Carol about her discovery first, in the hope that she'd save her the job of telling everyone else. Carol, of course, did exactly that, and over the course of the next few days all of Laura's neighbours – and new friends – came over to tell her how sorry they were. Carol brought round a home-made cottage pie, Arthur offered to mend the broken fence panel between their front gardens; Jane came round with a bottle of wine and they shared sob stories about terrible exes, Sonja came over to talk to her about the legal implications of Jim's bigamy which, it turns out, is her speciality, while Marjorie and Faye came round with biscuits and an offer of a tarot reading whenever she feels ready.

Then there was Ben. Kind, loyal Ben. He stayed away at first and Laura began to worry that he didn't want to know her any more – that he'd seen her at her most vulnerable and didn't want anything more to do with her. She couldn't admit even to herself how confused and hurt she was by this, but eventually, a week after their trip to London, she knocked on his door, ready to give him a piece of her mind.

The door swung open. 'Laura!' he said. He seemed pleased to see her but didn't invite her in.

'Hello, stranger,' she said, hoping he'd detect the anger simmering in her voice.

'I—' He stopped and ran his hand over his face and his body deflated like an empty potato sack 'God, I'm sorry, Laura.'

She took a step closer. 'Is everything okay?' He looked up at her with his deep blue eyes and held her gaze for a moment.

'Yes, fine. I'm so sorry I haven't been to see you. I—' He hesitated again. 'I wasn't sure you'd want to see me.'

'Why would you think that?'

He looked over her shoulder, then stepped back. 'Look, do you want to come in? I feel like we're on display standing here.'

'Sure.' Laura followed him into his kitchen where he flicked the kettle on.

'Tea?'

'Thanks.'

He took two mugs from a mug tree then turned to face her, leaning back against the worktop. 'So. How are you?'

'I'm all right,' Laura said. 'Getting there.'

He nodded. 'Good.'

'Ben.' She swallowed. 'Is everything all right? With us, I mean?'

'Us? Course.' He gave a nervous laugh.

'Right. Only, I haven't seen you since – well, since we got back last week after... everything. Have I done something to upset you?'

He cleared his throat. 'God no, absolutely not.' He ran his fingers through his hair and she tried not to notice how attractive he looked with his hair all dishevelled. The air between them pulsed for a moment, pulled taut like a piece of string, thrumming with tension. 'I'm sorry, Laura, it was wrong of me to ignore you. I just – I didn't want to intrude. I didn't know if you'd want people coming and going all day.' He looked at his feet. 'I should have come to check you were okay.'

She shook her head. 'I don't need looking after,' she said, looking him right in the eye. 'But I do need friends.'

'Of course you do. I know.' The kettle clicked off and the steam rose into the air but neither of them moved. Then Ben's mouth curled into a grin. 'I see Carol's been over quite a bit.'

Laura smiled back. 'Yes, she has. She's been very kind.'

'I bet she's loved every minute of it.'

Laura let out an unexpected burst of laughter. 'Yes, she has. But she means well.'

'I know she does.'

The laughter broke the tension, and Laura stayed for a cup of tea and made Ben promise to come and see her. He kept his word, and they've seen each other a few times a week at one or the other's home since then – along with Jane and Simon and anyone else who happened to be around. She's been so grateful for everyone's kindness, for their unexpected friendship when she needed it the most. Especially Ben's.

As she goes to answer the door now, she checks her appearance in the hallway mirror before she opens it, and finds herself hoping that it's Ben.

'Hello, dear!' Carol says and Laura can't help but smile. It's the second time Carol's been over today already. Arthur hovers behind his wife, looking apologetic.

'Hi, Carol, Arthur. Everything okay?'

'What? Oh, yes, absolutely fine.' Carol clears her throat loudly. 'Arthur and I couldn't help noticing that you've been doing some decorating, and he – *we* – wondered if you'd like some help.' She turns to her husband behind her. 'Didn't we, Arthur?'

'Yes, we did.' He grins at Laura and she smothers a smile back.

'That's really kind of you but you don't have to do that,' she says. 'I'm getting on fine.'

Arthur steps forward now and Laura can see he's already dressed in a pair of scruffy, paint-splattered trousers and a matching jumper. 'I'm more than happy to help,' he says. 'It'll keep me out of Carol's hair anyway. Might even get a bit of peace and quiet.'

'There's no need to be cheeky, Arthur,' Carol says, lifting her chin defiantly.

Laura takes pity on him and steps back. 'Well, if you're really sure, I'd love a bit of help painting the skirting boards,' she says.

Arthur hurries inside and heads straight into the living room.

Laura turns back to Carol, who's still on the doorstep, looking a bit sheepish.

'Is everything all right?' Laura says. Carol flushes a deep shade of crimson.

''Yes. I—' she stammers. Laura has never seen her look so nervous. Then Carol holds out a square pink envelope with *Laura* written on the front in neat handwriting. 'This is for you, from everyone.' She gestures behind her with a flourish and snaps her mouth shut.

'Oh, I – thank you,' Laura says. 'Shall I open it now?'

'If you like, dear.' Carol seems to have recovered some of her composure.

Laura carefully opens the envelope and pulls out a card, decorated with a drawing of flowers. She opens it up and several notes slide out and almost drop to the floor. Laura manages to catch them before they do.

'Oh...' She trails off, unsure what to say. She looks back at the card and sees that everyone has signed their name inside – Carol, Arthur, Ben, Jane, Sonja, Simon, Tracy, Marjorie, even Faye. She looks up at Carol questioningly.

'I – we knew you wanted to freshen the place up a bit and we thought this might come in handy to help you get what you wanted.' She seems uncomfortable. 'I – I hope you don't think it's inappropriate, only none of us knew what your taste was so we didn't dare choose anything ourselves.'

Laura glances down at the card and the bundle of notes in her hands. There must be more than two hundred pounds here and she finds herself overwhelmed with emotion.

'I don't know what to say,' she says. 'It's – this is too kind. Thank you.'

Carol claps her hands together. 'Oh, thank goodness, I'm so glad. I was worried you'd think it was vulgar, giving you cash, but

everyone else said it would probably be better than a voucher.'
She stops, gives a wry smile. 'Sorry, I promised Arthur I wouldn't
waffle on.' She lays her hands on Laura's forearm gently. 'We just
wanted you to know that we're all here for you, and if there's
anything you need, you only need to ask.'

Laura feels a tear forming in the corner of her eye and she
blinks it back. She can hardly believe how kind everyone has been,
and this – well, this has almost pushed her over the edge. Because
Carol is right. She does want to brighten the place up. She hasn't
spoken to Jim since the showdown in Putney, but through solicitors he's agreed to let her keep the house, which it turned out he
paid for in cash. She's always known he earns a lot but had never
realised quite how much, and knowing he can well afford it is
helping to allay the guilt she feels at living here mortgage-free.
The police are coming down hard on Jim because of the bigamy,
and a part of her felt sorry for him when it was explained to her
that he could even end up with a prison sentence. But there's
nothing she can do to change the outcome either, so she's chosen
not to think about it too much. After all, as Debbie has said count-
less times, he made his bed, the least he can do is lie in it without
making a fuss.

This house is the one good thing to have come out of everything that's happened, and she's decided to stay here, at least for
the foreseeable future. But she also wants to purge it of any memories of Jim, to make it a place where she wants to live, alone.
Because for the first time in years – since she met Jim, even before
that – she's finally starting to feel like herself again. She's learning
that Debbie was right all along: she is stronger than she thought
she was, she doesn't need anyone else to protect her, and she's
perfectly capable of looking after herself.

'Thank you,' she whispers, then closes the door and goes to
find her helper for the afternoon.

33

NOW – 5 JANUARY 1993

'I need your help.' Laura stands on Ben's doorstep, pieces of paper piled haphazardly in her arms, sheafs in danger of being lost forever to a sudden gust of wind.

'Come in, quick,' he says and she rushes past him into the peaceful calm of his hallway. He shuts the door and turns to face her. 'What's going on?'

Laura lets out a huge sigh. 'I was trying to fill in all these forms —' she indicates the stack balanced in her arms '—because I was determined to do them by myself, but it turns out one of the consequences of having spent the last seven years letting someone else do everything for me is that I've entirely forgotten how to do anything for myself.'

'Give them here before they go all over the floor.' Ben reaches out and takes the uppermost papers and shuffles them into a neat pile. 'What are they?' He starts to walk through to the kitchen and Laura kicks off her damp shoes and follows.

'Remember we talked about me starting my own catering business?'

'Ye-e-s-s-s?'

'Well, that's what this is. Only it turns out there are quite a lot more hoops to jump through than I'd anticipated.'

Ben places the papers carefully on his tiny table and opens the fridge. 'Drink?' He pulls out a bottle of wine. 'Or are you still trying not to...?'

'Actually I'd love one, thanks. It's been one of those days.' Laura has been trying to cut back on her drinking over the last couple of weeks, but it's going to take some time. This evening, she really needs a drink. She sits as Ben pours them a glass each, then he sits down beside her. She's aware of his proximity, but she doesn't move away.

'Why didn't you tell me you were doing all of this? I could have helped you. I mean, I have done it all before.'

'I know.' She puffs out her cheeks and looks down at her hands. 'The thing is...' She meets his eye, his gaze steady. 'The thing is I'm sick of being helpless, of always having to rely on other people.'

'You're not helpless, Lau.' She tries not to shiver with pleasure at his use of the diminutive of her name. It feels so familiar. So intimate.

'I am. I've always had someone to do things for me. Practical things, I mean. My parents, then Debs, then Jim. I—' She stops. 'I've never had to learn to look after myself. Not really. It makes me feel ridiculous.'

Laura's hand is on the table next to her wine glass, and as Ben reaches for his own glass his skin brushes against hers. His hand stills beside hers, resting on the base of his glass, and she tries not to think about it moving across, just a tiny distance, hardly anything at all, and touching her. God, it's been a long time since she could even contemplate a man touching her, even Jim. What is happening to her?

She looks up at Ben and his face is thoughtful. He reaches out with his other hand and lifts her chin. 'Listen to me, Laura.' His voice is low and serious. 'You are the least ridiculous person I know.'

She hardly dares to speak, her breath caught in her throat, her heart fluttering against her ribcage. She gives a small nod instead.

'You are so strong,' he continues, and his hand moves from her chin to rest on her cheek. She wants to turn her face so her mouth rests against his palm, and leave a trail of kisses from his hand down his wrist—

He pulls his hand away suddenly and her skin where it has been feels cold. She searches his eyes, trying to work out what he's thinking.

It's odd, she thinks, that Ben was the first person she thought of when she needed help with this. Getting back into cooking felt like a huge step for her. It reminded her of the darkest days, of the night of the attack. It reminded her of being someone she wasn't any more. But Ben was the one to encourage her.

'Think of it like therapy,' he said the first time she mentioned it. 'It's something you've always loved. I think you'd soon find your stride.'

So she's started small, baking cakes, making shepherd's pies and bolognese, a chilli, then some steak – a shared dinner with Ben that she didn't like to think of as a romantic meal for two. Until Ben made a suggestion.

'Why don't you start a small catering business?'

She looked at him as if he'd gone mad. 'I can't do something like that.'

'Why not?' He shrugged. 'You're a chef, and you said yourself you need to start earning some money soon, now that you don't have Jim's wage coming in every month. It means you can work from home, at least at first.' He held his hands out. 'Seems like a no-brainer to me.'

Although she dismissed it at first, the seed was planted and over the weeks it grew, spreading its fronds and petals into every corner of her mind until she couldn't ignore it any longer. Ben was right. Jim might have let her keep the house, but the condition was that he wouldn't be giving her anything else on top of that. She really did need to start earning some of her own money, and soon.

She drags her mind back to the present, to her and Ben sitting at the table together, her paperwork spread out in front of them. She clears her throat and tries to ignore his distracting presence beside her and concentrate on what she came here to do.

'So, will you help me?' She can't look at him, but stares down at the papers before her instead.

'Of course.'

Over the next hour, they work through the forms together. As she gathers the paperwork afterwards, she can feel her head spinning – from the wine, from too much concentration, from Ben's proximity? It's hard to know, but she closes her eyes for a moment to focus. When she opens them again Ben is watching her. He's moved closer and she feels the air vibrate between them.

'Thank you,' she whispers. Her vision is filled with him and all she wants, she realises, is to feel his touch. She pushes the thought away. She's betraying Jim, she— She stops. There is no Jim. She owes him nothing any more.

She sits statue-still, hardly daring to breathe as the seconds tick by. Then slowly, inch by agonising inch, Ben starts to move closer. He watches her, a question in his eyes – *is this okay?* – and she nods imperceptibly. For the first time since the attack, she wants to be touched. She almost needs it. Her breath hitches as his lips brush hers oh-so-softly, and she shudders with desire. Then their mouths are against each other's, his tongue seeking hers. He presses his hand to the back of her head, gently, and she rests hers on his thigh, and it feels as though they've always meant to be together. She no longer feels scared of being wanted.

The phone peals out and they leap apart, Laura's heart thrumming, Ben's face flaming.

'I—' Ben starts.

'You—' Laura says.

The sound of the ringing phone fills the room. The moment is broken and as Laura catches Ben's eye she starts to laugh, the sound rising up from her belly, through her windpipe and bursting out into the air. It rips through the room as the ringing stops, and Ben looks at her, surprised. Then he starts laughing too, at the absurdity, the released tension, the desire – all of it comes rushing out at once.

Slowly, the laughter starts to subside, and they sit, their hands still touching, Laura's lips burning.

'Well, that broke the mood,' Laura says.

'It did.' Ben looks suddenly serious.

'What's wrong?' Is he regretting it already? Oh God, he is, isn't he? But then he reaches for her hands and threads his fingers through hers. He doesn't look Laura in the eye and she feels sick. What is he about to say? She can't bear it.

Then he finally looks at her and his eyes are filled with warmth, with desire. 'When Helen died I didn't think I'd ever be able to love anyone again,' he says, his voice cracking. 'She was everything to me, and when I lost her I couldn't ever imagine being happy again, let alone finding someone who made me laugh the way she did. And for the last three years, I haven't. But then—' He coughs, suddenly unsure of himself. 'Then there you were. On my doorstep looking so sad and so lost and so, so... beautiful.' He reaches up and runs his fingers across Laura's cheek and she shivers. 'I think that day changed everything for me and, even though I knew I couldn't be with you because you were married to Jim, I knew that I needed to have you in my life, no matter what. As a friend, if that was all you could ever be. But I knew I'd found someone special.'

Laura looks at him, her heart pounding.

'Me too,' she says, and as the words spill from her mouth she realises they're true. Although she wasn't in the right place to fall for anyone when she met Ben she realises now, as she studies the curve of Ben's lip, the stubble on his chin, the long lashes that frame his sparkling eyes, that something changed in her that day too. She's been lost for so long, so scared of everything, so reliant on Jim. But now she feels like a new flower emerging in the spring.

She is falling in love with Ben.

'I know you need time, that you're still getting over Jim, and I'd never push you but...' Ben looks down at their hands, entwined on the kitchen table. 'I hope that this can become something, eventually. Me and you. However long it takes.'

She smiles, leans forward and kisses his lips, gently.

'I hope so too.'

EPILOGUE

NOW – 17 JULY 1993

Laura waits until the last few people have left, then she closes the door firmly behind her, and lets out an enormous sigh. Today has been the first day running her own catering business, and after finishing an order for a hot and cold buffet for a local party, she feels absolutely exhausted.

'Can I go now, Laura?'

'Yes, thanks, Abbie. I'm not sure I could have got through today without you.' She hands Jane's daughter, Abbie, a couple of twenty pound notes and the girl grins and races off, the door banging shut behind her.

Laura stands for a moment, surveying the mess around her. Pots and pans litter the worktop, baking trays, knifes and measuring jugs, a whisk, eggshells, potato peelings.

She would never have put up with this mess in her old restaurant kitchen but somehow she can't bring herself to care too much today. Because this is her dream come true. Her own little kitchen, above a row of shops a few streets away from home, and her first order has been a roaring success. She feels so lucky.

She heads to the sink and starts filling it with hot water, steam billowing up around her. She switches on the radio, and begins to load the dishwasher, placing the dirtiest items in the sink of scalding water to scrub later. She's so preoccupied with her work she doesn't hear the door opening behind her, or the footsteps creeping across the floor.

'Well, that couldn't have gone any better.' Laura almost jumps out of her skin as a pair of arms snake round her waist and a gentle kiss is planted on her neck. She spins round, her heart still thudding from the shock.

'You made me jump!'

'Sorry. You just looked so cute, singing along to the radio, lost in your own little world.'

'Yes, well, I'm afraid I'm still working *very* hard, which means that this—' she indicates the arms round her waist, the face pressed close to hers '—is entirely inappropriate.'

She tries to keep a straight face but she can't do it, and when Ben moves in for another kiss she gives in.

'Hey, hey, that's quite enough of that, you two.' They spring apart sheepishly as Debbie enters the room and she laughs at them. 'God, you two are like a pair of naughty schoolchildren,' she says. 'I was only teasing. Go ahead, snog all you like, don't mind me.'

Ben and Laura grin at each other, and he reaches for her hand.

'So, it went pretty well, by the looks of things,' Debbie says.

'It really did.'

'Don't sound so amazed.' Ben brings her hand to his lips and presses a kiss onto her knuckles. 'We were never in any doubt you could do it, were we, Debs?'

Debbie looks round. 'Absolutely none.' She studies her best friend for a moment, struck by how different she seems. So relaxed, so happy. So herself. She turns and plunges her hands into the sink of hot water. 'Right, let's get started.'

'You don't need to help,' Laura says. 'I'm fine here.'

Debbie peers over her shoulder. 'Don't be daft, the quicker we get away from here, the quicker we can get... er...' She shoots Ben a panicky look.

'Home,' Ben finishes, lamely.

Laura looks from one to the other and back again, wondering what's going on. But they both refuse to look her in the eye so she sighs and starts clearing the worktop, shoving things into black bin bags.

The three of them work in comfortable silence until the kitchen is back to its former sparkling self. Laura straightens up and groans. 'I'm going to ache like mad tomorrow,' she says. 'I'm not used to working this hard.'

'You love it,' Debbie says, throwing a damp tea towel at her.

'You're right, I really do.' She stretches her arms above her head and yawns. 'But right now I just want to go home and collapse on the sofa and watch some terrible TV.' She glances at Ben to see if he's with her, but instead catches him looking at Debbie again. 'Right, what's going on with you two?' she demands.

'What? I don't know what you mean.' Ben smiles at her sweetly.

'You're imagining things,' Debbie adds, picking up her bag and slinging it over her shoulder decisively. 'Let's get you home.'

Still not convinced, Laura follows them out of the room. When she reaches the door she casts one last glance back into the room and smiles. This is all hers. Then she switches off the lights, locks the door behind her, and follows Debbie and Ben down the stairs, clutching Ben's hand all the way home.

When they get back to Willow Crescent, however, Debbie and Ben both start acting strangely again, peering over their shoulders, jumping at the slightest bang, and Laura feels Ben's hand tighten its grip. She stops dead in the street and crosses her arms over her chest. They both stop and face her.

'Come on, out with it.'

Debbie and Ben glance at each other but say nothing.

'Okay, well, if you're not going to tell me what you're up to then I'm not moving another step,' she says.

They glance at each other again, then Ben steps forward and takes her hands again. 'Okay, don't get mad.'

Laura looks from Ben's face to Debbie. 'Oh no, what have you two done?'

'It's nothing bad, it's just—' Ben stops.

'Look, it's nothing to worry about, okay,' Debbie says. 'You just need to trust us.'

Laura's not convinced, but what choice does she have? They're clearly not going to tell her. 'Okay, but you two are in serious trouble later.'

Ben grins. 'I look forward to it.'

They reach Laura's front door and step inside the hallway. All the lights are off and she stands for moment, listening for any movement inside. But there's nothing. She flicks the light on, takes her shoes off, and Ben and Debbie do the same.

She's just beginning to relax when she steps into the kitchen and light floods the room. She gasps as she takes in the scene in front of her.

The first thing she sees are the people – her new friends and neighbours, all squeezed into the small room, smiling at her. Then she sees someone else, someone she hasn't seen for a long time, and her heart does a somersault.

'Hello, love,' her mum says as she steps forward uncertainly. And in that instant, all the pain and regret and heartache over the last few years evaporates and she throws herself into her mum's arms, enveloping her into a tight bear hug. She feels as though she could stand there all day, but eventually she pulls away. Tears course down her face and she can see her mum is crying too.

It's so good to see you,' she squeaks.

'I wasn't sure if—' Her mum stops, the words caught in her throat. 'I've missed you, Lorrie.'

'I've missed you too, Mum.' She frowns. 'But how are you here?'

Her mum looks sheepish.

'It was me,' Debbie says, behind her. 'Well, me and Ben. We both thought it was about time you patched things up...' She trails off.

'Tonight seemed as good a time as any, so we invited her along,' Ben adds. 'You don't mind, do you?'

Laura looks at her mum and her heart floods with love. She's missed her so much. She swallows down the lump in her throat.

'No, I don't mind.' She hooks her arm through her mum's and rests her head on her shoulder.

There's so much more to say, but now is not the time. Instead, she takes a glass of something sparkling that Carol's proffering, and turns to look at everyone again in awe.

'I do mind that there seem to be about a dozen people standing in my kitchen and I knew nothing about it though.' Her eyes sparkle as she speaks, and that's when she notices the transformation in the room. She spins in a circle, taking it all in: the freshly-painted cupboards, no longer a faded pine but a soft, pale grey; new pans hanging from hooks along the wall, the tiles, freshly scrubbed and gleaming.

'We wanted to do something to celebrate,' Jane says.

'You did all this in one day?' Laura says, in awe.

'With a little help,' Jane says. 'We knew you were redecorating and that you'd struggle for time now you're so busy with work and – well, other things.' She gives Ben a wink and he flushes a deep crimson. 'We all know what a tough time you've had recently and – we care about you. All of us.' She holds her glass in the air. 'To Laura. And Ben. And fresh beginnings,' she says. 'Cheers.'

'Cheers,' everyone chants.

As she takes a sip of her champagne, Laura is filled with happiness. She spent so long in a dark place that she could never have imagined her life would turn out like this: new friends, a new home. New love.

ACKNOWLEDGMENTS

I always have lots of people to thank at the end of my books. Sometimes it's moral and emotional support I'm thanking people for, such as my lovely boys Tom, Jack and Harry, my Mum and Dad and my fabulous friends – both writing buddies and non-writing buddies. Some of this book was written at the fabulous Chez Castillon writing retreat, so also thank you to Janie and Mickey for letting me come and stay and providing me with excellent food, wine and company, and Rowan Coleman for talking through the half-written plot and helping me work out where I was trying to go with it.

Sometimes it's thanks for believing in me and trusting me to write a good book – and for that I have to thank my wonderful editor, Sarah Ritherdon. I know you love this book, Sarah, so for your sake even more than mine, I hope it flies!

Other people need a huge dollop of gratitude for giving up their precious time to share their expert knowledge with me on various subjects, all of which helps to make the book better and more authentic. In this case, and in no particular order, I want to thank Nicky Lidbetter, CEO of Anxiety UK, for talking to me about agoraphobia, which helped to ensure I made Laura's experience true to life. Thank you also to the wonderful and very generous Graham Bartlett, Police Procedural Advisor and Author, who helped me with some sticky details to do with bigamy. The same thanks must go to Emily Watson of Rayden Solicitors in

Berkhamsted who also helped with that subject. Any mistakes are mine – intentional or otherwise.

I've loved writing this book, and I couldn't have done it without the support of my husband, Tom, who always believes in me, and never lets me give up – even on those days when I feel like throwing my laptop out of the window...

And of course, thank you to my wonderful readers. I love hearing from you, and it really is amazing to know that my words are out there being enjoyed by people all round the world. Thanks so much to each and every one of you!

MORE FROM CLARE SWATMAN

We hope you enjoyed reading *The World Outside My Window*. If you did, please leave a review.

If you'd like to gift a copy, this book is also available as an ebook, large print, hardback, digital audio download and audiobook CD.

Sign up to Clare Swatman's mailing list for news, competitions and updates on future books.

https://bit.ly/ClareSwatmannews

Explore more from Clare Swatman.

ALSO BY CLARE SWATMAN

Before We Grow Old

Dear Grace

The Mother's Secret

Before You Go

A Love to Last a Lifetime

The Night We First Met

ABOUT THE AUTHOR

Clare Swatman is the author of five previous novels, which have been translated into more than twenty languages. *The World Outside My Window* is her seventh novel. A former journalist, she spent the previous twenty years writing true life stories and health features for *Bella* and *Woman & Home*, amongst many other magazines, but now writes fiction full-time. Clare lives in Hertfordshire with her husband and two teenage sons.

Visit Clare's website: https://clareswatmanauthor.com

Follow Clare on social media:

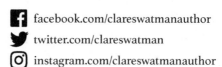

facebook.com/clareswatmanauthor

twitter.com/clareswatman

instagram.com/clareswatmanauthor

Boldwⓞⓞd

Boldwood Books is an award-winning fiction publishing company seeking out the best stories from around the world.

Find out more at www.boldwoodbooks.com

Join our reader community for brilliant books, competitions and offers!

Follow us
@BoldwoodBooks
@BookandTonic

Sign up to our weekly
deals newsletter

https://bit.ly/BoldwoodBNewsletter

Printed in Great Britain
by Amazon

42224038R00195